W9-AGA-981

PRAISE FOR JESSIE HUNTER'S RIVETING SUSPENSE

ONE, TWO, BUCKLE MY SHOE

"Effectively moody and engrossing . . . *One, Two, Buckle My Shoe* fulfills the promise of Hunter's *Blood Music*. First rate."
—*Kirkus Reviews*

"The tension never lets up."
—*Anniston Star*

BLOOD MUSIC

"Smart, modern, riveting. It's better than a page-turner. It's a page non-turner. . . . You are afraid to find out what happens next."
—*Newsday*

"Frightening and disturbing, and beautifully written."
—Jonathan Kellerman

"Much to admire . . . an authentic sense of nightmare."
—*Kirkus Reviews*

Books by Jessie Hunter

One, Two, Buckle My Shoe
Blood Music

ATTENTION: ORGANIZATIONS AND CORPORATIONS

Most HarperPaperbacks are available at special quantity discounts
for bulk purchases for sales promotions, premiums, or fund-raising.
For information, please call or write:
Special Markets Department, HarperCollins_Publishers_,
10 East 53rd Street, New York, N.Y. 10022.
Telephone: (212) 207-7528. Fax: (212) 207-7222.

One, Two, Buckle My Shoe

Jessie Hunter

HarperPaperbacks
A Division of HarperCollinsPublishers

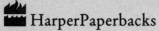

HarperPaperbacks

A Division of HarperCollins*Publishers*
10 East 53rd Street, New York, N.Y. 10022-5299

If you purchased this book without a cover, you should be aware
that this book is stolen property. It was reported as "unsold and
destroyed" to the publisher and neither the author nor the
publisher has received any payment for this "stripped book."

This is a work of fiction. The characters, incidents, and
dialogues are products of the author's imagination and are not to
be construed as real. Any resemblance to actual events or
persons, living or dead, is entirely coincidental.

Copyright © 1997 by Jessie Hunter
All rights reserved. No part of this book may be used or
reproduced in any manner whatsoever without written
permission of the publisher, except in the case of brief
quotations embodied in critical articles and reviews.
For information address Simon & Schuster Inc.,
1230 Avenue of the Americas, New York, N.Y. 10020.

ISBN 0-06-101325-0

HarperCollins®, ▬ ▬ ®, and HarperPaperbacks®
are trademarks of HarperCollins*Publishers*, Inc.

A hardcover edition of this book was published
in 1997 by Simon & Schuster Inc.

Cover illustration © 1998 by Peter Fiore

First HarperPaperbacks edition: June 1998

Printed in the United States of America

Visit HarperPaperbacks on the World Wide Web at
http://www.harpercollins.com

❖ 10 9 8 7 6 5 4 3 2 1

To my sister, Linell Prichard Hunter,
who went through it all with me

And to the woman who washed
the windows

DANIEL ANGELO
January 14, 1989–May 5, 1993;
age 4 years

OLIVER PLUCIENKOWSKY
April 8, 1987–January 15, 1994;
age 6 years

ANDREW TIMMONS
April 23, 1985–July 8, 1994;
age 9 years

RONALD CHIN
December 9, 1988–December 17, 1994;
age 6 years

PETER HUBERT
May 12, 1990–August 25, 1995;
age 5 years

ANDREW TONATA
January 2, 1988–December 13, 1995;
age 7 years

JAMES OSSI
October 18, 1991–September 15, 1996;
age 5 years

December 23, 1996
1:20 P.M.

THE CHOCOLATE MAN SAT AT THE KITCHEN TABLE, his collection spread out in front of him. From his chair he could see lead gray out the window over the sink. It had been sunny a moment ago; it had been snowing. The day before Christmas Eve.

The Chocolate Man looked around the kitchen, at the table and the things on the table, at the spotless floor, the empty sink, through the open kitchen door to the hall. He could see the tightly shut bedroom door, and the patterned rug in the hallway, bright near the door and fading to blackness as the light followed it. Mentally he went down the hall. He liked to think about each room in turn. This was his house, what he could control.

The hall itself was dark and empty, running the length of the house from front to back. The walls in the hall were white (all the walls in the house were white, and spotless), the carpet dark brown relieved by pink and blue flowers. The first room, off the hall in the front and to the left, was the living room; the carpet was brown there too, with no relief. The sofa was a brown-and-beige weave, the two chairs dark blue. The TV sat like a blank eye in empty silence. All the furniture was covered with clear plastic. The

Chocolate Man never went in that room, except to clean it, Tuesdays and Fridays.

There was a large Christmas tree standing in the farthest corner of the living room. It didn't have any decorations on it.

The next room was on the right of the hall: the guest room. Dark blue carpet, a hard dark-wood bed, a dresser; plastic flowers on the night table, a picture of Jesus holding a glowing red heart. A lamp with a cream-colored shade. The Chocolate Man changed the sheets Wednesdays and Sundays.

The next room on the left was the dining room. It was completely anonymous, with a bare wooden floor and a lot of spotless glass. The Chocolate Man only went in there to dust and vacuum, Tuesdays and Thursdays.

The next room was the Chocolate Man's own. He scrubbed his white walls Mondays and Thursdays. His bed sat against the far wall; his sheets were white, his pillowcases and blankets were white. There was a pine dresser next to the door. There was never anything on top of the dresser. There were white sheet curtains that were always left closed at the one window. There was no other furniture. The carpet was brown and gold; he didn't like it but it was the same colors the one in his childhood bedroom had been. He vacuumed all the carpets on Tuesdays and Fridays.

The last room on the hall, besides the blank antiseptic blue-tiled bathroom (which he cleaned Wednesdays and Sundays), was the kitchen. Everything in the kitchen was white and silver; under the bright fluorescent light the room hurt his eyes. In the kitchen the Chocolate Man sighed and looked at the table in front of him. His collection. Seven pairs of shoes, fourteen socks. A large, leather-bound album, open now to a headline: SIX-YEAR-OLD MISSING. One two three four five six seven. The Chocolate Man turned the page. FIVE-YEAR-OLD'S BODY FOUND. One two three four five six seven. He reached for one of the pairs of shoes, which were laid out in a meticulous line on the Formica table-top.

Peter Hubert. None of the shoes were labeled. This pair was a size two—one two three four five six seven—white sneakers. Scuffed, the laces frayed; without looking the Chocolate Man knew that the socks that went with this pair were also white, with red stripes at the rim. Dirty at the toe and heel. Jimmy Ossi had blue socks. Ronald Chin had green socks with trains on them. The newspapers were calling the Chocolate Man a monster.

He wasn't sure what he thought of his crimes. He felt an expansiveness at the description: "his crimes." The expansiveness of pride; the pride of creation. His crimes stood apart, each a memory encapsulated in a sock, a tiny shoe. Each a memory for others, too. The Chocolate Man pushed back his thin blond hair; unconsciously he was smiling.

There were mothers with memories. He liked to see their pain. He kept an empty videotape in the VCR, he clicked the "record" button as soon as he saw one of their faces. He watched stupid made-for-TV movies so that he could find out if there was going to be a segment about his crimes on the eleven-o'clock news. One two three four five six seven.

"Whoever you are, please send our Petey back to us," Mrs. Hubert had said on his television. "For God's sake, he's only a little boy." The Chocolate Man had watched that one over and over.

Jennifer Chin had also made an appeal on television. She had been angry. She said, "If you can hurt a child you are the lowest creature on earth." He didn't like having to kill them, but he didn't regret it. They were a means; even the molestation brought him little immediate pleasure. Only the pleasure of being able to say, "I have molested him."

And it had to be true, there had to be identifying signs to prove the molestation. So that he could imagine the mother's face when she found out it was true.

By the time he had killed three or four, the mothers knew it was true from the moment their children were discovered missing. One two three four five six seven, one two three four five six seven. The Chocolate Man caressed the dirty canvas of Peter Hubert's sneaker. He ran his finger inside; the lining was worn. Peter's mother used to slide this sneaker onto her son's foot; often it stuck at the heel. The Chocolate Man liked to think that maybe that was true. The mother's hand, firm on the heel of the foot, the boy's face laughing, his foot squirming out of reach; the mother mock-angry: "You bring me that foot this instant, Mr. Smarty—" He liked to think about that.

After a while he put the sneaker back in line

with the others. It must be just so—there. Not one
fraction of an inch out of place. One two three four
five six seven. The Chocolate Man looked at his collection and he sighed. He stood up.

It was time to go. Another mother was going to
cry tonight.

THE FIRST DAY

"EMILY!" LAURIE LOOKINLAND STOOD AT THE DOOR to her daughter's bedroom.

"Emily!" she called again. The sheets on her daughter's bed were pink flannel with roses. Laurie felt a familiar stab of irritation: the bed was not made.

"What?" Emily's voice was coming from downstairs. The bed was not made, and the floor was a mess, and Emily never came when Laurie called her, she just yelled, "What?"

A whole shelf full of stuffed cats had fallen on the floor. The top of the music box with the ballerina cats on it had broken again, Laurie saw; it was lying ignominiously on Emily's white desk, one cat's hopeful blank china eye staring up at nothing. Nobody, her mother used to tell her, can make you angrier than your own children.

Emily had promised she would clean that room. At the top of the steps Laurie called again. "Emily!"

"What?"

"Come *here*."

There was a silence.

"Why?"

And Laurie found herself smiling as she walked downstairs.

✗   ✗   ✗

Emily's mother was calling her. *Mr. Drew grinned broadly. "And you thought your old dad had met his end, eh?" he teased.* Emily didn't want to stop reading. "What?" she called absently. *Nancy heaved a sigh of relief. "I'm glad nobody was shot."* Emily didn't see why her mother had to call her, anyway. It wasn't like she'd sneak out of the house or anything. Her mother could just come find her.

"Come here!" *Mr. Drew said the stranger was thin, dark-haired, and had a scowling expression.*

"Why?"

"Oh, he might be the same one who was following me—the one Bess and George saw!" Nancy exclaimed.

Laurie could see her daughter lying on her stomach under the dining-room table, reading a book. As she walked into the room she resisted an urge to tell Emily that her bedroom was dirty, and if she was going to read why didn't she put on the light? Emily's long legs stuck out, in blue jeans and red socks. *She's too thin,* Laurie thought, and shook her head: she'd always thought that. And of course Emily lived on air and worried about getting fat.

Laurie leaned under the table. Nancy Drew, of course. *The Moonstone Castle Mystery.* "Has Nancy's father come to save the day yet?" Emily's legs had been bouncing gently in rhythm with her reading; now they scrabbled and tucked up as she turned, smiling, to her mother.

"Nobody here but us chums."

"Oh, God, chums," Laurie said, kneeling on her heels. "I always liked Georgie best."

"So does everybody," said Emily. "Why does it say that Bess is pretty and then call her 'plump'?"

Laurie laughed ruefully. "Oh, I'd forgotten that. Plump Bess. Well, a long time ago plump women were considered beautiful."

"Yuck."

"Not a long time ago it wasn't yuck."

"Yuck."

"I just hope that by the time you get to be a teenager women are allowed to have bodies again."

Laurie got up without using her hands; "You were supposed to clean your room," she said, and immediately hated her tone of voice. She sighed. So much of motherhood seemed to be negative power: Don't do this, don't do that, not here, not now, not there, because. She taught, as mothers have always taught, by negative example, creating as she went a shadow Emily of bad habits, unclean rooms, and coarse manners, and she set it up as a monster, a mirror of what the child might, if not for her, become.

And of course she couldn't know how much was Emily really, even negative Emily. Was she really prone to throwing things when she got mad? She had been three years ago, when she was six. Did she really put perfectly good food in the garbage? She had when she was eight. Did she dislike peas and artichokes? Laurie hadn't served her any in four years. Laurie didn't even know, really, whether her daughter still loved cats the way she had when she was a tiny child. She still seemed to love them; Laurie had seemed, she knew, to love the ballet lessons her own mother sent her to for seven years, the hours of tortured embarrassment she suffered for the sake of her mother's obvious pride. Laurie, by the time she was her daughter's age, had a whole rich secret life, of books read and games played and streets walked alone. Emily too must have her secret places. She was an ordinary child, and no one knew her.

Father and daughter sat down to enjoy the snack and to wait for—whoever thought plump could be pretty? Even though Emily was only nine, she knew she was getting a little fat. She tried not to notice it, but all the models and women on TV were really skinny, and so were the teenage girls on the bus. A friend of Emily's had already gotten her period. Emily didn't even have bumps yet, not a thing; she felt ashamed sometimes because she was secretly pleased. She didn't want to be like the teenage girls and the women on television; she wanted to lie under the dining-room table and read Nancy Drew. But she shouldn't, really: she knew she was getting fat, she ought to be exercising instead of reading.

Her mother was looking at her. Did she want lunch?

She closed her book; she smiled. Right now she just wanted to be with her mother.

✗   ✗   ✗

Emily was shaking her head *no* to lunch. Laurie considered and abandoned trying to get her to eat. "Listen," she said, "do you want to go to the park?"

"Yeah!" Emily scrambled out from under the table; Laurie had to stop herself from saying, *Be careful*, as her daughter's dark head grazed the tabletop.

"Why don't you have a play date today?" Laurie asked as they left the room. "*I'm* hungry," she went on, and hated herself, instantly, as though the words were a confession instead of a fact.

"'Cause I wanted to be with you." It was the day before Christmas Eve; most of Emily's friends were away for the holidays, but Laurie knew that Emily would want to be with her even if they weren't: it was on Christmas Eve four years ago that Emily's father had walked out on them.

Laurie had married her childhood sweetheart when she was nineteen years old. She didn't have to; there was no child on the way. She was certain of her love in the way that young people are certain. She believed in forever.

Laurie thought she had been so careful. Dick was steady, Dick was trustworthy, Dick was ambitious, Dick was of course entirely the wrong man for Laurie to have married.

Dick was six years older. He worked in real estate, and later Laurie often thought she should have known there would be trouble in the marriage, because she found real estate deadly dull. She never cared what happened at the office.

They decided they didn't want to have children.

Laurie never knew Dick's reasons, but her own reason was simple: her father had left the family when she was seven. And she could not bear to take the risk of passing that pain to a child.

Laurie wished Dick had gone to college. She went, nights, after days spent in a series of negligible jobs: waitressing, typing, standing behind counters. She studied European history and women's studies and learned to speak French, and Dick never wanted to hear about how her classes had gone.

Then Laurie got pregnant. "Oh, Emily was definitely planned," she would say later, "but not by us!" And she realized almost immediately that her marriage had died—had, in fact, been dead a long time.

But Dick was a fact, and her pregnancy was a fact, so she hid her primal fear—*he's nothing like my father*—trundling heavily to classes not feeling the winter cold, sitting at the backs of classrooms holding her hand over her belly so she could feel the little one kick.

She had tried; she would never know if Dick had tried.

The marriage dragged on until Emily was five. It was ironic that Dick should choose to leave on Christmas Eve: he had always thought Laurie melodramatic. He took her blank acceptance of pain as a surprisingly mature stoicism; he pretended pride in her even as he walked out the door. Perhaps he could feel guiltless then; Laurie sat in the living room alone and thought only, *This is familiar, this pain. It has not changed in twenty years.*

She hardly remembered the two months that

came after that; for all its familiarity this pain was not familiar to her daughter, and watching it become part of Emily was the hardest thing Laurie had ever had to do.

She didn't know what Emily thought, because Emily would not talk about her father. If Laurie could have assumed her pain she would have, but the truth was that when she thought of Dick at all she had a hard time imagining his face. She was almost ashamed that there was no more to their story than that: when she was sixteen Dick had seemed like the prince from a fairy tale.

Now he was hardly even a memory.

And Emily had not heard a word from him in four years.

After the divorce Laurie learned that college had not changed her status in the working world. The same jobs were open to her now as had been open to her when she was a teenager: counter jobs, service jobs, jobs that required ill-fitting uniforms and hours and hours of standing. She worked ten hours a day, six days a week, as the manager of a video store. When Emily was little she played behind the counter; when she was big enough for day care Laurie got a grant to send her to a good private school, nursery through sixth grade.

There was never more than enough money just to pay the bills, but Laurie made do, going without new shoes, new dresses, so that Emily could be as much like the other, more affluent children as possible. Dick's steadiness had brought him and Laurie a house shortly after they were married; it was tiny, with a living room, dining room, and kitchen on the first floor, two small bedrooms on the second—but Laurie knew how lucky she was to have it. The mortgage payments would not have been high if Laurie had had what she thought of as a "real" job, but she could pay her bills—and that was reward enough for work, that she could pay them.

Emily loved school, she loved learning for its own sake, as Laurie did, and she was bright and motivated but there seemed to be a hole in her somewhere, a place Laurie could not reach: whenever Emily cried it was as though she would never stop.

And every Christmas season, when Laurie had a few days off, Emily wanted to be with her mother all the time.

Emily had cried at night for a long time after her father left. Laurie would ask her if she missed her daddy and she would say yes, but always with the slightest hesitation; when Laurie's own father had left it was not for him that she had cried but for the ending of things. His loss taught her the irrevocable death of the past. She had said good-bye to her father in a dim room (with a red rug on the floor? and a big red-shaded lamp on the table?); that was "forever." His leaving—forever—was the hole in the universe that Laurie had never been able to fill, the presence of the death of things that she had carried with her—a part of her, an empty space—for twenty years. And now Emily too was incomplete.

Laurie tried to make sure the empty space was filled. Christmas had always been magical to her, the death of the year and the birth of hope, and she wanted it to be magical to Emily, too, more than the reminder of what she had lost. Each year Laurie bought, forgoing her own comforts, something to mark the time as special. A soft cloth Advent calendar with Velcro-backed toys to stick day by day on a green cloth tree. A delicate china angel with a whisper for a smile. A manger made of angular wooden puzzle pieces fitted together: a sheep, a cow, three Wise Men with brightly painted robes; a tiny crib, a baby; the pieces nested, interlocking, in a thin stable. Every day for a month before Christmas Laurie and Emily took out their treasures and played with them.

That morning they had played with the manger. Emily liked to take the pieces out and set them up just so. She told her mother elaborate stories about the baby Jesus: he never had a father; Emily made the blue-coated Joseph an uncle or a brother or simply there, with no explanation. Laurie knew that if she were to marry again she would get no complaint from Emily.

The manger pieces lay across the dining-room table, next to today's *New York Times*. Laurie had been reading it but she'd had to stop: sometimes the news was too sad, it made her cry, and Emily didn't need that right now. The children in fighting lands, the children in her own city, could sap Laurie's courage and hope, and she had her own child to take care of. The newspapers drove her away from her seat at the table, the comfortable chair; this morning she had been driven into the kitchen for hot chocolate neither she nor Emily wanted. For Laurie the straight-and-narrow of normal emotional balance—the ability not to live in a world of other people's suffering—was often too narrow. She felt too much. And so she had stood above the warming milk, and images ate her happiness.

The paper was folded to the last story she'd been reading. MOTHER OF SLAIN CHILD FORMS SUPPORT GROUP. Pat Angelo had begun the group in November, and already there were more than five hundred members, parents banded together to fight their grief, including other parents of children kidnapped and murdered by the Chocolate Man.

The Chocolate Man was a nightmare grown wings. There had been seven children so far, all boys. The kidnappings were maddeningly similar. They took place in safe residential neighborhoods all over New York City: from a park or a playground a boy would disappear. The youngest had been four, the oldest nine. After the boy had been missing exactly six hours there would be a telephone call. A soft-voiced man; always the same three sentences: *I have your child. I have molested him. If you do not pay me $20,000 in unmarked bills I will kill him.* Sometimes the calls were made from pay phones on the New York Thruway, sometimes from residential areas like Fresh Meadows or Brooklyn Heights. One of the bodies had been found not two miles from where Laurie lived, in Rego Park, Queens.

The first killing was taken to be an isolated incident. In May of 1993 a four-year-old boy named Danny Angelo disappeared from his driveway on a quiet street in Flushing, Queens. It happened at two o'clock in the afternoon. The boy was with his nanny at the time; she had run inside the house for a moment to get him a sweater: the air was cool for May. After the body was discovered the nanny suffered a nervous breakdown and had to be returned to her native Denmark.

Six hours after Danny's disappearance, his parents received a telephone call from what his mother later described as an "eerily quiet" man who told them that he had taken their boy. "I have molested him," he said. The caller demanded $20,000. But he was so softspoken, Danny's mother said, "that he seemed to be asking if it was all right."

The Angelos notified the police, who readied the money; the man called back in the morning. Eight o'clock tonight, he said, "at the corner of 159th and Cove, down by the yacht club."

The police located the spot, a cul-de-sac across the street from the Beechhurst Yacht Club in Whitestone, Queens. They staked it out. When Danny's parents went to drop off the money there was nothing there.

The police at first thought that police presence, however disguised, had spooked the kidnapper. Then a motorist spotted something eight miles away, in the weeds at the edge of Kennedy Airport, in Queens.

It was Danny's body, laid stiff and straight in the weeds at the side of the busy airstrip. Clearly it was intended to be found. The body was clothed, but the boy's shoes and socks were missing. Danny had been killed by a person of medium strength approximately twenty-six hours before. He had most likely been strangled with a knotted cord or stocking. There was evidence of sexual abuse. When the man had called to arrange the payment of the $20,000, Danny was already dead.

The other crimes had been almost identical. Six more times little boys had disappeared. Six more times parents received the call: *I have your child. I have molested him.*

No man had been seen loitering near any of the kidnap sites. There were never any witnesses at the time of the kidnapping. The police were not sure how the man got the children to come to him.

Only once had there been a lead. Six months after the second killing, a blond man of medium height and build was seen talking to a very small boy at a park in Fort Greene, Brooklyn. The boy's mother rushed over, but by the time she reached her son the man had disappeared. "He want give me chocolate," the boy said. He said it to his mother, he said it to the police. "He want give me chocolate." The killer became "The Chocolate Man."

Laurie felt sick for all the parents. All the boys had been murdered approximately four hours after having been kidnapped. The parents would have to live with those four hours for the rest of their lives.

Laurie was certain that if it were her she would go mad. She was so relieved that her child was not a boy! She regretted Emily's short hair. But she couldn't tame her daughter's unruly ringlets, a mass of tangles every morning; no matter how Laurie tried to cajole the knots, calling them birds' nests or bears' picnics, Emily always cried when her mother tried to brush her hair. (Laurie's own hair was mouse-brown and straight.)

Laurie had taken to putting bright barrettes in the soft dark hair above the ears: bells and clowns and starfish, yellow and orange and red. Things a boy would never wear.

"Which one shall we wear today?" Laurie asked her daughter as they got ready to go out, "the clown or the bear?"

"Oh, Mom, I don't like those things."

"Don't you want to look pretty? The bear, maybe," smoothing her daughter's soft hair.

"I *do* look pretty," Emily said, pushing her mother's hand away.

"The clown, then." Laurie fastened the barrette in Emily's hair and held her by the shoulders to see how it looked. Emily bent her head and squirmed.

"Hold still, pumpkin. You're such a wiggle—" Laurie suddenly crushed her child to her. Emily pushed, then gave in and wormed her arms free and threw them around her mother's neck. Laurie put her face down to her daughter's neck, but Emily wiggled away. For such a short time they clung to you without thought.

"Can we go out now?" Emily asked.

"Where shall we go?"

Emily started to laugh. "You said the park!"

"Maybe today we'll go to France instead." Always Laurie and Emily talked about going to France—as if it were not a country but Wonderland, or Oz. It had been a long time since Laurie had thought that she would wake up smarter, or happier, or different in a different bed: France was the only dream she allowed herself. Someday she and Emily would float up the Eiffel Tower in a glass elevator;

would walk through the Cimetière Père Lachaise, where Laurie would show her daughter Colette's grave.

Emily laughed. "Susan says that in France the girls start douching when they're seven years old," she said in her most annoying grownup voice.

"*Douche* means shower in French, and we do that here, too. Now come on, or it'll start snowing and we'll miss the park."

Every Christmas vacation, no matter how cold it was, Laurie and Emily went outside in the afternoon. Rego Park was a quiet, safe neighborhood: small, almost suburban lawns, shops down on Queens Boulevard, cement-and-grass parks with baseball fields. Hewlitt Park, four blocks from Laurie's house, even had a small duck pond, with three greedy white ducks.

When it was too cold for the park they went to Giorgio's Café on the boulevard, where they drank hot chocolate and played poker or gin rummy. Emily was a shark. She hoarded aces; sometimes she cheated. Sometimes while they played they talked about France.

But this afternoon Emily wanted to go to the park. The weather had been unseasonable, without snow or wind, and although the temperature was not quite forty there was a phantom of spring in the air, a gentle mirage. "It's not going to snow," Emily said with scorn as Laurie went to the closet to get their coats. Children had changed: Laurie didn't remember knowing everything until she was at least fourteen.

But: "Mommy, look!" Emily was at the window, actually jumping up and down with excitement. "Mommy, snow!" Laurie looked out the window at the weak slanting sunlight and the snow. The snow fell straight down through the sunlight. Emily had forgotten her superiority. "I didn't know it could snow when it's sunny," she said. She looked suddenly littler than nine.

"Look, it's going," said Laurie, kneeling at the sill next to her daughter. And the sun faded into gray and the snow stopped with the dissolving light.

"Happy first snow," Laurie said, kissing the top of Emily's head. And suddenly she was afraid. She thought of those seven children, missing and dead. She had a vision of herself staring out at the snow and Emily was missing, Emily was dead.

Laurie shivered violently. "What was that?" asked Emily, laughing.

"A goose just walked over my grave."

"Mom, that's *gross*," and Laurie reached out and grabbed her daughter and hugged her again, until Emily squirmed free and said, "I want to go to the park now," and Laurie sighed and let her go and said, "Okay, honey, come on."

GEORGE RIEHLE BEGAN HIS HAND-WASHING RITUAL
when he was eight years old. His mother was in the
bedroom with a man, and his father was counting a
small stack of bills at the kitchen table. George had
been listening to the noises the man was making—
his mother never made any noise—and all of a sudden his hands felt sticky. He had to walk by his
father and the bedroom door to get to the bathroom.

"What's up, sport?" his father asked genially as
he went by.

George locked the bathroom door and turned
on the water. *My hands are sticky*, he thought to
himself. The thought seemed to mean something
outside of itself. The word *sticky* seemed to mean
something. His hands were disgusting. When the
water was running he couldn't hear the man in the
bedroom. The water felt wonderful—clean. As if
he were washing away his disgusting skin.

But when he turned the water off, instantly his
hands were sticky again. He heard the bedroom
door open, heard a voice saying, "Oh, hi, Joe," and
felt the revolting dirtiness of his hands.

He turned the water back on and while his
hands were wet and soapy there was nothing but

the clean feeling. George washed until he was certain he had gotten every trace of the terrible stickiness off his hands.

But when he turned the water off it was still there.

George washed his hands five more times before his mother started to bang on the door. It was a torture to have to stop washing. George was convinced that his mother would see his hands, would be revolted by his hands.

But his mother didn't notice anything.

George sat in the living room in an agony of confusion until his parents went to bed. Two more men came by, nodding to his father on their way into the bedroom. George sat on his hands so that his father wouldn't see the stickiness, but his father drank gin out of a bottle and fingered crumpled bills, staring with no expression at the closed bedroom door.

After his parents finally went to bed, George washed his hands seven times, then seven more. Then he was able to go to bed, but he had to get up after half an hour to wash seven more times. Then he was able to sleep through the night.

It was just like that: one moment there was no compulsion, then there was. Neither of his parents ever asked him why he spent three or four hours in the bathroom every night. And they didn't ask him why he began pausing before answering questions, began mouthing to himself all the time.

It was because shortly after the need to wash had come an even more compelling need: George started counting. Every time he heard a number, or saw a number, or thought of a number, he had to count to seven. Seven was his magic, his balm. Seven times seven times washing his hands. Count to seven if you think of a number. Touch each corner of the kitchen table seven times as you go by. (George's father never asked him why he walked around him at the table, pausing briefly at each corner, a finger surreptitiously tapping.)

George's grades began to slip. He was accused of dawdling. When he walked up the aisle in the classroom he touched two corners of the desks on his right; on the way back he went down the next aisle, touching the corners to his left, with a quick count, one two three four five six seven, tap-tapping lightly. He had to stop walking every time he counted; his numbers paralyzed him. He left the classroom last, going stop-start slowly up the aisle, tapping at the corners of the desks, pretending to forget something so he could make his way, stopping and starting, up the next aisle to touch the other sides.

He was left back twice. His parents never answered the school's calls.

DETECTIVE FIRST GRADE ED HOAG SAT ASLEEP AT his desk, his head in his arms. A cigar stub lay burned out on the floor next to him. The computer terminal in front of him blinked silent toasters with tiny wings. A woman walked up talking—"Ed, you got the—?" and stopped, her hand halfway to her mouth. He didn't stir; she stood watching him sleep.

He was beautiful, the way old buildings are beautiful, in his imperfections: Detective Second Grade Marcy Fleischer had been partnered with Hoag for eight years, and she'd never gotten accustomed to his beauty, even as it aged and changed. Dark curly hair thin now, high angry cheekbones and skin gone from fresh to ruddy, a rich slack mouth and eyes almost black from rogue ancestral blood: an American Indian, a black slave woman. Marcy couldn't look at him this way when he was awake; in animation Hoag's face lost its rough unaware beauty. He was a good man who hid his goodness behind aggression and pride and banter. He was impossible; Marcy knelt quietly and lifted the cigar stub and dusted it with her fingers and dropped it on his head.

He started, eyes open and blank with surprise,

and then he sighed and settled his head back in his arms and said, "Fuck off, Fleischer," without looking up.

"Rise and shine," said Marcy. She had short, colorless brown hair and a thin mouth. Her hips measured wider than her bustline; her legs were not long. No one ever seemed to notice her body, and she considered herself lucky to be out of that particular maelstrom, and no resentment ate her heart. She loved being a police officer. She had two cats and a lot of friends and no regrets.

Marcy rubbed her temples with her fingertips. Her head hurt. She'd been at work since noon the day before, taking calls and sifting through tips at the Chocolate Man Task Force headquarters at the 909th Precinct, in Queens. The mayor had realized the need for a task force after Andrew Timmons was killed; he was the third victim of the Chocolate Man. And he was found within the borders of the Nine-O-Nine. The force was made up of sixteen officers, supposedly working in eight-hour shifts. But at any given time there would be thirteen or fourteen officers present, answering telephones, logging tips into computers, reading and rereading the individual case reports, cross-referencing every detail of every case, brainstorming about new ways to investigate the dozens of tips that came in every hour.

Marcy was tired. The minutiae of her search wore at her nerves: a thousand calls, a thousand tips, and no way of knowing which held the grain of truth she needed. She may already have taken the crucial call, may even have interviewed the guilty man. Murderers do not wear any sign of their evil; there was never any way, after a case was closed, to say, *The moment we saw him we knew*. Because evil wears an ordinary face, even as it kills and mutilates little children.

Marcy had been a policewoman for nine years when the Chocolate Man murders began. She had never wanted anything so much as she wanted to be a member of the task force handling the killings. She had no children of her own; she had never married. She was thirty-seven years old, and she knew that there would probably be no children for her. But she loved her work. She had no illusions about what she did: evil and good were equally real to her, and equally strong, and neither was a matter for the gods. To Marcy the world was black and white; there was no evil so petty that it should go unpunished, just as there was no kindness so small that it should pass without thanks. Her path had always been clear to her.

And children had always seemed almost holy to her: their wants, their imaginings, even their direct and explosive anger, had for Marcy an almost totemic purity. Marcy had seen horrible crimes. The death of children is common; the murder of children. Beaten, starved, and tormented for being what their parents are themselves: weak, needy, selfish, angry. A two-year-old cries; a six-year-old takes change from his mother's purse; a baby throws food. A child may be the mirror of the inmost self, and be punished for it. Children with chain-link collars around their necks, children marked with cigarette burns, Marcy had seen them. It wasn't often that she could help while a child was still alive. Ed called her the Avenging Angel—it wasn't a compliment. Marcy believed in God, and she had never felt that a reconciliation was needed between her belief and what she saw. God had given humans free will. Nature's free will is chaos. Innocence is the victim of chaos. Marcy could be there only after the fact; she could bear witness and promise vengeance. Because that is what justice was to her, an evening of accounts. She didn't believe in rehabilitation. She didn't ask God to solve her cases.

Ed had gotten up from his desk; "Your hair's trying to get away again," Marcy said, reaching to smooth it. He pushed her away without annoyance and flattened the wild curls. "What's left of it," he said. He reached for the coffee mug on his desk ("HAVE A F✷✷KING DAY"), pointed to the cigar stub where it had fallen to the floor. "Get that for me, will you?" he said to Marcy, and she said, "Yeah, right," and headed for the door. The hallway was dim green, with yellowy cream running halfway down from the ceiling. There were several officers heading for the squadroom—"You still here, Fleischer?" "Hey, Renny, is there any more coffee?" "Mohammad, you get any sleep yet?"—and Marcy and Ed joined them.

Marcy took a seat at the back of the room. As always when she was in the Task Force squadroom her eyes were drawn to the large map of New York City and environs on the front wall. Red plastic pushpins were scattered over blue and black lines and patches of green: one for each kidnap site. A yellow pinpoint for each ransom drop. An orange pinpoint for each body-drop site. Little blue tags linking each red, yellow, and orange pushpin: Peter Hubert had a blue five, a piece of sticky notepad with a scrawled number on it, suspended from red and yellow and orange. Red at Myrtle Avenue and Cumberland Street, in Fort Greene, Brooklyn; yellow at Jamaica Avenue and 182nd Place, in Jamaica, Queens; orange at the side of Kissena Lake, in Kissena Park, Queens.

Marcy had gone to each of the kidnap sites on her own time, and to each ransom site and body-drop point; Ronald Chin was kidnapped in Prospect Park, Brooklyn, his ransom was left in Lake Success, Long Island, and his body was found in the Cypress Hills Cemetery, just along the Brooklyn-Queens border. The killer had placed Ronald's stuffed panda next to his head; he had been clutching it when he was kidnapped. At first it looked almost like a kind gesture, the little black paw touching Ronald's cheek—but there were eight small stones, two cigarette butts, and a crumpled McDonald's hamburger wrapper lined up on the other side of the panda.

Ronald's socks had had trains on them. Marcy remembered that from the reports of each crime, which she read after midnight when the phones were quieter; she remembered pictures of Ronald now, his bare feet innocent and shocking, placed carefully side by side so that in death he looked like a toy soldier at attention.

Marcy knew all the children; she had talked to every parent, sister, cousin, friend. "You've got to learn to let it go," Ed had said to her more than once, "it'll eat you like cancer, you'll burn out." And Marcy could feel herself burning.

As soon as all the officers were seated Lieutenant Monsey, a short, stocky black man who reminded Marcy of the drill sergeant he had once been, began speaking. He didn't say, "Good morning," he said, "As you know, we've been expecting a new abduction for the last week or so. In the three years since the Chocolate Man killings began, they've been getting progressively closer together. And we know that our man likes to do his thing around Christmastime. That's classic, even people without personality disorders tend to become agitated or even depressed during the holiday season. And I think no one here will dispute me if I say that the Chocolate Man has one *fuck* of a personality disorder."

The whole room burst into laughter. Marcy caught Ed's eye and shook her head; he winked. "Okay," Lieutenant Monsey was saying, "okay, people. Tomorrow morning a Ms. Alethea Howard, of the psychological-profiling department of Quantico, is coming up to speak to us. You know we've been waiting for Quantico to put together a profile on our guy. Well, they finally did." There was some applause; "Okay," Lieutenant Monsey said again. "Now, I haven't seen this report. Ms. Howard is bringing it up from Virginia herself. She wouldn't fax it, she wouldn't E-mail it—she wants to present it herself. Said the report shows some interesting twists on the typical multiple-killer personality— whatever that means."

There was more laughter. The members of the FBI working out of Quantico never hurried; they didn't guess. They were responsible for almost everything the police, in this country and abroad, knew about multiple murders. Every police department in America that was faced with serial killings contacted Quantico; their experts regularly put together profiles based on each killer's individual MO and traveled with their reports to talk to the officers handling the case. The Chocolate Man Task Force team had been waiting for months now, every day expecting a murder, every day neglecting everything in their lives that wasn't about murder. They weren't tired, they were restless with fever, they were waiting for something none of them wanted, and yet with each fresh murder came the possibility that this time the killer had made the mistake that would lead them to him.

Lieutenant Monsey was finishing up: "—tomorrow at thirteen hundred hours," and Marcy got to her feet. "Think this Howard woman is going to know something we don't?" Ed asked her as they went back down the hall to what they all called the Information Room, the room with the telephones and the computers. He was trying to get his cigar stub to light; he had been trying throughout almost the whole meeting.

"'This Howard woman'? If it were a man would you refer to him as 'this Howard man'?" She took the cigar stub from his hand and lighted it with her own lighter. "I'll bet you refer to me as 'that Fleischer woman.'" She handed the stub back lit.

"Showoff. Actually, I don't think I can tell

you how I refer to you. Your virgin ears couldn't take it."

"Please."

"You know," Ed said, suddenly serious, "what I can never understand is, how does this guy hide it? We already know he's crazy, and now Quantico is saying he's even crazier than we thought. I know they say it's possible—hell, I've read the books. 'Family Man Found with Fourteen Skeletons in Basement.'"

"'Crazed Sniper Was Model Citizen.' I know. There are people right now who know him, who see him every day. He's probably got a job. He might even have a family. And they don't have any idea what he really is."

"Hell," said Ed, "*I* don't have any idea what he really is. After all this time I still don't understand—hell, I'm not naive—" Marcy said, "Ffff," —"but if he just wants to kill them, why does he call the parents? Why ask for money when you don't want it?"

"He likes to keep their hope alive. It's part of the game."

"Game? Shit. What kind of—" And they went on like that, down the hall; a conversation they had had a hundred times, familiar but necessary, to remind themselves that the particular horror behind the facade of "the Chocolate Man," with its images of bunnies and Santas, and the term "serial killer," with its automatic shock and disgust, was a human being, with the motives and feelings of a human being. So that when they found traces of him they wouldn't take them for more or less than what they were: evidence of one man's pathetic attempts to make himself whole.

"Shit," Ed interrupted himself, "my cigar went out again. Hey, you Fleischer woman, would you light it up again for me?"

AS EMILY AND LAURIE CAME OUT OF THE HOUSE Laurie noticed the already anticipatory emptiness of the street. The plastic Santa on the plastic sleigh and deer romping up the roof of a neighbor's house seemed not in flight but waiting; the unlit lights on front-lawn evergreens were waiting; the last dead perfectly still brown leaves were waiting in the gutter. The whole block was blank, like an empty stage. In two days the street would be alive, with grandparents and children and teetering towers of presents going up front walks. *And it'll still be just Emily and me,* Laurie thought. No grandparents, Laurie's mother dead now of cancer and her father so long ago disappeared. And Dick's parents as silent as he was. On holidays Laurie sent them cards and pictures; she would never understand how they could let Emily grow up without them. While Laurie and Dick were married his parents hadn't visited often, busy with their own lives in Oregon, but they had seemed, just as Dick had seemed, to treasure Emily: and yet with the death of the marriage they had been able to let go. Laurie wanted to ask them, *Doesn't it hurt? Don't you think about her, don't you wonder if she's forgotten you?* Laurie wished she could believe that Emily had forgotten them.

Emily didn't cry for her losses anymore. She rarely mentioned her father and never asked about her grandparents at all. A lot of her friends' parents were divorced; it was not, nowadays, a disgrace. It was normal. But its normality had not dulled its impact.

Laurie watched her daughter now, running ahead to look at the climbing reindeer; Laurie could never tell whether Emily was "normal" or not. She had never thought she'd find herself troubled because her nine-year-old daughter *didn't* want to wear a bra. But Emily evinced none of the petulant anxiousness of her friends to be "grownup"; if anything she was more childlike than they, with none of the parodying of adult attitudes that characterized so many children Laurie saw: she didn't swear, or clumsily ape poses of seduction, or assume what she thought to be adult mannerisms. Emily still loved her stuffed toys, she showed no interest at all in boys, and she didn't plead to stay up late to watch *Baywatch* or *NYPD Blue*.

Laurie was grateful, in a way. She didn't relish the inevitable time when the arguments would begin, when Emily without realizing would begin to sever the bonds that held her so close to her mother. All the other women Laurie knew with girls Emily's age were already grappling with their daughters' new hunger for independence; Emily was still leaning against her mother on the sofa to watch old black-and-white movies on the VCR.

Since Emily was three Laurie had been watching old movies with her. Garbo, Davis, Cagney. At first Emily had just liked the pretty dresses the

actresses wore, and their hair, but she had come to
love the world inside the movies as much as her
mother did. Laurie didn't much like the world as
she saw it around her every day; for her the movies
were a necessary escape. She didn't know what they
were for Emily, exactly, but they were important,
she knew that. They gave her and her mother a
vocabulary of images and stories that were theirs
alone. Laurie knew that Emily was an extraordinar-
ily imaginative child with a voracious appetite for
fuel for her fantasies: perhaps Emily was not comfortable with the world as she saw it around her, and
fantasy was a necessary escape for her as well.

Emily was always pretending something. When
she was little she told elaborate stories to her stuffed
animals; now she and her best friend, Susan, acted
out magic and drama in Emily's bedroom after
school.

Emily ran ahead of Laurie down the block,
intoxicated by the blandishing air. The sun shone
wan, but the breeze was out of spring; Laurie
caught the taste in it of other springs; she could
remember a tantalizing "before." Before Dick,
before Emily, before even work or school: a spring
morning like the first bite of a honeydew melon.
Emily would remember that too, someday. When
Emily was little Laurie used to stand by her bed at
night and watch her sleep, and cry. Her daughter's
purity of heart, of conception, hurt Laurie terribly;
all Emily cared about when she was four was what
goodies there would be to eat at her next birthday
party. And still Laurie hurt terribly: all Emily
seemed to care about lately was whether she was

going to get a Victorian dollhouse for Christmas. Not yet boys; not yet fear of the actual in the dark, far worse than monsters; not yet the consuming decoy caring about face and hair and muscle tone and appetite and too-tight shoes and should I have and I'll never be.

What Laurie was afraid of, she knew, was that Emily was going to have to grow up, someday, to be a woman.

When George was twelve he burned his house down. His mother was in the bedroom with a man; his father had fallen asleep at the kitchen table. George put some crumpled newspaper in the sink—*The New York Daily News*—he could see the date, May 8, 1968, and he stood unmoving over the sink while he counted, once for May the fifth month, once for 8, once each for the numbers in 1968. *And one and nine is ten,* he thought: one two three four five six seven. *And once for ten and six*—he stood over the sink a long time.

When he lit the match there was nothing in the world but the flame. George forgot his numbers, forgot his hands. Then he walked away from the sink and out the door.

No one was badly hurt in the fire. His mother and the man she was with smelled smoke; by the time they dragged Joe from the room the curtains over the sink had gone up, and after that it was too late to save anything.

George stood across the street, watching. The flames shot with astonishing swiftness out the kitchen windows. George's hands didn't feel dirty, and there was a stillness in his head. When he saw his mother and father stumble out the door he felt nothing at all.

Emily ran up the block ahead of her mother. The people next door had put the plastic Santa and sleigh up last night; when Emily and her mother came out of the house the familiar figures greeted her. The Santa's red was worn away in spots and he had a crooked smile on his face that made him look angry instead of jolly. Rudolph was beaming idiot glee. They were all like friends of Emily's by now: she couldn't remember a Christmas without them.

Then the hurt came, and Emily ran up the street away from it. A Christmas long ago, Emily on her father's shoulders looking at the Santa and sleigh as her father pointed out Rudolph and told her the story. "Rudolph the Red-Nosed Reindeer"—in her mind her father had a beautiful voice, even though she knew she wouldn't recognize it if he called her on the phone. *But he'll never call:* and Emily ran away from that.

Her mother was quiet behind her; just walking. But suddenly Emily felt guilty, as though her mother knew what she was thinking, as though it were wrong to think it. To feel the hurt. That's what Emily called it: the hurt. She stopped and waited for her mother, and when she caught up Emily said, "Nancy Drew just discovered a secret passageway at the old mansion."

"Nancy Drew *always* discovers a secret passage-way at the old mansion," said her mother. "But at least you don't read any of the ones that have been updated." And Emily got bored in an instant, and that was good. She took her mother's hand and didn't listen while she went on about Nancy Drew.

Her mother went to a lot of trouble to make sure that Emily didn't read the updated Nancy Drews. Sometimes her mother found the original versions at garage sales; and now there were reprints of the original books in the stores, and about once a month Emily would find one at the end of her bed when she woke up.

In the books that had been revised there were no roadsters, no chums. Bess wasn't plump and George wasn't quite so boyish. Emily had heard her mother telling her friend Carolyn about that, they both laughed and Emily didn't really understand, but she knew she wasn't supposed to ask. Her mother thought it was really important for Emily to read the books the way they were originally written; she said that children should be exposed to things that were from other times; she seemed angry and sad and said she felt betrayed when she found out the books had been updated. Emily sort of under-stood that: she liked the roadsters and plump Bess. Sometimes when she read the books she felt as though she were right there, all that long time ago. And when she finished reading it was like coming back from somewhere, for a while she was still back in that long-ago place.

Her mother was still talking about Nancy Drew. Her mother talked to her about too many things:

advertising and underwear and slavery and Shakespeare and China and how women are always made to seem helpless or if they're not the strength they have is not real, it isn't woman's strength but just an idea men have about it. Emily got bored, and then she felt guilty, but sometimes she loved to listen to it all, it was like reading or watching a movie, she had that same sense of having gone somewhere and come back by the time her mother was through. Her mother said Nancy Drew was a copout because she always got saved at the last minute by her father or her boyfriend. Emily was so embarrassed when her mother said *copout*.

Now Emily's mother was watching her, she knew, that way she had; as though Emily were glass. Emily didn't like it but she understood: there wasn't anybody else to care about. Emily wished her mother would get married again. She stepped into the street and the street was a river. Her class was studying the two world wars. *The survivor was swimming away from the* Lusitania. "Be careful," her mother said behind her. That was World War I. Her mother didn't know Emily was swimming.

"Mom, can we go to Giorgio's after the park?" Emily was walking backward, fast; at what age had Laurie stopped doing that?

"Sure, hon," she said; she resisted the urge to tell her daughter that the sidewalk was about to end, and Emily turned gracefully without looking and stepped down into the street.

"Be careful," Laurie said, too late.

THE BLACKJACK WAS WHERE THE CHOCOLATE MAN always kept it, on the backseat. He had to look for it; it was underneath a lot of empty containers from McDonald's, some soda cans and Styrofoam coffee cups, and newspapers that lay crumpled and spilled-on in the backseat. It had been three months since he had last killed. One two three four five six seven. He really should clean out that seat—but that he did only after. Never in between.

He reached back from the front seat of his car to touch the cold metal of the blackjack. The first white-hot horror of Marilyn Ossi's grief must be easing now. Maybe she could eat now, maybe some nights she slept. The Chocolate Man's pleasure in her suffering was getting stale.

When he held Jimmy's little shoe he no longer felt the visceral thrill of memory. The first night the leather had felt soft as skin. The mother's face on the eleven o'clock news had been poignant with tears as he played his tape of her over and over: "Please bring my Jimmy back to me." Over and over—and now he hardly played it at all.

The blackjack felt good in his hand. Absent-mindedly he lifted it, up and down, up and down. It was a clear day, about forty degrees. One two three four five six seven. An unusually balmy day for late December.

There were numbers in a random sequence along the spine of the blackjack. The Chocolate Man counted, one to seven, fourteen times. While he was counting, his face was utterly blank. Once he was jolted from his task by the sound of a child's laughter. But the numbers were in his head now, perfect in their meaningless order.

When he finished counting he looked up and down the street, but there was no sign of a child.

He let the blackjack fall and turned to grip the steering wheel. There was a playground in Rego Park; he had discovered it only a week ago. Three months ago—one two three four five six seven—he had sat on a swing in Van Cortlandt Park, in the Bronx, at four in the morning—one two three four five six seven—kicking his feet against the ground, seeing nothing. He had thought about the children who had sat on that swing, who would sit there the next day. He had taken Jimmy Ossi because he had promised himself that he would take the first boy child he saw sitting on that same swing. Jimmy had been standing, actually, brandishing a plastic sword and yelling to his friends to come on, they had to get away from Rita Repulsa and the evil space aliens. In the Chocolate Man's bright kitchen Jimmy had told him all about the Power Rangers, which the Chocolate Man had never seen.

The new park he had found was small, it would be dangerous to take a child. But he felt lucky: it was almost Christmas.

He was tired of Marilyn Ossi. He started the

car, his mind already ahead, the Long Island Expressway, trees along the side of the road, there were certain to be children in the parks today.

Exit Twenty-three. One two three four five six seven. As the car slid out of its parking space the Chocolate Man was smiling.

LAURIE WATCHED FROM A PARK BENCH AS EMILY let herself be chased by a much younger child, three or four, a darkly beautiful South American girl with eyes like a doe's.

There were a lot of children at the park today. The snow fell intermittently, a few tantalizing flakes, a tiny flurry; but always the sun broke; and it was getting warmer. An odd day for December.

Laurie liked this park, with its expanses of faded green and its openness. She liked always being able to see where her daughter was. The park was a dull green diamond, with a swing set, a slide, and an ungainly wooden sculpture for the children to climb. The water fountain had been vandalized years ago and never replaced. There was a field where people let their dogs loose and didn't clean up after them, and a clear patch of grass where sunbathers lay in the summertime; there was the tiny duck pond. There were chestnut trees, and sycamores, and a fire cherry. There was a mulberry tree and a tangle of bushes where Emily liked to play hide and seek with the littler children.

The little girl was screaming as she ran after Emily, a high, undulating wail; if you weren't watching you might think she was being hurt.

But her face was cut with a wide grin; Emily had hidden behind a low bush and was crouched, waiting.

The child faltered in her run, her cry faltered. She stood poised, looking back and forth. Laurie was afraid she was going to burst into tears.

The girl said something, called. *Where is her mother?* Laurie thought, looking around.

When she turned back they were both gone.

Laurie started from her seat, she opened her mouth to call; but Emily appeared around the side of a World War I monument, soldiers and a child and even a pug dog in bronze. (the little girl's shrill, happy cry reached Laurie and she settled back, chiding herself).

And here was the girl's mother. "I was watching from across the park, but then I lost sight of them."

The mother was beautiful, too, with the same eyes.

"If I lose sight of mine for a minute I panic," Laurie said. Like a confession, because for a moment she hadn't watched.

"You have to let the children be children," the woman said. "I have four, and you have to. They run? They have to run."

Laurie thought of the things she'd read in the newspapers lately, the child found at the bottom of a garbage chute, the baby shaken to death by a nanny, the two-year-old dropped and dropped again to the floor, for crying.

"We have to go home now," the woman said. "I found my boys, but Ulla she outrun them all. Every day she run."

"Emily!" Laurie called.

"Ulla! *Ven acá! Tenemos que irnos a casa!*" the woman called, and Laurie could hear in her voice an echo of her daughter's happy cries.

"It's so dangerous in the city," Laurie said, watching the girls stop, and turn, and head running toward them; this time Emily was chasing, slowly so the little one could win.

"We can only watch, it is all we can do," the woman said. She scooped up her child and said to Emily, "Thank you," and to Laurie, "She is beautiful," and, as she turned to leave, "Only watch. The rest is in God's hands."

When George Riehle was ten he murdered a dog. It was a stray, wet-nosed and friendly. George was walking in a narrow strip of woods off the highway that ran two blocks east of his house. If he didn't look right or left he could pretend he was in a real forest.

The dog had been following him for about three blocks. George ignored the peaks of houses rising out of the corners of his eyes, and he tried to ignore the dog, too; he wanted so much for it to keep following him.

It did follow him. He could hear its paws rustling up leaves. As George and the dog got near his house and the trees thinned, George stopped, and turned and knelt.

The dog jumped up and comically away. "Here, boy, good boy," George said. The dog leaned its nose down and growled.

Instantly George was angry. Angry, he put one knee to the mulchy ground and reached out his arm. "Here, boy, good boy." The dog eyed him without fear or trust.

It cocked its head. George became enraged with its stupidity—its refusal of his love. It would not come to him. He rustled the mulch with his fingers and the dog took a step, sniffing. The mulch smelled wet and dead and sweet.

"Here, boy, good boy." The dog inched its nose close to his fingers—it was almost impossible to keep his voice soft, his fingers slow—inched and leaned, snuffling, and George grabbed it by the neck and twisted.

The dog's hind legs kicked even after its neck was broken.

George brought the body home in his arms, as if it were a baby, past his father snoring at the kitchen table, and went to his own room and bent and pushed the dog's body under the bed.

A few days later his mother said, walking in a dirty cream-colored slip from the bedroom to the bathroom, "This place stinks, Joe, it really stinks."

Joe didn't say anything. George went into his room and breathed in the fetid smell. He took the sheet off his bed and wrapped it around the dog and carried the body back to the woods and left it there.

He took a bone. He kept it on his windowsill for a long time and then he forgot about it. He must have lost it.

✗   ✗   ✗

When Emily was six years old she ran through a glass door.

She was at her mother's friend Carolyn's house. Carolyn had a dog, a little mutt, wiggly and friendly. Emily liked to play a game she called Mad Dog, which her mother didn't approve of. Emily pretended the dog was chasing her. Carolyn had a big backyard, grassy-green, with dandelions. If Emily started to run and yelled. "Mad dog!" the dog would chase her. It would yap, and when she couldn't see it behind her it got bigger, she could hear its fast, uneven breathing and the sound of its paws thudding against the grass.

This time the thing behind her was very big. She wanted to get to Carolyn, in the house, past the cement steps up to the porch and the closed glass door.

The breathing was close and Emily was almost to the steps, she was tripping up the cement and her arms went out. *Like Superman,* she thought, and the glass was right in front of her and something was loud, a moment of black and then her arms red so red, the dog was running in circles and yapping and Carolyn was trying to catch Emily because she was running, too, away from the red, running in circles on the lawn, and she knew, running, that she could have stopped, that she had hit the glass wall on purpose.

2:20 P.M.

THE BOY WAS STANDING AT A LOW BOX HEDGE OVER by the bushes in Hewlitt Park; maybe he was looking at something. The Chocolate Man walked slowly in his direction, his sneakers loud against the brittle winter grass.

The boy reached out to touch the bushes' bare twigs, and the Chocolate Man hesitated. There was something yellow, shiny, among the bare branches. *Was* it a boy? The short, tousled hair, yes, the scuffed brown bucks. But the tip of the nose, the line of the cheek—yes, a boy.

He was holding a toad, the Chocolate Man could see. A little green one. It should have been hibernating, but it had been lured out by the counterfeit warmth.

The boy didn't notice the Chocolate Man at all, walking quietly toward him across the grass. The toad was kicking its legs. The boy stood at two o'clock to the Chocolate Man's six.

One two three four five six seven, one two three four five six seven.

The Chocolate Man stopped walking while he counted. He had the blackjack in his coat pocket. There was nobody—a gaggle of women stood across the field, gathered around something one of them was holding.

One two three four five six seven. The Chocolate Man stood, unable to walk. A baby, most likely.

Nobody was looking at him. The boy didn't even know he was there. American Indians put the full weight of each step evenly on the heel of the foot and on the ball; the Chocolate Man had read that when he was a boy. That was the way to walk quietly.

He could hear the boy breathing. He could see the pink of his tongue, stuck out in concentration; could hear a soft snuffle of exhalation. The Chocolate Man didn't like talking to them. That was always the hardest part, the talk right at the beginning. The pretending he was interested:

He took the blackjack slowly, silently out of his coat pocket. He opened his mouth to say something, but he stopped—his car was about seventy feet away—one two three four five six seven.

The boy lifted the toad up to his cheek.

I can take him, the Chocolate Man thought. He moved three steps forward.

One two three four five six seven.

If he were quiet—he walked gently, keeping his weight evenly distributed along the heel and the ball of each foot.

The boy looked up.

There was no fear in his blue eyes. *Nobody ever hurt him,* thought the Chocolate Man.

"I've got a frog," the boy said. The Chocolate Man bent to look at it. It was dull green, with tiny malignant eyes.

"All toads are poisonous," he said. The nearest person was a young woman with a baby carriage, walking about sixty feet away.

One two three four—

"It's a *frog*," the boy said.

—five six seven.

But she was not walking toward them.

"Oh," said the Chocolate Man. "Are you going to take it home?"

"My mom would like a frog."

His voice was too light—but a girl wouldn't want to give her mother a frog, would she? The Chocolate Man was snapping the fingers of his right hand, over and over; he always did that when he was concentrating. The other hand held the blackjack behind his back.

"Is that your mom over there?"

"No, she's by the bench," pointing toward the group of women standing next to one of the benches, surrounded by toddlers and bottles and gummy toys in the dust. They were about a hundred feet away.

One two three four five six seven.

Girls don't like frogs.

The Chocolate Man and the boy looked at the women for a moment; they weren't looking back. The Chocolate Man watched his careful boy's hands, one finger stroking the toad's belly. "If you pet them like this they like you."

They piss on you, thought the Chocolate Man.

"I have flies," he said suddenly.

"You do?"

"For the toad."

"It's a—hey, it peed on me!" But the boy didn't put the toad down; he held it up as it emptied its bladder on the grass. He wiped his hand unselfconsciously against his pants, looking with interest at the toad's bottom. "Neat," he said. "How many?"

"A dozen," said the Chocolate Man.

One two three four five six seven.

The boy was looking at him with interest now.

"You want to come with me to get them?"

"Well—" The boy hesitated. The toad waved its little arms and legs. "My mother wouldn't want—"

"We'll be right back. Look, he's dancing."

"He's not *dancing*," the boy said disgustedly, "he's trying to get away," and for a moment the Chocolate Man thought he had lost him. They looked at the toad together in silence.

"What kind of flies?"

He suspected nothing. "Bluebottles."

"You said a dozen."

One two three four five six seven.

"Yes. Big ones."

The Chocolate Man felt a familiar thrill of fear, up his legs and through his groin and up over the rest of his body. Anyone could see them now, a nine-year-old boy—one two three four five six seven—and a man in his mid-thirties—one two three four five six seven—of medium height with receding sandy hair and watery blue eyes. The boy's mother would see them, and call out. The woman with the baby carriage would see them, and remember.

"I'd better not," the boy said finally. "My mom would be mad."

The Chocolate Man's heart was racing and his palms were sweating.

"All right," he said to the boy, "I'll go get them for you."

He was holding his breath.

But the boy only said, "Okay," not looking up from his hand.

The Chocolate Man's eyes darted back and forth: no one there, or there. He raised his hand slowly, looking at the top of the boy's curly head.

For a moment there was no movement, nothing in the world but the oblivious child and the toad.

And then the boy started to turn his head and the Chocolate Man hit him once with the blackjack.

One two three four five six seven.

"HE'S SO BIG, HOW OLD DID YOU SAY HE WAS?"

"Two weeks." A cluster of mothers stood around Laurie's friend Maureen and her new baby. Emily was over by the bushes at the edge of the park; on the way home she would have a story to tell her mother about a dark wood, and poison berries.

"Is this the first time you've taken him out?" someone asked Maureen. Laurie loved the pretense of being a full-time mother. Usually she saw the other mothers only on the weekends, when they were with their older children and their husbands. There was something choreographed in these weekend park visits, a sense not of the preciousness but the oppressiveness of time. Laurie herself was always aware of the precariousness of the moment, which would, no matter how she tried to hold it, change, and change Emily.

But on weekdays the casual urgency of the weekend dissolved into comfortable routine. The mothers sat on benches, rocking their baby carriages with one foot while they talked about teething and the terrible twos and their toddlers clambered on the slides and the monkey bars. Laurie joined them gratefully and with no little envy.

"Well," Maureen was saying, "it's such a warm day for December—" Laurie glanced across the park to where Emily was playing. Was her jacket warm enough?

"Hey, Charlie," she said, bending to wave a finger in front of the baby's unfocused eyes, "you smile for your mama yet? Huh?" The baby grinned; it didn't even know it was alive yet. Sometimes Laurie wanted a baby so much she cried, at home alone in the bathroom, after a morning in the park. The baby smelled of powder and milk. Laurie looked up. What was Emily holding over there? She always seemed to be picking up bugs. When Laurie was a little girl she never even touched a worm.

The baby reached for Laurie's finger and the mothers *oohed*.

"He has Juan's ears," somebody said.

"May I touch him?" Laurie asked. When Emily was a baby it seemed as if somebody was always trying to touch her without asking. Strangers. The same people who had insisted on touching Laurie's pregnant belly to feel the baby kick; people for whom a woman's or a child's body is not real, with a real body's boundaries and rights. Again Laurie's eyes went to where her daughter was standing. Emily was bringing a finger up to pet whatever she held in her hand.

There was a movement at the corner of Laurie's eye. A man was standing about twenty feet away from Emily. He had light hair. He wasn't looking at her daughter. What had caught Laurie's eye was a movement at his side—for one horrible instant Laurie thought he was masturbating. But he was just holding his hand up near his crotch and snapping his fingers over and over.

Laurie almost cried out. She almost said something—"Do you see that man over there?"—when the baby began wailing, a high, keening, kittenish cry.

"Oh, my," said Maureen, "it's feeding time."

"Do you breast-feed?" somebody asked. Laurie remembered breast-feeding Emily, how much it had hurt. Even after six months her breasts were sore all the time. The man was not moving; Emily hadn't even noticed him.

"Are you having any trouble?" she asked Maureen; she wished she could have another baby even if breast-feeding did hurt. She worried too much, it was not so odd that there was a man there, he was probably somebody's daddy.

"My nipples hurt for about a week, I guess," Maureen was saying. "The second day they *really* hurt, and then Charlie vomited blood, and I thought there was something terribly wrong with him until I realized it was just that my breasts were bleeding."

"Do you use that cream, what is it called?"

"I've heard that cream clogs the pores," somebody said, and Maureen looked into her baby's face: "You're not hungry? So what's the matter?"

"May I hold him?" Laurie asked eagerly.

"You sure can," and the little bundle was in Laurie's arms.

The baby's head lolled back; his mouth was open. "He can't even hold up his head yet," Laurie said softly. She supported the back of his head with one hand, and his hair was soft like kitten's fur. She leaned his head against her shoulder and he reached forward with his face, looking for his mother's nipple.

Laurie laughed. "He tells me he *is* hungry," she said, and held him out to Maureen; as he left her arms she felt a sharp pain, a cramp in the heart. Emily had been smaller, lighter, when she rooted for her mother's breast it had always made Laurie laugh. She glanced up again to where her daughter was standing.

There was no one there.

Laurie gasped, and Maureen said, "Lau—"

"Emily's not there," Laurie said calmly. She was looking around and her blood was racing. Even as she waved the suddenly concerned mothers off— "It's all right, she's around here somewhere"—she felt a rush of dizziness. *I'm going to fall down,* she thought.

Someone put a hand on her arm. Emily wasn't where she'd been standing. Not to the left, near the swings.

"Where was she, Laurie?" someone asked. Not over by the duck pond. Laurie began walking quickly toward where she had last seen her daughter.

"She's probably right behind a tree or something," Maureen said behind her; Laurie's blood was pounding in her ears.

"Emily!" she yelled, and her voice was shrill and she was immediately embarrassed. Emily was out of her sight for two seconds and she was getting hysterical.

"Emily!" she called again in a more normal voice. Not down by the basketball court, not on the baseball field.

"What was she wearing?" somebody asked, and Laurie was surprised to see that two of the mothers had followed her.

"Ah—blue jacket, jeans, boots." Here. Laurie stopped and looked around. Not behind the bushes. Not back over by the benches.

"Laurie—" one of the mothers said, but Laurie stood as though stone, staring at the little yellow clown barrette caught in the box hedge. Her little girl was gone.

GEORGE AND HIS PARENTS MOVED INTO A HOUSE in another neighborhood. There had been insurance money from the fire, and an out-of-court settlement for his father's smoke-damaged lung.

Men no longer came to see his mother. She lay in the bedroom and his father sat at the kitchen table and sometimes nobody said a word for days.

George kept up with his rituals, washing and counting; he dropped out of school when he was fifteen. He started some more fires but none approached the cleansing beauty of the first one, so he gave it up.

He seldom made friends his own age, preferring instead to play with the little children who lived on his block. Always he felt he was on the verge of something, as if each time he counted to seven he might finally know—something.

The kids on the block liked to play counting games. Sometimes they got impatient with George's slowness. Only the very smallest ones didn't care. And their mothers seemed to accept the slow-talking adolescent who knelt with such concentration next to their toddlers.

Once George was asked to baby-sit. The boy was four years old; it was just for a couple of hours in the afternoon. As soon as the mother left the house George took the boy into his parents' bedroom. "Sit here," he said, and, "Pull these down. Like this." But he wasn't actually excited—until he thought, *What would his mother think if she knew?*

After George was done he told the boy that he must never tell his mother.

"Why?"

"Because she'll spank you." And although George was never asked to baby-sit again, he was reasonably sure the boy had not told. No one, after all, came to stop him as he knelt with the little children on the sidewalk.

But he was no longer comfortable around the four-year-old boy; seeing him made George want to wash his hands. Soon he didn't play with the children anymore.

THERE WAS A MOANING IN THE BACKSEAT. THE Chocolate Man had caught the small body as it fell, slipping his arms around it and cradling the lolling head. There was a little bit of blood where the blackjack had hit.

The curly head fell so that the face lay across the Chocolate Man's arms as he walked quickly out of the park and toward the car. He could not pretend he wasn't carrying a body.

As he walked he almost looked at his license plate: Q4—one two three four five six seven. He must not think; he would be frozen by the numbers and found, holding this small unconscious child.

He reached the back passenger door. A moment—*Where are my keys?*—a bend, and it was done: the body was in the car.

And then around to the driver's side, and nobody was moving, the women were still grouped around the baby at the far end of the field; it couldn't have taken ninety seconds. One two three four five six seven.

Now he was on the Long Island Expressway, and the boy was waking up. He wasn't supposed to—none of the others had. The Chocolate Man looked for a spot where he could pull over. There were woods on either side of the highway, high trees and wheeling crows. He watched one flapping slowly across the sky as he pulled the car up onto the grass. He must not have hit the boy hard enough.

"Uh-uh-uh," the boy said thickly; he was coming around. Usually they didn't wake up until the Chocolate Man got them back to the house.

He looked out the window for a moment: branches, clouds, another crow. Then he turned and faced wide frightened blue eyes.

"Daddy," the boy said—but his face was crumpled with fear, and to the Chocolate Man's horror he realized: it wasn't a boy's voice, and it wasn't a boy's face. He watched. "Da—" the child said again, and shook its head, and brought a hand up to its temple, and stared.

"The man," the child said.

It was a girl. The Chocolate Man sat frozen, looking into her eyes. Large and blue and terrified.

"You fainted," he said.

"No I didn't."

"You did. Your mother asked me to take you to the hospital." It was almost his regular routine, except the bit about the hospital. He would say he was a friend of the mother's and that she would come to pick the child up. Sometimes it worked and sometimes it didn't.

"What's my mother's name?" The girl was rubbing the back of her head. Usually they didn't get to that question so fast.

"I call her Sassy," said the Chocolate Man. He had thrown the blackjack into the backseat. He faced the little girl across the seat back, defenseless.

She was looking at him through narrowed eyes. "You're the man," she said again.

The Chocolate Man's left hand gripped the steering wheel, it hurt. "What man?" he asked.

"The Chocolate Man." Her lip was quivering but she didn't cry. "The man who steals little kids and kills them."

"I'm not."

"You *are*. You stole me."

To this accusation the Chocolate Man could think of nothing to say.

"I'm taking you to the hospital," he said, "where your mother will come get you."

"You don't know my mother! She would never leave me—you *don't* know her. You—" The Chocolate Man could see she was getting hysterical. She was waving her arms, somebody would notice them.

"The Chocolate Man only kills boys," he said suddenly.

The girl stopped. Slowly she put her arms back down to her sides. "Yeah," she said, "he does." Her cat's eyes narrowed to slits. "So who are you?"

"I told you. You fainted. Your mother is waiting for you."

The girl tilted her head, assessing him. "Nobody calls my mother Sassy," she said.

"I'm an old friend," said the Chocolate Man, and he risked turning to start the car. "We have to go, okay?"

"I can't get out anyway," the girl said matter-of-factly. "You have the doors locked," and he turned to see her hand on the door button.

"That's so you won't fall out." The car was rolling now.

"There isn't anything I can do."

"Don't worry." They were back on the highway, and the car was picking up speed. The Chocolate Man looked at her in the rearview mirror; there were tears on her cheeks.

"I won't hurt you," he said suddenly; he hadn't been aware he was going to say it. The girl lifted her eyes to meet his in the mirror.

"Do you really know my mommy?"

A girl. He could not touch a girl child. He could not set her shoes next to the seven pairs on the kitchen table. One two three four five six seven. Even with the boys it was difficult—everything but the killing. He thought of the only time he had touched a woman. He could not imagine himself touching this girl. He felt nauseated.

"I won't hurt you," he said again into her frightened eyes. "I can't."

LAURIE COULDN'T REMEMBER WHAT THE POLICE officer had just asked her. Her head hurt and she felt dizzy. She rubbed her fingers in a circle on her forehead.

"I'm sorry, what did you say?"

"What was your daughter wearing at the time of her disappearance, Mrs. Lookinland?"

Laurie couldn't think. "A pair—a pair of jeans, a blue jacket—" Emily was missing. Kidnapped. Something was happening to her right now and Laurie didn't know what it was.

"—red socks—" It had been twenty-five minutes. Emily's socks had reindeer on them. Laurie leaned forward in the hardbacked chair, but it didn't ease the pain in her head or the ache in her solar plexus. She felt as though she had a hole in her body. The hole was getting bigger every minute Emily was missing.

Laurie looked around the police station, where people were going about their business as though her daughter was not missing and maybe dead. The walls were green halfway up and dirty cream to the ceiling; Laurie felt as if she were back in school and had done something wrong: her feelings were out of place here, where no one else was showing an emotion at all. All the police walked purposefully, with the same expression of irritated competence; Laurie could see only two other people, a big man in a gray suit arguing with an uninterested officer, and a bored-looking teenager sitting alone on a scarred wooden bench.

An officer stopped at the desk where she was sitting. "Coffee, Mrs. Lookinland?" he offered, holding out a steaming cup.

"Thank you," Laurie said gratefully. The warmth of the Styrofoam cup felt good in her hands, the anticipation of the hot, bitter liquid felt good. As Laurie raised the cup to her lips she thought, *While I drink coffee, Emily is*—and her mind could not complete the thought, and she put her coffee down untouched.

When the car pulled up in front of the Chocolate Man's house he expected the girl to say something. After their initial conversation she hadn't said anything at all. She must have seen the number of the exit when they left the highway. She was going to see his address, dull metal numbers on the front door. 17–84. One two three four . . . He looked up to see the girl watching him in the rearview mirror.

"We're here," he said. She wasn't crying anymore.

"This isn't a hospital."

The Chocolate Man tried to smile reassuringly. "You didn't seem sick enough to go to the hospital, so I took you here instead. This is my friend's house. We'll call your mother from inside."

Again the tilted head, the catlike look. "You say."

The Chocolate Man sighed. "Yes, I say. Come on, let's get out." Two doors away the Christmas lights were already lit, orange and deep blue along the lintel of a neighbor's door. One two three four five six seven. The Chocolate Man got out of the car quickly and opened the back door for the girl. She was looking at the colored lights. "I don't believe in Santa Claus anymore," she said, and she got out of the car.

"I answered all these questions twice already," Laurie said to the officer in front of her. He was looking at her with a policeman's unsentimental compassion.

"I know, ma'am. This is the last time. I just have to get it down for the APB."

"You mean nobody's *looking* for her yet?" Laurie could hear the hysterical edge in her voice; she wasn't far from breaking.

"Mrs. Lookinland, within five minutes of your call we sent officers to check the park and adjacent areas. Believe me, we are taking this seriously."

Laurie rested her forehead against her hand. "I know. But . . . to think that something is happening . . . or *happened* . . . and not to know—"

"Ma'am, I have an eleven-year-old at home."

Laurie looked up. "A girl or a boy?"

"A boy. Elliott."

"A boy." Laurie was quiet a moment. "It's that man, isn't it?" she asked finally.

"What man, ma'am?"

"The Chocolate Man—all those boys. He has my Emily, doesn't he?"

When the Chocolate Man had shoved the child's unconscious body into the backseat, he'd thrown an old piece of flooring rug over her; usually he carried the bodies up the walk wrapped like rolled carpet. He also kept some carpeting folded in the trunk of the car: periodically he carried it up the walk to the house. If they were asked, most of his neighbors would likely think that he did something with carpeting for a living. Sold it, laid it. Work on the side. Now the girl stood next to his car, looking up and down the street. He had never had to walk up to the house with one of them before.

The Chocolate Man took her by the arm; she stiffened. "Come on," he said.

As always when he went up the front walk he was careful not to step on any cracks. One, two steps, a crack. He stopped while he counted to seven twice. Then two more steps, and again a stop. Like a blind man, unsure. The girl stood uncertainly and moved forward, out of sinc with his steps, slowly up the walk.

Ronald Linderman was taking his afternoon constitutional along Dogwood Terrace. "Everything else is broken," he liked to tell his grandchildren, "but I can still walk."

Every day at eight-thirty in the morning and again at two-thirty in the afternoon Mr. Linderman walked the length of the block, up the east side and down the west. "I know everything about everybody," he liked to tell his son Walter. "You'd be amazed at what people are willing to say around an old man. As if it didn't matter, because I'm only going to die, so who am I going to tell?"

Mrs. Imperle was suffering from her asthma again. All her windows were shut tight, even though it was a balmy day for December. Mr. Linderman waved anyway: she might be looking out. The man in 17–80 had had another fight with his wife last night. Mr. Linderman had seen the police cars. Mrs. Lindsey's two boys were playing superheroes on their front lawn.

He could see a figure in the house across the street; that would be Mrs. Rosenberg. He waved to her. She turned abruptly from her window and he smiled to himself: that one was always angry, always talking about how noisy the children on the block were.

"Argh—I got you!" one cried out now, kicking at the air in front of him as the other fell to one knee. "Get back, you evil space alien!" Mr. Linderman couldn't keep up with children's games anymore, they all seemed to be from TV shows. Mr. Linderman used to play Krauts and Allies when he was a little boy, after the Great War. And then he had fought in World War II, and after the war he started a family and began a career in insurance. His wife, Rachel, was gone now. His six children had been blessed with children of their own: he had fifteen grandchildren, and three great-grandchildren. He had never been sick, never been in debt. Mr. Linderman was a lucky man, and he knew it.

That odd fellow who lived in 17–84 was going up the front walk that way he had; Mr. Linderman could never figure out what he was doing. Riehle, his name was. A couple of steps and he stopped; a couple more and he stopped again. Sometimes after he got to the door he went back to the end of the walk and did it again.

He had a little boy with him this afternoon. Curly-haired, cute. He was stopping just where the man stopped. Mr. Linderman hadn't known that man had a boy.

The man held him by the arm. Mr. Linderman wondered what the boy thought about walking like that. Must be a son from a failed marriage. When his daughter Esther got divorced, he thought it would kill Rachel. "It takes stamina to stay married," he liked to tell his niece Janice. "And it helps to have a terrible memory."

He couldn't imagine who would have been married to a strange man like that.

The man and the boy had stopped again, just short of the door. As the man got his keys from his pocket the boy turned and saw Mr. Linderman; he made as if to move and the man reached out and grabbed his arm.

Mr. Linderman wouldn't want to have that man for a father. No point in saying hello; that one never answered. His own father had been gone these twenty-eight years, God rest him. Mr. Linderman raised his hand in greeting to the boy, but the boy only ducked his head guiltily. He seemed almost afraid. Mr. Linderman knew that Riehle wasn't right.

A moment later his face broke into a smile. He didn't see the man and the boy go into 17–84.

"Miss Wiedow," he said genially to a young woman coming down the block. "You look lovely today. Like fresh fruit. Stop and talk to an old man. How was your day at work?"

They kept asking Laurie questions, the same questions over and over. What had Emily been wearing? How tall was she? What did she weigh? Color eyes, color hair? Laurie kept seeing the face of Maureen's baby, its tiny waving hand.

How could I have let her wander so far away? Why wasn't I watching her? Laurie had seen the man, standing not twenty-five feet away from her daughter. There was no voice inside her head telling her she couldn't possibly have known. There was only the cold damning voice of reality: *Emily is gone, and it's your fault.*

The man was holding her arm. It didn't hurt. He kept stopping suddenly, almost making Emily fall. Two steps, then a stop. Emily snuck a look at him. His lips were moving. He and Emily were on a residential street; there were big sycamores up and down the block. She didn't know this neighborhood. There was an old man across the street, some children playing in a front yard a few doors down.

Emily shifted her weight to her right foot; she pulled very lightly with her left arm, where the man held it. His grip tightened instantly, but his lips kept moving. He was staring, now, at the brass address plate on the front door. 17–84. Emily knew she had to remember that. *Pretend it's a story, and it's about Emily. 17–84; what street are we on?*

She was sure he was the man. The Chocolate Man. Her mother always said if you're in trouble scream, but she couldn't. The man's hand was like ice. Emily had seen what he did, the little bodies wrapped in black tarp on the television news, the crying mothers. *This is a story about Emily who was kidnapped but got away.* She just had to write the end part.

The man was moving again; nobody ever called her mom "Sassy."

"Mister—" she said, and the man jerked her arm. It hurt, so she was quiet, moving with the man like a blind person up the front walk.

As the man reached into his pocket for his keys, he let go of her arm. The old man across the street raised a hand in greeting. If she ran, would the Chocolate Man stumble after her like a blind person?

She took one step.

"Don't," he said, grabbing her arm. His eyes were a very pale blue; Emily ducked her head away from his eyes and the old man's wave.

"Your mother will be here soon," the man said, opening the door.

✗   ✗   ✗

"Mrs. Lookinland, there is nothing to indicate that your daughter was abducted by the Chocolate Man. In fact, there's nothing to indicate, at this point, that your daughter was abducted by *anyone*. She might simply have wandered off, gotten lost—"

"Emily has lived her whole life in New York City," Laurie said flatly. "She would never 'wander off.'"

The policeman's expression didn't change. "Sometimes these things aren't as bad as they seem at first."

"No," said Laurie, dropping her head to the desktop. Emily was missing, Emily was gone. Emily was almost certainly with the man who had raped and murdered seven children. "No," she said again. She raised her head to the policeman's empty face. "Sometimes they're worse."

That man across the street was coming home. Iris Imperle sat in front of her living-room window, looking out at the street. She peeked around closed curtains: her asthma was bad today; a pity, because she liked to have the windows open, and it was such a pretty day, so warm. But when her asthma acted up she couldn't bear the fresh air.

There was Mr. Linderman going by. Every day, like clockwork, at two-forty-five, Mr. Linderman walked by. He waved to her drawn curtains, then stopped to wave hello to the man across the street.

There was a little boy with the man. Mrs. Imperle had never seen him with a child. He did something with carpeting, laid it or sold it or something; he was always going in and out of the house carrying bundles of carpet.

There was something wrong with that man. He didn't walk normally; he kept stopping. Maybe he had arthritis. Such a pity, he really was a young man.

Mrs. Imperle tilted her head around the closed curtain to see better. She had never thought of that man as having a child. He was so solitary. No friends on the block, no visitors.

Mrs. Imperle couldn't make out whether it was a boy child or a girl child. Her own little girl, her Sarah Louise, had had hair down to her waist. Mrs. Imperle had always plaited it into two braids; she wove pink ribbon down the length of each braid.

This little child had dark curly hair in a cloud around its head—and it looked frightened. Mrs. Imperle felt nervous all of a sudden. Sarah Louise had died when she was three years old.

No, the child wasn't looking in her direction any longer. Maybe it was just tired. Mrs. Imperle watched as Mr. Linderman raised a hand in greeting to the child and the man; the child ducked its head. Oh, it was just shy. Such a pretty child. It must be a boy, with those shoes.

The man and the boy were going into the house now. The child had been very good about going slowly so the man could keep up. He must be the child's uncle; Mrs. Imperle had dearly loved her Uncle Frank. She hadn't thought about him in years. He used to pretend he was going to swing her by her pigtails.

Mrs. Imperle reached for her inhaler. Such a lucky little child, to be visiting his uncle.

"Would you like something to eat?"

The first thing the man had done when he and Emily came into the house was to go down a dark hallway and into the kitchen. The light was already on; Emily stared at the table. It had several pairs of shoes sitting on it, right in the middle. Emily's mom would never let her leave her shoes on the table.

This is a story about Emily who was kidnapped by the Axis powers in World War I. She was concentrating hard: if she was in World War I she wouldn't have to think about what the shoes meant.

Before touching the shoes the man stood in front of them a long time. Emily could see part of his face; his mouth was moving, and then suddenly he bundled all the shoes into his arms and stuffed them into a cupboard above the sink. It didn't look like a place anybody would keep shoes.

"Would you like something to eat?" His smile was funny, as though he didn't use it much.

Emily stepped back. She didn't like having him facing her. His eyes were very pale. Her daddy's eyes were pale; in the picture of him on her desk they were like clear water. In the story about Emily the little girl was being very brave. *Emily must escape and warn the villagers in Alsace-Lorraine.* She didn't cry when the man smiled at her.

"Why are you crying?"

"Where's my mom?"

The man turned away, toward the refrigerator. "She'll be here soon," he said. In the story Emily looked around. There was a door beyond the refrigerator. That was the back door. There was another door behind Emily, which led to a long hall and then the front door. They had just walked through it.

Emily took a step backward. The man was leaning into the refrigerator. *The soldier guarding Emily had his back to her; he was checking coordinates on a map.* "I have some yogurt," he was saying doubtfully, "and some salami—"

Emily turned and ran for the door to the hall.

As Laurie left the precinct house she instinctively ducked her head. Lights flashed around her and voices called: "Mrs. Lookinland, how are you?"

"Look over here, Laurie!"

"How was Emily doing in school?"

Laurie's step faltered at that: *was*. She kept her head resolutely down. The hand of the policeman escorting her was reassuring against her arm.

Her dear friend Carolyn was at the bottom of the steps. The officer handed Laurie to her as though she were a parcel, and Laurie realized she was crying.

"Have the police got any leads, Mrs. Lookinland?" a voice called from the crowd of reporters, and for a moment Laurie felt, with sickening clarity and longing, the weight of her daughter in her arms, when Emily had been three, three and a half, before she got too big and grownup to be carried. She would hold her arms out to be picked up and then she would lay her head on Laurie's shoulder in a little miracle of trust.

This was his house. The Chocolate Man knew every item in every drawer or closet: the 17 pairs of white socks in the dresser in his bedroom; the 46 videotapes in the guest-room closet, marked "All models guaranteed 18 years or older," which was a lie; the 216 magazines, also in the guest-room closet, most of them with no such caveat; the Polaroid camera in the upstairs hall closet with the seventy Polaroid photographs stacked neatly next to it on the closet floor, the only color to be seen upstairs, where dirty white sheets covered forgotten pieces of dead lives: all of his parents' belongings. He had lugged their lamps and chairs and clothes and pictures and half-empty liquor bottles and the trash from their garbage cans and their half-used soaps and bottles of shampoo, their makeup and razors and books and his mother's three cream-colored slips up the stairs and into these rooms. His old bedroom was down the hall from the photographs in the closet; he had covered everything with white cloth and gone away from all of it.

But the photographs belonged there, somehow. Each one was labeled, each stacked in chronological order, the latest on top, face down: James Ossi, September 15, 1996, 6:07 P.M. The Chocolate Man didn't often go up to look at them, but he was always aware that they were there, waiting; they watched him, like an open eye; everywhere he went in the house they watched him, and he knew each image by heart.

The rug in the hall careened crazily in front of Emily, up and down with each step. The front door was far away.

Emily could hear her own footsteps, dull against the carpet. She had been running for a long time, but the door wasn't getting any closer.

In the story Emily was running through a minefield outside a town in Alsace-Lorraine. Above her head bombs burst with blinding light. Escaping from the enemy soldier, determined to warn the innocent villagers, she raced across the grassy expanse. Her rifle had been lost, her helmet abandoned; only luck and courage could save her now.

It was not the Chocolate Man chasing her.

There were three locks on the front door. She could see each one clearly, even though everything else was a blur; the walls were throbbing and the patterned floor threatened to rise up and swallow her.

One of the locks was a deadbolt—Emily could hear the man's footsteps behind her, slow and halting—and one was the kind you turned, and one was the kind with a chain.

"Out, out, out," her mind said with each step; in the story Emily's mother was just behind the door.

For a moment it was true.

Out, out, out.

In a minute—the man's footsteps were getting faster, he was gaining on her—in a minute Emily would be close enough—she reached her hand up and her fingertips touched the cool hanging metal of the chain.

"Laurie, are you all right?" Carolyn was leading her to her car, her arm firmly linked through Laurie's. Laurie's arms were empty.

Her head was still down, her hair a screen in front of her face; she felt blind animal hate for the reporters and the lights: she was their story, their prey. She would have hurt them if she could.

"Just get me out of here," she whispered to Carolyn; she felt savage and her voice sounded pathetic and small.

"Hey, Laurie, what's it like to have your daughter missing?" She did not raise her bowed head. Her arm in Carolyn's was shaking.

"Take me home," she said, and lights flashed and voices shrilled and Laurie saw nothing, felt nothing, but the long-gone weight of her daughter's body in her empty arms.

When the man's hand grabbed her ankle Emily wasn't surprised. She fell onto the carpet and the ceiling skittered up in front of her eyes. In her mind the ground exploded under her feet.

The man's hand was cold. Emily bumped her cheek against the floor; in the story she didn't cry. The enemy guard had recaptured her, that was all.

But in the dark hall the nine-year-old child closed her eyes against the patterned rug and sobbed.

2:45 P.M.

"I HATE TUNA FISH." ED WAS LIFTING UP A CORNER
of his sandwich, a complacent disgust on his face.

"Then make your own sandwiches." Ed was
shaking his head; he looked up and laughed.
Marcy's eyebrows were raised. "You love it," she
said. "It shows she cares."

"'Cause she makes me shit I can't stand?" Ed's
voice held no affection for his wife's idiosyncrasies,
but he smiled to show he didn't really mean it.

"Because she wants to make sure you eat right."
After many years it didn't hurt much: there was no
one to see that Marcy ate right. "Here, I'll trade
you half."

"Oh, no," rearing back in mock horror, "it's
probably some fucking tabbouleh shit." The way he
said "tabooli" made her laugh. She wasn't really
alone; there were people who cared.

"You're off tomorrow, right?" Ed asked, leaning to look at her sandwich, which was avocado and
cheese and sprouts. "See? Fucking tabooli."

She slapped his hand away. "It's *sprouts*."
Tomorrow she would be at midnight Mass, singing
Christmas in from the choir stall. She loved to sing:
she rarely ever made rehearsals but her voice was
pure and true, and every Christmas and every

Easter she stood among the members of the choir in the balcony stall and sang. The people in the pews below could see her, but she could see nothing but light.

"Sprouts? Gimme a sprout. Where do they grow these things?" holding it up with mock wonder; "Sprout farms! I'll bet—"

"Hoag." And Marcy knew before she looked up.

"—twenty minutes ago." It was Detective Renny Argule, and he had his hand on Ed's shoulder. Marcy had lost a moment—"Rego Park area, nice and residential, just like he likes it—"

"Did you say a girl?" Marcy was so surprised she thought she couldn't have heard right; Ed's fingers hung suspended with a tiny quivering sprout between them.

"Emily Rose Lookinland," Renny said kindly. *I must look sick*, Marcy thought, and, *What a pretty name*.

"Nine years old," Renny was saying—"Why do we think it's the Chocolate Man?" Marcy interrupted. Ed had said nothing at all, and he wasn't looking at Renny or Marcy. The sprout spun in his fingers, back and forth.

"The mother saw a man standing about twenty feet away from her daughter just before she disappeared. Her description fit the only possible sighting."

"But—there've been a thousand possible sightings. Every day we get ten or twelve more. The papers just love that Chocolate Man name, it looks good in print—"

"The mother said he was snapping his fingers."

Marcy was silent. The newspapers didn't know about the snapping. That when the blond man had tried to give the little boy chocolate he'd been snapping his fingers. Over and over, as though he didn't even know it. And the papers also hadn't printed that there had been blond hairs found on the bodies of Danny Angelo and Anthony Timmons and James Ossi.

Marcy leaned back in her chair; she didn't remember leaning forward. "Then it's him."

"Yeah," said Renny, "it's him." He patted Ed's shoulder; Ed still had not spoken but he looked up and back and nodded slowly. He brought his hand down to the table; he dropped the sprout. He was breathing shallowly through his mouth.

"Where's your cigar?" Marcy asked. She reached into his breast pocket and pulled out a stub.

"You hate it when I smoke at lunch," Ed said. He met her eyes; she breathed deeply and she wasn't crying. "Some fucking merry Christmas," Ed said as Marcy handed him his cigar. She lit it with her lighter, striking two, three times until the tobacco caught.

"Yeah," she said softly. "Some merry Christmas."

THE EMILY IN THE STORY WAS VERY BRAVE. SHE WAS not afraid, even when the man dragged her back to the kitchen by her ankle. *I will lie very still so the enemy soldier will think I'm dead.*

Then she saw her mother in her head, not saw, really, just felt her; as the rough nap of the carpet bit her cheek she felt her mother's lips: it was just that spot she loved to kiss. "Red as a cherry," she'd say, "and twice as tasty."

The rug scraped against Emily's cheek and she started to cry. *This is a story,* she thought vehemently, *about Emily who was recaptured but escaped again.* She let the carpet scrape her face, and she didn't lift a hand to brush her tears.

"You shouldn't try to get away," the man was saying, "your mother will be here soon." They reached the hard linoleum of the kitchen and he let go of her ankle. The light around her was too bright; it vibrated. This was not a story.

"My mother is *not* coming," Emily screamed suddenly, sitting up. The man made a move as if to comfort her and she flinched away. If he hugged her she would die right there. She kept screaming. "You're lying to me! You're the man who kills children and my mother is *not* coming and—" she stopped; in the story Emily swallowed hard and didn't cry.

"*You—sit—there*," the man hissed. "*You*—I don't even *like* little girls." Emily was crying in earnest now, rubbing her ankle. A moment ago she'd thought he was going to hug her and now he seemed so angry. He walked across the kitchen with his back to her but she made no move. She had never seen anyone so angry. When he turned around he was holding a knife.

Emily shrank back. She took her hand off her ankle, as though that might appease him.

But he walked toward her with the knife.

Suddenly Emily became an animal, she stopped thinking and scrambled across the floor like a cornered mouse; she forgot to stand up.

The man was behind her. She could hear his slow breathing. He was walking steadily, and then there was a shadow in front of her and a flash, a bright sharp light, and she squealed and turned, rolling, and his weight was on her, and something wet, and she rolled out from under him and to her knees; her breathing was short and ragged.

The man was looking at her. His mouth was open. He was kneeling on the linoleum and there was red running down his left arm, red on the floor.

The knife hung limp at his side. "I don't—I don't like blood," he said. He was panting from exertion.

In the story Emily looked at him. His blond hair had kicked up in the back in a cowlick. He looked stupid, with his pants hiked up and his thin socks droopy against his white skin: he looked like a bug from under a rock. She and the man looked at each other for a long time.

Emily had no tears on her face anymore.

"Put down the knife and I'll take care of the cut," she said at last. A drop of blood fell and splattered on the linoleum. The man held the knife out toward Emily. She flinched away from the naked blade.

"Oh. Oh, I'm sorry," the man said; he spoke very softly and he seemed almost unaware of her. He placed the knife carefully on the floor and turned its blade around; it slid a little in his blood.

"Do you have any peroxide?" Emily asked. In the story she was ministering to the wounded enemy soldier. She was just like her mother, all smiling competence when Emily hurt herself. "You don't have to cry," she said. That was what her mother would say.

But when she looked at his face it did have tears on it.

"Does it hurt a lot?" she asked.

"You yelled at me."

Emily was so surprised she forgot to breathe; and then she had to take a big breath before she spoke.

"You scared me."

"But you—you *yelled*."

"You won't let me go."

"No."

Emily felt her own tears starting again: *I will be like my mother I won't cry.* "You came at me with a knife."

He was looking at her with such a sad expression.

"Nobody ever said that to me before."

"What?"

" 'You don't have to cry.' Nobody ever told me I didn't have to cry."

Emily rubbed her elbow. "Do you want me to fix your arm? I had First Aid with the Girl Scouts."

"You're a Girl Scout?"

"Uh-huh." She got up and began looking through the kitchen cabinets. As long as she was concentrating she was not afraid. It must be sad never to have anyone tell you not to cry.

"It was mean of you to pretend my mother was coming."

"I didn't want you to be afraid." Emily had found some peroxide and a clean rag. She hesitated before she touched him. "I don't think this will hurt," she said, reaching out an uncertain hand.

He did not move or say anything. As she knelt down she kicked the knife away across the floor. "Can I ask you something?"

The man had his head turned away from the cut. Curiosity had overcome her fear. "Didn't you have a mommy?"

The man's head sank lower. He mumbled.

"What?"

"I guess so."

" 'Cause you said nobody ever told you you didn't have to cry. Did your parents get divorced?"

"No." It was like touching anybody's arm. And when she cleaned the cut she saw it wasn't very big at all. "I know five other kids whose parents did."

The man lifted his head. "Other?"

"Yeah. It's just me and Mom."

"Your mom? What's your mom's name?"

"Laur—I'm not going to tell you."

The man ran his tongue absently over his lips. "I'll bet your mom misses you," he said.

"Of course she does." Emily didn't want to talk about her mother. *The enemy soldier's wound was not serious. Perhaps he would be grateful and let her go.*

Suddenly he asked, "Did you ever want to kill anybody?"

The wound was already clean but she kept dabbing at it.

"I don't know—I got really mad at my friend Sue once—but I don't think I wanted to kill her. I might have wanted her to be dead, for a minute."

"I wanted to kill my mommy."

Emily didn't stop dabbing at his arm. She didn't say anything.

"Did you ever kill anything?" he asked after a moment.

"No."

"Not even bugs?" He sounded surprised.

"No. Boys do that."

"Oh." There was a long silence. Emily stopped cleaning the wound and bandaged it the way she'd learned at Girl Scouts. *Surely the enemy would remember her kindness.*

"I'm sorry I got mad at you," the man said finally. Emily was done. He got up off the floor. "Would you like some Yoo-Hoo?"

"Are you the Chocolate Man?"

He stood at the refrigerator with his back to her. "I'm going to have one," he said. Then he was silent a moment. "No, I'm not the Chocolate Man."

Emily raised herself up without using her hands. The man's back was still to her. He was lying.

"But I can't get away, can I?" she asked.

"No."

Emily looked around. *The prisoner assessed her choices.* The door to the outside was closed, and anyway there was a glass door behind it; she would never get through both in time. The hallway was in back of her, long and hopeless.

The police would be looking for her by now. Emily lifted her hand to touch the scrape along her right cheek. "I'll take a Yoo-Hoo," she said.

When he was twenty-three George got a job in the liquor store around the corner from his parents' house. He had gotten to know the owner on his many trips to the store to buy gin for his father. It was hard work, carrying and unpacking crates, but George was alone a lot of the time, in the back room. There was the distraction of the numbers on the crates, the dates, inventory; sometimes the owner, Bill, would come into the back room and find George frozen, staring at a pile of numbered boxes.

But after a while Bill let him sit at the front counter and take care of customers. He was very slow. There were numbers on the bills he handled, and people asked him prices. "Six seventy-five," he learned to say quickly; then he counted three times, one to seven. If he was very fast he didn't have to pause between the numbers.

George lasted a long time at the liquor store. Bill was tolerant of his idiosyncrasies; he didn't mind that George spent his entire lunch hour in the bathroom.

George's father died, then his mother. By the time he was twenty-eight George was alone. There had been a woman once—or there had almost been a woman. A small, fine-boned brunette who came to the liquor store every Thursday to buy wine for her grandmother. Seven bottles. Her grandmother had a bad back, she explained. Wine dulled the pain. The woman had brown eyes; she was about twenty-two. She worked as a bookkeeper, she said. She seemed to like talking to him. One Thursday he found himself asking her out, and to his surprise she accepted. Tomorrow, he said, around eight? One two three four five six seven. Around eight, she agreed. One two three four five six seven.

George and the woman went to the movies. She didn't seem to expect him to talk much; she liked to talk. Her name was Roxanne; she really did live with her grandmother. Roxanne had a great many complaints about the place when she worked. When George picked her up at her house he could smell the wine sweet on her breath.

George and Roxanne went to the movies four or five times and then George asked her to come to visit his home.

There was a table in the kitchen, just like in the apartment that had burned. Everything was scrubbed shining. There was never anything on the table because

George ate his meals standing up over the sink so as not to get anything dirty, and when he was done he washed the sink out, sometimes for more than an hour.

"Nice place," Roxanne said, and George knocked her down onto the kitchen floor and ripped her pantyhose off.

Roxanne didn't make a sound. She looked at the ceiling, seeming as far away as George himself when he was counting. George looked at her brown eyes and they looked dead.

After he got her panties off he almost stopped—until he thought of her grandmother watching, her face a mask of revulsion.

George had brought a bottle of wine up from the liquor store. He had imagined himself and Roxanne sitting at the kitchen table, talking about their lives. She would tell him her dreams, and he would take her hand.

When he was done, George helped Roxanne to her feet. "Do you have something to drink?" she asked. He had to pull her panties back on by himself, had to put the band of her ripped pantyhose back snug around her waist. He got her the bottle of wine out of the cupboard; when he put it on the table she tilted it to her mouth without asking for a glass.

Roxanne never came to the liquor store again. George spent three nights scrubbing the kitchen floor.

CHRISTMAS EVE DON'T MEAN SHIT TO ME," KEISHA Barry said amiably to another girl as they stood cold in the afternoon gray. The sky still threatened snow, it was a false white-gray that didn't look like real sky. It was dark, and the air had been getting colder—but still there was a hint of spring, like a memory of spring, on the air. Keisha didn't believe she could even have a memory of spring in a place like this.

Storefront churches, liquor stores, and bars lined both sides of Northern Boulevard, which ran four lanes wide; the liquor stores had orange or blue neon signs, that was the only difference. The bars had no names. Brick row houses faded down the blocks off Northern; even in daylight everything seemed bathed in gray. The crack houses didn't look much different from the other houses: a window might be broken, or a front door missing and covered with a plywood slab. One time at the crack house over on 101st Street a girl lay on the floor for three days before anybody noticed she was dead.

At night men gathered around big metal bins of burning trash; on certain corners men and boys hung out, outside a bar or a liquor store, and sometimes they spilled out into the street and frightened the businessmen heading east on Northern Boulevard, toward Long Island and the suburbs. Sometimes hookers flashed the businessmen commuting home late from work. But the trade wasn't very lively two days before Christmas. Keisha had been standing on Northern for two hours and had only done one trick.

"You hear?" the other girl had been saying. "That Chocolate Man, he got another little kid today. Ain't that something awful, the day before Christmas Eve?"

"Christmas Eve don't mean shit to me. But, man, I hate that fucking Chocolate Man. What age the kid?"

"Nine. The TV said. A girl. You got anything?"

"Girl, you know I don't do no shit. The Chocolate Man always does boys, don't he?"

"Yeah. I got my Dorian out in Floral Park with his great-grandma. I'm not taking chances. And I *miss* him, shit yeah. But one of those boys was black, Andrew something."

"Timmons."

"Yeah, that's right. He only lived, what? ten or eleven blocks from here. And I ain't seen no police patrolling this neighborhood, we could all—" Keisha saw a car slowing and she smiled while Dian talked. The car was black. The driver was white, and he had red hair. "You want this one, Dian?" She didn't feel like working. She was sick of the smell of men. Dian was stupid to ask her for shit, everybody knew Keisha hated drugs; "They killed my mama, they got me two brothers in jail and one dead, too. You do what you want," she'd say, "I ain't no preacher and I ain't no fool." Keisha would do anything for anybody; she was nothing but heart. But she never asked anybody for anything.

"No, you take him, Keisha. He's got his dick pointed at you anyway. Probably another daddy." Keisha looked younger than she was, and she could act younger still; she just had to look afraid. It was her mode, the daddies all knew Keisha.

Now she sighed and put her mouth in a pout and headed for the car. She wasn't really ever afraid, by now; Keisha couldn't afford the luxury of being afraid. She ignored the little wrenching jump her heart made every time she leaned over a car's passenger-side window. Once, when she was fourteen, she'd had a dream. She'd been tricking for three months, her mother lost to crack, her brothers coming by once in a while with presents and new scars, her father not even a memory. She was living with her great-aunt, which meant she slept there. What she did and what she ate were up to her; she had to eat and she had to have clothes, and tricking seemed an easy enough thing to do.

She was still afraid then: she had a dream. A maggot-white man in a maroon sedan was parked ahead of her where she walked at twilight on Northern Boulevard. She woke shaking; he had met her eyes. And that night she walked on Northern Boulevard, heading for the grocery store or the next trick, whichever came first. Ahead of her, cruising to a stop, was a maroon sedan. It meant nothing; and then she was closer and the driver's head turned.

She would never forget that dead white skin.

Most of the other girls had the same radar. There were men they waved away, fifty-dollar bills they turned from. The deft furtive check of the front seat was second nature now: a knife? a gun? a twist of cord? A tarp in the backseat got a girl out fast; if the backseat had been removed, only the most desperate crack junkie would get in.

Keisha smiled as she leaned into the passenger-side window of this car. Just a redhaired man and a pile of magazines and videos on the backseat. "Hi, Daddy," she said to the man, "what you looking for today?"

"I'm looking for a little girl to take to a party."

Cigarettes and whiskey; Keisha breathed out and down. He looked harmless enough, with his gray suit and brown coat; "Bet your wife don't know where you are right now," she said, opening the door with a sudden jerk and sliding into the passenger seat.

"I told my wife I was going to an orphanage to make children happy. But now Daddy wants to be made happy, too." Keisha gave a quick look around. *Family Fun* and *Family Letters;* a picture, taped on the dashboard, of a small, pretty girl.

Suddenly Keisha was angry. "You like what that Chocolate Man did today? Taking that little girl?"

"Heck, no, honey, I *like* little girls. I wouldn't ever do anything to hurt one. That Chocolate Man's a pervert, anyway, he usually does it with boys. That's sick. But, no, sweety, I wouldn't hurt any little girl. Why, I belong to a club," he said, smiling and putting his hand on her thigh, "we've got a slogan. *Before Eight or It's Too Late.* We'd like to make sure all little girls learn about love from somebody who cares, somebody who knows what a little girl likes."

Keisha felt queasy; it was the windows, they were closed and the air smelled from cigar smoke. "How old are you, little girl?"

"Fourteen," she said.

"Fourteen." The man tasted the age on his tongue. "You want to party, Fourteen?"

"How old was the girl the Chocolate Man got?"

"Honey, you got to stop thinking about things that might upset you." He was beginning to sound annoyed.

"We can party right here," Keisha said hurriedly. "You got a drink?"

"But, Fourteen, I got plans for you. And do you think you're old enough to drink?" That was better, Keisha knew girls who'd been beaten for less.

The man handed her a bottle from under the front seat. Keisha took a flowered handkerchief from her bag and wiped the top of the bottle with it.

"Fancy," the man said.

"Spit's a bodily fluid," said Keisha, losing for a moment the false softness she had put in her voice. Seeing his face harden, she added, "Daddy." The handkerchief was red and white with poinsettias on it. Jimmy gave it to her, he was a boy who lived in the apartment across the hall. "You should always do ordinary things with beautiful objects," he said. The handkerchief was a birthday present, two months ago. Seventeen.

"Daddy," she repeated, his hand between her legs. Ordinary things. "I don't want to go anyplace today. I want my Christmas present right here." The girl in the picture had red hair too; she looked about nine or ten. Too late. "First you have to show Daddy what a good little girl you are," the man said, and Keisha slid down in the seat and opened her legs.

THE YOO-HOO TASTED GOOD. WHILE EMILY WAS drinking it she didn't let herself think about anything else. She really liked the chocolate-flavored best, but strawberry was good, too.

"If you're not the Chocolate Man, who are you?"

The man was standing at the sink counter making sandwiches. He turned around. "My name is George."

"George."

"Yes."

"I had a boyfriend named George last year."

"Oh?"

"In school. We used to fight in the schoolyard."

"Did you love him?"

"I guess so. He had two white rats."

George—the Chocolate Man—stood very still, looking past Emily, for a couple of seconds. He shivered.

"A goose is walking over your grave," Emily said. His face frightened her. She sat and watched as he walked toward her across the kitchen floor. In the story Emily leapt to her feet and ran—but the real Emily sat very still.

Just before he reached her she held up the Yoo-

Hoo bottle and said, "Do you have any more of this?" and he stopped.

"Yoo-Hoo," prompted Emily. Her mouth had gone dry; she really did need something to drink.

"It was right here," the Chocolate Man said. "My only time with a woman."

"You didn't know any women?" Something in his eyes had changed, shifted away. Emily continued to hold up her Yoo-Hoo bottle.

"I didn't like it," he said. He took the bottle.

"Like what?"

The Chocolate Man was back over by the refrigerator. He stooped to take out another Yoo-Hoo; when he turned back toward her he said, "What's your name?"

Emily reached out a hand for the bottle. *The interrogation of the prisoner had begun.*

"What if I don't tell you?" she asked without conviction.

The Chocolate Man looked at her. "If you want to go home you'll have to tell me."

The Emily in the story knew what to say, what magic words to make him release her. Tears did not start to that Emily's eyes.

"You don't have to cry," the Chocolate Man said.

Emily swallowed. "What if I don't tell you?" she said again. There were no magic words.

"I'll get it off the TV." Emily bit her lip.

"You're going to call my mother."

The Chocolate Man shrugged.

"Drink your Yoo-Hoo," he said. He had gotten another bottle for himself, too.

"My mother never lets me have two," said Emily. The Chocolate Man stood very still. His lips moved.

Emily almost asked, "What are you doing?" but she stopped herself. *A clue,* thought Emily in the story. *Why does he do that?*

"My mother told me there were men who touch little girls where they shouldn't. Are you going to do that?"

The Chocolate Man looked at her a long time. He didn't answer.

"If you want money, my mother doesn't have any."

"I don't want money."

Emily tried to think of what he could want, if it wasn't money. He hadn't said he *was* going to touch her. In *The Rescuers* the bad lady kept a little girl prisoner to send her into a cave to look for a special diamond.

"Do you want me to do something?" Emily asked.

He looked confused; he cocked his head.

"Do you want me to go down into a dark tunnel and find the treasure you're too big to reach?"

The Chocolate Man smiled. "You believe in magic," he said.

"Sometimes kids can do things grownups can't."

He picked up his bottle of Yoo-Hoo and wiped at the tabletop underneath it; he got up and put the bottle in the sink and pulled some paper toweling off a rack and got a bottle of Fantastik from under the white counter. Carefully he cleaned the area of

the table where the bottle had stood. He rubbed
the tabletop a long time. When he looked up, Emily
was tilting her bottle and a tiny rivulet of strawberry
was running down her chin.

"Stop it!" The Chocolate Man screamed. He
threw the Fantastik bottle savagely in her direction.
"You dirty little—" and he was around the table and
her bottle was lying on the linoleum, a splatter of
strawberry pink across the floor.

He grabbed Emily and threw her down. He
held her arm twisted underneath her, his weight on
her stomach. "You're *dirty*," he hissed. "You made
a mess."

Emily didn't make a sound. He was so heavy on
top of her that she couldn't breathe.

"You're as dirty as she was," he whispered. "It
doesn't matter if you're a girl, I could—" and then
he stopped; he released her arm and stood abruptly.

Emily lay unmoving. Her arm hurt but she
didn't dare rub it. Very slowly she pulled it out from
where the Chocolate Man had pinned it behind her
back. He was over by the sink, breathing heavily.
He'd turned on the water and although his back
was to her she could tell he was washing his hands.
The prisoner lay wounded on the cold ground.

He ran the water a long time. Emily sat up and
rubbed her arm. There was strawberry drink all over
the floor. She sat there and waited.

"My name is Emily," she said finally. But she
couldn't tell whether he could hear her.

He said nothing. Emily got up. There was a
dish towel hanging next to him, on the handle of a
drawer. Emily walked very softly over to it and

reached out, behind him; he did not move. The water sounded loud in Emily's ears. She was certain he was going to turn and strike her.

"If you give me a rag I'll clean it up."

The towel slid easily off the handle. The Chocolate Man kept washing his hands. Emily knelt and began wiping up the strawberry, and in an instant he was standing over her.

"I have to do that," he said, and he knelt beside her and took the towel, gently.

"It's no good if you do it," he explained. "I have to use Fantastik and four paper towels"—here he paused a moment—"and clean the dirty spot in circles six"—another pause—"times." When he paused he stared straight ahead and his lips moved. When he stood up he took Emily by the arm—she flinched—and helped her up, too.

"Why?" she asked.

The Chocolate Man picked up the bottle of Fantastik and got some more paper towels from the counter. "Just because," he said.

"Oh."

The Chocolate Man lined his equipment up on the kitchen table: the bottle and four carefully spread sheets of paper toweling. He looked at them a long time.

"Can't I help?" Emily asked. The Chocolate Man shivered as though he'd been unexpectedly touched.

"Help? I said no. Now just go sit over there until I decide what to do with you."

THE WATER WAS VERY HOT. HE HAD ALMOST DONE IT to the little girl. For a moment, on the linoleum floor, he had felt the brightness, the silence, the closeness, as though she were part of his own body: the things he always felt, just before, just after. During the act he was lost to himself. All light magnified and fractured, and all sound died.

He had almost felt it, almost sunken into the familiar voluptuousness. And then abruptly he was lying on top of a little girl.

He wanted to take a shower. The water from the kitchen faucet was too hot but it could never be hot enough; he wanted his skin to slough off.

The girl was behind him on the floor. She was gasping for breath, just as he was breathing hard where he stood at the sink. She had made a mess and he had almost been able to kill her.

He rubbed so hard at his left hand under the scalding water that it sang with pain. He had touched her neck with his left hand.

"If you give me a rag—" he heard her say. The fluorescent light flared around him with unbearable brightness, but he could still hear her: "—I'll clean it up." When he turned she was on her hands and knees.

106   JESSIE HUNTER

"I have to do that," he said, and he showed her how. The light abated, and when his hand accidentally brushed hers he flinched away. He was going to have to kill her, but he knew he couldn't touch her skin again.

The girl was sitting obediently at the table watching him wiping the paper towel in a circle, six times. One two three four five six seven.

That is, unless the brightness came again.

"MYSTERY MOM REFUSES TO TALK." LAURIE SAT IN the living room with the lights off even though it was already dark. There she was, in full color but small, on her television screen. Her hair was a curtain in front of her face; she was not surprised to see that her fist was clenched. The voiceover continued as the Laurie on the screen walked down the precinct-house steps. "Lauren Lookinland left the Nineteenth Precinct stationhouse this afternoon, after questioning in the disappearance of her nine-year-old daughter."

Laurie lighted her third cigarette in twenty minutes. "The search continues for Emily Rose Lookinland, who was reported missing this afternoon from Hewlitt Park, located at Third Street and Seward Avenue in the Rego Park section of Queens. The girl was being looked after at the time by her mother."

It was four-twenty. Emily had been missing for two hours. In the half-light from the windows the living room looked strange; Laurie didn't recognize the chairs she loved, russet velvet and oak, or the poster on the wall for *Dark Victory* she had found at a garage sale, or the pictures on the mantel, pictures of Emily mostly, unrecognizable now in the dark. "Although there is no indication of foul play at this time, the eerie specter of the Chocolate Man has arisen in many people's minds, not least the police. The Chocolate Man, as every terrified mother or father of a small child in this beleaguered city already knows—"

Laurie smashed out her cigarette. Carolyn had gone home to pack an overnight bag. "Are you sure you're okay?" she'd asked, and Laurie had almost laughed, but she'd said, "Yes," and, "Don't worry about me." The police had suggested she go home, "in case." In case Emily called, having wandered too far. In case some Good Samaritan called, having found and befriended her.

In case the Chocolate Man called early.

The police had said they'd be back to monitor surveillance; they had already put a wiretap on her phone. Laurie had never seen that done except in movies. If it was the Chocolate Man who had Emily he would call at exactly eight-twenty. He was methodical that way, predictable.

"Mrs. Lookinland, who is not at this time a suspect in her daughter's disappearance, refused to talk to, or even look at, reporters who waited for her on the precinct steps."

On the television Laurie made a sharp, repeated motion with her left palm, as if to drive back the intruding cameras, microphones, and lights. In her living room she pushed back her chair and left the room. She was obscurely proud of her veiled face, her refusal to let the cameras capture part of her soul. As she walked to the bathroom she felt again the rush of adrenaline and rage that had swept through her as she left the station-house. The vultures wanted to feed off her grief; her raw wounds gave them a chance to feel something.

In the bathroom her ravaged reflection swung out of sight as she opened the medicine cabinet. Little gray and black makeup containers stared out at her with reassuring vacuity. Black Stallion mascara, Beach Sand eye shadow. Laurie's hands were shaking badly. Barely Blush foundation, Perfectly Plum lipstick. Aurora Rose for her cheeks.

Laurie seldom wore makeup. Her eyes were swollen with tears. Unconsciously she squared her shoulders before the mirror and began.

The Chocolate Man was in another room. Emily didn't know what he was doing; she didn't want to know. He had tied her wrist and her ankle to a kitchen chair with scratchy rope and left the room. Emily had pulled at the rope, had worked at the knots with the fingers of her left hand. Now her wrist was raw, and her fingers were raw.

"Are you being a good girl?" the Chocolate Man called from the other room. Emily didn't answer. He had already called to her several times; it made her angry. He didn't have to check. He knew she couldn't get away.

She didn't care what he did to her. *The prisoner was no longer afraid*. That wasn't true, but Emily had discovered that even fear could be controlled. The nights she had cried for her father's leaving she had abandoned control; and then she had learned.

Don't think about it. Put it away, like a coat or a hat. When the fear of death leaps out in the night, turn on the lights, the radio; keep away from mirrors (which show too clearly the ephemeral skin at the eye sockets, the shape of the skull). When the hole inside gapes, and yawns wide, run from yourself into another room, to conversation or the TV.

Or sing. Emily loved to sing. She was in the chorus at school. They had learned a madrigal, *Il est bel et bon, bon, bon* . . . to sing at the Christmas show. Emily had worn a red velvet dress, and a green ribbon in her hair. The song was about how wonderful somebody's husband was.

Emily's mother liked to sing, too. ("I'll be through in a minute," the Chocolate Man called.) She and Emily had been singing together since Emily could remember. Rounds, carols, things her mother's grandmother had taught her. "Hush, Little Baby," "Down in the Valley," and Emily's favorite, an old song her mother had sung when she was a little girl herself, a song about a swallow and a calf.

The Chocolate Man was moving something in the other room. Emily heard a thump, a heavy bundle falling. *Outside her cell the prisoner could hear the enemy soldier: was he loading his rifle?* She could hear him walking, back and forth, back and forth. Sudden fear washed over her like water, and without thinking she began to sing.

In a wagon, bound for market, there's a calf with a mournful eye.

The Chocolate Man's footsteps were coming.

High above him there is a swallow—The footsteps stopped outside the doorway. Emily's eyes were closed.

—*wheeling swiftly across the sky.* If she didn't hear him or see him he wasn't there.

And the winds are laughing, they laugh with all their might. He was back in the room.

Love and laugh the whole day through—

"What are you singing?"

—*and half a summer's night.*

Emily stopped. She looked down at the table, the rope. She said nothing.

"I want you to teach it to me." His voice was hard.

Emily closed her eyes again. That was her mother's song.

He took a step toward her; she heard him. "Teach me," he said.

Emily breathed once, heavily, and with her eyes still closed she began to sing.

Stop complaining, said the farmer, who told you what has to be?

Why can't you be like the swallow, flying swiftly so strong and free?

The melody was old, old. Emily's voice was thin and true. Behind her eyes her mother was singing to her.

And the winds are laughing, they laugh with all their might. And she heard the Chocolate Man sitting down next to her.

Love and laugh the whole day through, and half a summer's night.

And they sat together in the kitchen, Emily's

wrist taut against the rope, and she taught him,
and together they sang the old song.

*Calves are easily led to slaughter, never knowing
the reason why.*

*Bow your head, it will soon be over, like the swal-
low you'll learn to fly.*

*And the winds are laughing, they laugh with all
their might.*

*Love and laugh the whole day through, and half
a summer's night.*

As Laurie smoothed the pale brown shadow across
her eyelids she thought of nothing but the arc of
color she was creating. Like a knight girding for
battle she penciled liner under her sore eyes,
brushed a swatch of rose onto each cheek. The
eyeliner pencil slipped and she flinched away from
the small smarting pain. *What is Emily feeling right
now?* Tears sprang and stung and Laurie blinked,
hard: *I am putting liner on my lower lids, Charcoal
Haze; Carolyn is coming and the police are coming
and I am smoothing Aurora Rose on my cheekbones.*

When she was finished her face looked, worn,
calm, and entirely unfamiliar.

The phone rang.

The sound cut right to her solar plexus. *I have
your child. I have molested her.*

The phone rang again. Laurie stood over it,
her arm extended toward the receiver, her hand a
fist. It rang again.

Laurie snatched up the receiver. "Yes," she
said. *I am wearing Beach Sand eye shadow,* she

thought, and at the same time she saw Emily's prone, silent body. At the other end of the phone somebody sighed.

"Mrs. Lookinland?" A man's voice. Laurie was aware of the little mechanical bug on her phone; the tape would have clicked on automatically by now.

"Yes," she said again.

"Mrs. Lookinland, this is Jack Davies from the *Daily News*. I'd like to ask you a few questions—"

Laurie slammed the phone down. Her hands were shaking violently. She pushed the button that activated the answering machine, but before the little box stopped its elaborate clicking she turned it off again. "Coffee," she muttered to herself, turning toward the kitchen.

The police will be here soon. Carolyn will be here. Mechanically she washed old grounds out of the espresso pot and filled the bottom half with cold water and spooned coffee into the metal catch basin. She was furious and afraid and she felt nothing at all: she was just moving her hands.

The news media wanted a quote from the distressed mother. They wanted her brave, hysterical, stoic, self-possessed. They weren't interested in her at all; they just wanted a hook for the nightly news. Laurie knew the media hadn't told everything they knew about the Chocolate Man. Between the reports of children missing and children dead there was only one word: *molested.* That word was frightening enough—but what lay behind that word? Someday a book would be written, no doubt, that cataloged the wounds of the victims, each and every aspect of their last hours as the forensic scientists found it etched into their skin, their tiny bones. What would Laurie find out then, was her daughter even now—

The phone rang.

Laurie jumped. She sighed; she had almost screamed. As she reached to flick the stove flame on, her hand clenched back into a fist. When she picked up the phone she spit, "Yes?" into the receiver.

"Mrs. Lookinland?"

"Yes."

"I am sorry to bother you, Mrs. Lookinland. My name is Peter Bjornstand, and I would like to talk to you, if I may."

"What do you want?"

"Please hear me out, Mrs. Lookinland. I may have important information concerning the whereabouts of your daughter."

Laurie sat abruptly on the sofa. She felt as though she had been punched in the stomach.

"What information?"

"Mrs. Lookinland, I am a psychic. I have reason to believe that your daughter is being held on the Island of Barbados—"

Laurie slammed the phone down. She kept slamming the receiver against the box, over and over, until she heard the coffee gurgling up into the top of the espresso pot.

The door would open; her grandfather would be there. Laurie had no memory of his face at these times, only his voice and the brown pants he wore. That was more than she wanted to remember. But there was more: his hand guiding hers, something hard beneath the zipper; his hands snaking around her from behind, fingering her nipples through the cloth of her shirt; sitting uncomfortable and ashamed in his lap; her oldest brother appearing white-faced in the doorway, staring at her grandfather until he let her off his lap.

Emily didn't know anything about her mother's memories. Emily wasn't going to have memories like that. That was to be the great achievement of Laurie's life, that her daughter would not be molested. Laurie could remember being four years old and thinking, *This has been going on all my life*. When Emily was four she bossed her mother and begged for ballet lessons. When Laurie was eight she had made a conscious decision not to tell her mother or grandmother; she didn't want to hurt them. When Emily was eight she came to Laurie and cried: why didn't Sue and Esther want to play with her?

It was only years later that Laurie realized that her mother and grandmother had both known, had to have known, her grandfather sticking his tongue down her small throat in the front hallway, saying hello; how could he have done that with people around?

Laurie had been such a "good" girl; she didn't tell because she didn't want anyone to be hurt. And years later, when her mother was dying of cancer, she said, "Oh, yes, your grandmother and I had an agreement, we always stopped Grandpa. One of us would say, 'He's on his way up to Laurie's room,' and we would stop him." And Laurie looked at her mother's pale, pain-racked face and she was not surprised.

And now she was waiting for the phone to ring, to find out if her daughter had been raped and murdered by the Chocolate Man.

"WHY DO YOU DO THAT?" EMILY ASKED.

"What?"

"Talk to yourself." Emily's hand was still tied to the kitchen chair. She was looking at where the row of little shoes had been. The Chocolate Man was sitting in a chair across from her; he was leaning forward and snapping the fingers of his left hand, over and over, above the Formica tabletop. Every time Emily moved—to shift her leg or rub her eye—the Chocolate Man leaned a little farther forward. *The guard and the prisoner were talking through the thick bars of the prisoner's cell.*

The Chocolate Man didn't answer but he stopped snapping; he looked almost comically surprised and then he scowled and turned his head away. "I don't."

"Yes you do. I've seen you. You move your lips."

The Chocolate Man started wiping at the kitchen table with his fingers. There was a window opposite Emily: it gave no light, it was nothing but black.

"It's okay," Emily said. "Once my mom caught me talking to myself, only I wasn't really, it was Vicky, she's a skeleton who was my friend."

"Isn't she your friend anymore?"

"Oh, no. That was baby stuff."

"What did your mother do?"

"When?"

"When she caught you talking to Vicky."

"Oh, nothing. She just laughed and tried to make sure I knew Vicky was really pretend."

"Did you?"

"Well—I guess so. But she was real at the same time, you know?"

"Uh-huh. I had something like that. But my mother never asked me."

The interrogator spoke only imperfect English; the prisoner had to strain to understand him.

"Is that who you've been talking to?" Silence was dangerous, Emily knew. And when he snapped his fingers it made her even more scared; it seemed very important to keep him talking.

"My mother?"

"No, the somebody."

"Oh—no."

"Who was the somebody?" It seemed safer to ask about a long time ago.

"Just—I didn't have any friends, so I made some up, I guess. Like Vicky."

"I've always had lots of friends. Vicky was because I wanted a monster friend."

"I already lived with them." the Chocolate Man said very softly.

"What?"

He was silent a moment.

"Did Vicky ever talk to you when you didn't want her to?"

"How could she do that?" *The prisoner looked around her cell: there was no way out.*

The Chocolate Man didn't say anything for a long time. Emily couldn't think of anything else to say. When she looked at him he was staring past her and his lips were moving.

"Do you have anything to eat besides salami?" Emily asked quickly. He started as though awakened. "I don't usually—" he said vaguely; he went to the refrigerator and looked dubiously inside.

"Could I get up and look?" Emily asked.

He didn't answer. Suddenly Emily wasn't as afraid as she had been. *I just can't make him mad,* she thought, *or talk about my mom.* It was like with her friend Sue's dad, who was nice and then hit Sue's mom, and sometimes Sue too, and they didn't always know why. "But I try not to do anything wrong," Sue had told her. "I try to be a good girl and never upset him." Sue was very quiet and she cried easily. Emily loved her.

Emily upset her mother, she knew that. Sometimes her mother yelled, and then she held Emily and said she was sorry but people get mad, and sometimes Emily got mad at her, didn't she? And Emily did, and she yelled too, or more likely kicked something or slammed a door. Once she called her mother a silly bastard, she'd heard somebody on the street say that, and her mother wasn't mad, she hugged Emily and said yes, she was, but don't ever say that again, it's naughty.

Was her mother upset with her now? Emily had gone too far away across the park. Of course her mother must know that somebody had taken her—

but what if she just thought Emily had run away? Then she would be angry. Maybe she wouldn't even look for Emily. *Yes she would,* Emily thought, but she had already started to cry.

"What's the matter with you?"

"Nothing. I just—my mom is going to be worried about me."

"Yes." The Chocolate Man was looking into the refrigerator himself. He stood with his back to her.

"Tell me about your mother," the Chocolate Man said. Emily froze in her seat. His voice sounded different. "Tell me something you two like to do together." There had been something on the television—"mutilated," a word Emily didn't know. But Perverts touched little children. Her mother had told her. And the Chocolate Man was a Pervert.

She didn't want him thinking about her mother. She didn't like the way he sounded, like he was out of breath. She couldn't stop looking at him, though; his back was moving as he breathed and she didn't think his hands were in the refrigerator. If thinking about her mother made him act funny, she just wouldn't talk about her.

"So, who do you talk to?" she asked.

"What?" The Chocolate Man stopped doing whatever he was doing; Emily had looked away. He didn't turn around.

"ET was my imaginary friend too," Emily said desperately, "the same time I had Vicky. I had two." When he turned around she forced herself not to look at his pants. He was still breathing funny, as though he'd been running. But he wasn't snapping his fingers. For a second Emily thought he looked scared. But his breathing was slowing. Emily's eyes darted to his pants but she didn't see anything strange. Men have penises and women have vaginas. Women can have babies and men can't. Maybe the Chocolate Man wanted to give her a baby. It comes out from between your legs, not your belly button. Sue said she had seen her father's penis once, he had tried to get her to touch it. She wouldn't and he hit her and she cried. "It looked like a big pink bologna," she said. Emily didn't know what that meant. "Like a sausage," Sue said, "but pink like bologna."

"Don't do that," the Chocolate Man said.

"Do what?" It was impossible to know what to say. There were minefields everywhere.

"Just—don't." And he stood, his back to her, and he started to snap his fingers again.

"I'm sorry," Emily said softly, and suddenly he turned around and he was holding up a bag of potato chips and a tin of dip. "Is this okay?" And Emily nodded, her hands shaking and her head hurting: yes.

The Chocolate Man put the chips and dip on the table, but Emily was afraid to eat. What if she made a mess? It was her right wrist that was tied to the chair. She felt awkward reaching across the table with her left: what if she dropped a chip, or dripped dip on the table? She sat, looking down; and then she looked up at the Chocolate Man. He wasn't even looking at her; he was looking past her, at the closed door to the hall.

"Do you ever feel dirty?" he asked suddenly.

"I brush my teeth," Emily said cautiously. If the Emily in the story had any magic she would use it right now. Emily's mother had told her that prayers are a kind of magic. She would say one. *Our father who art in heaven, hollow be thy name. Please don't let him touch me. Don't let him make me touch his penis.*

But now he was smiling. He didn't have a sausage in his pants. "Go ahead and eat," he said.

Thy will be done, on earth as it is in heaven. He was looking at her expectantly. She couldn't think of anything to say. There was nothing outside the window at all. She reached for a chip with her left hand and said, "Thank you," very softly.

Detective Second Grade Marcy Fleischer was not a pretty woman. It seemed her whole life had been built around that fact. She was not grotesque; she was not deformed. She was overweight but not obese. She laughed readily, and she was, she knew, more intelligent than most of the people around her. But she was worse than ugly: she was plain. There was nothing about her at all that could catch and capture the eye, even in surprise or derision.

No one ever noticed Marcy; no one ever had. She had never dreamed the typical little-girl dreams: ballerina, princess, movie star. She had always known that even the dream worlds were closed to her. Her mother was a beautiful woman. She had expected to have a beautiful child. She took Marcy's looks to be a personal affront from God; at least that's the way it always seemed to Marcy.

Her mother liked to sit in front of the mirror in her bedroom and look at herself. She liked to stand in front of the full-length mirror in the dining room and spin into different positions and look at herself. Marcy loved to watch her; women still wore grownup clothes then, high heels and stockings and cinched belts and perfume and a whole fake careful face out of bottles, and beautiful shiny unmoving hair.

Marcy herself, now, wore only lipstick. She wore unobtrusive shades and did not paint an ideal faddish mouth over her thin natural lips. But she loved lipstick; at any given moment she owned eight or nine tubes, in barely changing hues of rose: because lipstick was her entrée into the adult world, the world she had never been inside, the world she suspected did not exist at all. Her perception of that world had changed very little from the time she was a girl. It was a surface world; it lay in mirrors and television screens and shiny magazine pages, it came out of tiny pots and powder compacts and glossy tubes, and it smelled wonderful. Marcy allowed herself only the magic smell of lipstick, the many different-hued tubes, as the only symbol of that world she would accept.

Marcy was not an innocent. She had known men, she had fallen in love. But no feeling had ever consumed her the way the Chocolate Man case did. She hadn't had a regular meal in months; she hadn't slept a regular night's sleep. Her friends felt abandoned; her partner said she was possessed. And she was. Possessed by a fever hotter even than love: vengeance, and hope.

Sometimes she lay awake at night and looked at the ceiling and saw the crime-scene map. It was always there, behind everything she saw, blue veins and red arteries and thick black highway scars. It haunted her, it plagued her like a memory: Here is where they found Danny, here is where they found Andrew Tonata. Here is where the Chocolate Man wanted the ransom for Ronald Chin to be left. He didn't kill for money; he didn't want the money. He wanted the pain. He wanted the parents' anticipation: even when they knew, after the third and fourth killings, the parents of Oliver and Ronald and James had spoken with hope. *Maybe this time— maybe if we*—even when they knew. And then, *Why? Why did he torture us this way? Isn't it enough to lose a child?* And Marcy looked at the crime-scene map and knew that there were answers there. Not to all the questions; there would never be an answer for *Why?* But the riddle of the Chocolate Man's mind was written in red and yellow and orange pushpins on the crime-scene map, and Marcy knew that if she could solve that riddle no more children would have to die.

Multiple killers always have a pattern. It may not look like one, because the mind that can plan to kill and kill again cannot be made like other minds. But such a mind will always approach its victims the same way, will kill, again and again, the same way, will create over and over the same grotesque beloved tableau. And the mind that had kidnapped one by one seven little boys and demanded ransom each time with the same words, then each time lied, each time killed and left the body out in plain view to be found—that mind was executing, each time, the same plan, enacting each time the same fantasy, receiving each time the same satisfaction. And with so much of each crime similar to the last crime, there must be some significance to that mind's choice of ransom drop and body drop. The site of each kidnapping was identical: a public park, a playground; a busy day. Except the first, which the Task Force believed must have been a strange, fortuitous accident that marked the birth of the Chocolate Man in the death of Danny Angelo. And after that death the course had been set, all phases of the kidnapping and killing had assumed their unique, necessary order and solidified in the mind of the Chocolate Man.

And they were all in plain sight on the crime-scene map. Marcy spent hours in front of it. She stared blank-faced at the colors, the death and desire and deception spots strewn random across its width. "Marcy," Ed would say, "he's just jerking our chains. He says Richmond Hill, he means Boerum Hill. He just likes us to run in one direction while he goes in another."

But it was more than that. Marcy knew, could hear his cool, keen satisfaction in each taped mocking ransom demand: *Leave twenty thousand dollars at*—each time the same, with the same pause after *twenty thousand*. He was relishing the number, each time stopping to let the same meaningless number float like a buoy to a mother or father drowning in loss and fear.

Marcy knew every location the Chocolate Man had called from, demanding money he didn't want, exacting the pain he needed. It was easy, nowadays, to trace a phone call. Alert the telephone company, press the star and the number three when the call comes in. But it was never enough. The Chocolate Man said the same three sentences every time he called; it always took him between twelve and four-teen seconds to say them. The trace was almost immediate, but it didn't matter, by the time the police cars screamed to a stop at a public phone booth in Cobble Hill, Brooklyn, or Sunnyside, Queens, or TriBeCa, the Chocolate Man was gone, and he was never remembered. Usually the phone booths were on empty streets, sometimes in dan-gerous neighborhoods. Or right in the middle of a neighborhood so busy with tourists that no one remained who had been there for the fourteen sec-onds of the Chocolate Man's call.

Marcy knew that the riddle of the Chocolate Man was written in red and yellow and orange across the expanse of the crime-scene map, and she was determined to be the one to solve that riddle, and stop the killing forever.

"It's getting so warm," Emily had said sadly to her mother as they walked to the park that afternoon, a life ago.

"You wanted snow for Christmas."

Emily was silent. Laurie was aware that she didn't know, hadn't known for years, what Emily really wanted for Christmas. She touched her daughter's shoulder. "I heard on the weather that the barometer is going down. And look, there's a mackerel sky."

The steel-gray clouds above them floated past, they looked like scales on a fish.

"You're just saying," said Emily. "You wish I still believed in Santa Claus."

"I believe in Santa Claus."

"*Mom.*"

"In the spirit of love."

"I've been trying to understand that." Emily's face was scrunched up with a child's concentration. "Like you told me, the spirit moving across people's souls. How do you know?"

"I can feel it, honey."

"I can't."

"Yes, you can. You can feel that I love you, can't you?"

"I know. When I was a little baby you always used to wake up at night just before I started to cry."

"Mama-love."

"Yeah. But what's *spirit?*"

"It's like a voice. You feel it but you don't hear it. You feel God's love, right?"

"I guess so. I say my prayers. But, Mom—there are so many bad things that happen to people—don't they pray?"

"Some of them do. And every prayer is answered. It's just that sometimes, the answer is no."

6:00 P.M.

THERE WAS TO BE A MEETING IN THE SQUADROOM, no exceptions. The expert from the Behavioral Science Center at Quantico had caught a flight out of Dulles the moment she heard about the latest Chocolate Man kidnapping. Marcy was supposed to have gone off duty hours ago; her body was a nuisance now, needing sleep. She had been resting her head on her desk in semiconscious dreams when Ed came to tell her about the meeting. He'd gone ahead; when Marcy got there she wasn't surprised to find that there were officers she didn't know, and some she did, from precincts all over the city, from every precinct, in fact, where the Chocolate Man had struck.

Ed had saved her a seat. There was a black projector set up at the back of the room, a flimsy white screen at the front. There was a woman already speaking, leaning on Lieutenant Monsey's desk. Dr. Alethea Howard. Marcy tried to listen to what she was saying as she excused herself down a row of policemen.

"Now, this latest abduction—of the girl Emily Rose Lookinland—differs from all the previous kidnappings in one important respect. The Chocolate Man abducts, sexually abuses, and murders chil-

dren—boy children." Marcy looked around her.
Every face was attentive, every pen was scratching
paper. She wasn't the only one who hadn't slept in
twenty-four hours: there were men here who had
made this case a personal crusade. Marcy had no
children; Sergeant Benthazar Mohammad, a member of the Task Force out of the Two-O-Seven, had
two boys and a girl, and he had attacked this case as
though it were his own who were gone. Marcy
looked for his face—but he had been assigned to
stay with the mother. Mrs. Lookinland. Marcy
couldn't bear to think of her, of any of the mothers.
"We have obtained photographs of Emily from the
One-Two-Eight—" Dr. Howard was saying; she
signaled toward the back of the room and the lights
went out. Emily's smiling face appeared on the
white screen and Marcy gasped.

The child was beautiful, with thick dark curls
and a small unconscious half-smile. She held a viola
to her chin; she wasn't looking at the camera but
above and behind it, and her eyes were half-closed.
She was unaware of the camera and of her own
startling prettiness. At first Marcy thought, *How
could he have mistaken this child*—? That was why
she had gasped. But as she looked—and Dr.
Howard was quiet for a long time, as they all
looked—she realized how much she had brought
with her to this picture. A beautiful child with curly
hair, an old-fashioned bow mouth. Change her
clothes, her expression, her setting, and this child
could as easily be a boy.

"As you know, we at Quantico agree with the
decision to treat the apparent kidnapping of Emily

Rose Lookinland as the latest in the series of kidnap-murders by the serial killer the media refers to as the Chocolate Man. The description of the suspect in this case tallies quite exactly not only with the physical description of the Chocolate Man but also with his modus operandi, as well as with forensic evidence found on three of the murder victims.

"First we will address the particulars of the profile I and my colleagues in the Profiling Department have drawn up. After careful consideration, we had to agree to a somewhat unusual diagnosis of this particular multiple murderer." Marcy was wide awake now, leaning forward in her seat. "The man who committed these crimes," Dr. Howard continued, "is almost certainly suffering from obsessive-compulsive disorder. This is a fairly new category of psychological disorder, but we are discovering that it is much more widespread than we had previously thought. You see, the disorder itself is so bizarre—really quite hard to believe, in some instances—that at first we were loath to categorize more than a few variations: hand washing is one that probably is familiar to you. Lady Macbeth was a compulsive hand washer. Compulsive hand washers will scrub their hands until they bleed—forty, fifty times a day. And then there are people who have to pick up every piece of paper they see on the street—literally *have* to. They lose their jobs, their families—it takes them three hours to get to work because they're stopping to pick up every single piece of paper they see! Or they can't stop singing the first two lines of 'I'll Never Fall in Love Again'—that actually was one of my cases in private practice. Fortunately the man worked in a bakery, where nobody minded if he sang. They even put up a plaque commemorating his millionth live rendition of the song.

"But if that man had been a salesman, say, or a banker, he would have lost his job. Because he was not capable of stopping—he *had* to repeatedly sing the first two lines of that song.

"Now, we at Quantico believe that the Chocolate Man is obsessive-compulsive. Our reasons? The timing. The kidnapper calls the parents exactly six hours after the abduction. *Exactly* six hours. Oliver Plucienkowsky was taken at four-seventeen—his parents were contacted at ten-seventeen. Exactly. Again, in Oliver's case the kidnapper called the second time precisely twelve hours after that—at ten-seventeen the next morning. And he arranged for the money dropoff at ten-seventeen that night—exactly twelve hours later. And every single case has had that same pattern. Six, twelve, and twelve.

"Very likely it is not the particular numbers themselves that have meaning to the murderer, but the repetition of those numbers, the *exactness*. And each of the seven bodies has always been laid out in nearly identical tableaux."

Dr. Howard paused while all the officers looked at those tableaux in their minds. "The material found near the bodies," she went on, "has always been the kind of things left over from a fast-food meal: napkins, paper cups, bits of meat, and french fries. In obsessive-compulsive disorder there is no middle ground. No gray. So you line the body up in a perverse, ritualistic way—but you also use the

detritus from the backseat of your car. It's very
likely that in his home environment the Chocolate
Man is either meticulously neat or extremely
slovenly—or both, in rotating cycles. These cycles
could be lunar-related; that is, subject to the phases
of the moon. That's very common; every police
officer knows that the rate of violent crime rises
sharply around the time of the full moon. But the
Chocolate Man's cycle has never been clear to us. A
spring kidnapping followed by a winter one, a full-
moon killing followed by a killing at the new moon.
And what appear to us," gesturing at the map
behind her, "as random decisions"—pointing to
the red pin for Ronald Chin and then to his yellow
pin, then his orange—"may in fact indicate a very
precise methodology we simply have not been able,
up to this point, to identify. That is, I know, one of
the most frustrating aspects of this case."

Marcy rolled a lipstick tube absently between
her fingers; her head hurt.

"Now, we've had to ask ourselves, Wouldn't the
killer's compulsions get in the way of his ability to
carry out the abductions and murders?

"Since we don't know for certain what his compulsions consist of, other than an exactitude involving time, or possibly numbers, and the two
extremes of order and chaos, it's difficult to say
what effect they might have on his modus operandi.
Obviously he is able to kill."

Marcy remembered touching the tops of dining-
room chairs as she went by, when she was nine or ten;
she remembered not walking on the cracks in the
sidewalk: *Step on a crack, break your mother's back.*

Things all children do. And she could not imagine now what a continued slavery to the trivial would have done to her mind.

"And OCD accounts for another apparent contradiction. As you know, serial killers usually have a 'type'; that is, they repeatedly abduct and kill similar-looking victims. Blonde women, Causasian males under the age of twenty." Marcy was still rolling the lipstick, back and forth, the tube making a clicking noise against the rings on her fingers. "And you would think the Chocolate Man would operate within such a pattern. But in fact he takes what he can get: any little boy is fair game, so far as he's concerned. Danny Angelo was Caucasian; Ronald Chin was half Asian; Andrew Timmons was black. What this tells us is that this killer isn't looking for a specific type—perhaps because all the minutiae of his particular compulsions do not leave room for him to make even one more decision. He is very likely to be straitjacketed by the parameters of his disorder.

"Now we come to Emily Lookinland. It is highly unlikely—not to say impossible—that the Chocolate Man intended to abduct a girl child. His compulsions would almost certainly not allow for that. But Emily Looklinland was dressed boyishly, she has short hair—there is no reason to think that the Chocolate Man diverted from his regular routine on purpose. And we do know," leaning forward, her arm stiff on the desktop—this was what these people were here to find out—"that when the obsessive-compulsive is confronted with a situation contradictory to his expectations, it becomes impossible to predict what he might do. He may be unable to kill the girl." Marcy's lipstick tube fell unnoticed at her feet. "He may instead inflict harm on himself. But he may, after a period of indecision, be able to carry out his original intentions."

Marcy raised her hand. "Can we count on having some time before he kills the girl?" she asked before Howard acknowledged her.

"We can't count on anything." Howard's face was calm and sad. "We'll know more when he calls—if he calls. You see, the fact that he's taken a girl child could change every facet of his usual M.O."

"So you're saying we don't know—anything could happen now."

"What I'm saying," her voice hard and compassionate, "is that the X in this equation is suddenly Y—and nobody, not even the Chocolate Man, knows what is going to happen next."

For years nothing changed. George went out to work and came home to clean. The need to wash his hands ebbed over time, but the counting did not. But by then it had become such a part of him that he didn't mind it much anymore.

One day, when George was twenty-nine, he took a walk around the neighborhood. It was spring. George hadn't taken a walk in a long time. He looked at the houses and the trees; there were some sort of little white flowers on some of the trees. As he rounded the corner George saw a little boy standing at the end of a driveway. He wasn't doing anything; he was just standing there.

George stopped. He looked at the boy. "Are you lost?" he asked.

"I'm waiting for my nanny."

"Your nanny asked me to take you to the candy store," George said, and the boy put his hand out to be held, and that was all.

George asked the boy his name and his telephone number; like most children he had been taught to recite these on command. George made a telephone call: *I have your son. I have molested him. Give me twenty thousand dollars in unmarked bills or you will never see him again.*

George had no intention of returning the boy.

It was so easy the first time that George didn't dare try again for almost a year. He went to the liquor store to work, he came home. He had kept the boy's body under his bed overnight; it took a long, long time to get the space clean after it was gone.

George kept the boy's shoes, and his little socks. The shoes sat soldier-straight in the center of the kitchen table, and George dusted them every night and every morning. The socks he kept folded neatly in front of the shoes; sometimes he picked them up and held them, thinking of the mother's face as he had seen it on the television news, anguished and begging: *Send my baby home to me.*

He knew he would do it again. It was winter the next time, summer the time after that. Seven times. It was always so easy. Learning to drive his father's car had been difficult, but he couldn't keep taking children in his own neighborhood. George taught himself, driving five mph down the block in the middle of the night. The feeling of power he got from being behind the wheel was almost as intense as the feeling he got while killing. But he drove very carefully, almost too slowly, even when he had taught himself enough to venture out onto the highway during the day. He had an orgasm in the car the first time he did that; he wasn't aware of any feeling at all, and then he was coming. That happened again every so often; after a while it no longer frightened him.

And he could count while he was driving. Normally George couldn't perform even the simplest motions while counting; he couldn't even walk, but he could drive. And he came to love the seamless rolling of the numbers and the tires beneath him.

George found his quarry at parks and playgrounds; never again was he lucky enough to find a child simply standing, waiting for him. That first time had been a sign, a symbol of the rightness of his actions. It was not God that smiled on him but his compulsions. After that first killing George cleaned every inch of his house for hours.

And the catharsis! Scrubbing the kitchen floor, scrubbing under the bed! For a little while, on his knees, his hands raw from scrubbing, his breath short from exertion, George was safe, and George was happy, and George was free.

"I HAVE TO GO OUT FOR A LITTLE WHILE." THE CHOC-olate Man was on his hands and knees in front of the bedroom closet; he had asked Emily to stand where he could see her. His bedroom didn't look as though anybody ever slept in it. It was all white, and there were big pieces of blue and green and gray carpet outside the closet; Emily thought maybe that was what he'd been doing when she was in the kitchen, taking carpet out of the closet. Now she watched him stack the pieces one by one against the wall.

"I have a place where you can stay." They had just finished watching *I Dream of Jeannie* on the Chocolate Man's TV in the living room. He had sat on the sofa; he had carefully tied Emily's wrist to the end table. Even though it was dark he hadn't turned on any lights. There was a Christmas tree in the corner with nothing on it; Emily had asked why but he wouldn't tell her. *The prisoner seemed to have no hope of escape.*

The Chocolate Man seemed to be pleased with himself. "I'm fixing it special," he said. Emily stood behind him and to the left—"Now don't you run off," he'd said playfully, "I want to see you every minute." Now he was pulling shoes out of the bottom of the closet, boots and sneakers and loafers with tassels. None of them looked worn. "That's it," he said; he leaned back on his heels and smiled at her.

"The closet?"

He nodded happily. There was a dull gold key in the lock on the outside of the door.

"You want me to stay in the closet?" He seemed so pleased, as though he were doing her a favor. He was going to lock her in.

Emily couldn't say a word. She could not get any air into her lungs.

The Chocolate Man was looking at her expectantly. When her heart started beating too fast she was certain he must hear it. Its thudding filled her ears, her heart was galloping out of her body. She brought her hand up to her heart. It took a long time; from far away the Chocolate Man was still looking at her. He said something, his mouth moved and there was thunder in her ears and she was going to die.

"—okay?" She heard him say, and the thunder stopped as suddenly as it had started. Emily gulped in great drafts of air, she bent slightly, as though she had been running, her hand on her heart.

"Emily, are you okay?"

It was the first time he had said her name.

"Don't put me in there," she whispered.

"It's okay. It has a light. See?" A hard glare sprang up inside the closet; Emily could see a cord swinging from the ceiling.

"Please don't put me in that closet."

"It's okay. Look." The Chocolate Man stepped

away: a bare wooden floor illuminated by a flat light; wooden slatted walls. In the corner was an empty saucepan; at first Emily didn't know what it was for.

Emily tensed her body to run. She emptied her lungs. The Chocolate Man had pulled the cord again and darkened the closet, and now he was facing away from her; he was walking away across the room. Emily waited, her breath suspended: *now*.

The Chocolate Man turned. "See?" he said. "TV!" and Emily lurched forward and caught herself before she fell.

He was holding a small television. He looked proud.

"So you won't get lonely," he said.

Emily stared.

"And I have cookies," he went on, kneeling to put the TV in the closet, "and a salami sandwich." Emily hated salami. "And magazines, and Coke. You like Coke?"

Emily nodded. "You're going to lock me in there," she said faintly.

"It won't be for long. I have to make a telephone call."

"Why don't you just kill me!" Emily screamed suddenly. "Just do it and get it over with! You're nothing but a murderer!"

The Chocolate Man was looking at her with puzzled eyes.

"I hate you!" Emily was screaming. "You can't put me in that closet, I won't go in that closet!"

The Chocolate Man took a step toward her. She looked behind him, at the open closet door, and without thinking she charged him and pushed, and he was falling backward and he looked so surprised, Emily had time to think, *He's frightened,* and everything was vibrating, he was in the closet and she slammed the door and the Chocolate Man said, "Oof," quite distinctly. Emily heard a sharp thump and her hands were frantic at the keyhole. She turned the key—but the key would not turn.

Emily could hear the Chocolate Man bumping in the dark. She jerked the key right, left. She wasn't sure, and then the key was stuck. She wrenched it and it moved a little way out of the lock, she pushed it, hard, and she was running out of the room and she couldn't hear him behind her, there was nothing but a shushing in her ears.

It was dark, and he couldn't breathe. That smell, that smell. Where was he? There was something, a long way away—"Mommy?" he said softly. If she heard him she might be angry. He couldn't remember what he'd done wrong. It must have been very bad, she didn't put him in the closet often—but there was yelling. Why was she yelling? Maybe she was hurt; maybe she needed him. He tried to listen but the dark was so scary: *Don't you put that light on, I'll see it under the door if you do.* But the yelling was still—the Chocolate Man sat up; he'd hurt his head. It was the child. The girl child.

And she was calling for help. The Chocolate Man stood up—*Don't you put the light on*—and the lightbulb cord slapped him in the face. He had never been so frightened. He was crying: why would she do that? He hadn't done anything wrong. Sometimes he even put himself in the closet, if he thought he'd been a bad boy. But he hadn't done anything to upset his mother. "It's not right," he said aloud, and he reached for the doorknob.

He knew just where it was; as if it hadn't been a long time ago. It stuck, for a moment he thought she'd locked it again, she did that when he was really bad, other times he was allowed to come out when he thought he'd been punished long enough. The doorknob stuck and moved and stuck—he pushed hard, and the door was open.

Emily could hear the Chocolate Man behind her: "Mommy?" A little voice, a scared voice. This couldn't be real, running down the hall of a mad-man's house—again, "Mommy?" tentative and afraid—it wasn't happening. She was just a kid, this couldn't be happening to her. On the other side of the door it wasn't happening, there was nothing happening at all. If she could get there, where the old man was, where it was just the day before Christmas Eve and everybody was wrap-ping presents—she was crying but she didn't know it, crying: *it's not real, it's not*. She wasn't thinking as her fingers fumbled at the deadbolt, *it's not*.

She knew that as soon as she opened that front door it would be over, because it had to be.

✗   ✗   ✗

"Don't you open that door," the Chocolate Man said loudly behind her, "I'll know it if you do." "Help!" the girl yelled again; she wasn't his mother, she didn't have any right to put him in the closet. He walked evenly down the hall—his mother had never run, never hurried, even when she came out of the burning house she had not moved quickly, holding his father up with the other man. "Help!" the child yelled again, and he was angry now.

The three locks were looking at her, waiting. The highest one was almost too high; the lowest was a chain and it slipped off easily: Something creaked and then banged behind her, louder than screaming. The second lock was a deadbolt, it should have been easy but it wasn't. And he was behind her in the hall. Left—but no, right, and she snagged her finger, it was bleeding, there was blood on the brass.

"Please please please." Emily was whispering; on the other side of the door none of this was happening, it didn't exist.

I am going to escape I am I am I am.

But she could hear the Chocolate Man's footsteps, coming slowly down the hall. "I'll hear you," he was saying.

The deadbolt gave with a shriek. The Chocolate Man's breath was against her neck. "Please," she said, he said, "What's the matter, Mommy?" and when he grabbed her it hurt, but when he gripped her and pushed her up against his neck it felt like an embrace.

✕   ✕   ✕

The Chocolate Man was looking at her with something like fear. He was angry but he was afraid
too; it was like a nugget of fire in Emily's heart,
that he was afraid.

"Why did you do that?"

Emily was silent. What was she to him now? He
held her hard by the shoulders but it didn't hurt;
and he looked as if he might cry. "You were doing a
bad thing," she said bravely.

The Chocolate Man looked down at the floor.
His mouth was ashamed. "A very bad thing," Emily
went on. He had said, "Mommy," maybe he
thought she was his mommy.

"I didn't mean to," he mumbled: Emily shivered: *There's a goose walking over your grave*, and she
almost broke then, the Chocolate Man's hands sliding slowly down her arms; "I'm sorry," he said.

But when he raised his eyes he was smiling.

Emily gasped.

"You're not my mother," he said contemptu-
ously. "She wouldn't have tried to lock the door.
She always knew I wouldn't come out."

"Why?" Emily asked. He sneered, he lifted her
roughly by the arms, he pushed her before him
down the hall toward the kitchen. "Why? That's a
stupid question, you're just stupid, you're *stupid*."
With a little push for each *stupid*, when they got to
the kitchen Emily shocked them both by turning
and fiercely saying, "Don't you do that to me, don't
you call me that! You're not my mother, and she
would never say anything like that to me!" and she

didn't care, she really didn't, he could kill her right now she was so mad.

But the Chocolate Man just looked at her. "She wouldn't?" he asked seriously.

"'Course not. I want something to drink. Besides Yoo-Hoo."

The Chocolate Man was regarding her dubiously. He was like two people; Emily knew how dangerous he was but he was something else simple too; sometimes he listened to her as though she were the grownup one.

"You have to say please," he said finally.

"Please," with narrowed eyes.

"Okay." As he passed her to get to the refrigerator he grabbed her shoulder and she gasped; "Your mother doesn't call you any names?"

Emily was forced to walk close to him, she could smell his sweat. "Once in a while she calls me a pain in the butt," she admitted.

The Chocolate Man laughed. He opened the refrigerator door. "It's not so bad in the closet," he said. A minute ago she'd thought he was going to kill her.

"Are you mad?"

"What? Oh—not really. I thought everybody—I mean, if you've never been put in the closet—" questioning, his silhouette haloed by the refrigerator light.

"No."

"Oh. Well. It's not so bad. My mother used to let me come out myself. Not when I was little. When I was bigger—like you. She used to let me come out by myself when I knew I'd been punished enough. I've got some lemonade."

Emily said nothing. *When he thought he'd been punished enough.*

"It looks kind of old," he was saying. And "I never would have talked to my mother that way," and Emily couldn't tell whether he was angry; he sounded almost proud of her.

"Well?" He was looking at her with expectation.

"Okay. I mean, lemonade sounds just fine. I guess—" slowly, because she didn't know the rules, anything could make him be mean or be nice, "—I still have to go into the closet, huh?"

He had let go of her shoulder; "Just a minute," he said, reaching for the lemonade pitcher and sniffing it; "It's really not so bad. Nobody else ever stayed there, just me. And that was a long time ago. And I put in the TV and the sandwich." Maybe he was getting mad. "Okay," said Emily, "anything you want."

"That's a good girl. Come on," taking her shoulder again but gentle this time, "I've got to go. The pot's for you to pee in. I thought of that myself." And he snapped his fingers while he told her about the closet as they walked to his bedroom, and Emily thought, over and over, *You didn't get away. That was the last chance, and you didn't get away,* over and over and over and over.

THE NIGHT WAS WARM; TOMORROW WAS CHRISTMAS Eve. There was a memory of spring in the air. Laurie had called Dick; she had gotten his number from Chicago information, matching the address on his checks to a 312 telephone number with the help of a patient information lady.

When Laurie dialed the number a taped female voice told her that Dick and Evie weren't home right now but would she leave a message? "Emily's been kidnapped," she said into the dead air of the answering machine. "They think—they won't say but I think it's the Chocolate Man. Pray for her, Dick."

That was an hour and a half ago. There had been no reply.

Every month Dick sent Laurie a check, and if Emily was the one to find the envelope in the mail she was always quiet for the rest of the day. Laurie wrote once a year, at Christmas, sending photographs of Emily and assuring Dick that he could visit her anytime.

There was never any reply.

This year Laurie had included pictures of Emily playing the viola, taken at a performance of the school orchestra. Emily had a look of serene concentration on her face, the dark-wood instrument enormous in her small hands.

"What do you think about while you're playing?" Laurie had asked her, studying her daughter's relaxed half-smile.

"Oh, I guess—clouds. Like I'm walking on clouds, like all the notes are cloud-steps and I'm going up. Kind of stupid, huh?"

Laurie lighted a cigarette. She had not looked at any photographs of her daughter since Emily disappeared. Now she reached for a stack that stood on the living room table next to the sofa, rejects from the three she'd sent Dick four days ago. There was another one that the police had taken.

Laurie's hand hesitated; she watched the smoke from her cigarette twisting up into the lamplight and knew she was only hurting herself. Even when the police had asked for a picture she had not looked, just said, "They're over there." *But I can't hurt any more than I do already,* she thought, and lifted the first picture from the stack.

Emily, standing in the kitchen looking self-conscious but with a gleam in her eye: Laurie never knew when she was going to pull a face or jump toward the camera just as Laurie clicked the shutter.

This time Laurie had shot before Emily could do anything, but Emily fell theatrically to the floor anyway, crying, "They got me! Top o' the world, Ma!" They had been watching James Cagney movies all week, snuggled in blankets on the living room sofa, with popcorn and Raisinettes.

Tears were streaming down Laurie's face. She bent forward until her forehead touched the surface of the cool anonymous photographs. As sobs wrenched her body she could only think, over and over, *Top o' the world, Ma, top o' the world*.

As the door closed in front of her Emily took a deep, unconscious breath, and she reached for the doorknob as it clicked and quivered and the bolt slid home.

The walls were breathing.

Emily could not think for fear. She rattled the knob and half-expected it to turn: it had to turn.

But the door shook slightly, that was all. It was white, and the walls were white. The whiteness expanded around her, choking her, blinding her. There was nothing but white.

There were tears streaming down her face, she was rattling and rattling the doorknob.

Suddenly she stopped. There was a brown wire snaked under the doorframe, which was old and warped. The wire slipped through easily: a cockroach or a spider could slip through, too. Emily looked at the white door and the half inch of space at the bottom and anything could have been out there. She moved farther back—but there could be a spider on the wall in back of her. She scooted abruptly forward. She was trying to make herself small.

"This is a story about Emily," she whispered, "who was held captive by the Axis powers outside Alsace-Lorraine."

✗   ✗   ✗

The police came. Two male officers who made the house strange. Big and young and healthy, they made the small rooms smaller. *It's been a long time since there was a man in this place,* Laurie surprised herself by thinking. The officers took over the kitchen, clearing off the counters, the tiny table; Emily and Laurie ate all their meals at the kitchen table, looking out the windows over the sink for birds, for clouds, for rain or snow.

The policemen were named Sergeant Mulrooney and Sergeant Mohammad. Mulrooney was big and Irish, Mohammad was big and black. Like partners on a TV show. Mulrooney was quiet, moving almost noiselessly with electronic equipment, plugging and unplugging wires to check the tap on the phone. Mohammad was aware of his strangeness in these rooms. Whenever Laurie looked up he was looking at her, sympathetically and without pity. He was solicitous without intrusion. Laurie was grateful. Her house didn't seem like her house: her and Emily's home. The men's physical presence displaced more than air and order; Laurie found herself distanced from her pain. She and Carolyn watched them take over Laurie's home and turn it into a police outpost. Carolyn offered to make them coffee but they refused her, and in a little while Laurie could smell burnt roasting coffee, and the smell cheered her. Once she heard the refrigerator door open, and the sound comforted her. And she began to search, when she looked up from her seat on the living room sofa, for Sergeant Mohammad's clear and calming eyes.

✗   ✗   ✗

The Chocolate Man got into his car and sighed as he slipped the key into the ignition. He was already tired. It was much harder this time; usually everything simply unfolded and he didn't have to think at all. From the moment of selection the familiar story played itself out; there was no alternative, no choices to be made after the first choice.

His victims need only be boys, and unwatched. Unwatched meant unwanted. The Chocolate Man could not remember ever looking up to see his mother's eyes on him, in pleasure or affection or even in anger. He had washed his own clothes from the time he was six, the washer a white swallowing monster above him, the settings gleaming silver out of reach; so he had climbed, jumping off as the monster sprang to life.

His mother was always, in his memory, wearing the same cream-colored slip, lacy at the hem, one strap fallen from an expanse of shoulder like a mountainside, a steep drop and slope, dangerous. She smoked cigarettes; she drank brandy; she ate cold meat sandwiches standing over the kitchen sink, scattering crumbs. The Chocolate Man had heard her sing only once, and he didn't know if she knew how to read. She played solitaire. She smiled often and absently at his father, over his own tow head. She never called him by name.

The children in the parks were often unwatched. The nannies and mothers sat blind and unconcerned, ignoring their charges while they talked about their own stupid needs. His mother had often talked of her needs: another bottle, a new deck of cards, money, a hot bath. The children played far from their mothers, running and laughing. The Chocolate Man did not remember ever needing anything. He would tell them he had lost his dog, his own son: children love to help people. So they would follow him, calling for Spot or little George.

If the girl's mother had been watching, the girl wouldn't be in his closet now. If she had cared. The Chocolate Man smiled as he got into his car. They always seemed to be so upset; but that was after. And after lasted a long time—a lifetime. So that all the mothers could think about their uncaring, selfish before. The engine whined, the wheels started to move. Maybe he would tell her mother that. Maybe with this death he could scream that, across the country and across time, and finally be heard.

Directly above Emily's head hung a rack of shirts. A long, dirty string hung from a naked lightbulb in the ceiling. Emily didn't realize that she could stand up.

She stared, crouched like an animal, at the glare from the bulb.

After a long time she lowered her eyes. There was light speckling everything. The shirts, the white walls, the small TV. Emily stared at the TV a long time. When her hand reached out to turn the knob it didn't seem to be her hand.

But the moment the TV went on Emily's body relaxed almost completely. Television. The most familiar noise, perhaps, in her short life.

"—too many lovers, not enough love. We'll be right—"

She switched the channel. "—Chuck E. Cheese's, where a kid can be a kid."

Again. "—body cover. Because nobody's perfect. Available at—"

Again. "—search for the missing nine-year-old, Emily Rose Lookinland. More at eleven."

Emily flicked through the dial as fast as she could. "—or I'll fill you with so much tranquilizer you'll be out for a week." There was nothing else about her on any of the other stations.

How strange to see your own face on television.

She remembered when her mother took that shot, it was only a week ago. They were taking pictures to send to her dad.

"—not a very romantic reason." Now there was an old movie. *Camille.* Emily and her mother loved Greta Garbo; they had been watching her movies together since Emily was three years old.

Greta brought a chocolate daintily to her mouth. "I'm sorry," she said languidly, "one needs friends," and for a moment Emily forgot her captivity.

Laurie sat with her head on Carolyn's shoulder. She could smell the tea-rose perfume Carolyn wore. As always it brought back the moment of Emily's birth.

When Laurie became pregnant, Dick was not pleased—he never said so, but he showed no interest in her burgeoning body or the tiny, energetic kicks from within. When it came time to take Lamaze courses he said he was too busy. He didn't want to be in the delivery room, anyway. So Laurie went to classes with her friend Carolyn from night school; she went to a midwife instead of a doctor. Childbearing became a completely feminine experience. And forever afterward the smell of the tea-rose perfume Carolyn wore would bring her instantly back to the hospital room. The midwife had turned off the overhead and lighted candles. Carolyn held her hand and she gripped like a woman drowning—and then she screamed, and Carolyn's tea rose brought that back to her, too, the screaming that seemed to come from outside herself, and Carolyn saying, "It's okay, go ahead and scream. Push. Get it out. Scream."

And the final, impossible push, and the tiny bundle suddenly in her arms—all this came rushing back with the smell of tea rose.

Emily had lain quietly, looking around slowly, and Carolyn said, "Another woman," and Laurie said only, "Emily."

"Carolyn?" Laurie said softly; Carolyn had been stroking her hair, and she kept stroking it as they talked.

"Yes, honey."

"I can't live if she doesn't."

"Shh. They'll find her."

"It feels like she's still alive."

"I know."

"It does to you, too?"

"Yes. You know how much I love Emily."

"Yes. So you would know, too."

"Yes."

They were silent awhile. Carolyn looked at the night outside the window, not seeing. When Laurie spoke again it seemed to Carolyn that she wasn't aware she was speaking.

"Do you know much about the Lindbergh kidnapping? A long time ago—sixty years. Emily and I"—not faltering on her daughter's name—"watched a documentary about it a few weeks ago. The baby"—but here she did falter—"the baby was less than two years old. He was taken in the middle of the night. His mother kept her hope alive for ten weeks—it might have been longer. But when they came to tell her the baby was dead, she realized that she had known all along, that the instant she knew he was missing she also knew he was dead. And I'm searching myself, Carolyn," turning, leaning forward, her eyes lit with tears, "I really am, but I can't see her dead, I don't think she's dead, and I would know, wouldn't I?"

"Shh, honey, shh now. She's alive, Laurie. She's alive."

And she held Laurie to her as she sobbed. "If she's dead I will be," Laurie kept saying, muffled into Carolyn's shoulder, "If she's dead I will. I will. I will." And Carolyn stared out the window at the blackness there, until she couldn't see it for her own tears.

Emily thought about turning the television on really loud. Maybe somebody would hear it and call the police.

But there was a man in the house next to Emily's who played classical music loud all the time, and the police had never come. And it was only just after six-thirty—Emily knew because *I Love Lucy* reruns came on at six-thirty.

An image popped into her mind: the figure of the old man waving to her from across the street. There were people in all the houses around her. There were probably people walking up and down the street right now, past this house, this closet.

"The answer to all your problems is in this little bottle," Lucy was saying on the television. The smell of salami was overwhelming. "It's so *tasty*, too," Lucy said, and Emily turned the volume knob as high as it would go.

"Laurie?" Laurie was almost asleep and she jumped when Carolyn said her name. A park, a green lawn, a black shadow.

"You haven't shown me the dollhouse you got Emily for Christmas." Carolyn was smiling with her lips tight; "Oh, Carrie," Laurie said, "don't."

Carolyn still smiled, she tilted her head. "Come on, Laurie, I want to see it."

Getting up from the sofa was almost more than Laurie could do. The air was so heavy against her arms. Movement felt like a violation: against Emily, against her own grief. She didn't want even to talk. Only her fingers were busy, lighting cigarette after cigarette that she barely smoked; as she got up she noticed that she had burned the tabletop, and her fingers were dirty with ash.

Laurie knew she shouldn't be angry at Carolyn. Inside she was shouting. Paralysis was a blessing; she didn't want to be roused from her lethargy.

Sergeant Mohammad was standing in the kitchen doorway. "Go ahead," he said, "I'll take care of things down here."

Carolyn helped her up; *I've gotten old,* Laurie thought. She felt old, as though her body were already preparing to die. As they reached the stairs she stopped and looked at the Christmas tree, which stood in the corner of the living room blinking red and green and blue. Somebody had turned on the lights, Laurie didn't remember when that could have been.

"I always let Emily pick the tree," she said. The sergeant was looking at her quite normally, as though she weren't already almost dead inside. She paused. "At least I always make sure she thinks she picked it, you know?" And she turned and shook off Carolyn's arm and started up the steps.

The dollhouse was in two boxes under Laurie's bed. She hadn't wrapped it yet. That was something she and Emily did just before bed every Christmas Eve, Emily in her bedroom and Laurie in hers, with doors closed and a mock veneer of suspicious seriousness and much rustling of paper.

"Let me see," Carolyn was saying; she also spoke normally. Laurie was beginning to think she had already gone insane and so could not hear the horror in their voices. But Carolyn was pulling the boxes out from under the bed and she didn't seem insane, her hands were shaking badly and

Laurie suddenly wanted to ease her pain: "Thank you," was all she could think of to say.

"Don't waste your energy on me," Carolyn said; she was opening one of the boxes and that was all she said; then, "Laurie, this is beautiful," softly and naturally, and Laurie found herself leaning over the tissue paper to take out a tiny sofa and a green-leafed tree.

"I found it at a flea market," she said eagerly, "remember when I had you take Emily that Saturday, when was it, May or June?"

"May."

"Right. I remember, you had a dentist appointment but you took her anyway."

"I knew how much you love that particular flea market."

"Oh, yeah, I love that one. The Mount Olive Baptist Church. All these little old ladies who have no idea what they've got. And I bought this there, the whole thing was fifteen dollars. And the lady who sold it to me was practically apologizing, she said she couldn't lower the price because the owner wanted it firm."

"What's this?" Carolyn was holding up a small wooden bench. "Oh," said Laurie, "I love that, that's a church pew. I don't know why it was in there. Don't you love the thought that somewhere there's a toy church it once belonged to?" All the furniture was wood, "and look at this! A school bus, can you believe it?" There had been a box of stray things, the pew and the school bus and several battered wooden people, a little girl and a man and a tiny dog. Laurie picked up the wooden girl and suddenly she was angry, she hated Carolyn.

"What the hell do you think you're doing?" She stood up, furious, Carolyn had made her betray Emily, she had forgotten about Emily. "I *hate* you," she said, and Carolyn stood up, too, she said, "I'm sorry," and Laurie fell into her arms.

"It's no use," she sobbed, "I don't want to forget, not for a second, please don't try to make me forget."

And Carolyn said, "I'm sorry," over and over, until Laurie's sobs had eased and she was quiet in Carolyn's arms.

Mrs. Rosenberg thought she heard something. She was watching *I Love Lucy;* it was her favorite episode. Lucy was doing a television commercial for Vitameatavegamin.

Mrs. Rosenberg thought she heard yelling. And somebody was listening to the TV awfully loud. That would be next door, where that strange man lived. Mrs. Rosenberg had asked the mailman what the man's name was. George Riehle. Every once in a while she heard noises from over there.

Lucy was getting drunker and drunker. "—is in this biddle ottle," she said. The noise sounded like the TV too loud and a child yelling. Mrs. Rosenberg had never seen a child go in or out of that house, but there must be one, because sometimes she heard it crying. Now it was yelling, and there was a kind of banging noise, very regular.

"Are you unpoolular?" demanded Lucy. "Well, *are* you?" and Mrs. Rosenberg reached for the remote and turned up the volume.

✗   ✗   ✗

There was a pair of shoes at the back of the closet. Brown loafers.

Out of the corner of her eye Emily saw them move.

Then she dared look and they were only brown shoes.

If somebody just hears the TV they won't think anything is wrong. Emily picked up one of the shoes and started banging it against the wall, on level with her head, over and over and over.

He'll come back—and the rhythm faltered. *I have to,* Emily thought, and she yelled.

"Help!" Her voice sounded puny. Help me!" Would anybody really think there was something wrong? In the Nancy Drew books screams were always "piercing." Nancy Drew never screamed herself; she was too brave. Emily didn't feel brave. She felt as if she might start to cry and never stop. Nancy Drew wouldn't cry. Even Bess wouldn't.

Plump Bess. Emily started to cry, and she banged louder with the shoe, and she yelled as loud as she could without thinking at all.

The doorbell rang. Laurie was up and across the living room before the echo died; but her hand, shot out, stopped short of the doorknob. Suddenly her chest was tight. *My heart is in my throat,* she thought. One of the officers appeared at the kitchen door. "I and my partner can—" he began, but she shook her head and turned the knob. She didn't know what she expected on the other side of the door.

It was Mrs. Konstantius from two doors down. She was carrying a large square Corning Ware dish and a small package wrapped in bright Christmas paper.

"I know of your troubles," she said; Laurie could see that she'd been crying. She and Mrs. Konstantius had been saying good morning to each other for years, ever since Emily was a baby. In the mornings Mrs. Konstantius sat outside in her clean cement front yard, where flowers grew in earthen pots and the Virgin Mary stood vigil between two narrow columns of brick, with bent tin over her head for shelter. When Laurie passed by each morning on the way to day care, she would say hello to Mrs. Konstantius. At first the old woman looked surprised and suspicious; she didn't answer. But she leaned to look at the baby as they passed by.

And leaning became "Good morning," and "Good morning" became short daily stops in which Mrs. Konstantius and Laurie would look together at the baby and say what they could to each other. Laurie never knew how much Mrs. Konstantius understood of what she said; the old woman understood the baby's smile. And they all became friends, and each Christmas season Mrs. Konstantius would have, waiting on her lap on the day before Christmas, a small or large package, brightly wrapped and with a stiff plastic card of the Virgin or St. Veronica or St. Catherine Labouré. Mrs. Konstantius would tell Emily the story of the saint, and Emily would take the plastic card and put it on the top of her bulletin board. Eight cartoon-colored pious faces and humble hands; they all meant something to Emily, Laurie knew, but she never asked her about them, and Emily never talked about the cards.

And now Mrs. Konstantius stood firm and old on Laurie's front stoop. "I didn't know you could walk," Laurie blurted.

"Of course I can walk, but it is true I have not walked this far in many years."

Suddenly Laurie wished desperately that she knew even a few words in Greek; she took the casserole. *Thank you. I love you.* "In the package is a present for Emily, just like always. Because we know she come back, and we want when she come back to home it should be like it always is." Even just *Merry Christmas.* "A pink sweater this time, I know how much little girls like pink." Laurie was shivering. She took the package. A sweater; suddenly her hands were shaking and the package was on the floor. And Carolyn's hands were on her shoulders and Mrs. Konstantius had taken her elbow. "St. Jude," the old woman said, tapping the plastic with a long finger. Laurie noticed that the nail was painted pink, that Mrs. Konstantius's hands were beautiful, long and slender with nails like seashells. "I never normally give you this saint, but today I do. You know this saint?"

"Would you like to come in?" Carolyn offered; it was insane, Laurie thought, how normally they were all behaving around her, Carolyn massaging her shoulders and the old woman speaking quietly in the cold: but Laurie could breathe now; she couldn't smile because her lips had forgotten that, but she tried, reaching for Mrs. Konstantius's sleeve, missing and finding only air. One of the officers had knelt and picked up the Christmas present from where it had fallen beside her.

She couldn't speak. For some reason it seemed very important not to cry. "St. Jude," said Mrs. Konstantius, "is the patron saint of desperate people. He is hope where there is no hope. I will go home now," abruptly, "and say a prayer. And perhaps tomorrow we wake and find our prayer answered." She turned to go, brushing off the policeman's offers of assistance. Laurie stood in the open doorway and didn't speak. But for a moment something moved and stilled inside her, and when Carolyn turned her gently around and led her back to the sofa she did not resist.

Keisha and Dian were cold, served up in their little skirts and tall shoes off the curb of Northern Boulevard after the evening rush. The cars were thinning out now, everybody hurrying home to start the holiday weekend; Keisha and Dian were all the family either one of them had, they shared a coffee Keisha'd bought down on the corner. "Now, over in Jackson Heights, I hear it's fat there," Dian was saying, while Keisha watched Frank hassle a man trying to use the pay telephone.

The man in the phone booth was white, that was his mistake. He was as far inside the booth as he could get, his right side pushed up against the glass;

but the booth had no door. Keisha touched Dian's arm and tilted her head: "Frank's really dissing this guy."

"Motherfucker you want to *move?*" Frank spoke with the rapid-fire rhythms of a rap song. "Motherfucker you ain't done *yet?*" And he kicked, high and graceful and threatening, in the air very near the white man's head.

Frank was crazy. He was older, twenty-five, twenty-six. He'd been standing over by the street-light, holding a bottle of vodka in both hands, tilting it, turning it around. He thought he was the Messiah sometimes: "You ain't never seen a *good* person before in your whole motherfucking *life*," he was telling the white man.

"Frank, leave 'im alone!" Keisha yelled, and Dian laughed and shook her head: "Girl, Frank don't listen to nobody, you know that."

"Fucking cunt," Frank said amiably to Keisha; the white man had finished talking. He replaced the receiver but he held on to the silver metal coil.

"Somebody gonna catch a beatdown!" Frank called out. Keisha started over to the phone booth.

"This ain't no place for you," she said to the man in the booth. And softly, to Frank, "Now you have your fun, but don't you go hurting nobody, you hear?"

Frank reached toward Keisha's breast; "You got *that* down!" he said. Keisha smacked his hand, hard. "I don't take shit from shit," she said. But she wasn't really mad.

The man in the phone booth hadn't moved. His hand was still clutching the telephone cord, and his face, pasty under pale blond hair, looked pathetically vulnerable.

Frankie was standing directly in front of the booth's door. "Motherfucker I am *talkin'* to you," he was saying. The white man looked up and down Northern Boulevard; there were cars but nobody was looking at Frank or the man. One car honked for Keisha; she waved it away but the white man jumped at the noise.

"Hey, Keisha," Dian called softly, "come on over here. Don't fuck with Frank, you know what he's like."

"I know what he's like sure as shit and I ain't lettin' him scare that poor bastard. He's only white."

"White the reason we live this way," Frank said. He finished his bottle and threw it down. The glass shattered with a sound like a gunshot and an odd delicate tinkling.

"Hey, motherfucker, you almost got my stockings. These things don't come from nothin'."

"What you doin' in this neighborhood, Ivory Snow?" Frank was saying. "This is the land of *glory.* You Puerto Rican or Irish?"

The man mumbled something. "I just want—"

"Give it a rest, fucker," Keisha said, "he ain't done nothin'." She could hear the far-off whine of sirens, getting bigger, closer.

The white man froze; suddenly he didn't seem to see or hear Frank at all.

"I'm gonna take you *apart,* motherfucker. I am the Holy *Ghost,* you dig? I am the—" and Keisha saw the whirling lights of the police cars and Frank turned his head and the white man broke past him at a flat run and disappeared around the corner.

Laurie had just made herself a cup of coffee. Carolyn had offered to make the coffee herself, but Laurie wouldn't let her: "I have to at least pretend *something's* normal." The two policemen in the kitchen tiptoed between anxious attention and unnatural naturalness. Laurie was aware of every move she made. Taking the coffee beans out of the refrigerator (after turning down offers of coffee from the pot Sergeant Mohammad had already made), she was acutely aware of the officers' not watching her; as she ground the coffee she could feel them behind her, turned away and talking softly but aware of her, too, aware as she moved to the stove, "Excuse me" and shuffling of feet and soft self-conscious demurrals: as she left the room she could feel the air sucked out and the men's shoulders relaxing. Laurie stopped to take a sip; the coffee was still too hot, burning her tongue; but the pain was good, better than anger or numbness.

The phone rang.

Carolyn jumped; but Laurie walked steadily toward the phone. Carrie rose and touched Laurie's shoulder as she passed the sofa; but Laurie shook her off. She wondered what her face looked like: she was aware of her face. The phone rang again and she picked up the receiver. "Laurie Lookinland," she said, her voice calm and empty.

✗   ✗   ✗

The word BULLETIN appeared suddenly on the television screen: a slash of black, as though hand-written, on a field of red. In the lower right-hand corner there was a picture of Emily's face, smiling. It was bordered in blue and yellow.

Emily had stopped banging, stopped screaming. She had tried to stop thinking. Nobody could hear her in this place. She tried not to think the word: *closet*. Locked in a closet. Even the thought was dangerous.

The words disappeared, and a man's grave face took their place. "As the apparent abduction of nine-year-old Emily Rose Lookinland stretches into the evening hours, a nation holds its breath." How long would she be here? *Look at the man on the TV. Listen to the man on the TV.* Behind his head was her picture again, with the same border of blue and yellow and the words TOT TERROR in the same hand-written scrawl.

"If the kidnapper is indeed the brutal serial killer known as the Chocolate Man, he should be phoning Mrs. Lookinland at precisely eight-twenty this evening." The door was locked; there was no way out. *Look at the TV. Listen to the TV.* "Stay tuned to this station and we will keep you updated on the crime that has all of America in a grip of terror."

George's mother put him in a closet. Emily was shocked to find herself thinking about him that way: George. *When he was bad she locked him up in the closet.* She thought of that: maybe it was this closet. Maybe George had sat here the way she was sitting. *I'll bet there wasn't a TV.* It was funny, she could think of George as a little kid; that was easy.

And she was in the closet right now. But her mother would never put her here. That was the part she couldn't imagine: that her mother would lock her in a dark place and go away. And George had said that sometimes his mother didn't even lock the door, that he just stayed there until he thought it was time for him to come out. Until he thought he'd been punished enough.

She looked at the TV and the voice came suddenly clear—"Is Emily Lookinland still alive? And if she is, what horrors has she suffered at the hands of the Chocolate Man?" Emily felt lightheaded. *The same closet. George was a kid once. Maybe he had banged on the door the way she did at first.* "Stay tuned to this station for up-to-the-minute headline news on what may be the latest Chocolate Man kidnapping." The announcer sounded as if he really wanted that to be true. And George had sat right here, all alone in this closet, without anything to listen to or look at or eat, until he thought he'd been punished enough. There was music now, the same squib of melody over and over, like the music for the O.J. Simpson trial. *They're making me sound like a miniseries,* Emily thought.

Nobody had even known about George being in the closet when he was a kid. The music had ended; there was a commercial for toilet-bowl cleaner on now.

Poor George.

"I have your daughter."

Laurie was still looking out the window. At

nothing. "Yes," she breathed. It was just after eight. He wasn't supposed to call this early.

There was a long silence. "I have—" the man said, and stopped. Laurie closed her eyes. She could hear words, adrift in the wires: "You want to *move?*" After a long time she said, "Yes." It was not a question.

"I have—" the man said again. Laurie leaned her head back against her neck. "—in your whole motherfucking life," said a floating voice. The kitchen ceiling was dirty. He must be enjoying this.

She said nothing.

"I have molested her!" the man blurted, and for an instant Laurie was filled with wild hope.

"No you haven't," she said calmly.

There was no reply. If she hadn't heard the voices in the wires—"am the Holy *Ghost*"—she would have thought the line had gone dead.

"I have molested her," the man repeated firmly. "Give me twenty thousand dollars in unmarked bills or you will never see her again." A pause. "I know your phone is tapped. It doesn't matter. They won't find us." And he was gone.

Laurie was caught between hope and deadly fear.

" 'Us,' " she said aloud. He had called early, he had hesitated over the word *molested*. He had said, "us."

But her resolution slid from her face in a mascara tear. "We got a trace," Sergeant Mohammad said from the kitchen doorway. Laurie carefully gathered the black tear onto her finger. Mohammad's voice was calm, but his face was sad. " 'Us,' " Laurie said again, firmly. "He said, 'us,' " she told Carolyn; her eyes were dry. "And he hesitated. He couldn't say he—couldn't say he—" and she collapsed on the sofa into Carolyn's arms, and she was laughing. "He couldn't say it, Carrie, he couldn't." And Carolyn met Sergeant Mohammad's eyes while Laurie shook her head against Carolyn's neck and laughed.

Was that what had made George be what he was now? Being locked up when he was a kid?

Emily reached for the salami sandwich. She didn't like seeing herself on TV. It made her think of her mother. *I can't think of her. Emily is a prisoner of war she cannot think of her mother it hurts too much.* Is this what it was like for the Chocolate Man, to come back again and again to the thing that hurts you? Like trying not to think of an elephant. No wonder he was so mad. It didn't make him right but it made Emily sorry she'd been so mean to him. Just like his mother.

Emily took a bite of the salami sandwich.

Poor Emily.

Poor Emily.

Poor George.

The Chocolate Man's palms were sweating, there was sweat under his shirt. The sirens had stopped just as he put his foot to the gas. It had been hard not to floor it. He forced himself to drive slowly up the street, reasonably; it was not until he turned the corner that he dared pick up speed.

Over one block—one two three four five six
seven—up another. Over two—one two three four
five six seven—and up four. One two three . . . As
he drove the dark streets he wasn't really thinking;
he was driving by instinct, absorbed and calmed by
the familiar ritual counting.

The streets around him were desolate, the lid-
less eyes of abandoned buildings stared with blank
malice and burning garbage cans loomed up at
street corners, surrounded by flickering shadows of
men.

By the time the Chocolate Man found himself
in more familiar territory he was hardly aware he
was driving at all. Fear had energized him. He had
been afraid of that black man. Even through the
thick safety of his car windows he was afraid of black
people.

As he drove he thought with disgust of the
things that frightened him: black people, and
Jews, and women; homosexuals, toads. He began
to feel angry as he drove. Babies. The anger
started as a tightening in his lungs and moved
downward into his solar plexus. Spiders; the dark.
He could feel the throbbing of his heart just
behind his scrotum.

Bats. Loud noises. He felt a familiar stirring.
Confined spaces. Groups of children.

He thought of the girl. He had made it nice for
her and she was mean to him. Prostitutes. He
hadn't left her in the dark.

And all she would say was that she didn't like
salami.

Once, when the Chocolate Man was very little,

he went into his mother's closet, to see if it was like
the one in his room. He closed the door almost all
the way. The closet smelled of perfume and sweat. A
man came into the bedroom. He was carrying a
beer.

Then the Chocolate Man's mother came into
the room and lay down on the bed. She didn't
know her son was in the closet. She was wearing a
bra and a half-slip.

The man sat on the bed; they shared the beer,
passing it back and forth. The Chocolate Man had
to go to the bathroom.

The man climbed on top of his mother. He
pushed her legs apart and began to grind his pelvis
against her. She lay back with her eyes closed and
did not move. She might have been sleeping, or
dead.

The man made grunting noises. The Chocolate
Man shrank into a little ball at the back of the closet.
He drank in the smell of his mother's perfume. In
the sliver of light from the open door, all he could
see was his mother's face and the man's head, his
shaggy hair bobbing and the hard grimace of his
mouth.

The Chocolate Man's mother's eyes remained
closed; her mouth tightened and became rigid. He
needed to pee. The man's head bobbed faster and
faster. His mother's lips quivered with pain.
Although he wanted to cry out, he did not dare
move. The man might hurt him, too.

It went on a long time.

He wished that little girl were in the same
closet.

He had tried, years later, to find that perfume. He went into six or seven department stores, but he couldn't place it, not in little sterile bottles under bright lights.

He was afraid of the women who waited on him; of their flat, superior eyes watching as he lifted a delicate glass tester up to his nose.

He could do it to that girl. He had done it to Roxanne. That girl had been mean to him.

His closet at home smelled of detergent and sweat. He would make sure she made no sound. His groin was throbbing now, with a steady beat like a heart.

It would not be too hard to do her.

The patrol cars roared up to the phone booth and skidded to a stop. Four policemen jumped out and converged on the phone booth like a SWAT team. "Who was just in that booth?" one of the officers snapped at Frank. He glared at them, then pirouetted a leg above his head as he turned away.

"You," another officer was saying to Keisha, "you see anything here in the last five minutes?"

"I know you," Keisha said, "what's it say on your badge? Miller. You run me in last month."

"We don't have a lot of time here. One of you must have seen someone using that booth."

"I did," Frank said suddenly, spinning abruptly and walking too quickly toward the officer.

"Anything you could tell us would be appreciated," the officer went on calmly.

"By who? Some white motherfu—"

"We're just following up on a routine investigation."

"Damn straight. For some white trash—"

"Stop it," Keisha said.

"All right. Now, did any of you—"

"He was white," Keisha said. "He was—oh, Dian, how tall was he?"

"About as high as Frank kicks."

"So—about the same height as Frank over there." Frank stood with his back to the police; he was talking.

"What did you say?" one of the policemen asked him.

"I said *nothin'*," Frank roared, whirling around.

"He's the Holy Ghost," said Dian, laughing.

"Stop it," Keisha said again. "He had blond hair," she said to Miller.

"Which way did he go?"

"I am talking to you in the name of the Lord!" Frank roared; no one noticed.

"Around that corner," said Keisha, and the officer said, "How long ago?" Already two of the policemen were running for the corner.

"Just a couple seconds. Frank was playing with him but he heard those sirens and he ran."

"Thank you," the officer said, and he turned and ran to a patrol car. "Miller," he barked into the radio, "we have a positive ID. I repeat, we—"

"You motherfuckers come in here," Frank said, walking toward the car, "you think we good for nothin' but helpin' you find some motherfucking white—"

"Shut *up*," Keisha said sharply. Then, to Dian, "I got to go check on Tanzara now."

"You didn't leave your baby alone again, did you, Keisha?"

Keisha shrugged. "It's warm night. I thought I might do some business."

"I'll go with you," Dian said, getting up from against the wall. "I can watch her if you want to go back out."

"Dian, you're sweet."

"She's a *fool*," muttered Frank. Then, suddenly sober, "Anybody got any cash? I gotta go down to A Hundred First Street, gotta get me one hit."

"Like shit," said Keisha.

The officers who had run around the corner were already walking back.

George hadn't hurt her. Emily was staring at the screen without seeing it. He could have; even if she hadn't kept trying to get away he could have, anytime.

He had made her a sandwich. How was he supposed to know she didn't like salami?

He had brought her a TV.

Maybe sometimes he was lonely, too. Did he have any brothers or sisters?

He was the Chocolate Man—but he hadn't hurt her.

Why had he hurt those boys?

But he hadn't hurt her. Even in the car he had said it: *I can't.*

He had tried to make it nice for her in the

closet. He had spared her life: and he was going to let her out of the closet as soon as he got home.

He hadn't killed her. Always it came back to that. He hadn't killed her.

Maybe he wasn't going to.

Maybe he really liked her.

Maybe he was lonely. He had fed her, he was trying to keep her happy.

Emily took a bite of the salami sandwich. She was going to say she was sorry when he got back.

"Fleischer. Fleischer."

Marcy turned, protesting, into the softness of her pillow.

Her head hit the wall.

"Fleischer!" There was no pillow, just her pocketbook lumpy behind her head, and Ed was shaking her awake where she lay on a cot in the hall outside the Task Force room.

"He called," Ed said, and Marcy came completely awake.

"What time?"

"It's quarter past eight."

"No, what time did he call?"

"Nine minutes ago. Eight-oh-seven."

"It was supposed to be eight-twenty." Marcy sat up and pulled her fingers through her hair. "When did I lie down?"

"Sevenish. You said to wake you when he called."

"Uh-huh." Marcy reached into her bag for her lipstick. "What did he say?"

"Same thing he always says, except he said something at the end, something about 'us.'"

Marcy sighed.

"And the mother says he hesitated when he said he'd molested the girl. She doesn't believe he's done anything yet."

"Yeah, but what does the *tape* say?"

"He hesitated."

Marcy got up and walked into the Task Force room. Directly in front of her was the pushpin map. She walked over to it, unscrewing a shiny lipstick tube. There was a red pin in the middle of a small blank space on the map: Hewlitt Park. There was a tag—eight. To the right of the map there was a vertical line of photographs: seven little boys and one girl. All the children were smiling.

"We've got to get him this time, Ed." Marcy was putting on her lipstick without a mirror, staring at the little girl's smile.

"We don't know whether she's still alive."

"*Somebody's* got to see this guy sometime!" Marcy burst out. "He broke the pattern—apparently by mistake. Maybe he also broke the pattern getting her to his house—or wherever he takes them. He was off guard—he had to be. He had to make at least one other mistake. Come on," turning away from the map, the color perfect on her mouth, sliding the lipstick tube back into her bag. Ed smiled to himself, looking down. "Where are we going?" he asked.

"To recheck every sighting in the last six hours. The Chocolate Man is going to slip up somewhere along the line, and I intend to catch him when he does."

Emily heard the click of the front door opening. *He's trying to be quiet,* she thought. The front door slid open with hardly a sound. Emily imagined him opening it slowly, down at the end of the hall; she almost thought she could hear him breathing. Without thinking she rose and reached for the light cord. She reached over and cut the sound on the TV; for a moment little people moved in pantomime and then she cut the picture, too.

For the first time Emily was not afraid of the dark. She wished it were a big cloak she could wrap around herself. In the stifling closet she shivered.

As she listened to the Chocolate Man's footsteps coming down the hall she thought, *He's trying to be quiet in case I've fallen asleep.* She wanted to tell him that she understood about his mother. *He doesn't want to hurt me anymore,* she thought. *He tried to make it nice for me. He can't help it if I don't like salami.*

Emily sat in the dark, holding her arms around herself as though the darkness were a cloak, and waited for the Chocolate Man to open the closet door.

Laurie didn't know quite where she was. She had jolted awake; she hadn't known she was sleeping. Someone was holding her hand—Carolyn. Her hand was damp. Laurie looked up to see Carolyn's compassionate eyes.

"Where—" Laurie felt paralyzed. She tried to pull her hand from Carolyn's—there was a weight.

Emily.

Instantly she was sitting up and her mind was clear. "Why did you let me fall asleep?" she cried.

"You need the rest." Laurie resented the kindness in Carolyn's eyes. How could Laurie have let herself fall asleep? She dug her nails into the soft flesh of her upper arm.

"I'll make you some tea," Carolyn said. Laurie's coffee sat untouched on the living-room table. She dug her nails deeper to keep from screaming.

She didn't want tea. Emily liked camomile, with lots of honey. Laurie's stomach growled and she felt revulsion at the treachery of her body: how could she feel hunger or fatigue? When Emily was with that man. Even through the thick nap of her sweater Laurie could feel the hard crescents of her nails digging into her skin.

"Yes," she said. "Tea." Suddenly she felt nothing. She tilted her head back against the sofa and looked at the ceiling. There was a physical sensation in her arm, that was all. She saw her own reality as if it were a story: *She is sitting on the sofa. Her child is missing. She is waiting for her friend to make her a cup of tea.*

Her child may be dead.

The pain hit so suddenly that Laurie could not breathe. A shaft of pain so wounding that she reflexively leaned forward, her hands to her stomach.

After a moment she realized she had cut her

arm; that it was bleeding. She lowered her head to her knees and breathed convulsively: there was not enough air; her lungs refused to accept air.

"Laurie? Are you all right?" Carolyn stood in front of her, holding a teacup with orange roses on it, a delicate rose-strewn saucer. Emily's favorite cup and saucer.

"Yes." Laurie raised her eyes to Carolyn's. She breathed in once, deeply, and extended her hand.

"Thank you," she said. She could breathe but there were crescents of pain under her left sleeve. Small red spots had seeped through the blue wool. As she reached for the saucer her arm hurt, a little: enough.

"Thank you," she said again.

The Chocolate Man did not turn on the light in the hall. He stood in the dark and listened. He was not afraid. When he moved it was quietly: if she was sleeping he didn't want to wake her.

He looked down the hall. It was twenty-one paces from the front door to the kitchen. One two three four five six seven. Thirteen paces from the kitchen door to the bedroom. One two three four five six seven. He started walking very slowly down the hall. On the rug there were pink and blue flowers irregularly arranged against a brown background. Even in the dark the Chocolate Man knew the path he must take to avoid walking on the flowers. This afternoon when he had to go after the girl he hadn't been able to keep from stepping on them; if he hadn't been so angry he wouldn't have been able to do that. And then again before he went out: it made him feel powerful.

Now he went slowly, making up for before: he would count three times for each step. Light from the kitchen lit the rug bright and faded out as it trickled up the hall. The Chocolate Man kept his eyes on the light. He could feel where the girl had bandaged his arm. It itched a little under the binding. With Roxanne it had been impulse. He had never planned before to do this to a girl.

One step: one two three four five six seven, one two three four five six seven, one two three four five six seven. There was no sound coming from the bedroom. Another step: one two three four five six seven, one two three four five six seven, one two three four five six seven. He wanted to hurry but he couldn't.

He wouldn't think about what he was going to do. One two three four five six seven, one two three four five six seven, one two three four five six seven. After he was done he could put her body under the bed and go to sleep. One two three four five six seven, one two three four five six seven, one two three four five six seven.

As the kitchen door drew closer the Chocolate Man stopped. His breathing was shallow and fast. *Don't think about anything but after.* He was already tired. One two three four five six seven, one two three four five six seven, one two three four five six seven. He always slept so well, after.

NIGHT

THERE WERE THREE CHINA FLOWERED CASSEROLES on the kitchen table, and two hot Thermoses of coffee. There was a bag of doughnuts on the Formica counter and a bag of sandwiches in the refrigerator. Laurie didn't know the names of most of the people who had come and left these things; some of them she hadn't even seen before this evening, people with stricken faces and embarrassed eyes. Mr. Giorgio from the café had come; he had been almost unable to speak, standing in front of her with a box of cookies: finally he said, "Your Emily, she like this kind." Toffee oatmeal. When Laurie took the box she could feel the warmth of the cookies, just made.

One woman Laurie was certain she'd never seen before appeared at the door with two buckets of soapy water and a squeegee. The woman stood for a long time and then blurted, "I'm going to wash the windows," and disappeared around the side of the house. Every once in a while Laurie could hear the thud of a bucket against the house, the squeal of the squeegee on wet glass.

The Chocolate Man opened the closet door to the girl's shy smile.

"I ate the sandwich," she said. She was holding out the crumpled wax paper like an offering from a cat. The Chocolate Man recoiled as though it were indeed a bug or a half-eaten mouse.

"I saw myself on the news," the girl said tentatively. She was still holding out the paper; there was nothing for the Chocolate Man to do but take it.

The light in the closet was out, the TV dark. He looked down at the blank screen as though her picture might still be on it.

"It'll be on again at eleven."

One two three four five six seven. *Now*, he thought. *In the dark where I don't have to look at her.*

"I'm sorry I locked you in the closet," the girl said, slipping past him. Involuntarily he shrank from her body, light in passing like a feather's touch, her shoulder only, no more nervous than his own shaking hands.

He turned; he could see her silhouetted against the light from the kitchen. He wished he had a weapon. He had never used anything but a twisted and knotted slip, before. Something with a blade. This afternoon he hadn't been able to use the knife. He was ashamed of that. He reached toward the girl, uncertain in the dark of the distance between them. She did not flinch.

"I didn't mind it *too* much, myself, but it must have been worse for you," she said, "because you're bigger." His hand stopped, and because he could feel it shaking he made a fist.

"I thought about you," she continued, "I thought about your—about how you had to stay in the closet when you were a kid." He couldn't tell if she was looking at him. "But don't worry. Everybody's got secrets."

He brought his fist down to his side. She *was* looking at him, he realized; she could see his face in the light from the kitchen. Only she was in darkness.

"I have a secret, too," she said. "I've been pretending." When he didn't respond she went on quickly, as though she had rehearsed what she was going to say. "Before, when I was really scared, I pretended this was all just a story about a girl named Emily. And Emily was in the war, she was very brave and she didn't cry and the bad guys held her captive but she was just like Nancy Drew, she wasn't afraid and she didn't cry."

The Chocolate Man was silent a long time. He didn't know who Nancy Drew was. "Which war?" he asked finally.

"The Great War. That was at the beginning of the century, right, and the Germans took over Paris—"

"That was World War Two."

"Oh." And after a moment, "Did every country in the world really fight?"

"Ah—no. Germany and France and England and—which one, the first or the second?"

"Which was the war with Alsace-Lorraine?"

"I think that was the second."

"What was the first one?"

"The *Lusitania*, I think."

They stood together in the dark, contemplating war.

"What time is it?" the girl asked suddenly.

"About ten, I think," said the Chocolate Man, squinting at his watch and counting.

"There's news on Channel Five at ten o'clock. Do you want to see me on TV?"

One two three four five six seven. One two three four five six seven. He sighed and shook his head. "The hall—when you ran away before—was that minefields?"

"Uh-huh," she said. "And bombs."

"Okay," he said, and he knelt at the closet door to turn on the TV.

After a while Laurie let the police officers answer the door. She could hear them saying thank you, hear the murmured replies, all of which sounded like apologies: "I'm sorry to bother Mrs. Lookinland . . . ," ". . . such a difficult time," ". . . all praying for Emily . . ."

Laurie told the officers to eat whatever they wanted, to take what they wanted when they left. She sat, her hand in Carolyn's, and each visitor registered: the voice, the click of the front door softly shutting, the sound of the policemen's shoes walking toward the kitchen, the smell of meat or cake. Her hand in Carolyn's became hot, then sweaty; she remembered holding hands with boys, years ago, wondering if she could or should move her sweat-soaked palm; she gave the same mental energy to each thing she heard or saw or thought, like a botanist examing specimens of plant life. Coffee, sweat, a young boy's hand, a small, tarp-covered body—and she would start up in her seat, and

Carolyn would pull her gently back down, with soft hands and soothing noises. She didn't ask any questions; Laurie didn't look at her. Laurie must have cried out once, because one of the policemen appeared at the kitchen door; at a look from Carolyn he disappeared again.

Laurie couldn't have said what she was thinking, even when she jumped from her seat: to do what? to go where? Every moment was like waking from a dream. Every single time she thought of Emily the pain was new. And everything reminded her of her daughter: Emily drinking decaffeinated cappuccino and pretending it didn't make her feel terribly grownup and sophisticated; Emily on one knee, kneeling to show Mrs. Konstantius an orange-legged beetle she'd found; even the faint protests of the squeegee were signals of Emily: Laurie was aware, somewhere behind her pain, that from now on, no matter what happened, the sound of wet glass squealing would always make her think of Emily.

"It's time to go to sleep." Emily and the Chocolate Man had just finished watching Emily on the eleven o'clock news. They were in the living room, Emily's wrist lashed to the end table. The announcer's shrill predictions had irritated the Chocolate Man and frightened Emily.

After the program they were both silent.

"I told you my mother doesn't have any money," Emily said at last, looking at the bare Christmas tree.

"I don't want any money."

"Then why did you ask her for it?"

"I always do. It's really time for bed now."

"Do I have to sleep in the closet?"

"Oh, no." The Chocolate Man sounded offended. "I had to think a long time before I thought of a place. Come with me." He reached over to untie her wrist (she flinched away) and left the sofa without waiting to see her follow. "How do you know I won't run away again?" she asked.

"You've already tried. I have a nice place for you to sleep." He continued walking into the bedroom; there was nothing for Emily to do but follow.

"Here," the Chocolate Man was saying. Emily couldn't see what he was pointing at. "Come on, I'll get some sheets."

For one horrible moment Emily thought he intended her to sleep in his bed. But as she came around him—*the prisoner of war is led to the torture chamber*—she couldn't tell where he meant at all. She'd thought he would put her back in the closet. "I don't—"

"There! See?"

But she didn't see. He seemed to be pointing under the bed.

"Under the bed?" she asked slowly; her hand was covering her mouth.

"Under the bed," he affirmed. He was proud again, the way he'd been when he showed her the closet. "This is a special place."

Emily considered, tilting her head; it was spotless under the bed, without any stray socks. The color of the wood was even a little lighter than in the rest of the room, as though it had been recently scrubbed. Emily didn't want to go into that place.

"What's so special about it?" she asked bravely.

The Chocolate Man was silent a long time. And then he smiled. "You know you're going to sleep there. Be a good boy." His eyes were shining. "Be a good boy and take your nap."

He wasn't looking at her, he was looking under the bed. Emily was shaking all over and she couldn't control it, and when she tried to speak she made no sound. Then, "George," and the Chocolate Man jumped at the sound of his name.

He was looking at her blankly; Emily gave him a moment to come back from where he had gone. "What's your last name?"

"My—?"

Emily tried not to clench her fists. If she concentrated on her fists she wouldn't scream. "Your last name, George. Everybody's got a last name."

She was trying to sound sure of herself; and from the expression on his face she was succeeding. *The prisoner spoke with a tone of authority unsettling to the gaoler: she had thrown him off his guard.*

"My name's Riehle," he said finally. He seemed suspicious but that was better than a minute ago; "Why do you want to know?"

For a moment Emily surprised herself, and she laughed. "Is that really your name? Like 'real'? I'll bet you made that up."

The Chocolate Man was offended; that was better than a minute ago, too. "I did not. It's a good German name."

"German? Like World War One?" Emily felt giddy; she was safe again.

"Are you still playing that?" he asked. He didn't seem angry.

"Sometimes."

"Then you can make believe this is a foxhole," he said with satisfaction. "This is a foxhole and you're going to hide there tonight."

He was right: she was going to have to get under the bed sometime. "Okay," she said, "but now we're on the same side, right? If I'm in the foxhole you're going to stay up there and watch for enemy fire." *I'm only nine years old*, she thought, watching his face, *there isn't anything I can do*.

He was smiling again; which wasn't necessarily good, but then he nodded his head, up and down, up and down, and he looked like a big bird. "Your hair's sticking up," Emily said unkindly, and she slid gracefully underneath the bed. And she lay down, and even though she was shivering, and cold with fear, Emily closed her eyes and fell asleep almost immediately.

That little girl on the news—Mrs. Imperle couldn't sleep. The digital clock on the night table glowed 3:27. If her husband, Dan, were still alive he would know, even though she hadn't moved or made a sound, that she was not asleep; and he would know why. She had their son, Tony, thank the Lord, and Tony was a good boy, never any trouble with girls or drugs. And Mrs. Imperle told herself and told herself that Suzette was like a daughter—but she was really only Tony's wife.

That little girl on the news had looked a bit like her own Sarah, thirty-seven years gone now. Mrs. Imperle was crying quietly, looking at the ceiling. The hair was just the same, the soft unruly ringlets.

I've got tears in my ears/ from lying on my back/ in my bed/ while I cry over you. Dan would have sung her that. Something was teasing Mrs. Imperle's memory. She wiped at her eyes with the back of her hand. Everybody who knew about Sarah was dead now, and if Tony had ever found the photographs, the single long lock of hair, the birth certificate, he hadn't let on.

What would he think if he knew that he should have a sister five years older? With long dark curly hair.

The girl on the television. Mrs. Imperle sat up in her bed. A tear dropped past her lip and into her lap—salty, for self-pity. The child going up the walk of the house across the street.

Iris Imperle tried to see the child in her mind: was it a boy or a girl? Hadn't she doubted, in the first instant of seeing, hadn't she thought it was a girl?

The child had been walking slowly up the pavement, timing its steps to the man's. It—he or she— had seemed familiar with the man's peculiar way of walking.

Or was she frightened, and moving slowly out of fear? Hadn't she taken a tentative step away from the man?

And hadn't the man reached out to stop her?

Iris's eyes were clouding with tears. *Not a child; not that child.*

Sarah would be forty years old now. How old had the child been? Eight? Nine?

Iris got out of bed. Dan used to keep his slippers handy, right under the bed, but Iris could never remember.

What time did I see the child? What's the address across the street? Iris forgot the cold against her bare feet as she went downstairs to call the police.

Until the creaking of the mattress woke her, Emily hadn't known she'd been sleeping. She was thinking about snow, about watching the snow fall through the sunlight. Then the mattress creaked.

Emily was under the Chocolate Man's bed. It smelled like Lysol. The Chocolate Man had just gotten into bed above her. He had left her here a few minutes ago—or a long time, she didn't know.

She had lain staring at his feet. He wore heavy black boots. When he walked out of the room she almost cried out; but he left the door open. It was open still. It looked strange at this low angle, a bright wedge of light, a stream of light seeping across the floor into the room. For some reason Emily thought of a movie she had watched with her mother, last week or last month: *Dark Victory*. It was her mother's favorite movie.

They had watched that movie many times. It was Emily's favorite, too. Bette Davis was Judith Treherne. She was sick with a tumor in her head. She knew she was going to die but she wasn't afraid

of anything. She wore wonderful dresses and
Humphrey Bogart was in love with her. (The
Chocolate Man moved above Emily in the bed.) In
her story Emily was Judith Treherne behind the
lines at Alsace-Lorraine and Humphrey Bogart was
saying a prayer for her in an Irish brogue.

Emily lay quietly with the Chocolate Man
above her. The wedge of light made her think of
sunlight, and snow falling in sunlight. Judith
Treherne walked in the snow with her dogs, she
brought sandwiches to her handsome husband, she
dug in the hard ground and planted bulbs that
would not bloom until after she was dead.

The smell of Lysol was almost unbearable. The
Chocolate Man was snoring fitfully. If Emily crept
out from under the bed, would he wake up?

When the light disappeared Judith Treherne
was not afraid. She continued to plant bulbs,
scratching with awkward fingers at the hard winter
ground.

The wedge of light looked very far away.

The Chocolate Man turned; the mattress
creaked. There was a big sag just above Emily's
head. She started to move her shoulder very slowly,
easing it loose from his weight. She kept her eyes
fixed on the light, and soon she was flat on her
stomach.

She started to crawl out from under the bed.

The light was an eternity away. In his sleep the
Chocolate Man grunted and moaned, and Emily
froze.

In his sleep he mumbled—"heaven," or
"seven"—and Emily stopped crawling. The light

was very close now. Six feet, five. *The village was just ahead; if she was just strong enough, and brave enough—*

"You can't go away yet," said the Chocolate Man. He was sitting up in the bed. Emily laid her cheek against the cool wood floor.

"I made the bed up special for you," he said. "You promised you'd stay in the foxhole, and I promised to guard you."

Emily sat up and faced him. "I want to go home," she said.

"It's not time to go home. It's time for bed." The Chocolate Man sat, a dark lump on the bed, talking in a reasonable voice.

Emily stood up. "I hate you," she said to the darkness.

"Be a good girl."

"Can't you just let me go?"

"No. You see, I have to call your mother again in the morning. She has a pretty voice, your mother. Don't you like the idea of me calling her?"

Emily hesitated.

"I could tell your mother really misses you," he went on. His voice sounded a lot more awake now. "I'll bet—"

"I'm coming," Emily said. She walked back to the bed and ducked down quickly before he could touch her. "I'll stay here."

"I could tie your hand to the bar here."

"No." Whatever courage she'd felt had completely left her. "I'll be good."

"I'm a very light sleeper, Emily." Now his voice was hard.

"Yes."

"Very light. My mother used to wake me up all the time with her—go to sleep."

"Yes."

"You said you'd stay in the foxhole."

"I'm sorry. I will."

"Good. And in the morning I'll call your mother."

"Yes." And Emily put the soft nap of the blanket against her cheek and looked across the vast impassable length of the room toward the light spilling in the open door.

Mr. Linderman opened his eyes to the blank ceiling. He had been dreaming: the smell of hay in the barn loft when he was a child; his favorite silent-screen actress, Nita Naldi, the size of a movie screen, her shoulder bare and her face turned away.

But he was in his own room, in his own house, and Nita Naldi had been dead more than thirty years; he had seen her last movie more than sixty years ago.

His daughter Rosalie looked out at him from a silver frame across the room. His wife on the bedside table smiled toward a pale green wall. There was something wrong, some business unsettled or thought unfinished. He often woke this way, his old-man's alarm rousing him in the middle of the night: *It's time to think now, time to plan.* And he would think till dawn, and get out of bed and drink his orange juice and wonder: *Why do you*

*want me thinking, God? I'm old. I'm going to die
soon, what do you want from an old man?* But he
had never really questioned God. "You just do
what's right," he told his grandson Brian once,
when Brian asked him about the purpose of life.
"You just do what's right and God will take care of
the rest."

He thought about his dream now, looking at
his memories on the wall, the table; even the view
out the window was full of memories. There was
nothing moving on the street; every tree branch
was still. Mr. Linderman looked awhile, remembering, and then he thought again of his dream.

A rabble of young boys playing at war, hiding in
the hay below the barn loft; the giant image of Nita
Naldi beginning to turn, looking out the window
Mr. Linderman saw again how beautiful she was,
smoky dark and full, her bare back like an avalanche
of skin, her cloudy hair swinging; the boys laughed
raucously; she turned, and the boy he was in the
dream was flushed with anticipation of her kohl-
rimmed eyes, her half-open mouth: she turned, and
her face was a little girl's face, and her eyes were
blue and frightened.

Mr. Linderman was breathing hard, and there
was a familiar tightness in his chest. He could still
see the blue eyes ducking shyly from sight. He
closed his own eyes, but she was still there.

That little child, walking hesitantly up George
Riehle's walk. Riehle's hand hovering above the
child's arm: but when the child tried to move away,
hadn't he grabbed her, hard?

"Old fool," Mr. Linderman said aloud, sitting

up in his bed. There was nothing out the window at all, and he was alone. "Old fool."

Marcy leaned back in her chair; she had a crick in her back. She had been hunched over the phone for six hours. It was 3:45 in the morning but there were still calls coming in.

As she stretched her arms over her head the phone rang again. "Task Force, Detective Fleischer speaking," she said; it would be another crazy lead, like the man who insisted an hour ago that he had just seen Emily Lookinland and a tall black man getting into a rocketship on the Brooklyn-Queens Expressway.

"Ah—is this the task force dealing with the kidnapping of that little girl?"

"Yes. What can I do to help you?"

"Well . . ." There was a silence on the line. Most callers had this hesitation; each seemed about to confess. "It's about that little girl." An old woman with a spiderweb of a voice, all hushed breath.

"Yes," said Marcy.

"I think I saw her."

"Where was this, ma'am?"

"Across the street. I don't know the number. She was with a man."

"May I have your name, ma'am?"

"Oh, well—" This was where Marcy so often lost them. Even when it concerned the life of a child few people were willing to commit even their names.

"You don't have to give your name," she said gently. Anonymous it was easier to lie—or tell the truth.

"Oh. All right, then. I saw them this afternoon—the little girl and that man. He's a strange man."

"Do you know his name?"

"Oh, no, But he's very odd. He—"

"What makes you think it was Emily Lookinland you saw?"

"I didn't think it was. I thought at first that it was a little boy. But then I saw her picture on the news and then I thought, well, it's that little girl. I had a girl of my own, you know—oh, it was a long time ago. Her name was Sarah Louise—"

"Ma'am, about Emily Lookinland. Can you describe the man who was with her?"

"He isn't tall. Let me see. Blond hair. Blue or green eyes. He's about five foot nine, I think. My son Tony is five eleven, just like his father. I don't know weights. He isn't fat. He's a very strange man, he has such an odd way of going up his front walk—"

"Can you describe the child to me?"

"Well, as I said, at first I thought it was a boy. She had short hair, like a boy's. Beautiful curls, though. My Sarah had curls like that, that's why when I saw that little girl's picture—"

"Can you describe what the child was wearing?"

"Oh. Yes, I think. Something blue—a blue jacket? A heavy blue jacket. And blue jeans—that was the other reason I thought it was a boy. I would never dress a little girl in blue jeans, I don't think—"

"Ma'am, how old would you say the child was?"

"Well, the news said she was nine. So I guess nine."

"But when you saw her—" patiently, drawing out facts like fish on a line, slowly, inch by inch— "what age did you think she was?"

"Well—I guess eight or nine. I wasn't really thinking about that, except that it made me think of Sarah, and how Sarah was just three when she died." Marcy was quiet for that, feeling the old woman's ancient pain even through the telephone wires.

"I'm sorry, ma'am. We really appreciate your calling with this information. Now, where did you say you were calling from?"

"My home. I couldn't sleep, thinking that maybe that dreadful man—"

"I need to know what street, ma'am, what borough. Where are you calling from?"

"Oh. Dogwood Terrace. It's in Flushing. Queens. There was a terrible kidnapping three years ago, wasn't there? Just two streets down. A little boy—"

Marcy felt a surge, of adrenaline or hope. Danny Angelo had disappeared from his driveway at 17–62 Juniper Terrace four years ago. The first known victim of the Chocolate Man.

Marcy put her hand over the receiver and signaled to Ed across the room. She pointed at the phone: "Extension sixty-four," she mouthed. And then a finger to her lips. Ed picked up the phone and pressed the extension.

"—hope it's not the same awful man," the woman was saying. "I never thought—" Ed was signaling Marcy to hurry her up.

"Ma'am," she said, "I just need the address."

"But I told you, I don't know the address."

Marcy sighed. "I have to know at least what the cross streets are."

"Oh. It's between Union Turnpike and Seventeenth Avenue. It's right across the street. Two doors down from the house with the orange and blue Christmas lights."

"By 'down,' do you mean north, south, east—?"

"I don't know. It's closer to Seventeenth Avenue."

Ed was slicing his finger across his throat; "Thank you," Marcy said gently, "you've been a great help. We'll be sure to check it out."

"I hope you find that little girl." The voice, web-thin and lonely; then nothing.

Ed was looking at her. "So, what do you think?"

The old woman would be looking at the phone or out the window or at an old photograph of a little girl with beautiful curls.

"Ed," said Marcy, "let's take this one."

Keisha couldn't sleep, and the baby was crying. Cutting a tooth, having a bad dream—"You dreaming, baby?" she asked as she crossed the room to Tanzara's crib. "You having a bad dream?" The whole apartment was one room, Keisha was across it in eight steps. Little babies dream in static pictures; Keisha had read that in a book she got at the library: as the babies get a little older the pictures start to move. "What was it, honey, you see a monster?" Eight steps, over dirty linoleum in a pattern of blue and white squares lit by the glow from the streetlight outside her window.

As Keisha picked the baby up it quieted and laid its head for a moment against her cheek. "Oh, Tanzy, a kiss! Thank you, sweet baby," walking to the refrigerator to get milk; Keisha couldn't afford formula, "The price at the drugstore ain't believable," she'd told Dian, and, "I can't be going over to the ShopRite sixteen blocks away every time I need formula." So the baby got regular milk. "Shit, honey, this one says it's expired," and she sniffed the carton in the light from the refrigerator. "Smells okay."

She closed the refrigerator door and reached for a pot off the stove and filled it with water, all without having to move from the spot where she stood. She lighted the stove with a match she lit with one hand—"Don't you go near that, Tanzy-girl"—and put the bottle in the pot and turned, while it heated, toward the TV. It sat in the corner like an eye, open and meaningless; the sound was off. The pictures were always there, so that when Keisha couldn't sleep, which was often, she could look at them and feel like she wasn't alone. She got frightened sometimes, as though she were the only thing breathing in the whole world.

There was a commercial on. Keisha closed her eyes and the streetlight's glare was reflected, red and jagged, against her eyelids. She could still see Northern Boulevard, black tar and headlights behind her eyes. There were no Christmas lights slung across that wide street, no false Christmas snow in store windows. One of the bars had put up a single strand of crooked lights; Keisha thought of them blinking now on the empty street. Dian was going to like the bag she'd gotten her, and the scarf. She'd gone to Astoria on the bus to buy them, to Steinway Street, where garlands of heavy tinseled stars were strung across the street at every corner and every block was full of holiday shoppers and every store had a Santa in the window, or a Christmas tree, or elves and packaged snow.

That Frank was crazy. Keisha heard something, a pop and an echo; that was gunfire. An image of Frank was in her mind, toe pointed and leg extended with the grace of a dancer. No need to call the police, some fool was always shooting something. Keisha wondered what that white man had done that the police were after him. He looked like such an innocent white-ass fool. But the cops had sure been hot to get him.

Keisha walked over to the set and turned the volume up.

There was a news program on. Keisha looked at it absently while she carried the baby back to the stove and felt the bottle and turned the gas off and wiped the bottle dry and put it to Tanzy's mouth; the baby was fussy, it took her a moment to realize that she was getting what she wanted.

"—in the case of Emily Rose Lookinland, who was abducted from Hewlitt Park in Rego Park,

Queens, at two-twenty this afternoon." The girl was pretty, with dark hair and blue eyes.

"At eight-oh-seven Emily's mother received a telephone call from a man claiming to be the brutal child killer the Chocolate Man. As the search continues, police are focusing their attention on finding witnesses to the kidnapping. Only moments before Emily disappeared, her mother noted the presence of a Caucasian male, thirty to thirty-five years old, five-foot-eight to five-foot-ten, weighing approximately one hundred forty-five to one hundred sixty-five pounds, with receding, sandy-colored hair. The man was wearing dark clothing. He fits the description in what is commonly considered to be the only other genuine sighting of the Chocolate Man, at a playground in the Fort Greene section of Brooklyn almost three years ago. Anyone having any information about this mysterious stranger is urged to come forward by calling—" There was an 800 number running across the screen.

"God," Keisha breathed, sinking to her knees with the baby in front of the TV. "That was the guy," she said softly, wonderingly. "Tanzy, that was the guy I saw. On the corner, at the phone booth. That was why the cops were in such a fit." What was he wearing? Had they said on the television? Tanzy was quiet in her lap; she had suddenly stopped sucking and was almost asleep.

"He had a hooded jacket on, it said something," Keisha said to the baby. "Some bird thing. Now, what was it?" She closed her eyes again and searched the red space behind her lids. "Drugstore? No, *liquor* store. Something liquors. Some bird.

With an *S*. What birds I know, sparrow, swallow? I've got a baby, too, I've got to call the cops." When she got up Tanzy gurgled, once, and let out a tiny cry. But Keisha held her against her shoulder and the baby fell asleep before she finished dialing.

The Chocolate Man stood in the dark next to the bed. He watched the girl; she tossed, she moaned and sighed. It was strange to see the body under the bed moving and making sounds.

The sight of her for a moment excited his desire: she had been naughty, trying to get away. He was holding a kitchen knife in his hand. She had taken him off guard when he got back from making the phone call. He would not make the same mistake again.

He had seen her mother on the TV news, the curtain of hair and the clenched fist. She had not issued any statement. She had not allowed the cameras even a glimpse of her face. The Chocolate Man's breathing became heavy and fast. Lauren Lookinland was not asleep. Every mother of young children was thinking about him tonight. It was, in fact, perhaps a good thing that this time he had taken a girl. Now it was not only the mothers of boys who were afraid.

The child under the bed shifted and sighed. Tomorrow morning he was going to have to call the mother again; tomorrow night she would drive out to Dover, Delaware, to leave twenty thousand dollars—one two three four five six seven—in a telephone booth opposite the train station.

He could still make it all come out right. In one hour he could be driving, the child a silent bundle in the backseat. One two three four five six seven. So that when he called, the body would already be in place.

It was four-seventeen now—one two three four five six seven, one two three four five six seven—the time gleaming blue across the room from the clock near the bed. He stood looking at it, his lips moving. Four-seventeen. Four hours and three minutes until the next telephone call. The Chocolate Man counted. He had already made the mistake of calling the mother too early; he wouldn't make that mistake again. And after the next call, twelve hours until the drop-off. The dropoff point was fifty-five miles away. Exit 68 on the Long Island Expressway. The Chocolate Man counted and counted. It would take two hours to get there. He would have to act quickly after the morning call.

The Chocolate Man stood in the middle of the dark room and counted. The girl slept under his narrow bed. He had never liked one of them before. He was sorry that he liked her. Because in about five minutes—one two three—

The doorbell rang.

The Chocolate Man dropped the knife; it hit the floor with a clatter and a thud. There was a silence, a ringing in his head. He leaned down and picked up the knife. Had there been a bell?

The girl shifted and sighed.

The doorbell rang again.

This time the Chocolate Man was ready. He tossed the knife onto the dresser; it skittered loudly and fell down the back of the dresser onto the floor. He didn't hear it; he was yanking the blankets off the bed, wrenching the topsheet loose. The girl made a sound—"No noise," he said softly, and she was quiet. He put one end of the sheet in his mouth and ripped it with his teeth; he took it in his hands and rent it with one smooth movement.

The girl had crawled partway out from under the bed. She was watching him. He grabbed one of his socks from the chair next to the bed and balled it up. "Open your mouth." The girl looked at him with big eyes.

"*Open*," he hissed, and he stuffed the gag into her mouth and secured it with the strip of sheet.

The doorbell rang again.

Emily didn't dare move. There had been a sound, an ordinary, civilized sound: the doorbell was ringing. At first she thought she must have dreamed it.

But the Chocolate Man was up, throwing his blankets. Maybe he was going to hide in them.

But when she came out from under the bed to see, his eyes were terrifying. He didn't need to speak for her to know she mustn't make a sound.

And when the Chocolate Man started ripping the sheet Emily knew what was going to happen next.

There were Christmas lights on the house two doors up the block, deep blue and orange. The blue ones must be old, Marcy thought, they

reminded her of the Christmas lights of her childhood; they hypnotized her.

"Son of a bitch isn't going to answer the door,"
Ed said.

"It's after four in the morning. Give him time."

The street was silent. Marcy was cold underneath her coat. She stared into the blue of the
lights—Ed was complaining, about the cold, the
time, but she didn't listen. When Marcy was nine
years old she wanted a pink plastic dollhouse, three
stories high, with polkadot curtains. She had seen it
on TV. All night for days before Christmas she
couldn't sleep: would she get the dollhouse? She
prayed to God and she prayed to Santa Claus, even
though she didn't believe in Santa Claus anymore.

Blue lights around the lintel. Ed was still complaining—and then there was the sound of footsteps behind the door.

Emily lay in the dark without arms or legs or
voice. She could hear the front door opening, the
miracle of people talking. One voice, maybe two.
Emily flexed her feet, she pulled at the bonds that
held her wrists. Panic threatened her: the foul-
smelling something the Chocolate Man had put in
her mouth would choke her, cut her breath.

She could not move her ankles or her wrists.

She could not make any sound.

Emily lay looking at the metal leg of the bed.
She began moving sideways on her belly, her head
held up as though she were in deep water, inching
herself sideways out from under the bed.

✗   ✗   ✗

Marcy knew better than to expect a monster, so when the man answered the door she thought she'd be ready. But when she saw his face she wasn't ready: adrenaline leapt in her fingers; she was dizzy. Because he was a monster, just for a moment, feral and afraid and utterly remorseless. And then the door was all the way open and the man in front of her looked nervous and sleepy, and Ed tilted his head, lightly, toward where Marcy's hand had found her gun, and she moved it quickly away and said, "We're sorry to disturb you this time of night—"

"—but we've received information that pertains closely to a case we're working on." There were two of them, a man and a woman. It was impossible, but here they were. The man was big. The woman was watching him as though he were a snake. "Mind if we come in?" the woman went on. The big man's foot was already in the door.

"Yes," said the Chocolate Man. How could they have found him? He became aware that his hand was clutching the door frame; he relaxed his hand. "You have no reason to come to my house in the middle of the night."

"But we do," the woman said softly. She had seen his hand. "Couldn't we come inside for just a moment? It's cold out here."

"Well—" The big man moved to open the door a little more, and the Chocolate Man let him. "If you'll tell me what it's about—"

"We're looking for information for one of our cases," the woman said. The Chocolate Man stopped; he moved his lips. He knew the woman was watching him but he couldn't help it.

"—saw anything out of the ordinary within the last twenty-four hours," she was saying. The Chocolate Man counted, helpless.

"—just want to come in for five minutes—"

The man stood as though hypnotized. Marcy watched as he made some private incantation while she and Ed tried to get into the house. He was about the right height, the right age; so were thousands of men in the city. He was wearing blue jeans and a white T-shirt; there was a bandage on his left arm. His hand on the door frame was bone-white.

"—want to come in for five minutes—" Ed was saying, and the man just stood there with glazed eyes.

But when Ed tried to push the door all the way open the man said, "No. I have a right to my privacy." He was speaking quickly and he sounded peevish. Marcy started to say, "Nobody likes to be woken—" when there was a sound. She stopped. A faint dragging sound, a bumping or scraping of metal against wood.

Emily had inched the lower half of her body partway out from under the bed; her head was farther under, almost against the wall, and her right shoulder was against the leg. She butted metal; the bed moved, protesting: it squealed. To Emily the sound seemed very small.

She pushed again, the metal leg resisting, pressing into her skin and hurting her. But the sound was bigger.

"—my privacy." The Chocolate Man didn't know what to do, how to keep these people out of his house. The woman was talking again—*Don't say a number,* he prayed—when he heard a noise behind him. A faint noise, but a noise.

"I don't see why—" he said, careful not to raise his voice to cover the sound.

"What was that?" It was the big man speaking; the Chocolate Man was afraid of big men.

"It sounds like furniture being moved."

"It's my dog," said the Chocolate Man. The man and the woman looked at him. "I keep him chained at night because he chews the furniture." Did dogs do that? "Sometimes he rattles his chain."

The noise went on, without rhythm but without stopping, a metallic bump and drag, bump and drag.

"I wish you'd tell me what you're doing here," said the Chocolate Man.

The noise seemed loud now; but if the people didn't hear it, would the Chocolate Man kill her when he came back?

Emily didn't know how far she had pushed the bed. She could hear the people talking while she stopped and breathed and clenched to push again.

Then there was nothing but blind pain and the noise, enormous in her ear but faint down the hall, probably, a little noise like a mouse rustling.

✕   ✕   ✕

"You were seen with a child this afternoon," the big man said roughly. "Is that true?"

"Why, yes." The Chocolate Man knew his voice was normal, his face perplexed but not angry. He did not offer information.

"A little girl," said the woman, "about—"

"No," the Chocolate Man said, "a boy."

The woman was watching him. He could hear the noise coming from the bedroom. He would wait.

"What were you doing with him?" The big man; the Chocolate Man didn't look at him.

"He lives around the corner," he said to the woman. The bump and drag went on and on; the Chocolate Man began to think it might just be in his head.

But the big man was looking past him down the hall.

"He needed to use the bathroom," the Chocolate Man went on. "I see him around sometimes." He was talking too fast: he stopped. But he didn't want them to hear the noise.

"What's this boy's name?" the big man asked; he had exchanged a look with his partner, and now the Chocolate Man was really afraid. He had never thought about what he would do if the police came to his house in the middle of the night.

Ed shot Marcy a glance: that noise, in back of the man, down the hall. The man was standing so that he blocked the partly open doorway. Marcy realized that neither she nor Ed had asked his name.

"Excuse me," she said suddenly, "but you haven't told us your name."

"George," the man said. Marcy could tell that he wanted to look behind him, down the hall.

"George what?" Ed barked; they all listened to the bump and drag, bump and drag.

"Riehle," the man said. "My name is George Riehle."

Emily couldn't keep moving the bed much longer. She could hear the people again but the pain in her shoulder was almost unrecognizable, at this point, as pain. It was so big. And the sound Emily was making was so small.

The woman and the big man were looking at the Chocolate Man. Bump and drag, bump and drag. The big man started to speak but the woman stopped him with a hand on his arm. "The child's name," she said harshly.

"Oh." The Chocolate Man stood hesitant only a moment. "Bill."

"Bill." The woman seemed angry now. The Chocolate Man was afraid of women when they were angry.

"His last name?"

"Uh—I don't know his last name."

"What time was he here?"

"Time?" Certain words were beginning not to make sense.

"*Time*," the woman snapped.

"Three o'clock," the Chocolate Man said quickly. One two three four five six seven.

"Where does he live?"

"I don't know."

The banging started again so suddenly all three of them jumped. Bump and drag, bump and drag.

Suddenly the woman said, "Is that Emily Lookinland making that noise?"

Bump and drag, bump and drag. The noise was stupendous in the night. The police officers' eyes glinted in the light from the streetlamp. The Chocolate Man opened his mouth.

The noise stopped.

"No," said the Chocolate Man, "it's my dog."

"Where did Hoag and Fleischer go?" Sergeant Hank Romano was sitting in the hall outside the Task Force room on a metal folding chair, drinking coffee and picking at the leftovers in three Chinese-food containers.

"Fleischer got a call." Detective René Argule dug into a fourth box with a chopstick. Inside the room the policemen could hear phones ringing; it was 4:25 in the morning, but still the calls came in: It's my brother-in-law, my husband, my landlord, my son. Romano had left the room ten minutes before to sit in semidarkness in the hall, where there were two metal folding chairs and an old card table; somebody had left the remnants of a takeout

Chinese meal. Argule had come out at the end of his shift manning the phones, but instead of heading home he'd sat down next to Romano and picked up one of the containers.

"Yeah?" Romano tilted a carton up. "Hey, a shrimp."

"Yeah. Some old lady in Flushing—I think Hoag said Dogwood Terrace. She thinks she saw the kid."

"Dogwood? That's near where the Angelo kid disappeared."

"Yeah, couple blocks over. But you know how many tips we get from the neighborhoods where kids went missing or were found. Probably half the old ladies in Flushing think they saw the Look-inland kid." Argule laughed. "Here, I don't like these things."

"Did you tell the Loot? It's a mushroom. I just got a call from there myself."

"No kidding. Old lady?"

"Old man. Said he saw the girl and a guy who fits the description of the Chocolate Man going up the walk of a house at—I don't know, some house near Seventeenth Avenue. Maybe we should tell the Loot."

"What for? What's this one?"

"It's a bamboo shoot, asshole."

"Fleischer and Hoag are already going over there, right?"

"Right."

"So don't worry about it. Give me another one of those things, will you?"

✕   ✕   ✕

It really was too much to be borne. She was trying to sleep, and there was noise coming from next door again. Mrs. Rosenberg sat up in bed. Some sort of banging. Again. She looked at the clock next to her bed. Four twenty-five. What on earth could that Mr. Riehle be banging about at this time of the morning?

Mrs. Rosenberg got out of bed. She could have sworn she heard something about a dog. And it was the second time in one night that there'd been that awful banging noise. It sounded like it might be a dog, dragging a chain, maybe, but Mr. Riehle didn't have a dog. Just a child—now, was it a boy or a girl? Mrs. Rosenberg stood listening. For a moment she thought she heard a name—Peony? Emily? Something like that.

So it's a girl, she thought, heading for the downstairs telephone. Sometimes she made an awful lot of noise, screaming and crying. *A very unpleasant child, Peony or Emily.*

Mrs. Rosenberg picked up the phone. Suddenly she couldn't hear anything anymore. The noise had stopped. *I've a mind to call anyway,* she thought. *Now he's got a dog, as if the child weren't bad enough.*

But there wasn't any noise anymore.

Mrs. Rosenberg turned to go back upstairs. *Some people are so inconsiderate. If I hear one more peep I'm definitely going to call the police.*

"No, Fleischer," Ed said softly as Marcy's hand went toward her gun. She turned slightly and paused, but she was still looking at Riehle. "I'm afraid we're going to have to—" she began, and Ed said, "No," again, louder, and put his hand on her shoulder.

Riehle was just standing there; he seemed disoriented. "I haven't done anything," he said.

"We know you haven't done anything, Mr. Riehle," said Ed, "and we're sorry to have bothered you."

Marcy shook away Ed's hand. "We're coming in, Mr. Riehle," and she stepped resolutely forward and knocked right into him.

"Oh, my," he said, and Marcy found herself unsteady on her feet with her palms against Riehle's chest.

"Detective Fleischer." Ed's voice was a warning but Marcy didn't hear it. She got her balance and pushed hard against Riehle's chest. He made no move to stop her. But he stood like a locked door; Marcy could feel the muscle in this man who had looked so soft; she recoiled, astonished at herself.

Her hands were shaking. George Riehle was staring at her hands. Ed jerked her backward and she almost fell.

"Of course, Mr. Riehle" he said smoothly, as though Marcy hadn't practically attacked the man, "we'd like to be able to contact you if anything else pertaining to our investigation comes up—but that would be later, tomorrow or a few days from now."

There was a silence. There was no noise from inside the house, no noise on the street. Marcy straightened her coat and looked at Riehle. His lower lip was quivering. Ed went on, "I'm sure you'll make yourself available—"

"Can I go back to bed now?" Riehle asked. He was still looking at her hands.

"Come on, Fleischer." Ed's voice was firm, like a father's. Marcy was about to hit him but when he turned she followed, not saying anything or looking at George Riehle. She said nothing down the walk, nothing as they got into the car, nothing as the engine turned over. Then: "What's the matter with you? He has that little girl in there, why didn't we go in?"

"Fleischer, it was his dog."

"It was not his dog, and you know it! We could have gone in there, it was an emergency situation! Why the—"

"You know what kind of shit could come down if he's not the guy?"

"What are you talking about? We don't need a warrant if we know someone's life is in danger, we could have gone in and—"

"Marcy, we didn't 'know' someone's life was in danger."

"Okay." Marcy took a lipstick out of her purse. "We both know the rules. Emergency doctrine: if we as police officers feel that there is an emergency situation involving life and death in which we must enter a premises for which we do not have a warrant, we are authorized—"

"Not *feel*. There has to be empirical proof. Not subjective feeling, empirical proof. Did we have empirical proof that Emily Lookinland was in that house? It could have been his fucking dog, and you know it."

Marcy lined her mouth with rose. She was near tears; that always happened when she was really angry.

"Besides," Ed was saying, "you know what would happen if we were wrong? If the media got a hold of it? 'Police Harass Innocent Man for Owning Dog.' Riehle could pull police brutality, you name it. They always do. And we'd be on desk assignment for the rest of our fucking lives—you know what the *Post* could do with this? It could blacken the whole department."

Marcy took a deep breath. "Are you sure it wasn't Emily Lookinland in that house?"

"I didn't see anything to indicate that—"

"Oh, Ed, for Christ's sake, this isn't a trial. This is me, your partner, asking you if you can say for certain that what we heard was *not* Emily Lookinland."

Ed looked out at the empty street for a long time. Finally he said, "Marcy, I'll do everything I can to help you get a warrant on this as soon as possible, and I'll be the first one out the door when we get it. But right now we just don't have enough to go into Riehle's house. You know how it is. They tell us often enough. Don't risk the good name of the Department. Before you act, be sure. Think of the consequences. Well, I'm thinking."

"Ed—"

"Never mind, Fleischer, I know what you're going to say."

"And do you know I'm right?"

"About me—I know. About Emily Lookinland, well, we'll just have to wait and find out."

Marcy rolled her window down. She closed the lipstick with a sudden click. The air outside was very cold. "And what if it was her," she said finally, "what will the papers say then?"

"Come on, Marcy, you know the drill. Procedure. However long it takes the warrant to come through, that's 'procedure.' We're in the clear."

Marcy leaned her head into the cold air. "God, this job disgusts me sometimes."

"Listen, I know how you—"

"Don't you even *care?*" There were tears in Marcy's voice. "There's a little girl being held captive under our noses and—"

"Jesus Christ!" Ed bellowed, slamming the steering wheel with his fist; Marcy jumped. "Of course I care! But I'm a trained professional, and so are you, and we can't go barging into people's fucking houses in the middle of the night because we hear a fucking noise!"

"We had a sighting," Marcy said evenly.

"Right. And Riehle confirmed he was walking with a boy, and gave us a name, without any hesitation. Which we're going to check out as soon as we get back to the station."

"The blue jacket—"

"Come on, Fleischer, grow up! Coincidence. Riehle's blond, you're going to say. Fucking coincidence. Boys wear blue jackets. Yeah, Riehle's weird. In fact, he's too weird. That old lady on the phone, she didn't even give her name, why do you think that was? So he's screwy—maybe his neighbors don't like him—"

"You're rationalizing. We should at least have called him on that dog business."

"How? Insist he bring his dog out?"

"Yes. Exactly."

"And how were we going to do that? How does that look? We are not permitted to just bust into people's houses in the middle of the night and order them to show us their fucking dogs!"

Marcy sighed. "Emily Lookinland was in that house," she said quietly.

Ed punched the steering wheel, once; then he put the car in gear. "We'll get a warrant," he said as the engine heated up. "We'll get a warrant."

If she's still alive by then, Marcy thought—but she said nothing, and she didn't look at Ed.

Marcy closed her eyes. After a few moments she felt the car start moving; she said, "Wait."

The car continued to roll. When Marcy opened her eyes Ed was regarding her with weary compassion.

"The dog," she said.

He nodded.

"The *dog*. If Riehle has a dog the neighbors have got to know about it." She was leaning forward now, resignation vanished. "You see? Let's just hit a couple of the houses on either side—you take that one and I'll get the one next to the Christmas lights." She was already leaning forward and reaching for the door; when the car stopped she lurched backward.

He looked at her for a moment. "Okay. You win. But, Fleischer," regarding her where she sat smiling with excitement and waiting for a fight, "don't get your hopes up."

✗   ✗   ✗

Mr. Linderman stood in the kitchen, in his slippers and his checkered robe. He had just hung up the phone. "They didn't listen," he said aloud. The voice at the other end of the line had been non-committal and abrupt.

Mr. Linderman reached a hand to the light switch, hesitated. "They didn't listen." There was an almost indiscernible brightness out the window. He hadn't realized it was so near dawn.

Krauts and Allies. One time he and Tommy Elfinger and some other neighborhood kids had gotten up before dawn and crept into an abandoned house down the block. Up and down its decaying stairways, in and out of its empty rooms, they had played Krauts and Allies until long after it was time to go home for breakfast.

Mr. Linderman's hand was still stretched out toward the light switch; it looked alien, not his hand. In a dim room Tommy held a toy gun. Mr. Linderman could see himself as a small boy, half hidden in his winter coat, creeping round a doorway, a stick for a weapon: *rat-a-tat-tat*, felling the enemy.

Mr. Linderman flicked the switch and his old man's hand was lit harsh, blue veins raised roads on freckled skin. He clenched his fist. There was a German Luger in the upstairs closet.

No one listened, and there was a little child being held captive across the street.

An old Luger, it hadn't been fired since the Great War. Mr. Linderman's father had brought it back; it had looked huge to his child's eyes.

Her eyes were blue, and frightened.

The gun was in a black suitcase at the back of the closet.

Mr. Linderman was halfway up the stairs before he realized he had left the kitchen light on.

Mrs. Rosenberg sat up in bed. The doorbell was ringing! She looked at the clock: 4:42. The doorbell—who would have the nerve? She allowed indignation to mask her sudden uneasiness. She listened, clutching the sheets to her beating heart.

The bell rang again. Mrs. Rosenberg was suddenly glad to think of George Riehle next door; even the child. But she wasn't frightened—no. Just angry.

She made no move to leave her bed. Out her window she could see a light on in Riehle's kitchen. Maybe he had heard the ringing; maybe he would go see who it was. He must know that a middle-aged woman lived alone next to him, even if she'd never spoken to him in fifteen years. And he had a child, he would know that children and older people need extra consideration.

The doorbell was ringing again, over and over now. He would know that she'd never spoken to him simply because it wouldn't be proper, speaking to a man she didn't know. He'd seemed odd even when he was a teenager; she glanced again toward his kitchen window: there was only darkness. Surely he would be at his front door now, concerned for Mrs. Rosenberg's safety.

Unless it was him at the door.

Banging now, quick loud sounds without reso-
nance. Like a boot against the door. What if it was
Riehle? Of course he didn't know she'd called the
police about his noise, there was no way he could
know that.

She closed her eyes. The noise would go away.

And so she sat, torn between fears, until at last
the noise stopped.

And then she opened her eyes and took a deep
righteous breath. The light in Riehle's kitchen was
out. Whoever had been banging on her door had
some nerve, interrupting her sleep. That George
Riehle or whoever, Whoever it was was going to
pay. In the middle of the night! Mrs. Rosenberg
snorted and reached for the phone.

Marcy stood for a moment in front of the house
with the colored Christmas lights. Ed was right;
but her veins were flush with adrenaline and it felt
more like certainty than hope. It could be so simple: either Riehle had a dog or he didn't.

There was a light on in the living room. Marcy
quieted her step without thinking, and she kept to
the right side of the walk as she neared the house, so
that whoever was up wouldn't notice her. But when
she rang the doorbell the sound was so loud she was
the one who jumped.

The door opened immediately. The man who
answered didn't seem surprised or upset to see a
policewoman at his door. "That thing last night,"
he said, "I already talked to the cops. My wife said
she didn't want to swear out a complaint."

"I'm not here about what happened last night," said Marcy; but she acted as though she knew. And she probably did: there was alcohol on the man's breath. He was immaculately dressed in blue silk pajamas and a black silk robe, and his slippers were soft leather. "I'd like to ask you some questions about another matter—this is just a routine investigation." Normally this was one of Marcy's favorite sentences; it made her feel like a character in an old film noir. The man was unimpressed. "Yeah? What do you want to know?"

"Is your wife available?" Marcy asked; just a hunch. "I know it's late, but—"

"My wife is out of town at the moment. She's staying with her mother in Rosedale. I already told the cops that down at the precinct this afternoon. You think I'm lying or something?"

His voice was rough and out of character with silk. "I only have one question," Marcy said coldly: "Do you know if your next-door neighbor, Mr. George Riehle, owns or has ever owned a dog?"

The man burst out laughing. "A dog? You wake me up in the middle of the night to ask me about a dog?"

"What is your name?" Marcy asked, all stiff formality.

"My name is Anthony Palmieri," he said, angry, and Marcy could hear the drink in his careful pronunciation, "and I'd like to know just who the hell you are, barging in here—"

"Tony?" A woman's sudden voice, frightened. "Who are you talking to, Tony?" Marcy couldn't see past Palmieri, but the voice came from upstairs.

Marcy noticed what a big man he was, with his liquor halo and mean voice.

"Shut up up there, you hear me? I can take care of whatever's happening here." And when he turned back to Marcy he wasn't trying to hide anything anymore. "Okay, you got what you wanted? What are you going to do, drag me down to the station again?"

"I am Detective Second Grade Marcy Fleischer. I believe you asked about that a moment ago. I'm not here to drag you to the station or anyplace else. I'm here to ask you a question and I already asked it: To your knowledge, does your neighbor George Riehle own a dog?"

Relief washed away all Palmieri's pretense; he was drunk and tired. "My wife and I have a problem once in a while. It's mutual, it's not just me. I mean, you should see the bruises *I* got yesterday, you think she got it bad." Marcy waited. "You want to come in? I got a bottle of real good scotch, they gave it to me at the office party." He was already turning toward the living room.

"No," said Marcy, "I don't want to come in. I don't want any scotch, and I don't want to hear about your bruises or your office party. I want you to answer my question."

Palmieri laughed again. He didn't seem to feel threatened anymore, he thought Marcy would keep his secret. "I wasn't trying—okay, okay, Riehle's dog. You want to know does he have a dog. Ah—" and Marcy knew: he was deciding what answer would please her. "—yeah. He has a dog, yeah. A little yappy thing, like a Pomeranian, right?"

"I'm asking you, Mr. Palmieri."

"And I'm answering. A little yappy thing. Like old ladies have. I see it time to time, you know, when he walks it."

"Can you tell me anything else about Riehle's habits?"

"His habits? I don't know, I never see the guy. That all you want to know? You sure you don't want a Scotch?"

"I'm sure. Thank you, Mr. Palmieri. I don't think I'll be bothering you again." She walked away and he said, "Merry Christmas, Detective—ah— Detective," and she nodded as she walked, thinking that as soon as she got back to the station she was going to contact the precinct captain and tell him Palmieri had lied about his wife. She wanted to say it now, to shout it at him, but she knew who would pay, so she was silent.

She met Ed at the foot of the walk. "Anything?" he asked, and she sighed and said, "Maybe. How about you?"

"I got one no answer and one lady who was so scared I thought she would scream or something. I kept saying, 'You don't have to call the police, I *am* the police.' She said she never saw Riehle with a dog. But she also said she never saw Riehle period."

"I don't think anybody has. Let's just take one more, okay? I skipped the house right next door because I saw a light on here. But the guy's a loser, beats his wife and Jesus did he smell. Said there was a dog. He would have said he'd just seen little green men from Mars if he thought I

wanted him to." They had reached the door of
the house next to Riehle's. "You're dating yourself, Fleischer," Ed said, "nobody talks about little green men from Mars these days," and he rang
the bell.

There was a wait; Marcy was glad, she didn't
want to talk to anybody else who was still awake at
four in the morning. As they waited she watched
Riehle's house: no light in the front, none in the
back. No noise at all. No curtain stirred, no window
creaked. He wasn't watching them. Maybe he really
did have a dog.

The door opened with a jolt. "Hello?" a
woman's voice said tentatively from behind a chain
lock.

"We're sorry to disturb you, ma'am," Ed said,
and Marcy let him handle it. She didn't want the
woman to know how important this information
could be.

Laurie sat up in the dark. Had there been a sound?
She was out of bed and down the hall. Quietly, she
didn't want to wake Emily. It was probably just a
bad dream; Emily hadn't called her name.

It was not dark in the hall. (Laurie was thinking
about Emily two years old: "What's my name?"
Laurie would say, and Emily would giggle. "Lauren
Loogilan," she'd say.

"But what's my *real* name?"

"Mommy!" And Emily would laugh and
laugh.) Laurie remembered leaving the light on in
the hall, dimmed, the way she always did. It shone

eerie now; Laurie didn't know why but she was frightened.

Emily was almost certainly just having a bad dream.

Right before her daughter's bedroom Laurie almost stopped; but she went in. There was a form on the bed, lumped up under the covers. Well, it was a cold night.

Laurie hesitated; something was wrong. She walked across the room softly, quickly, her daughter's things always looked different in the dark. A china cat caught light from the window; for a moment Laurie thought it was moving. But it only lay on its side and stared. There was a book on the floor, yellow and blue. Laurie could see part of the title:— *stone Castle Myst*—

Emily was breathing gently in her bed. Just a bad dream, all gone now. Laurie stood above her, her hand reaching out to touch Emily's hair—

"Laurie!" Carolyn gasped, sitting up abruptly. "Oh, you scared me! What—" and Laurie's hand didn't move, above the now-empty blankets, and Carolyn said, "What?" again, but Laurie wasn't looking at her, she was looking at her empty hand, and Carolyn stood and pulled her down to sit on the bed and put an arm around her and said, "It'll be all right," over and over. But Laurie wasn't listening she was looking at her empty hand and saying something; Carolyn leaned close.

"What's my name, Carolyn?" Laurie was saying, staring at nothing, "What's my name? What's my name? What's my *real name?*"

✻   ✻   ✻

The front window had fogged over. Marcy lighted
a cigarette and spat out smoke. She knew that Ed
would wait for her to speak first; if he said *anything* right now she would bite his head clean off.
It was infuriating to have somebody know you
that well who wasn't even a lover. Marcy surprised
herself by laughing out loud.

Ed was surprised too, of course; Marcy liked
that. He raised a quizzical eyebrow: "Thank God
you're not my lover," Marcy said.

Ed's eyebrow dipped, but he said nothing.

She thought her feet would never get warm.
Marcy didn't want to talk about Riehle's dog anymore. "Can you put the heat up higher?" Her feet
and her hands, she was cold to the bone.

"Sure," Ed said. And he said, "I'm sorry," and
she whipped him with her voice: "Don't tell me
you're sorry in that tone, okay? Just—don't tell me.
I had my one chance and now Emily Lookinland is
going to die because two people said Riehle has a
dog. One of them was drunk and one of them
was—I don't know what she was. I think she was
getting laid and didn't want to be interrupted."
Marcy lighted another cigarette; she didn't know
what was wrong with her.

"Could be," Ed said equably. "But she did say
Riehle has a dog."

"Yeah. But she doesn't know what kind of
dog. She thinks maybe a big dog. So what does he
have, Ed, a big dog or a little yappy one? Or does
he have two dogs now?" Marcy rarely raised her

voice; she didn't now, but her voice was metal against metal.

Ed sighed. "It doesn't matter what I believe," he said flatly. His hand reached to turn the key.

"Ed—" Marcy's hand touched his. "I'll take all the responsibility. Say I went against your orders. Say you couldn't stop me."

Ed was silent.

"But, Marcy," he said finally, "I would stop you."

And the car rolled away from George Riehle's house and nobody saw the door opening across the street.

As Mr. Linderman opened the front door he saw a car moving up the street. He thought it was a police car. He raised his hand—and the car turned the corner. And he noticed how cold it was. He hadn't put on a warm enough coat. George Riehle's house was dark.

Two houses down the block, across the street, orange and blue Christmas lights beat a lonely tattoo on the empty street. Mr. Linderman pulled his coat close and headed toward Riehle's house. He had checked the gun: it was loaded. But he had no way of knowing if it would fire.

As he stood at the door to Riehle's house, fingering the smooth metal in his pocket, he thought he heard footsteps: someone walking toward the back of the house. He rang the bell.

There was no sound at all for a long time. Mr. Linderman felt the cold seeping through the collar of his coat, cold air up the sleeves. The gun was reassuring but cold. He knew he was an old fool; he should go home.

But he rang the bell again. As he listened to the footsteps turn and come toward him he forgot the cold; he straightened his back and watched the Christmas lights blinking on and off.

Emily lay gasping on the bedroom floor. She listened to the Chocolate Man's footsteps coming toward her and knew she was going to die. There had been somebody at the door. The enormity of that, of there being another person, of someone *knowing:* but whoever it was had gone away.

After they left there was only silence for a long time. First Emily thought maybe the Chocolate Man had gone away, too. But now the Chocolate Man was coming, and there was nobody to care after all, and he was going to kill her.

The doorbell rang. Again the ordinary sound was monstrous in the night. It couldn't be the doorbell, not again; she was imagining it.

But the Chocolate Man's footsteps stopped. Was it the same people as before, with second thoughts about the small bumping noise they'd heard? Emily suspended her breath so she would be able to hear which way his footsteps went. When they turned and started toward the front door again she sighed hugely and closed her eyes. She had to be ready to make the noise again.

✗   ✗   ✗

The door was wrenched open and George Riehle stood panting, as though he'd been exerting himself. He was clearly angry, but in the moment after recognition his face changed, and softened, and Mr. Linderman saw how like a child himself he looked, with his confused eyes and irresolute mouth. And Mr. Linderman was unsure.

"Mr. Riehle?" Mr. Linderman was disgusted with himself: he knew it was George Riehle.

Riehle was just still looking at him, his mouth slack.

"May I come in?" What was he supposed to say? *Excuse me, but do you have a kidnapped child in there?*

"Yes," said Riehle, surprisingly, and he turned away without seeing whether Mr. Linderman was following him.

"I'd like to talk to you," Mr. Linderman said to Riehle's back as he followed him down a long, dark hallway.

"Yes," Riehle said ahead of him. Mr. Linderman didn't know quite what that meant. He was helpless to do anything but follow.

Riehle walked into a darkened room; when he flicked on the light Mr. Linderman saw it was the kitchen. Everything was very neatly arranged, and spotlessly clean. Riehle walked across the shining floor to the sink and stood there, his back still to Mr. Linderman.

"I guess you're wondering," Mr. Linderman began nervously, "why one of your neighbors would bother you at this time of night." He hesitated; Riehle said, "Yes," again, without any inflection.

Mr. Linderman stopped. He'd thought he heard a noise. Just a small noise: a creak or a whimper.

At the sink Riehle started laughing, and Mr. Linderman's head jerked away from the noise.

"That's my dog," Riehle said, laughing. He hadn't turned around. "Are you here to complain about my dog?"

Mr. Linderman shivered in the warm kitchen. He didn't have to know anything else.

"I have a gun," he said suddenly.

Riehle's back stiffened. When he turned around he was holding a carving knife. He was smiling. "If you shoot me you'll scare my dog," he said.

"I'm an old man." said Mr. Linderman, stepping toward him. "I'm not afraid to die. You have Emily Lookinland here. That's who I just heard. I want you to turn her over to me." The gun was out now, big and black; it looked like a prop; it would never fire.

Riehle was laughing harder. He gestured toward the dark hall with his knife. "Spot!" he called, waving the knife, "come out, Spot!"

The Chocolate Man was yelling something; it sounded like it was about a dog. Emily had been about to push the bed again, but she stopped and listened instead. Yes, he was yelling for his dog to come.

But the Chocolate Man didn't have a dog. Emily hadn't seen any bowl in the kitchen, or any leash hanging on the front doorknob.

"Spot!" he was calling. "Come out, Spot!"

Emily leaned her forehead against the floor. His voice was terrifying. He hadn't yelled like that before, even when he was really mad at her.

When she heard the other voice she brought her head up like an animal sniffing the wind. "Emily Lookinland, you can come out now!" She closed her eyes against the awful familiarity of her name. It must be the Chocolate Man. It had to be. Teasing her, seeing if she'd come.

But she wouldn't come. She brought her head back down and leaned her left ear, hard, against the floor. But she could still hear her name.

"Emily Lookinland, you can come out now!" Mr. Linderman's hand was steady on the gun. Riehle was shouting, nonsense and threats. It had to be that child in the other room. "Emily!" he called again, "it's all right!"

Riehle was still laughing and waving the knife. Mr. Linderman knew how dangerous he was: seven children dead. But he had been speaking the truth. He wasn't afraid to die. "Out of my way, Riehle. I'm going into that room."

"You are?" Riehle was red with laughter, crying with laughter. "You *are*? But what about my dog, my Spot? Don't you *dare*." All of a sudden Riehle wasn't laughing, and the knife stopped, and moved forward, and rested, just under Mr. Linderman's chin.

✗   ✗   ✗

There was somebody in the kitchen with the Chocolate Man. There really was. He was calling for her to come out. *It's all right,* he said. Emily was crying; she tried to lift herself, to get to the door, but she hardly moved at all. The strips of sheet bit her ankles and her wrists. Her shoulder and neck were just red pain.

And the dreadful thing in her mouth—she pushed it with her tongue, and it moved. The taste caught in her throat—but the gag had moved.

"Mmm-phmm," Emily said: *Help me.*

Mr. Linderman stood with his head tilted up. *Ridiculous,* he was thinking. *Like a bad TV movie.* But he didn't move. The gun was butted almost up against Riehle's stomach. *I'm going to have to shoot him,* Mr. Linderman thought incredulously, and as he pulled the trigger he felt the knife's blade sharp against his skin.

"Mmm-phmmm."

Emily was screaming. "Mmm-mm—" But there was no more noise outside the room. With a last dreadful effort she pushed the gag all the way out of her mouth.

No noise at all. Emily breathed in great gulps of air; she tried to breathe out the fetid taste in her mouth. The Chocolate Man had stopped yelling. She'd thought she heard a bump—"George?" she said tentatively, surprising herself. *Who else was in the kitchen? What if it was somebody bad—somebody worse than the Chocolate Man?* She tried to raise herself up into a sitting position. "George?"

"Fleischer—Marcy—even if she's there you know she's dead." Marcy and Ed were standing in front of the crime-scene map. It was after five in the morning.

"No," said Marcy. She was still clutching her tube of lipstick. She shook her head: *no.*

"Yes, Marcy." Ed's hand was at her chin, he forced her to look at him. "She's dead by now."

Marcy jerked her chin away. "Because of us." All her anger was in her jaw and her neck; she had stopped crying almost instantly.

"Yes."

"Because of *you*," Marcy hissed. "I was ready to go in. I'm still ready."

Ed had his head down. He was looking into the pocket of his shirt. He sighed; he pulled out the stub of a cigar.

"I'm sorry," Marcy said.

Ed shook his head: "It doesn't matter. If we'd gone in, any evidence we found probably would've been thrown out in court."

"The hell with court!" Marcy burst out. "The hell with the evidence! That little girl was in there— Ed," reaching out to touch his shoulder, "Ed, I know you don't care about your job enough to risk a child's life just to cover your ass."

"I do care about my job," Ed said tiredly. "I care so much I follow the book every step of the way. Every time. Because the way we handle an

investigation reflects on every police officer in every
city, every state. This isn't a computer job or a bus
route. Every time one of us fucks up it affects lives.
It affects the *law*. Look at L.A. Look at any goddamn city. Marcy, when we lose respect, police officers die. Every time the department fucks up you
may as well hang a target around every officer's
neck."

"'Every time one of us—'" she shook her head,
"'—it affects lives.' We messed up, Ed. Emily
Lookinland was in that house—"

"We don't know that."

"—and we left her there. Alive. Oh, we'll get
the evidence, Ed. When we go back to that house,
we'll have a body for evidence. And you won't have
to worry about our precious—" Marcy fumbled
with the lipstick—"*image*." It dropped to the floor.

Ed leaned and picked it up. He handed it to
her. She snatched it; she was being childish but she
didn't care. Tears had started up in her eyes again
and she hated Ed and she hated herself. "I should
have gone in," she said. She lifted her eyes to her
partner. "I'm going back now."

"Marcy, for God's sake—"

"I am. You don't have to come along." She was
checking her pockets, patting herself down: badge,
nightstick, gun. She took the gun out of its holster
and checked it; it was loaded.

The magazine made a loud, familiar click as it
slid back into place. Marcy was looking at Ed without defiance or even, now, blame. She slipped her
gun into the holster and it made a small satisfying
final sound. "Detective Fleischer," a voice said

behind her. Ed's face was sad and compassionate. "I'm sorry," he whispered, and Marcy turned to see Lieutenant Monsey standing in the doorway.

"Sergeant Hoag contacted me," Lieutenant Monsey said. He didn't acknowledge Ed, and although his voice was soft it was also iron. "Said he was afraid you were going to do something cock-eyed. Told me he thought you might be going off on a one-woman posse. Now, is that true?"

Marcy's hand was still on the gun in its holster; she did not move it. Ed saw it, and the lieutenant saw it.

She took a deep breath. "Emily Lookinland is in that house," she said, "and she's alive."

Lieutenant Monsey looked at her with no change of expression. "Tell me about it," he said easily. Marcy's hand went tight around the gun handle.

"Ed already told you."

"You tell me." He was talking to her as though she were holding hostages; she wanted to blast the even kindness off his face. She stood very still, but inside she felt like shattering glass.

"You and Hoag followed up on a tip tonight." He waited. Marcy nodded. Talk slowly, get them to agree with you. "You went to the house of one George Riehle." Again he waited, until Marcy spat, "Yes," to make him go on. "According to Sergeant Hoag, when you first confronted Mr. Riehle, he did not behave strangely in any way." Marcy stared; she denied him with a shake of her head. "You asked Mr. Riehle if you could come in. He said no."

Lieutenant Monsey's eyes darted past her, and

suddenly she became aware of Ed behind her. She almost smiled; she hesitated a moment and when Monsey looked back at her she lifted her hand away from her gun. "You won't have to disarm me," she said. "I'm not going to do anything."

"Marcy—" Ed began.

"Of course you're not," Lieutenant Monsey said.

"So stop the crap. Just tell me what you want to tell me."

"Sergeant Hoag says you both heard a noise at Riehle's house. A kind of banging, as though something metal were being bumped or dragged."

"Yes," Marcy said, suddenly eager, "as though somebody was trying to signal us, to let us know they were there."

Lieutenant Monsey looked at her evenly. "Or as though there was a dog pulling on its chain."

"No! It wasn't that! Riehle got really strange, Lieutenant. He was hiding something, I know it. Emily Lookinland was in that house. She was trying to signal us."

"But when you and your partner questioned the neighbors—"

"I know. We have two witnesses who say Riehle has a dog. But one woman said he *didn't* have a dog, and one other neighbor didn't even open the door."

Lieutenant Monsey said nothing for a moment; then, "What exactly did Mr. Riehle do that was, in your opinion, 'strange'?"

"He was moving his mouth. Talking to himself. He knew we could see it but it was like he couldn't

help it. And he was very nervous, I could tell that—"
and turning toward her partner she saw that he
wasn't looking at her but at the lieutenant, and
there was compassion in his eyes.

"I'm *right*," she spat, wheeling back to the lieutenant, "I am *not* losing it. We had two sightings of
Riehle this afternoon, going up his front walk with
a child that fits the description of Emily
Lookinland. And he fits the only known description
of the Chocolate Man. And—"

"*And* you put your hands on a civilian without proper cause. *And* we are going to check out
Mr. Riehle's house as soon as we have a properly
issued warrant to do so. Detective Fleischer, I've
been aware of your dedication to this case," and
now his voice was hard, "but I refuse to let any of
my officers turn it into a personal crusade. I know
how you feel about this. We all feel the same way.
But this Task Force is not going to cut corners.
And no member of this Task Force is going to cut
corners. And that means we go by the book. And
you don't take a step out that door until we get a
warrant—a properly issued, well-thought-out
warrant."

The lipstick tube was warm against her fingers.
She hadn't realized she was holding it. "Could we
at least set up a surveillance of the suspect's house
until the warrant is issued?"

"Frankly, Detective Fleischer, if it weren't for
Sergeant Hoag's recommendation, I don't know if
I would have bothered to call for a warrant at all. As
it is, we're waiting for the warrant."

Marcy stared; she opened her mouth to speak.

"Detective Fleischer, I advise you to get some sleep." She felt Ed's hand on her shoulder. "Hey, Fleischer, you got a light?" He stood with his cigar stub in his hand.

Marcy turned. She wanted to hit him. "Sure," she said, and, "Thank you, Lieutenant, I think I will." Above the flare of the lighter her eyes met Ed's. He nodded very slightly, and for one moment Marcy thought she was going to cry again.

"We are all aware," the lieutenant was saying, "of the quality of work you and your partner have been putting in on this case, Detective Fleischer." She nodded, still turned away. "I'm fine," she said.

"We're all tired to the bone," the lieutenant began; "No," Marcy said, squaring her shoulders and walking away from both men toward the hallway where the cots were. "Not to the bone, Lieutenant—to the heart. Tired to the bottom of the heart."

The click of the trigger had been enormous, terrifying. He looked down at the body on the kitchen floor and thought, *I didn't know I could really do that.*

"George?" It was the child's voice, uncertain.

"It's all right now," he said, looking at the body. The child was silent. "I'll come get you." He had to walk over the body to get to the door, and when he got there he was unsure, because of the dark.

"Emily?" he called softly.

"I'm sorry." The child still sounded afraid.

"You don't have to be sorry." He stood over her where she lay immobile on the floor. Then he knelt and began to work free the knots of her bonds. "That was a bad man out there."

"What did you do to him?" As soon as she could, Emily sat up and rubbed at her arms and her neck.

There was a long silence.

"He wanted to take you away from me, so I got rid of him."

Marcy looked up from where she was sitting, still awake, on a cot in the darkened hallway. Ed stood over the cot. His face told her, but she asked anyway: "No good?"

Ed was lighting a cigar, flicking a match against the grainy matchbook bar over and over. "What time is it?"

"Ed! For crying out loud!"

"Shit, Fleischer—okay." The match lit, and Marcy waited while Ed lighted his cigar and pulled, his eyes closed, smoke billowing out through his mouth and nose. "What time is it?" he said again.

"It's five forty-eight," Marcy said through clenched teeth. "Are you going to tell me or aren't you?"

"Sure. Judge Rosenkowski didn't buy it. Said we didn't have enough to go on."

"Didn't have—"

"Had to check out precedent. I told you we didn't have enough for emergency doctrine."

"Forget the emergency doctrine, okay? Just forget it. What about the telephone calls, the sightings—"

Ed shrugged. "Rosenkowski didn't see it. He was concerned about Riehle's rights—"

"*Riehle's* rights!" Marcy slammed her hand against the cot. "Riehle's—"

"Come on, Marcy, you know how it is."

"Yeah." She was looking with disgust at the dirty green canvas. "I know how it is."

"So," Ed said, sitting down next to her, "what do you want to do?"

"Want? I want to go back to that bastard's house and crucify him." She sighed and looked around; Ed had picked her lipstick up off her desk, he handed it to her. "But you won't," he said.

"No, I won't. Listen," straightening up, talking to Ed while looking at the dirty cot and the dirty walls, "we've got to get to another judge. I'll call Amy Bell over at the courthouse, she's a stenographer, she knows all the judges. You see if anybody here can rustle up a judge—any judge. Somebody's got to give us a chance."

"And there's alway morning, Marcy. We just might have to wait and take our chances with the day judge."

Marcy was tracing a rip in the canvas with her index finger. "I know. Parrish is on in the morning—I checked. He'll probably give us the warrant."

"He owes you?"

Marcy laughed. "He's a friend of my dad's."

"So call him now."

"Childhood friendships only go so far, Ed," she said ruefully.

Ed smiled, he touched her back. "Why don't you get some sleep, Fleischer?"

Suddenly Marcy wasn't angry anymore. "Thanks for trying," she said.

"I want him, too, Fleischer."

What had the noise really been? A child banging on a door? Marcy sighed.

"Get some sleep," Ed said again.

A bound child banging her head? "Okay," she said, "but I don't want to think about the kind of dreams I'm going to have."

There was blood all over the Chocolate Man. On his neck, on his shirt.

"What happened?" Emily asked; she was rotating her shoulder and rubbing her neck, but the pain wasn't going away.

"He was a very bad man." The Chocolate Man seemed unaware of the blood. Emily couldn't keep her eyes from it. "Did he hurt you?"

"What? No—no. He made me hurt him. He wanted to shoot me with his gun." The Chocolate Man sounded incredulous; he really didn't seem to understand what had just happened. Emily didn't understand either.

"Then why—you have blood on you."

The Chocolate Man looked down at his shirt. He lifted the collar away from his skin and the wet material stuck to him. Emily was making a face.

"The gun didn't work," he said, as if that were an explanation. "Now we have to clean up."

Emily swallowed. "We?"

The Chocolate Man looked at her. "It wasn't nice of you to make that noise."

Emily shrank back. "I'm sorry."

"It wasn't nice. They wanted to take you away."

"They?"

"The police were here. You knew that. That's why you were making that noise."

Emily was crying. *The police were here.* "I didn't know it was the police."

"Then why did you make noise?"

"Because—" Emily was crying harder. "I didn't know anybody was trying to hurt you." She was terribly ashamed. She hadn't thought of that: if she were rescued the police would hurt George.

"And then that old man—"

"Old man?" The one across the street, waving; she hadn't waved back. "The one from this afternoon?"

"Yes." The Chocolate Man sounded surprised. "How did you know?"

"I just guessed."

"You knew he was coming." Now he was accusing her of something.

"I didn't. Really I didn't. I'm sorry." She didn't know what she was sorry for: George had hurt that old man. But if the old man was going to hurt George? He didn't want anyone to take her away. That meant he cared about her.

"It's okay," he said, and he reached over and touched her neck. "What were you doing, anyway?"

Emily let him touch her. "I moved the bed," she said, ashamed.

He smiled. "Oh, I see. Well—just don't do it again." He sounded almost proud of her. Emily reached out a finger and touched his shirt. "Are you hurt?"

"Oh, no, that's *his* blood." Emily flinched. "It's okay—he didn't hurt me. He was a mean old man."

Emily dared to get up; the Chocolate Man did, too. "Is he—"

"Dead? Yes."

"And you want me to help."

"Only if you want to." The Chocolate Man was picking up the strips of bedsheet and putting them one by one on the chair next to his bed. He was moving his mouth.

"Do you have enough Fantastik?" It was all she could think of to say. *How do you clean up a dead man?*

The Chocolate Man laughed. "I have everything we need." He paused. "I usually put them—" Emily was looking at him with wide eyes. *Usually,* she was thinking.

"Never mind," said the Chocolate Man, "you just do the floor, and I'll take care of the rest. You know," starting toward the kitchen, "we were lucky this time. I guess you bring me good luck."

Emily followed him slowly. Her neck was starting to feel better. *I guess you bring me good luck.* Maybe it wouldn't be so bad.

THE SECOND DAY

THE SKY WAS GETTING LIGHTER. AT FIRST LAURIE thought it must be hope affecting her vision. But as she got up from the bed she saw pale red against the clouds: dawn. And as if she were a medieval nun or a prisoner she took dawn as her signal to get out of bed.

She walked downstairs to the kitchen; as she passed her daughter's room where Carolyn slept she did not look inside. There was a burnt-coffee smell coming from the kitchen, and the stale smell of smoked cigarettes. At the door she saw that one of the policemen was asleep and the other was just staring, without expression, at the Formica table-top.

Laurie stood inside the kitchen door. The clock on the wall read 5:58. "What are you going to do?" she asked.

The policeman looked up without surprise. It was Sergeant Mohammad. "The Task Force is putting everything we know about your daughter's abduction into its computers. They'll be able to cross-reference any information we have—for example, that the kidnapper speaks with a peculiar cadence suggestive of a speech impediment—with information already in the computer. Task Force officers have been taking tips all night. We get tips all the time—mostly they're bogus, but when something looks good we check it out. And it goes into the computer."

"But you haven't got enough yet to find him."

"No." the policeman looked down at the table-top, looked up. "Would you like some coffee? I could—"

"No." But she sat down at the table. The other officer snorted gently, his head on his arms.

"Jerry's been up since yesterday—"

"It's all right." *It's not his child,* she thought unkindly; but she knew that wasn't fair. "Officer Mohammad," she said, "do you have children?"

"Three. Two girls and a boy. We live three blocks from where Danny Angelo was kidnapped. Four years ago now."

"So he would be—?"

"Eight. Eight years old."

"He wouldn't believe in Santa Claus anymore," Laurie said softly.

"Maybe not. Does Emily believe in Santa Claus?"

Laurie was suddenly so grateful—he had said her name, he had spoken as though she were still alive—that she started to cry. He let her; he said nothing.

"I think I'll have some of that coffee now," she said finally, and he got up to make her a pot.

"Milk?"

Laurie nodded; she almost laughed. "This is supposed to be my house," she said.

"I can find my way around a kitchen pretty well."

"Were you at any of the other houses—?"

Mohammad stopped, a spoon in midair. She waited while he dipped it into the coffee, stirred.

"Yes." He took the spoon out and turned the water on in the sink; he rinsed the spoon and shook it. Laurie could feel the tears coming again.

"I was at Danny Angelo's house," he said finally, turning with the coffee cup. "My wife is very friendly with Pat Angelo." He put the coffee down in front of her. "Danny's mother."

Laurie nodded.

"We didn't know then—about the Chocolate Man."

"I don't know now. Tell me."

Mohammad looked startled; he turned back quickly to the counter and poured himself a cup of coffee. "I don't quite understand—"

"Yes you do. I want to know what he does to them. What the police make sure doesn't get in the papers."

"I don't think you should be worrying about—"

"What else should I be worrying about? You think there's any way I could *not* worry—" Laurie had stood up; she was almost shouting. The sleeping officer snorted and shifted in his seat.

"I'm sorry," Laurie said. "And of course you're not going to tell me."

"Mrs. Lookinland—Laurie—the Chocolate Man has never kidnapped a girl before. We don't know what he's going to do. *He* probably doesn't know. And that's the best possible thing in a situation like this. That's our hope. Because he probably *won't* do what he's done before."

"But you won't tell me what that is."

Mohammad and Laurie were silent for a while, drinking their coffee.

"Last night," Laurie said finally, "where did the Chocolate Man call from?"

"A phone booth on Northern Boulevard."

"Where on Northern Boulevard?"

"Does it matter?" Laurie met Sergeant Mohammad's eyes over the rim of her coffee cup. Suddenly it mattered very much.

But she only nodded.

"A phone booth at the corner of One Hundred Second and Northern."

Laurie thought of boarded windows and asphalt skies. "That's not a very good neighborhood, is it?" The Chocolate Man had stood in a phone booth at 102nd Street and Northern Boulevard last night. He had spoken—there had been voices in the background. "There were other people there," she said excitedly, rising from her seat, "at least one person. Did the police—"

"Actually there were several people present," said Sergeant Mohammad. But his voice precluded hope. "And the police already spoke to them."

"But"— feeling desperately that there should be more—"aren't they at least having a police artist work up a sketch?"

Sergeant Mohammad smiled involuntarily at her easy appropriation of police language. "I'm sure the police at the scene did everything possible under the circumstances." He saw her darting, uneasy glance: "Laurie, the people at the scene were drug addicts. That's what I've heard so far. Drug addicts are notoriously unreliable witnesses. If they think you want—Laurie," again, more firmly, because he saw the angry hurt in her face at her hope's being so easily batted down, "you have to trust us. We're doing everything we possibly can to get Emily back."

Laurie sat for a long time, looking at her coffee cup. "You know," she said at last, "Emily doesn't believe in Santa Claus, and neither do I."

6:07 A.M.

BEFORE SHE OPENED HER EYES SHE FELT A FAMILIAR fierce, queasy excitement: *It's today, Christmas, it's here, it's*—and the smell of Lysol split anticipation into cold fear.

Emily put her hands in front of her face: they would be the first thing she saw. But she didn't open her eyes. She listened for him; he had been so happy last night, so happy, he thought he had saved her from something. He had let her do just the final wiping of the floor: she told him she would rather die right then than help him clean up a dead man. She opened her eyes and looked at her hands, and her right thumbnail was dark with dirt—but it wasn't dirt.

Emily could hear him now, moving around in the kitchen. He had said he would make her something nice for breakfast; she gagged now, she hadn't gotten the blood out from under her thumb, and the smell of Lysol was so strong.

"Emily?" he called cheerfully; she must have moved, or made a sound. It seemed as though he could hear everything, even what she was thinking. "Are you ready for breakfast?"

"Coming," Emily called softly. He probably

wasn't going to kill her; she still hated him but she wasn't so afraid all the time anymore. She crawled out from under his bed, her back and neck and shoulder still sore. She thought she was going to throw up. And he was standing in the bedroom doorway, smiling at her.

"I don't want breakfast," she said, and "I'm sorry," immediately, because his face changed and he was still the Chocolate Man.

"I made you pancakes," he said in a hurt voice. "They made a mess."

"I'm sorry," Emily said again and walked into the kitchen. "I like pancakes." Now he was going to say something about her mother again.

"Do you like cartoons?" he asked. Emily was sitting at the kitchen table without rope around her wrist or her leg; she was surprised, she said, "Sure, but I like *Leave It to Beaver* better." The kitchen clock said a little after six. Emily was surprised; she'd thought she'd slept a long time.

"Do you have cable?" she asked. It was almost like talking to anybody: *I just can't hurt his feelings. I have to be careful, like when I play with the littler kids at the park I can't tease them or get them too excited, 'cause then they'll hit or bite or have a tantrum.*

"In the living room," said the Chocolate Man. "I like *Leave It to Beaver*, too. You want butter and syrup?"

"Sure," said Emily. "Could I have some Yoo-Hoo?"

The Chocolate Man laughed. "For breakfast?"

and Emily was suddenly afraid. But, "Okay," he said, still smiling, "I guess today's a special day."

Almost like talking to anybody. She just had to make sure she didn't make him mad again—or make him laugh.

LAURIE STOOD IN THE BATHROOM, LOOKING AT HER reflection in the mirror. Her eyes had purple circles under them, and her hair hung lank and straight. *She's got her father's hair,* Laurie thought. *And she has my eyes, and tomorrow will we be speaking in the past tense, She had her father's curly hair and her mother's river-blue eyes?*

If she is dead I will be, Laurie promised her reflection. She opened the cabinet—the Laurie in the mirror swung out of sight—and stood in front of the open shelves a long time. Beach Sand eyeshadow, Helena Rubinstein eye-makeup remover. Aurora Rose blush, a blue plastic razor.

As Laurie's hand reached for the razor she was thinking about the time Emily fell down the stairs and cut her eye and had to be taken to the emergency room. Laurie had to throw out the sweater she'd been wearing when she rode in the back of the ambulance, cradling her daughter's head. There had been so much blood.

Emily hadn't cried. Laurie picked up the blue razor. Emily had sat on her mother's lap in the emergency room, one hand holding a washcloth up to her eye and the other clutching her mother's hand so tightly that it was numb for a long time afterward.

Laurie took the razor out of the cabinet, almost absently: Emily had been five years old. She still had a scar that looked like a tic-tac-toe board on the outer corner of her left eye.

The razor had a new blade; Laurie had changed it two days ago. Emily had not cried when the doctor put the stitches in—eight stitches. Laurie held the razor up; she closed the cabinet. She stared at her reflection; she had nearly fainted at the sight of the doctor sticking a needle and thread into the transparent skin just at the outside of her daughter's eye.

Laurie held out her left arm. There was a blue artery that ran from the wrist to the elbow. Laurie placed the blade of the razor about an inch to the right of the blue highway. "You don't have to cry, honey," she'd said to Emily, and Emily said, "As long as you're with me I'm not scared."

Laurie dug the blade into the skin—it felt like butter—and pulled it down, parallel to the artery.

The hurt was deep and clean. Laurie watched the red blood spring and run, one long straight line of red against her pale skin.

Emily was not dead. Laurie moved the razor and turned her arm; she had the feeling she was just slicing chicken. The razor bit and blood jumped. Not so long a line this time, the clear pain of the blade was sufficient.

Laurie put the razor down on the sink top. There was red on her hands, on the white porcelain. There was red running in two lines on either side of the artery down her left arm.

The hole in Laurie's solar plexus shifted and filled. She looked at the woman in the mirror and her face was calm.

Laurie didn't want to wipe the blood off her arm. But it was not enough. The police didn't know what to do. Nobody knew. The Chocolate Man was playing them all like piano keys, playing them for fools. She pulled down her sleeve without cleaning the two narrow wounds. She wasn't going to sit anymore and hold Carolyn's hand, sit and make small talk with Sergeant Mohammad. She was going to find the man who had her daughter. The Chocolate Man.

There was a phone booth, on Northern Boulevard in a bad neighborhood where she had never been. Surely evil so dense had left its residue somewhere there, on the pavement or in the booth or in the memory of someone who'd seen it. Because this evil was a man, he must have been seen, registered his presence somehow at the point where he stood, solid flesh like anyone, and said things too awful to be true.

There must be something to help her, somewhere, someone. Laurie couldn't sit another moment without acting. She was going to find the Chocolate Man and kill him and bring her daughter home.

"ARE YOU OKAY?" CAROLYN WAS SITTING NEXT TO Laurie on the sofa; when she reached out a compassionate hand Laurie flinched away.

"Laurie, what's the matter?"

Laurie laughed with a horrid, dry sound. "What's the *matter*? What's the—"

"Laurie, what's the matter with your arm? It looks hurt."

Laurie carefully peeled back her sleeve. Already the blood was getting tacky; when she couldn't pull the material away she tore it impatiently.

"Oh, my God—"

"Shh. I don't want them to hear," nodding toward the kitchen.

"But Laurie, what happened? How did you—"

"It's the only part of me that feels real. It's not so bad, Carrie. Just two scrapes. There's a lot of blood, that's all. Listen, I have to get out of here."

"But where—"

"I've got a hunch. Or maybe I do. Carolyn, I've got to move. I can't sit here one more minute. I figure I have almost fourteen hours before I have to deliver the ransom. If she's alive I've got to find her."

"Laurie, let the police do their job."

"The police aren't doing anything. They're in there having coffee."

"Laurie, there are police all over the city working on this case. Sergeant Mohammad told you—"

"I don't give a damn. I *can't* just sit here."

"That arm looks bad. Let me call a doctor."

"They'll sedate me."

"Laurie, you need a doctor."

"I don't need a doctor, I need a friend. Just cover for me, okay?"

"What if—he—calls while you're not here? Are you going to put Emily in danger?"

"He's through calling. The next step is she turns up dead. And Emily *is* in danger—if she's alive. I've got to at least try. Will you help me?"

Carolyn gathered Laurie into her arms. "Of course I'll help you. I love her too, you know."

"I know. Now go in there and chat the boys up for about five minutes. That'll give me time to get out of here."

THERE WAS A REVOLVER IN A BOX AT THE TOP OF THE bedroom closet. Dick had left it. Laurie stood on a chair; was it the blue shoebox or the white one? The closet shelf was filled with the detritus of ten years, boxes and piles and bundles of anonymous life. A stack of paperbacks fell past her and made a terrific racket on the wood floor.

Laurie froze: the sound had been tremendous. But there was no answering noise from downstairs. It was the white shoebox, Laurie remembered. As she carefully extricated it a few hangers fell, clattering, but again there was no answering noise, no call of concern.

Laurie put the shoebox on the bed; had Dick even loaded the gun? He had planned to take lessons, he was interested in target shooting. He had planned to do so many things. And then he left, and Laurie knew there was a gun in the closet but it was up high so she didn't think a lot about it, she made sure it was under a lot of other things and Emily was a good child, she wouldn't go into her mother's closet without permission.

Laurie stood above the bed; she shook away thought. She didn't know how to shoot a gun. Its dull metal seemed to suck up the light around it. She was afraid to touch it.

But she did touch it. It was not cold—she had thought it would be. She clicked the barrel open and checked the chambers. She hadn't known she knew how to do that.

All six chambers were full. In how many movies had she seen the hero tilt the revolver just so, releasing the catch and checking the chambers?

I can shoot this, she thought. Her left arm hurt with every movement; it felt good.

She clicked the barrel closed and tested the heft of the gun in her hand. She put her fingers around the handle as she had seen actors do, put her index finger on the trigger.

I can shoot this.

Laurie slipped the revolver into the pocket of her coat and left the room.

7:00 A.M.

THE POLICE WERE ASKING ABOUT LAURIE, BOTH OF them coming out of the kitchen; one walked over to the sofa where Carolyn was sitting and one lounged against the kitchen door, watching.

"—Mrs. Lookinland upstairs?"

Carolyn lurched forward on the sofa; Sergeant Mulrooney reached to steady her. She'd thought he was turning toward the stairs.

"She's sleeping," she said. Of course he would know she was lying. "Upstairs."

"Ah," said Mulrooney. "Well, I don't want to disturb her." He stood a moment; Carolyn glanced over at Sergeant Mohammad where he stood in the doorway. They didn't know anything. She leaned back a little.

"May I ask you some questions? I didn't mean to disturb you, but—"

"No, no, it's okay." Carolyn moved to make room next to her.

"We just need," Mulrooney said; he did not sit, "to know a little bit more about Emily's life. For instance, what is her relationship with her father? Has there been any friction between Emily and her mother lately? Perhaps you could fill in the gaps."

"Well," said Carolyn, picking up her coffee cup;

it was empty and she put it down hastily, "Laurie is my best friend. We've known each other since night school. She was my matron of honor, and I—" She was babbling; what had he asked her?

"Mrs. Heffernan, would you like a cup of coffee?"

"Yes. Please. Emily doesn't see her father—she hasn't seen him since she was five. Every Christmas Laurie sends him pictures. She keeps track of where he is by the child-support checks. He moves a lot. I think he's living in Chicago now. Thank you." Mohammad had relayed a cup of coffee from the kitchen. As Carolyn took the cup her hand was shaking. She sipped, casting her eyes down to her cup so that she wouldn't have to look at him.

"I know this is difficult for you—being so close to the mother—"

"I'm Emily's godmother." Mulrooney was quiet a moment, and then, "Did Laurie and Emily have any major disagreements?"

"Oh, no, of course not. Why did you say that, 'did'? Do you really think—"

"I'm sorry. Of course I mean 'do.' Do they have altercations? Fights?"

"No. No. Emily is a very stable little girl, considering. Very centered. She loves her mother."

"What did you mean by 'considering'?"

"Well, her father being gone. And—it's been very hard for Laurie, raising Emily alone. She makes hardly any money at the video store, she's working all the time—"

"But yesterday she wasn't working."

"She got yesterday and today off because she's

supposed to be working Christmas. She really needed this time. She's been really—stretched, I guess. Tense. And now—"

"Mrs. Lookinland has spent considerable time in the care of a psychiatrist. The last four years." It was not a question.

Carolyn sighed, leaning her head back and exhaling heavily toward the ceiling. "How did you know that?"

"We've spoken to her ex-husband."

"That son of a bitch." She sighed again. "It doesn't have anything to do with anything. I mean, she started going when Emily was five. Dick had just left, and Laurie was working really hard, and she didn't know if she was going to be able to make it—"

"Didn't she threaten at one point to harm herself? To commit suicide?"

Carolyn's hand had gone to her mouth; she hastily put it down to her lap. "Suicide? God, no. I mean, she may have said something, she was pretty stressed out. But she got help, and she's been able to handle things really—what are you saying?"

"Do you mind if I smoke?" Mulrooney asked, patting his pockets. Camels, Carolyn noted, no filter. He didn't have matches. "There are matches in the kitchen."

And then she had to wait until his partner found matches and brought them, and while Mulrooney struck a match and lighted his cigarette and inhaled.

"Please," she said.

"We've got to explore every avenue; Mrs.

Heffernan. If there's any history of emotional insta-
bility we have to take that into considera—"

"But Laurie isn't emotionally unstable! For crying out loud, if your child was with the Chocolate
Man—"

Mulrooney made a soft shushing sound. "It's
all right, Carolyn. We're just concerned about her
reaction to the abduction. Unstable people sometimes do things they shouldn't."

Laurie's arm had been slick with blood.

"What do you mean?"

"Well, I'd like you to help us here. We need to
keep a very close watch on Laurie. To make sure
she doesn't do anything—well, out of the ordinary. The psychiatrist's reports note that she is
'impulsive in the extreme.' That she is 'capable of
acting out revenge fantasies of a self-destructive
nature.'"

"How did you get the psychiatrist's reports? I
thought that was supposed to be confidential."

Sergeant Mulrooney sighed. "Carolyn, could
you go check on Laurie? I don't like to disturb her,
but—"

"Oh. Yes, of course." And Carolyn leapt off the
sofa as though Laurie really were upstairs and not
gone who knew where. She could feel Mulrooney's
eyes watching her as she headed up the stairs.

She was panting as she reached the top. She
walked to Laurie's room (past Emily's, where she
had slept; there was a Nancy Drew mystery open on
the floor, and a jar of flowers caught light from the
window). Carolyn stood at the threshold. Of course
Laurie's bed was empty; her closet was open and

there were things on the floor, and boxes askew on the shelf over her dresses.

Dick had a gun, Carolyn suddenly remembered. A handgun. He had left it, and Laurie kept it high up in her closet so Emily couldn't find it.

A gun. Had Laurie really gone to find Emily? Or, thinking Emily dead, had she gone to join her?

She had taken the gun. Outside a few flakes of snow were falling. Carolyn stood in the middle of Laurie's room. Even as she noticed them the snowflakes stopped coming down. Outside the window was nothing but gray. She turned to go downstairs and talk to the police.

7:00 A.M.

"Hey, Evelyn." Officer Miller walked with a quick sure unconscious step, he did not pause at the front desk. "Any calls? I'm expecting one," walking away already down the hall, "from my wife."

Evelyn laughed tightly; every morning when Miller came in from his tour of duty the same joke, with Miller divorced for almost a year now.

"John," Evelyn called, "there is a message," and Miller executed a perfect military turn and lifted his chin and his eyebrows, already impatient.

"It was some girl. And the lieutenant said something about did you arrange for a sketch artist—"

"Shit," Miller said to himself.

"What?"

"Just give me the message."

Evelyn was looking through some papers too fast, already intimidated, "Oh, she said she was—wait a minute," and Miller sighed, and Evelyn murmured, "something about the Chocolate Man," and Miller snapped, "What?" and Evelyn visibly jumped in her seat.

"—said it was about the Chocolate Man, some girl who—" and Miller said, "How old? What girl?"

Evelyn sighed. "Oh, just—I'll tell you when I find the piece of paper. I know I wrote it," her voice softening down again to a murmur, and Miller tightened his lips and swiveled on his heel and continued down the hall.

CAROLYN STOOD UNCERTAINLY THREE STEPS FROM the bottom of the stairs.

"Mrs. Heffernan?"

Carolyn breathed out; she thought she was about to cry. "I'm here," she said inanely. She felt like a child who had done something terrible: kicked the cat, eaten the last piece of cherry pie. As she reached the bottom of the steps her eyes were wet.

"Mrs. Heffernan—"

"I'm so sorry," she said, covering her face with her hands.

"What's wrong?" Sergeant Mohammad spoke with cautious compassion.

Carolyn couldn't stop crying. "She's going to hurt somebody. She cut herself, there was blood but she said it was nothing—"

"Mrs. Heffernan, come sit down and tell us what's happened." Mulrooney was already heading up the stairs. "Is Mrs. Lookinland all right?"

"I shouldn't have let her, I shouldn't have," Carolyn said as Mohammad led her toward the sofa. Mulrooney was already on his way down the stairs, shaking his head and holding his palms up: "Gone," he said.

"Jerry, get her some whiskey or something. Mrs. Heffernan, what happened to Laurie? Where is she?"

But Carolyn couldn't speak; Mulrooney brought her gin in a plastic cup and both men were silent while she drank. She could feel the tension pouring off them as they hovered solicitously above her. The gin tasted bitter and good; she swallowed and said, "I'm sorry," again, but her voice was firmer. "She's gone to find the Chocolate Man."

"Jesus, Jerry, call it in. How did Laurie expect to do that, Mrs. Heffernan? And what about blood? You said something about blood."

The gin had an absurd party smell, Carolyn would have liked some ice but she didn't ask. "She cut herself, I think with a razor blade; she had blood down her arm. And she took Dick's gun, oh, God, I shouldn't have let her go—"

"Took Dick's gun *where*, Carolyn? Where did Laurie go?"

"She said she had a hunch," Carolyn said miserably. Her stomach felt sick from the liquor.

"A *hunch*?" Mohammad was clearly incredulous.

Carolyn nodded. She held out her plastic cup for more gin.

"Did she say where she was going?" Mohammad took the cup. "Jerry, get me some more of this."

"I don't know where she went. She said it was the only part of her that felt alive—her arm. She seemed to think that she might really be able to find out something that would help."

"You said something about a gun." Carolyn

was ashamed to take the gin but Mohammad was holding the cup out to her.

She put it on the table. "Her ex-husband kept a gun. He left it here. I think she took it."

"It's okay, drink. When did she leave the house?"

"About twenty-five minutes ago, I guess. She asked me to keep you busy."

"Yes, well. You did that." Carolyn offered him the cup and he shook his head, smiling ruefully. "Carolyn, please think hard. Do you know if Laurie knows how to *use* that gun?"

"I don't think so. She never said anything about it. But it's not—I mean—she could probably load it, couldn't she?"

Sergeant Mohammad nodded. "Jerry," he said, "get an alert out. Quietly, though. We don't want the media to get this. They'd love it, they wouldn't care if it spooks the Chocolate Man into doing something"—seeing Carolyn's face—"hasty. Mrs. Heffernan," speaking sternly now, "didn't you realize that Laurie's actions could change the face of this investigation? Oh, not that she's going to find him, but if this leaks out, if the media gets a hold of the fact that Lauren Lookinland has gone off on some crackpot crusade, they're going to blast it all over the television, and if the Chocolate Man sees it—I don't know," shoving the air with a stiff open palm, and Carolyn burst into tears and said, "Oh, I didn't know! Sergeant Mohammad, may I go? I've got a car, I could—"

"Mrs. Heffernan," kneeling suddenly in front of her and taking her hands, "this isn't about blame.

And it's not about you," gently, squeezing her fingers, "or about me, or even about Laurie. It's about Emily, and doing what's best for Emily. What I need you to do is to stay calm. Can you do that?" Carolyn nodded, and, "Carrie, there is something else you can do." Carolyn nodded again, swallowing and sniffling. "The Chocolate Man is going to call here in about an hour and ten minutes. I could send for a policewoman to come over here and substitute for Laurie." Carolyn leaned forward. "But I'd rather you did it, Carrie. That is," rising lightly, freeing her hands, "if you feel up to it."

"Oh, Sergeant Mohammad, thank you so much! I'll do anything I—"

"But," the sergeant cut in calmly, "you're going to do exactly what I and my partner say to do, because if you fuck up this time," his eyes suddenly hard, "it's going to be Emily who pays."

LAURIE HAD HURRIED DOWN THE WALK, LOOKING AT her feet. How did the rhyme go? *Step on a crack, break your mother's back.* Laurie broke bones hurrying down the sidewalk to her car, which was parked, thank God, three doors down from her house. She felt naked, both more and less vulnerable outside her home, where the situation, bad as it was, was at least under control. Here on the street Laurie was not protected from her pain and fear, but neither was she defined by it. In a minute she would drive away and she could be anybody, a woman driving to the mall to pick up last-minute Christmas gifts; a woman with no children, no husband; a woman with both, and both safe, waiting in some home empty of pain.

A passing car slowed and Laurie paused, thinking without logic, *Maybe it's Emily.* She turned, and the man behind the wheel yelled, "I'd like to eat it, baby!" and honked his horn.

Laurie shied away, afraid only that the police might be alerted by the noise. And she thought, *Emily spoke to a stranger.*

The car door squealed as she opened it. Emily had gotten into a car with a stranger. Laurie had taught her, the same lesson over and over: Never go past a car with the passenger-side door open. When it's dark out, don't go near a parked car with the interior light on. Never go over to the passenger-side window to give directions. Never go with anyone who doesn't know the password. Emily and Laurie's password was *Armistice* this year, because Emily was studying the World War and liked the sound of the word. Never go with anyone who says his dog or cat is lost, his child. Never go to look at a promised kitten or puppy. What could the Chocolate Man have said to her daughter to make her go with him?

As Laurie slipped the key into the car door the alarm let out a piercing scream, once, and was silent. Any moment she expected to hear a voice, to hear quick, heavy feet, to be caught here running not away but toward. Going where she didn't belong, doing what wasn't allowed. Becoming a part of the crime, not just watching the way she was supposed to, offstage in her cocoon of suffering and protection, where it didn't matter to the investigation whether she was awake or sleeping.

But now—turning on the engine, which woke huge and growling—Laurie was going to become a part of it. Fidgeting in her seat, waiting for the car to warm up, the engine beginning to purr—even just a little part, scurrying at the edges of the crime like a cat underfoot; but she would know at the end, with her daughter alive or dead, that she had done something, that she hadn't just stood by and cried, that she had at least tried to find and help her daughter.

The car moved smoothly away from the curb.

What had Emily seen out the window of the Chocolate Man's car? Laurie felt a surge of power. Of real hope, of something like certainty. What had the Chocolate Man said to make Emily trust him?

She was going to ask Emily that, when she got her home.

THE CHOCOLATE MAN AND EMILY WERE WATCHING *My Three Sons* on the television in the living room. Emily sat on one end of the sofa, the Chocolate Man on the other. He hadn't tied her wrist or her leg; there wasn't anyplace to go. Emily liked *My Three Sons*. Ever since she and her mother had watched a movie called *No Time for Love* she'd had a crush on Fred MacMurray. He played a sandhog and Claudette Colbert played the lady reporter who fell in love with him. A sandhog was a man who dug the tunnels for the subways a long time ago. In the movie Claudette dreams that Fred is Superman and is coming to rescue her—Emily couldn't remember from what. In *My Three Sons* Fred MacMurray looked really old.

Emily knew that something was going to happen soon. The Chocolate Man was going to call her mother again. Maybe if her mother paid the ransom he really would let her go. Her mother didn't have any money; but the police would give her money, Emily knew. She wanted to ask the Chocolate Man questions: Do you tell them to put the money in a black attaché case? Do you ask for it all in small bills? *My Three Sons* was going to be over soon, and all of a sudden Emily was terribly afraid.

"Well," said the Chocolate Man; he turned toward her. He was smiling. "It's almost time to—"

"You don't have any ornaments on your Christmas tree," Emily said. She didn't know why she said it.

The Chocolate Man frowned; he was thinking. "I don't usually put anything up," he said finally. The credits had begun to crawl across the screen.

"Why not?" He moved to turn off the TV and Emily almost screamed. "Don't you like ornaments?"

"I don't know," he said, "but now I have to—"

"Don't you think they're pretty?" Anything that took him away from her was good. If he was thinking about something else he wouldn't think about her. About her mother.

"No." Emily couldn't tell if he was getting angry. It was so hard; one minute he was almost nice, and then—"That's not what I think is pretty."

So she'd said the wrong thing. His eyes had taken on that strange gleam. *That happened,* her mother would say when she was telling Emily a memory, *before you were a twinkle in your daddy's eye:* Emily knew what that meant. He was thinking something bad, she knew it. He was nodding his head very slowly; she didn't think he even knew he was doing it; and he was moving his lips again.

"Well," Emily said desperately, "what *do* you think is pretty?"

"Hmm?" It was almost like a normal conversation. But there were consequences here, and traps. Emily didn't know what she was supposed to do. She'd always been a good girl, and she was proud of that. Her mother was proud, too; she often told Emily so.

But how could she be a good girl now? Anything she said could make him look like that. Like he had a twinkle. The Chocolate Man smiled at her.

He wasn't completely back from wherever he had gone. Emily knew she had to get him back right away.

"I was in the school Christmas pageant," she blurted, not knowing what she was going to say next. "I was a Christmas bell." The Chocolate Man looked up at her; he had been staring at the floor. She closed her eyes against his. "I wore red," she went on, "and I carried a bouquet of dried flowers."

"Good girl." He stood up; she thought he was going to pat her on the head. "Good girl." If he touched her she would start screaming and never stop.

But he did touch her. "I'll be right back," he said gently, and Emily felt the familiar scratchy rope around her right wrist. And she didn't scream. At least if he was tying her up he wasn't going to take her anyplace.

"Okay?" asked the Chocolate Man, and Emily nodded: yes. And after a moment she heard him moving away. She kept her eyes closed as he moved across the living room toward the stairs; there was carpeting on the stairs so she couldn't hear very well, but it sounded like he was going up. Emily kept her eyes closed even when she knew he was gone.

LAURIE WAS CONCENTRATING ON THE ROAD. SHE hardly noticed that she was smoking cigarette after cigarette. Everything was at once familiar and extraordinary. She had felt this before: looking out at the cold asphalt she remembered. The day she went to a nearby obstetrician's office and confirmed that she was pregnant she had felt something like this. After leaving the doctor she had walked down Queens Boulevard and all the familiar things looked different. A river of yellow cabs swam by; Laurie had never noticed how buttery that color was. A traffic signal hung suspended red a long time; she was mesmerized by the light. Random items in a boutique window caught her eye: a blue-sequined dress, a strand of pearls. Laurie stood struck by the fact that pearls are forged in darkness. Someday she was going to explain that to someone. Someday she was going to hold somebody in her arms and teach her to raise her hand to hail a yellow cab. Because of Laurie someone else was going to see; to touch, to smell, to hear. Because of her.

Now she looked out the window of her car and everything looked dead. That house—the roof a bright incongruent orange against the lead sky—now someone might never see that color orange again. These cars, red and black and gray, with a rush of engine as they passed or were left behind—someone might never hear that sound again. The world in all its vastness and variety might no longer contain her daughter. As simply as an insect's life is stamped out. A moment, an act of will; a life gone. A world that did not contain Emily couldn't contain Laurie; but it did, if Emily was already dead. Laurie felt her hands gripping the steering wheel, and she hated her hands. Cold air blew against her face and she hated her face.

There was a child, four or five, in the backseat of the car in front of her. He sat facing backward, his palms flat against the window glass, his face serious. Laurie blinked, hard. She had to be able to see the road.

The child in front of her stuck out his tongue.

The pain Laurie felt was physical, like shock from electricity. The boy in the car was waving determinedly. Laurie watched her hand raise itself and begin to move, up and down; the boy laughed, silent and triumphant behind glass, and waved harder. He was mouthing something: her hand hung limp; she looked at it curiously and lowered it. The boy banged the window glass and mouthed again: *Merry Christmas*.

Laurie was crying. A knife would feel like this, a metal blade. And yet there was joy as well, piercing joy, which was all the unspoken memories that made up *Emily* for her. Her Emily, a thousand thousand layers of memory, some static like photographs, some so distant that they defied memory:

Laurie no longer remembered what Emily had looked like as a baby, but she knew how looking at the baby Emily had made her feel. How many times had Laurie looked at Emily? She knew her daughter's face better than she knew her own. On Christmas morning Emily would always come down the steps very slowly; she would have woken early and waited in her bedroom for her mother to wake up. She would end up in bed with Laurie—how many Christmas mornings was Laurie remembering? Dick wasn't in these memories, what happened Christmas mornings when he shared her bed?—fidgeting and squirming until Laurie pretended to get mad.

There were so many Emilys; Laurie was haunted. Not by the dead but by life itself, haunted and blessed and overwhelmed by memory. Laurie pressed her foot against the gas pedal; *odd that such a simple thing propels me faster.*

There was one crow, high in a tree. Laurie was aware of passing it, leaving it behind. There was one crow that flew every afternoon at four o'clock to an oak tree across the street from Laurie's house; it barked four times and waited. Often Emily ran to find her mother: *He's here again, he's calling.* And mother and daughter would kneel at the window—silently, as though the crow might hear them there—and listen, and wait.

And the crow would call: four times, four times, four times. And soon other crows would come, and call, and then all the crows would fly away east.

"Merry Christmas," Laurie said aloud. "Merry

Christmas, little boy." And suddenly the boy's car swerved out of her sight and he was gone. And Emily was gone, and Laurie was left alone at the wheel of her car, driving through the mist of her tears.

7:15 A.M.

EMILY HEARD THE MUFFLED THUD OF FOOTSTEPS from upstairs. It was odd to listen without her eyes. Thirteen steps, and then a door opening. Emily sat in darkness. There was no sound at all, and then a small repeated bumping, as though somebody were going through a pile of books or videos. It seemed safer in the dark; she opened her eyes. She had to look around, because this might be her last chance.

Out the sightless windows there was only gray, as if a shadow had settled over the whole house. Only gray, as though there were no world at all. No other lives. And inside the Christmas tree hung naked.

There were no pictures on the walls. At home right now Emily and her mother would have been trimming the tree, a nice big one from Canada. Emily had picked it herself, she always did, last year she'd made frames around every tree with her fingers and looked at them like that, because last year she thought she was going to be a movie director when she grew up. This year—there was a sudden small bump upstairs: Emily was looking at the rope around her right wrist now; all the while she was thinking she'd been trying with her left hand to move the rope even a little—this year she didn't want to grow up. The rope was scratchy and it burned her skin. She looked down the length of it to where the Chocolate Man had tied it to the table leg. She hadn't realized about not wanting to grow up until right now. She leaned over and tried to push the knotted rope down the table leg. It squealed—she lifted her head like a deer. She liked to put on her mother's lipstick; Emily was concentrating so hard on the knot in the rope, on moving it down the leg without sound, that she wasn't aware she was thinking at all. If she had to say what she was thinking—the rope squealed again, so softly, "grownup" used to be high heels and lipstick and pretty dresses but it wasn't anymore, it was danger, even before the Chocolate Man she'd sensed it—there was nothing but the rope.

There hadn't been any noise from upstairs for a long time. As Emily worked the rope, slowly, so slowly, she had a sudden visceral memory: her fingers delicately holding a metal ornament hanger, the fingers of the other hand tracing the ancient slope of a paper-thin rose-colored house, like a gingerbread house but so fragile, every year her mother let her hang it herself. It was an honor and a challenge still; it would lie wrapped, now, in old white crinkly paper in a box in the living room. Nancy Drew would slide the rope this carefully, a particle of an inch at a time, evenly so the rope wouldn't squeal. What was he doing up there? Layers of thought: Emily knew she was protecting herself, insulating herself: because who knew what would happen when the Chocolate Man came downstairs? Children are supposed to be innocent. Emily had heard her mother and Carolyn talking about it many times. Some of it was easy, like she shouldn't know too much about sex. Her mother made sex sound like a threat. The knot was more than halfway down the metal leg; there was only silence upstairs.

Some of it she didn't understand, about how pure her wanting things was, or how little it took to hurt her: she didn't know why that should be good. The Chocolate Man wanted her innocence (she was thinking about the rope, only that). He wanted to suck it out of her like a vampire. She froze: a muffled thump from upstairs, maybe a door being closed. But he didn't want to touch her, because she wasn't a boy. If he caught her trying to get away he might kill her right here, but if she was fast—her mother was right, Nancy Drew always got rescued at the end. Everything she did all through the story always came to the same thing: her father or her boyfriend.

There were footsteps from the stairs, and only an instant to think: Emily yanked the rope back up the table leg—it screamed—and leaned back, breathing hard, against the sofa pillows.

She was looking out the window when he came into the room. She didn't want to look at whatever he might have brought from upstairs. Whatever innocence was, she knew she didn't have it anymore.

IN THE MOVIES IT ONLY TAKES TWO MINUTES TO GET a warrant," Marcy said. She was flicking her lighter over and over, listening to the tinny click and watching the spark.

"Yeah, in the movies it only takes a phone call," Ed agreed; he was sipping coffee from a paper cup. "Who made this shit?"

"Renny or Church, I don't know." Click and spark, click and spark.

"Somebody ought to—Jesus, Fleischer, do you have to keep doing that? You're driving me fucking crazy."

"You're always so gracious, Ed. I appreciate your tact." Marcy flicked the lighter once more with a deliberate motion, then snapped the top closed, hard.

"Marcy—" Ed reached across the table toward her hand, and she pulled her hand away and made a fist. She was being childish but she didn't care.

"I talked to Lieutenant Monsey," Ed said.

Marcy hid her mouth behind her coffee cup.

She waited.

"I asked him to hurry up the warrant. Told him I was wrong, you were right."

Marcy waited. Ed sighed and warmed his hands

around his cup. "It's fucking cold in here," he said at last. Marcy's eyes flared. "Damn it, Marcy, I tried," he said.

"Monsey said no," she said calmly.

Ed sighed again: "He said no."

Marcy drank coffee and looked above Ed and behind him. When he put his hand on her clenched fist she didn't pull away.

"I'm sorry, Marcy," he said; she shook her head. "Thanks for trying, Ed." But she wouldn't look at him.

"Marcy—" His hand was warm over hers. "I had to stop you. You know that."

"I know." There was nothing behind Ed, green-and-yellow-cream dirty walls, no windows.

"Monsey said he respected your determination. But he couldn't—"

"The hell with my determination," Marcy said quietly. "I don't want brownie points." She sighed, as though speaking were difficult. "I just want that little girl—" and she broke, and laid her head in her arms and cried.

And Ed did nothing. Her hand in his clenched tighter; with his other hand he picked up her coffee cup and nudged it against her arm.

She looked up. "It tastes like—"

"Shit," said Ed, and Marcy almost smiled.

"It'll put hair—" he began, and she said, "Shut up," and took the coffee. And she drank it and lighted a cigar for Ed and they didn't talk about it anymore.

7:25 A.M.

EMILY LOOKED OUT THE BLANK WINDOW UNTIL SHE heard the Chocolate Man walk over and stop right in front of her. She looked at his hands.

"What are you doing?" he asked. She gauged his voice; it didn't have a twinkle. He was holding a small pile of Polaroids, with only the backs showing.

And he just stood, looking at her, until she said, "What are those?"

"Oh," he said. They looked at each other. He walked across the room and put the photos on the mantel. "Never mind," he said. Emily didn't know if she was supposed to say something. "It's not the same this year," the Chocolate Man said finally.

"Oh," said Emily. She was as crazy as he was; they were going to just talk to each other like this forever.

The Chocolate Man yawned suddenly, stretching his arms above his head. Emily shrank back and he laughed: "I'm not going to hurt you now," he said, as though that would make her feel better.

"I want to go home," she said fiercely, "I want to go *now*."

He regarded her with a faint smile. "Of course you do," he said. Maybe this was ordinary for him.

"What happens now?" asked Emily, surprising herself. She was afraid but she had to know. The Chocolate Man leaned over and tested the rope where it bit her wrist.

"I have to go to work now." The knot at Emily's wrist was still tight.

"So I go into the closet again."

"Uh-huh." He pulled at the rope, and for an instant Emily went tense. She'd made a fist. Consciously and not too quickly she relaxed it. "Do you mind?"

Emily laughed, a high, pure sound. "Do I have a choice?"

The Chocolate Man didn't laugh. "No, I guess not."

He hadn't noticed anything.

"You're going to have to let me go sometime," she ventured.

Suddenly he was shouting. "I don't *have* to do anything! If I want to I can—"

Emily shrank back in her chair, and he stopped. *This is not a game, there is no story, only me, Emily, and I got him mad again.*

The Chocolate Man had raised his hand, as if to strike her, and she sat up defiantly. "Go ahead," she said quietly. "My mom's going to love me no matter what you do."

The Chocolate Man looked as though he had been punched in the stomach.

"Your mom wasn't very nice to you when you were a kid," said Emily, "was she?"

"How—why did you say that?"

"'Cause you like it when I want my mom."

Emily pressed her lips together. *This is not a story. It doesn't matter if he's nice sometimes, he's still the Chocolate Man.* "'Cause you like it when I'm unhappy, or scared," she went on. "And maybe somebody made you scared."

The Chocolate Man made a sound like a bark: a laugh or a cry. Emily shrank back but she kept talking. "That's what you want, isn't it? For me to be scared and want my mom? So you can feel like—like a bigshot."

The Chocolate Man was shaking his head, back and forth; he might have been crying. He said something but she couldn't hear it.

"What?"

"I don't want to hurt you."

Emily stared "Then wh—"

"I want to hurt the mothers. All the mothers. Even if I don't take their kids. I want them to be afraid of me."

"I'm afraid of you."

"I didn't want any of the—I never knew one of them this long, before. I never took a girl, before."

"But—" Emily looked for words. "But my mother is still going to love me, even if I never come home."

"I know," the Chocolate Man said miserably.

"So you can't stop her loving me."

The Chocolate Man nodded, his head toward the floor. After a long time he said, "I really have to go to work now."

"The closet?"

"Uh-huh."

"Oh. Okay." Emily sat very still while he untied her wrist. Then she got up, and with her back to him she said, "Didn't anybody love you?"

And she turned to see the Chocolate Man slowly shaking his head, back and forth: *no*.

8:00 A.M.

THE CHOCOLATE MAN WAS IN THE BACK ROOM OF the liquor store, trying not to look at the numbers on the tops and backs and sides of the boxes stacked almost to the ceiling all around him. He had gone to work because he always went to work; even when he was sick. He wasn't going to stay—Château Lafitte 1989: one two three four five six seven—but he thought it would look better if he showed up. If he didn't, Bill might call the police or something. And he would go back to work after he made his call. That way no one would suspect—Bill wouldn't suspect. (Somebody must have sent the police to his house, and he guessed it wasn't the old man—Château Dordogne 1978: one two three four five six seven—because he would have come with the police if it had been him.)

George tried not to be nervous. Bill was nervous today; he was sharper than usual: "Move your ass, George, I got four deliveries have to be out before ten. And don't spend all damn day in the storage room." And Bill didn't talk like that, he never minded that George was slow. Maybe he knew something; George stood still with fear. Château Margaux 1987: one two three four five six seven. Bill thought George was stupid; that was okay. And if he knew something, he wouldn't just let George keep working, would he? George picked the box up and tucked it under his chin so he couldn't be distracted by the numbers. He closed his eyes as he left the room; he always did that. His feet were sure as a blind man's, but there was another danger. Three steps to the door; one two three four five six seven. Two steps around the big cardboard cutout next to the door; one two three four five six seven. And once he was among the aisles he had to open his eyes. He looked at the floor then, because there were traps everywhere.

He had become good at avoiding traps. He would sing songs in his head: "Mary Had a Little Lamb," "Michael, Row the Boat Ashore." Now he tried to remember the words to the song Emily had taught him: *In a wagon, bound for market, there's a calf with a something eye.* And soon he was at the front of the store, and he could say, "Where do you want this, Bill?" just like anybody.

"Over by the register. The sp—the Hispanic kid'll get it, what's his name, Jaime." And George put the box down and got caught: Château Margaux 1987: one two three four five—Bill was talking to a deliveryman at the counter. Six seven.

"Yeah, Phil, I've got to get another two cases of that red—the eighty-seven. George, go check the year on the Lafitte. The red. It's in the back room, we got I think one case, it's in the front, about two rows down, three boxes up, something like that."

George stood still until he stopped counting.

"George, go check the red. We got a million things to do here, so go." And as the Chocolate

Man started toward the back, "And don't take too long in there. Jesus," to the deliveryman, "sometimes I think—well . . . " and the deliveryman said, "Ah, hell, he's just slow. You got a heart, Bill. Anybody else would have put him out on the street." And they watched the Chocolate Man shuffle slowly back down the aisle toward the storage room.

NORTHERN BOULEVARD WAS NOTHING BUT GRAY. The sky, the buildings, the used-car lots with their scrawled white offers; all the cars could have been gray. It could still have been night here, where the bars looked the same open or closed, where the churches were ubiquitous and anonymous as the bars, and could have been open or closed.

The day before Christmas. Laurie searched the dirty sidewalks for a revelation. Ninety-eighth Street, Ninety-ninth. Two men standing outside a boarded storefront, gesturing anger with their hands. One Hundredth Street, One Hundred First. A woman and a small child, hand in hand, the mother pointing to three strutting pigeons; Laurie could see the child's laugh.

One Hundred Second Street. The phone booth stood alone on the corner, too bright a blue. Laurie slid the car to a stop, but the wheels were shrieking in her mind, she was already out of the shaking car and at the booth before she had braked smoothly to a stop.

The street corner was empty. Laurie didn't know what she had expected: the police, a curious crowd, the Chocolate Man's footprints in the dry cement in front of the phone booth? Laurie stood uncertainly. All her pain and rage and courage had taken her here. There was garbage on the sidewalk, broken glass in the street. A torn flier flapped on a storefront window: INTERNATIONAL DINNER, SATURDAY JANUARY THIRD. CHRIST CHURCH OF POSSIBILITIES. The phone booth hung spectral in the flat morning light. Somebody had written, FLY MAN, across one side of the glass in red paint; the glass was missing from the other side.

Laurie walked toward the phone. She was terribly afraid now, as if the Chocolate Man might actually be hiding behind the narrow steel shaft that held up the booth, might jump suddenly from the empty steps of a boarded-up church.

The phone hung neatly, ready to use. Silver that rejected light, refusing to reflect. Laurie couldn't hear the day around her, the cars going by and the fragmented voices across the street, down the block; it was night inside her and she heard the disembodied threats and flat truths of the Chocolate Man and whoever, whatever, had been speaking around him. "You gonna *move?*" "You won't find us." Laurie walked quickly toward the phone booth and stepped in.

And in a moment she was in the Chocolate Man's world. He picked the phone up—*here,* she thought, *and held it to his ear.* There was no sound at all inside the receiver; Laurie half expected the sucking sound of the sea. Her eyes were closed and she didn't know it, it was cold night inside her head. What had the voices said? *You ain't never seen a good person*—Laurie's eyes snapped open and her hand was sweaty on the receiver.

"—happening here?" a voice thundered at her ear. She broke away from the phone booth and the spell was ended: but a stocky man confronted her with an angry face.

"What do you think is happening here?" he yelled. "Now, on the corner of One-O-Two Street and Northern Boulevard, in these United States of America?" Great booming words without meaning; only intention.

"I'm looking for anyone who was near this phone booth last night," Laurie said steadily. This man could not be worse than the Chocolate Man.

"Is this a *free* phone here? Is this an *equal-access* phone here?"

"There was a white man here at about eight-fifteen last night," Laurie said carefully, "blond hair, medium height. I need to know if anyone saw him."

"You are not of this neighborhood." The man stepped closer and Laurie managed not to step back. "You are not of my color. Do you know what is happening now in the world today?"

"Yes," snapped Laurie, suddenly impatient, "someone has kidnapped my daughter, and he phoned me from here last night."

Her bravery seemed almost to frighten the man. He took a step back and drew himself up and executed a sharp balletic kick at the air in front of her face; she shied back. "And I've never seen a good person in my whole life," she said angrily. There was nothing he could do except slow her down. "You were here. I heard you. Please," quieter, searching behind his eyes, "he has my daughter. I have to—"

"The police are white," the man said abruptly, "why don't you talk to them?"

"Because the police didn't catch him. They weren't here. You were. Please—for a child—do you remember anything about the man?"

"The Man? Do I know anything about—"

"He killed a black child too," Laurie said desperately, "a little black boy. And I heard another voice," she said quickly, seeing pain and anger now for the boy, and fearing it, "a woman's voice. If I could find her and talk to her—"

" 'And I saw three unclean spirits like frogs come out of the mouth of the dragon—' There are black children dying right here in this neighborhood, dying in spirit, dying in soul—" Laurie turned away and slid down the metal support bar of the phone until she was sitting on cold cement. He was right, of course, why should he care about the particulars of her crisis? For a few minutes last night the Chocolate Man had not been invisible; he had walked up this street, put a coin in the pay phone. And the witness hadn't seen him. An intruder; prey; a threat to be threatened. Laurie was crying now, because this was the end, here on the cold ground in a place she didn't belong, with a lunatic for company and time running out.

"Keisha," the man said in her ear. Laurie jerked away from his sudden kneeling closeness and snapped the back of her head against the metal bar. "Her name is Keisha." Laurie's eyes filled with tears; the man's face was blurred. "She's just a girl. She was here when that man called. That Chocolate

Man." And he stood and laughed and laughed and laughed.

Laurie lifted herself slowly from the sidewalk, noticing the grit of dirt against her palms. "Keisha," she said.

"She works this corner. I was telling him—that Chocolate Man"—laughing and laughing—"what he was doing wrong, being here. 'He that hath ears to hear, let him hear.' Make you fishers of men. Now, do I look like a fisher of men?"

"No," said Laurie. Keisha. *She works this corner.* A prostitute. With a lunatic for a friend.

"Neither did he." The man bent into Laurie's face, his breath alcohol and smoke.

"Do you want a cigarette?" Laurie asked quickly. He was quiet while her hands were busy. There were more people on the street now, three boys with skateboards and bikes, a woman on her way to work; Laurie wanted to ask them about Keisha.

"Hundred Third Street," the man said placidly, lighting the cigarette from a match in Laurie's hand; she had not wanted to hand him a pack of fire.

The match burned Laurie's fingers. She dropped it and rubbed her fingers together and waited.

"Third house in. Third floor. Back, I think." He inhaled and smiled.

"Thank you," Laurie said. She wanted to put her burned fingers in her mouth. "I appreciate it."

"Appreciate? Ap*pre*ciate? Do you know who I *am*?"

"No," said Laurie softly, "but I thank you," and she turned quickly from what showed on his face. He was screaming at the phone booth as she got in her car, raining insults and straight-handed chops at the air all around it while Laurie drove slowly down the street toward gray sky and tenements and hope.

EMILY HAD BECOME USED TO THE CONFINES OF THE closet; the smell was a lot like the smell of her mother's closet at home: cedar and something that might be starch, or soap, and faint sweat. Her mother's closet also smelled of the perfume she wore, Cinnabar. Sometimes after Emily's bath her mother let her powder herself with Cinnabar talc; it made her feel like Greta Garbo or Bette Davis.

The Chocolate Man said he didn't want to hurt her. She was still afraid, in fierce flashes that took her breath and whipped her heart. Even this morning it had happened, when the closet door closed; Emily could not stop her hands from reaching for the knob, shaking it; but she was embarrassed too—he might hear her. And she was instantly afraid: he said he didn't want to hurt her, but he needed her suffering, it fueled whatever rage or sorrow that drove him.

He wanted to hear her cry again so he would be able to kill her.

Emily had held on to the doorknob with both hands, her head down, waiting for her heart to burst from beating.

George had forgotten to leave anything for her to drink, and she wasn't hungry. The police had gone away last night. Emily had tried and tried not to think about that. They had gone away, and George had killed the old man from across the street because he'd come to save her. The police thought she was Spot; she'd figured that out. And the old man was dead. So nobody would be looking for her here anymore. She might as well get used to it. *He tried to take you away from me, so I killed him.* It was funny how that made her feel. As though he thought she belonged to him. As though maybe she did.

When Emily got scared it came all at once, and then if she waited a minute usually it went away. It was Christmas Eve; how long would it be before the police stopped looking for her altogether? On Christmas morning Emily's mother made her hot chocolate with real whipped cream, she always said the cream came from Santa, even though she knew Emily hadn't believed in Santa for a long time. The cream was so rich it made her a little sick, but that was part of Christmas, too, opening her stocking at the kitchen table while her mother kept telling her not to get whipped cream all over everything.

After what seemed a long time she became aware of the television's familiar drone. Emily wished the Chocolate Man had MTV, but the TV in the closet didn't get cable. Even Channel Eleven was just a flickering blur that turned to red and green as she stared at it. The Chocolate Man had turned the TV to *Sesame Street* before he left. Emily was too old for *Sesame Street*.

She sat for a time looking at the once-beloved figures of Ernie and Bert, Telly, and the little red monster whose name she couldn't remember. He had been her favorite, in her dim memories of being very small it was his red fur face that occupied the television screen.

Watching now, she started quietly to cry. Maybe the Chocolate Man wouldn't kill her, but she knew now that he would never let her go. She had read a book her mother took out from the library, about a boy who was kidnapped when he was seven years old and not found again until he was twelve or thirteen. He lived for years with an older man who made him "perform" things Emily didn't understand, there was the word *fellatio;* her mother had forbidden her to read that book.

Emily had heard rumors about sex: to her it was the half-naked young women going by on the sides of city buses, the vague androgynous aggression of the fashion ads in magazines, the mystifying glances between Greta Garbo and Robert Taylor.

Was she going to have to live with the Chocolate Man and be his daughter, washing his clothes and making breakfast? Was he going to make her "perform" things, sex things, and go to a strange school under a different name, was he going to make her sleep under the bed every night?

When her mother found a picture Emily had drawn—a beach, a yellow umbrella, a cat in the water—tucked inside the book's pages, she had taken away Emily's library privileges for two weeks.

What if her mother didn't want her back? She had read that book. She had gone too far away in the park. Two months ago she had stolen a pen from Woolworth's, the gleam of the gold nib on a black-velvet bed too much to resist, the hard shiny body of the pen opalescent like the body of a dragonfly.

Her mother didn't know about that. Or did she? Had she guessed, did she know that Emily was not a good person—because that was the truth. Maybe God had let the Chocolate Man kidnap her because He knew she wasn't good. She hadn't cried for her daddy when he left; and she had lied to her mother about it. But how could her mother understand what Emily cried for? And that time when she ran through the glass door: wouldn't her mother hate her if she knew that Emily had done it on purpose?

Maybe her mother already hated her. Maybe she was glad to be rid of her. Emily stared at the brown snake of wire under the door. Now she was a news story, a freak. Her father had probably seen her on the TV, her friends at school had seen her. She was nothing but a name now, Victim Number Eight of the Chocolate Man.

It seemed as if everything had conspired to leave her, at last, here in this place.

She remembered them talking, yesterday on the TV news: "If the police were not proceeding on the assumption that little Emily Lookinland has indeed been kidnapped by the Chocolate Man, the FBI would not be called into the case until twenty-four hours had elapsed, in accordance with the Lindbergh Law, which was enacted in the wake of the notorious 1932 kidnapping of the Lindbergh baby." There was going to be a special on *Nightline*,

about famous kidnapping cases from the early part
of the century. Leopold and Loeb—names she had
never heard—and of course the smiling blond
Lindbergh child, dead now sixty-four years.

Emily stared now at the little red *Sesame Street*
monster. She and her mother had watched a documentary about the Lindbergh baby. Sixty-four
years. That was a long time to be dead. Up in
heaven, was the baby still not yet two years old,
unable to say more than a few words; did the angels
change his diapers?

Suddenly the TV picture seemed far away and
Emily could hear a thudding shush, like the ocean,
in her ears. She could not hear the TV. She seemed
to be floating above herself, and behind; she was
aware of the blood flowing through her body.

Someday I won't exist, she thought. It seemed
as if already she was diminished, she wanted to
look at herself in a mirror. *My eyes will be eaten by
worms,* she thought, and she wanted violently to
be completely outside her body, free of its
inevitable rot. *I'll just be bones and hair,* she
thought; *I can see the TV now but someday I won't
see anything, I won't hear, that's my blood thump-
ing, even if the Chocolate Man doesn't kill me I'm
going to be dead someday.*

Emily dug her fingernails into the palm of her
hand. *I can feel that. I'm not dead.* But still she
could not hear, or see; there was a film over her
vision and blood beating in her ears. "I'm going to
be dead," she said out loud. She knew it was true.
In an hour or eighty years she was going to stop
breathing and die and be nothing.

Emily curled into a fetal ball on the floor of the closet. *Elmo,* she thought inanely, *the little monster's name is Elmo, and I am going to die.*

And she waited for the Chocolate Man to come home.

8:17 A.M.

KEISHA WORE SWEATPANTS AND A SWEATSHIRT WITH a hood and stamped her feet against the cold. Dian was sitting across the kitchen from her wearing a thick sweater, Keisha's baby easy in her lap.

"You'd think Mr. Tasker would have fixed the heat before Christmas Eve," Dian was saying.

Keisha waved her hand, soapy with cold water from the sink. "Well, he didn't. You still got coffee or should I make some more?"

"I've still got. Keisha," causing Keisha to turn from the sink, "what's this? 'International Dinner, Saturday January Third.'" Dian was reading from a torn flier lying on the edge of Keisha's bed.

"We oughta go to that," Keisha said seriously, turning back to the dishes.

Dian was bouncing Tanzy on her lap. "Oh, yeah, I can see it: you, me, and the old ladies of the Church of Possibilities," and the baby screamed with pleasure, "discussing Christ's second coming or some shit."

Keisha shook her head and smiled. She would like to have an international dinner with the ladies of the Church of Possibilities. Dian had come over early, just at seven she was there at the door with coffee in Styrofoam cups. Keisha had known before she opened the door; she didn't ask Dian why she'd come. The smell of coffee filled the apartment and made it warmer.

Keisha started humming at the sink, "The Battle Hymn of the Republic"—*As he died to make men holy, let us die to make men free*—she remembered that from when she was little, her mother at the sink singing freedom. It was good to have Dian there. To be with somebody on Christmas Eve, not out on the street like most mornings looking for nothing at the side of Northern Boulevard, where it was no colder than in her own kitchen.

Keisha shivered at the sink. She was still humming but her back felt naked all of a sudden. She was looking at the soapy water, but all she could see was the Chocolate Man, over and over, coming up to the phone booth on the boulevard last night, fumbling with change. Taking a long time; Keisha hadn't thought she'd even noticed him before Frank started bothering him. But he was there now, in her head and on the street in the dark, how could she not have known? To have been that close to evil and not feel a thing.

She would have gotten into a car with that man.

Dian was still talking, why couldn't she go to church, have a normal life? Because she let men touch her. Keisha finished up the dishes and turned to her friend and her baby with that naked feeling still down her back.

"You're real good with her, you know that?" Keisha lighted a cigarette, her fingers dampening the matches; she lighted one for Dian, too. "Where's your little boy?"

"He's still out in Floral Park," Dian said, smiling into Tanzy's face. "Koo-koo, little girl, koo-koo. My aunt, she wants me to let her have him permanent. 'Cause the schools there are better—she says. He's only three, I tell you that woman—" The baby let out a howling chortle and batted Dian's neck with a balled-up fist. "Hey, girl, what're you doing? I swear, you're tougher than my Dorian. She takes after you, Keisha."

"She sure as shit don't take after—"

There was a soft knock on the door.

"That's Kitty," Keisha said, "she said she'd be coming sometime today to take Tanzy to see her cousin's kids, she's taking care of the whole lot of them"—walking toward the door shaking her hands to dry them, scooping Tanzy from Dian's lap as she went—"she's sure early though, I didn't think—oh."

The woman in the door was pale and resolute. "I'm sorry," she said, looking almost immediately past Keisha to Dian.

Her voice was calm and frightening.

"I was told this was where I could find a young woman who'd seen a man making a phone call last night on Northern Boulevard."

"That would be me," Keisha said, and she watched the woman's eyes dart from Dian back to her and Tanzy and back to her face, startled.

"Oh. Well—"

"Who told you?" Keisha was angry; she knew what the woman had been told.

The woman sighed. She seemed hardly able to stand. "There was a man by the phone booth when I got there this morning. He was—agitated."

Keisha took the woman's arm suddenly and pulled her gently into the room. "That's Frank," she said. She knew who the woman was; she felt fear in a fine line slither up her back. "Don't you mind what he says. He's just full of pain."

"Full of *shit*," Dian said. Keisha offered the baby and she took her; Tanzy mewed.

"You want some coffee?" Keisha asked the woman, ignoring Dian's asking eyes.

"You the police?" Dian asked. The woman turned to her, she seemed about to fall. "'Cause you don't look it."

"She's not the police," Keisha said, setting a pot of water to boil. "She's Lauren Lookinland."

Dian gasped.

"How did you know?" the woman asked. She seemed frightened and strangely placid at the same time.

"'Cause I know who that man at the phone booth was."

Dian lurched in her seat. "You mean—"

"I saw that man," Keisha said softly to the woman. She walked to her and looked into her face. "The Chocolate Man."

"Please," the woman said, "tell me what you saw." Tanzy laughed and they all looked at her for a moment. "Hush, girl," Dian said, soft and stern.

"Well," Keisha began, kneeling and taking the woman's hand, "I was—I was out. And Frank was there, he's crazy. And Dian, of course," nodding to the other girl, "'cause we look out for each other. I had to leave my Tanzy, I felt bad. Tanzy, she's my daughter."

The baby was sucking her fist now and staring with big eyes at the woman. She wore bright colored barrettes at the ends of little braids all around her head. A red bear, a purple duck, a white poodle.

The woman was staring at the barrettes. Keisha reached to touch her hand protectively to her baby's head and the woman shuddered. "Please," she said, "go on."

"I called the cop who was there. Miller. I know him. I called because I remembered something. Last night. I didn't talk to him, though. He was supposed to call me back." She sighed with disgust and said, "I can tell you, though. I'll tell you the whole story, just like you were the cops."

"Yes," Laurie breathed. "Please."

"Well—like I say I was out. This man—the Chocolate Man—he made a phone call. God, I wish I'd known what he was doing."

"He was calling me," the woman said with something like wonder. She seemed to be shaking herself awake; with each new piece of information she moved her head slowly from side to side.

"I saw your girl on the TV," Dian said. "She's sure a cute little girl." They were silent, looking at Keisha's baby; the woman's head was still moving from side to side.

Keisha sighed. "Well, he made his call, and Frank started right away going after him. Frank's *crazy*. He was kicking at him, and he was saying all this stupid shit, like he's the Holy Ghost and shit. And then the cops came. Man, that Chocolate Man was scared, he was more scared of the cops, though. I tell you he ran *fast*."

"Which way did he run?"

"Right up A Hundred Second, he was *gone*."

"Did you see his car?"

"No, I didn't see any car. The cops came, the guy went around the corner and two cops went after him but he must have got away, 'cause they came right back."

"Can you tell me anything—"

The baby was mewing aimlessly in Dian's arms again, almost singing. The woman was still looking at her; she began to shake: her hand in Keisha's was trembling. Keisha gripped it tighter and put her other hand on the woman's shoulder. "Hush, Tanzy girl. He wore blue jeans. Heavy boots. He wasn't carrying nothing. He had that look—like some white guys get—like he was an animal, you know? Scared like that. Frank scared the shit out of him."

"But he didn't have—" The woman's face was resolute and covered with tears. "He didn't have anybody with him."

"No," said Keisha. "I'm sorry."

The woman nodded; she started to get up.

"Wait a minute," said Keisha. "Before he left, when Frank was bothering him, I saw his jacket. I called that Task Force number last night about that jacket, but I don't think the man I talked to really paid me much mind."

The woman's head was lifted like a fox's, scenting the wind. "Was there anything special about his jacket?"

"Yeah. It was dark, blue, I think. And it had a lining, I could tell 'cause it kind of went out around him, you know? Like he was small inside it. And anyway, it had some writing on it, I forgot to tell the cops when they were here, they were in such a hurry anyway they didn't want to talk to no black hook— oh," with a little exhalation; "It doesn't matter," the woman said quickly.

"'Cause I've been run in before, six, seven times," Keisha said, and the woman said again, "It doesn't matter," and the baby chortled.

"Okay. So—it was a dark jacket, just to his waist, and it had writing on the back, I don't remember what it said exactly. I'm real sorry about that now. I was watching Frank, mostly, I didn't want him to hurt that man. Man, was I wrong." She laughed sadly. "Anyway, it was the name of a liquor store. It was a bird name, some bird Liquors. Like Sparrow, or Swallow, or something. I don't know many bird names. Like I say that man last night didn't listen to me at *all*."

A bird. Sparrow, or Swallow. "You're sure it began with an *S*? And that it was a liquor store?"

"Oh yeah. I don't do drugs like most of the other girls. I've got responsibilities. I know it was some bird, I only wish I could remember it. And it was a liquor store for sure, yes."

The woman was quiet. Keisha thought maybe she was praying. Then she said, "Thank you, Keisha. Will you do something for me?"

"Anything I can."

"Will you call the police again? Tell them you saw me. Tell them what you told me."

"'Course I will, but I don't know if those cops—"

"They'll listen. Tell them I told you to call and they'll listen."

The pot of water boiled, hissing on the stove.

The woman jumped as though she'd been sleeping. She was already shaking her head no to coffee. "I'm sorry," she said, "I have to—" and stopped, standing. She reached to touch the baby's little hand. "Tanzy," she said.

"Yeah," said Keisha, turning to take the baby from Dian. "Tanzara. She's my joy."

The woman's mouth was quivering. "She's beautiful," she said, taking a step backward. "Beautiful." She was at the door; she almost backed into it.

"Hey—lady," said Dian. She stopped abruptly. "Be careful."

The woman looked at the door; she nodded and said, "Thank you," again and opened the door. The water hissed and sputtered on the stove.

"Mrs. Lookinland?" Keisha began, and Laurie turned back. "My Tanzy, she likes to look at birds. You find that man, Mrs. Lookinland. You find your daughter. You'll be in my prayers."

"Thank you," the woman said. She looked for a moment more at Tanzy as the baby laughed. "You'll be in mine, too."

EMILY'S SONG WAS IN HIS HEAD, BUT IT WAS DIFFER-
ent. *In a wagon, bound for market*—but not in her
voice. Not in his. The Chocolate Man was walking
down the block away from the liquor store. There
was a phone booth two blocks away. He stopped
walking: one two three four five six seven. He
hadn't heard that voice in such a long time; not his
mother's voice. Not when he took a child, not after.
He had talked to Emily about it, in the kitchen. He
didn't like to think of her that way—Emily, with a
name—but he couldn't help it. When she spilled
the Yoo-Hoo he was so mad. He had to clean up:
the Chocolate Man stopped on the sidewalk and
counted: six times with the wipe, one two three four
five six seven . . . two Yoo-Hoos, one two three four
five six seven . . . When he was a child he'd heard
that voice sometimes. At first it had frightened him.
But then it said nice things: when he was in the
closet, when he put the dirty clothes in the washing
machine. Sometimes it sang. Not a woman's voice,
not a man's.

He had told Bill he needed to run an errand.
Bill was angry; and he almost said something, too,
but the voice started again, so the Chocolate Man
didn't pay attention to Bill. *You'd better be back here*

in five minutes; one two three four five six seven—
the voice had been in his head since yesterday. Since
Emily. At first he was frightened, but then he
remembered, and Emily had had a pretend friend
once. So he guessed it was okay.

Now the voice was singing Emily's song. *Stop
complaining, said the farmer*—he was going to call
her mother now. Usually that made him happy. But
it was different—*who told you what has to be*—
because he didn't know what he was going to say.
Even the first time—one two three . . . he had
known what he was going to say. But it would be all
right; the voice was going to tell him, and he would
say it. *Like the swallow, so strong and free.* The voice
was singing and talking. This time it was going to
be different. Not like the others. When he was a little boy he hadn't been able to stop the voice until
he burned down the house.

And now the voice was back. The voice would
tell him everything he had to do, and he would do
it. As the Chocolate Man walked down the street
away from the liquor store he was snapping his fingers, over and over and over.

8:19 A.M.

Carolyn looked at her watch; she had looked at her watch a moment ago; she would look again in a few seconds. Sergeant Mohammad stood next to the sofa where she sat, and periodically he put his hand on her shoulder. "He's not going to call, is he?" she asked. She was looking at the Christmas tree, which stood undecorated in the corner. Laurie and Emily always decorated the tree on Christmas Eve. Mohammad didn't answer; he squeezed her shoulder.

"You can trace him if he does call," Carolyn said hesitantly, not asking.

"Yes," said Mohammad, "it's not like it used to be, we can trace a call right away."

The Chocolate Man could call any moment. Carolyn was so afraid. Sergeant Mohammad had looked at her sternly and said, "This is not a game, any of it. If the Chocolate Man realizes that you're not Laurie—" and Carolyn hadn't had the right to cry; she wanted to tell him that of course she knew that, she loved Emily, too, she loved Laurie. But Sergeant Mohammad went on: "That was a childish stunt Laurie pulled, thinking she can solve this thing alone. Now I've got her to worry about, too. And it was foolish and childish of you to help her. Our only hope lies in listening to the Chocolate Man, seeing if we can get him to make a slip on the phone, give away something. Emily's life depends on it. And now Emily's life may depend on you. Now that Laurie's gone off on some cockamamie"—he made *cockamamie* sound like a curse word—"I understand," Carolyn said. He didn't have to lecture her, Carolyn was always going to have to live with this: this room, this weather, Mohammad's voice, and Laurie's voice pleading, "Help me." With the smell of gin. With the smell of coffee. With the still, menacing air before the telephone rang.

And when it did she was perfectly calm. She waited until the first ring died away completely and Sergeant Mohammad nodded his head. Carolyn was quite beyond nervousness; "Hello," she said, softening and deepening her voice. So it would sound like Laurie's voice.

There was a pause of dead air. Carolyn waited. And then a voice spoke rapidly and Carolyn turned, confused, to Sergeant Mohammad, who came in two strides and took the receiver roughly from her hand.

8:20 A.M.

ED WAS STANDING, LOOKING AT A GREEN WALL IN THE Task Force room. Behind him phones rang in shrill, uneven counterpoint and fingers hit computer keyboards without any noise at all. The paint on the wall was old and flaking. Marcy was taking calls; Ed felt awful for her but there was nothing he could do. Lieutenant Monsey refused to speed up the process of getting a warrant on George Riehle, and it was Christmas Eve, people were coming late to work and starting slow. Maybe Emily Lookinland was dead now. And maybe that was Ed's fault.

"Hey, Hoag," a voice called from across the room. It sounded too loud; Ed was already annoyed before he turned.

"You gonna get the phone?" It was Renny Argule, and he was annoyed, too. "These goddamn things are ringing off the hook." Already he was turning away. Ed felt a flash of anger; but Renny was right. Several times Ed had heard the other officers talking about "the wild-goose chase." Ed hoped Marcy hadn't heard it. Irritation and adrenaline hardened in his throat as he picked up the phone.

"Sergeant Hoag." Ed regretted instantly the impatience in his voice. Maybe this tip—but he was too late, the line already seemed dead. "Sergeant Hoag speaking," Ed said again, and he heard a little intake of breath and felt fear ripple over the skin at the back of his neck.

There was nothing. And then a familiar voice: "I like Emily."

Ed was so shocked—and so angry—that he couldn't say anything.

"Uh-huh," the Chocolate Man went on, "she's a nice girl."

Ed looked at the clock on the wall: it was exactly eight-twenty.

"Then bring her back," Ed spat, and was immediately sorry: now the Chocolate Man knew he had hurt him.

But he only said, "Oh, I can't do that." As though it were self-evident. "You have to give me a ransom." Ed couldn't see Marcy; he signaled to Argule, who said, "What?" in a perfectly normal voice, and Ed motioned quiet with his hand.

"Now, officer," said the Chocolate Man easily, "you're not trying to trace this call, are you?" And Ed said slowly, "What do you want me to do?" and Argule was standing next to him now and Ed signaled for a pen.

"Because I could just hang up and you'd never know where to look."

"These phones aren't wired for a trace." Ed sighed angrily and wrote *CM* on the edge of an envelope on the desk.

"Just tell me—" Ed checked himself; slowed, and softened. "—what do you want?"

"Dover. That's Delaware. Eight-twenty tonight." The Chocolate Man's voice had gone hard; Ed felt fear running down his arms and legs. "Exit Twelve on I-95." There was a pause. "First phone you see."

Marcy had told Ed it was going to snow. Only the man at the other end of the line knew if Emily would be alive to see it. Argule had disappeared; Ed could hear him excited in the hallway, he hoped the Chocolate Man couldn't hear him, too.

"Please—" Ed wiped at his eyes: anger, fatigue, hope. "—are you taking good care of her?"

But the line had gone dead.

When Marcy came into the room her partner was staring at the telephone receiver in his hand. And when he looked up his face was awful.

"For God's sake, Ed—" Marcy began, but his face stopped her. She walked quickly to him, searching his eyes: anger and remorse and a terrible, quiet fear. Marcy said nothing; she felt in his breast pocket for a cigar while she scanned his eyes.

His heart beat fast under her fingers. She found the cigar and held it to his lips. He didn't take it, he said, "I dialed star-fucking-sixty-nine and it just rings and rings and rings. It's still ringing."

The red-orange flame flared from Marcy's lighter. She waited. "It was him," Ed said finally. "George Riehle." He took the cigar from Marcy's hand and smiled ruefully at it. "We'll be able to get the trace off the line now. As long as I don't hang up."

"Ed," Marcy said, taking his hand; it was ice. "What did he say?"

Ed laughed. "He said he likes Emily. That she's a nice girl."

Marcy bit a sharp intake of air and sank into the chair next to the desk. "Did he say he'd molested her?"

Ed shook his head, he held the receiver up to his ear for a moment; "When are the phone guys going to get here?"

"Ed—"

"No, Marcy, he didn't. He wants us to go to Dover."

Marcy felt dizzy, she felt herself rising above her body; she leaned her head back and said, "She's alive."

"Marcy," said Ed softly—he seemed to have recovered himself—"Marcy, I know this looks good—you may not know how deeply I feel about getting Emily back, but—"

"Let her be alive!" Marcy cried. Tears were streaming down her face, and she was laughing. "Let her be alive for me, just for the next twelve hours." And inside she was thinking, holding on to Ed's hand and feeling her tears falling on his skin, *She's alive. It's not too late she's alive she's alive she's alive.*

And Ed said, "Shit," and slammed down the phone. Marcy looked up; "Somebody hung up the *fucking*—" and she forgot herself, and leaned and gripped his shoulder and said, "Don't worry, partner," smiling into his eyes, "we're going to get Emily home for Christmas."

THE CHOCOLATE MAN HURRIED DOWN THE STREET away from the phone booth. He shouldn't have said those nice things about Emily. Part of him felt bad because he did mean them. But he had only said them because he was told to. Something about hope—*Where there is hope there will be more pain.*

The Chocolate Man shivered in his warm coat. *It will be different this time,* the voice said; he walked along, looking up at the mackerel sky and listening. *Mackerel sky, someone's going to cry.* The Chocolate Man didn't know whether he'd heard that somewhere or made it up. Or if the voice had made it up.

There were a few flakes of snow falling. The street was busy here, Union Turnpike just two blocks down from the liquor store. The Chocolate Man looked away from the people, up into the empty sky, as he walked back to work.

LAURIE HAD TO FIND A TELEPHONE. SHE WAS FRIGHT-
ened in earnest now: that girl had seen the Chocolate Man, he was real. He had stood in that phone
booth by the side of Northern Boulevard in the dark:
had he spoken to the girl? Laurie wished she had
asked her to tell her everything, like a teenager with
a crush: What was he wearing? Did he talk about me?

But the Chocolate Man was an apparition after
all. Because he had disappeared completely. No car,
no strands of hair or flakes of sloughed-off skin.
What had the police found on several of the bodies?
(Laurie barely noticed the traffic; her hands were
shaking, she was nauseated and all she could think
of was that beautiful young girl and her tiny baby,
and how the girl had lifted the baby's hand to wave
good-bye.) Carpet fibers, blue and green. Where
was Emily? She had to be somewhere while he made
his calls: were there carpet fibers in her daughter's
hair?

Laurie had to pull the car over. There was an
exit and she took it: UTOPIA. She would have
laughed at that if she could.

She parked just after the exit slope, thinking,
I'm in Utopia. It was what she didn't know that
hurt the most. She gripped the wheel; she watched

herself grip the wheel. She made herself pay attention to how the wheel felt, how her skin felt. How her fingertips felt in the icy air from the car window.

These things were real. The blank gray asphalt out the window, the open bay of a gas station across the street, with faint white silhouettes of naked women in the walls. The blue and white of a pay telephone—and Laurie was out of the car and hurrying across the street. For some reason gas stations always made her think of summer.

The air was biting now, it slid up Laurie's arms and down the back of her neck. *Jack Frost nipping at your nose,* and Laurie was crying, it was so stupid, she couldn't find a quarter, that was all. She stood in the street feeling around in her bag for a quarter and that was all there was, until a car horn honked and she tripped up the curb and almost fell.

Her fingers were nearly numb. She didn't want to go into the gas station. The men in these places had hard eyes, Laurie didn't like to walk past them on a summer day; they said, "Bouncy, bouncy," to her light dresses, they made suggestions to one another behind her stiff, receding back. Laurie felt the same angry awareness of her body now. It was something else to them than it was to her. They had their own way of judging its realness, they could feel it in their bodies even after it was gone.

But she just walked into the gas-station office. The young man behind the counter looked up and smiled; unconsciously his eyes scanned her body, up and down; *I've got a coat on,* Laurie thought, *you can't even see anything,* but all she said was, "Excuse me, do you have change for a dollar? I need it for the phone," gesturing outside. The young man's eyes slid to her breasts and back up. Behind him a very young woman stretched and pouted on the wall. He saw Laurie notice it and smiled. "Do you have a telephone book?" she asked.

"No such luck," he said; a man to whom any contact is an insinuation; "but I can fix you up with some change."

Laurie looked away before he met her eyes. When she handed him a dollar bill she made sure their fingers didn't touch. She wanted to scream. *What the fuck are you doing, my daughter is missing.* But she just said, "Thank you." She didn't have strength for anything else: only Emily. It was as if she stopped thinking about Emily even for a moment her daughter would be dead. As long as she was looking, as long as she hurt, Emily was alive. It wasn't just that there was hope. Laurie couldn't help feeling that Emily really *was* alive because of her love, of her trying—that her trying was keeping her alive. Like a rope to a drowning man.

So all she said was, "Thank you," because for the young man behind the counter there was nothing happening at all, Laurie was just a pretty woman who wanted some change.

She took her quarters out to the phone, aware of the man's eyes on her. She was aware of her hips moving; she hated that man. When her fingers fumbled at the coin slot she said, "Shit"; she was aware of her fingers and the women on the walls in the open garage and the man's eyes.

But once the coin dropped home all she was aware of was the dial tone sudden in her ear.

Four-one-one. A wait, and then an electronic voice: "Welcome to Bell Eastern. What city, please?"

"Queens."

A pause. "What listing?" A pleasant voice, inhuman.

"I need a liquor store; the name is something—"

"An operator will connect you with that information."

Laurie waited.

"An operator *will* be with you."

Laurie waited.

"Your call *is* important to—" and a ring, and an ordinary voice: "What is it you're looking for?"

"I need the address of a liquor store in Queens, it's called Sparrow or Swallow or something, some name of a bird beginning with S. I'm sorry, I—"

"I'm afraid I need more information than that. Do you know the name of the store?"

"No, I just told you, it begins with an S, I'm sorry but—"

"I can't give you the information you want unless you know the name of the store."

"But I—"

"I don't have any listings under categories, ma'am. I can't access just liquor stores."

There was a pause, Laurie's impotent fury choking her throat. Traffic was moving past in a slow stream of color on the highway; someone had written *Words say more than violence* on the glass of the telephone booth.

"It begins with an S," Laurie said, quietly because she was so angry.

"Well—" This voice controlled everything. Laurie's fingernails drove unconscious cresents into her palm: everything, whether Laurie would be able to get to the Chocolate Man. *But violence feels better* was scrawled underneath.

"Why don't you suggest a name, and I can look it up?"

"Swallow," Laurie said quickly. She didn't dare even say thank you; the woman could stop helping at any time.

"Ah. Well, let's see." A long silence; Laurie noticed the pain in her hand and flexed her fingers.

"We have a Swallow"—Laurie stiffened, there was nothing but this woman's voice—"no, that's a jewelry store. In Astoria. No good. Another?"

"Sparrow." Laurie's mind was blank: what other birds began with *S*? While she waited she tried to think, but she could only think of the song she had taught Emily, the song about the swallow.

"I'm afraid there's no Sparrow Liquors listed." *In a wagon, bound for market, there's a calf with a mournful eye.*

"Okay. Then—wait a minute—" desperate now, suddenly desperate with that song in her mind crowding out sense, she couldn't think of any— "How about Swan?"

While she waited she tried to tame her suddenly wild mind: *And the winds are laughing,* what bird begins with—

"Here we go, Swan Liquors."

And Laurie said, "Oh, good," as though it were a normal thing. And she laughed; what must this woman think she wanted the information for? "I

need the address," she said quickly. "And thank
you, you've been very kind, but I need the address
more than the phone number," and the woman's
patience gave out and she said, "I have to give you
the number first," testily, and Laurie waited a little
eternity while the number played—but she remembered it—and longer, for the woman to come back.

And when she didn't, Laurie dialed Swan
Liquors.

EMILY SAT WITH HER BACK AGAINST THE WALL OF THE closet. The television was on loud, but she wasn't listening to it. Her eyes were closed and her fists were clenched in concentration. She could see the Chocolate Man in her mind; it was very important that she see him. She didn't know why it was important, and she didn't know why it was this image: the Chocolate Man moving haltingly up the front walk, with shuffling feet and vacant eyes; he was *doing* something, that was what teased her now.

Behind her closed eyes she wondered if she was losing her mind. There was a drumming in her head. The Chocolate Man would not leave her; he walked, hesitant and empty, over and over up the front walk.

Emily tried to keep her body calm. The drumming was the blood in her head. She was listening to her heart. She listened to her breathing and became afraid when her lungs emptied: she wanted to be able to breath again, she might die right now.

But she breathed, and the Chocolate Man was still there. He was wearing heavy black boots and his foot hung suspended above the sidewalk— above a crack.

Emily sat up; she forgot about her heart. The

Chocolate Man took another hesitant step in her mind. His foot wavered and came down: he wasn't stepping on the cracks.

The drumming in her head receded. She wasn't going insane. The Chocolate Man was being careful: *Step on a crack, break your mother's back.* That made her feel better. Now she knew something about him. A secret.

Emily made a face and reached for the salami sandwich. One secret. If she could figure out his other secrets, maybe she could figure out some way to get herself out of here.

The salami didn't smell good, but she was hungry, so she ate.

THE WIND WAS FIERCE HERE, ROLLING DOWN THE four-lane street from the east and north; the land was flat, the trees small and bent with wind. The liquor store was on a corner, bright with Christmas red and green, soft with half-clad paper women. A sign hung moving a little, unaware of its importance: SWAN LIQUORS.

Swan Liquors. Just sitting there on the corner as if it weren't the most important building in the world. In spite of what the young girl had told her, Laurie had expected something else, she realized— a cave, a desolate railway trestle, an abandoned building. More likely a bar, open early for the holiday traffic. Someplace dark and forgotten.

As she walked up the block toward Swan Liquors Laurie began to be terribly afraid. Not that she was going to finally face the Chocolate Man, that he was going to be there in the body, a real challenge and a real threat—but that he wasn't. What would she do if he wasn't there? If he refused to become real and stayed a specter, unknowable and therefore free? Laurie quickened her step. And if he was there? Standing ordinary behind the counter making change? It was ludicrous for Laurie to have thought that she could find him, could better the police who had been searching for years. To think that a young hooker could really know what no one else knew, and that Laurie alone could take and use that information. The girl had said that she'd already talked to someone at the Task Force.

And suddenly Laurie was filled with a wild, rushing hope—what if the police had already acted on the girl's late-night tip, what if they had already picked up the Chocolate Man and found Emily? Laurie had kept the news on in the car—"Emily Rose Lookinland, the nine-year-old girl kidnapped by—" She hadn't wanted to listen but she knew she had to. Every five minutes, like the score of the World Series.

But she hurried, now, because surely there would be police cars and TV news cherry pickers in front of Swan Liquors, where the Chocolate Man had been found. It was on a corner so the newspeople were just around the corner; in a minute Laurie would be there, and surely Emily was close by; the police would be happy to see her; they would take her to Emily.

But there were no newspeople, no police. There was nothing at all except a mechanical Santa in the window, and elves, and brightly wrapped presents and brightly colored paper women.

The bell over the door struck a cheery note as Laurie passed through. She stopped just inside the door, and then had to move politely as people went in and out. The store was busy, with hostesses picking up party orders and last-minute shoppers grabbing bottles of sherry or gin. Laurie thought it odd that the store was open, but it fit, somehow, with the rest of this crazy day: if the swan on the awning had barked a hello she would not have been surprised.

At first she saw nothing—rows and rows of bottles, fracturing the overhead lights—and then there was a gray-haired man, and a man in a brown shirt at the counter with his back to her, and a woman in a fur coat holding a bottle by the neck.

Laurie felt sharp disappointment. *There's nothing here,* she thought, and the man behind the counter turned, and Laurie knew.

He was tending to the woman in the fur coat. He was absentmindedly snapping the fingers of his right hand. He was looking right at Laurie.

For an instant she thought he recognized her. Something lit his eyes—and was gone. He was just looking at her.

"May I help you?" the man behind the counter asked. The Chocolate Man.

"A bottle of wine," Laurie said, surprising herself. She sounded, to her own ears at least, completely natural. She moved closer to the Chocolate Man. "Something Christmasy," she said pleasantly.

She saw nothing but his face. His blue eyes were entirely innocent. Laurie noticed that she was clenching her fists, and she made an effort to relax her hands, her face. Surely he would feel her hatred, it was pouring off her in waves. But he only smiled and said, "How about a red one?"

He hadn't noticed anything; Laurie could hear her own pleasant voice discussing the proper wine for poached pears. Suddenly she wished she were drunk, violent, crazy, no-conscience drunk.

But she was trapped in clear-cut reality, and the man who had kidnapped her daughter was getting her a bottle of wine.

She resisted speech, watching him. His lips were moving. It wasn't just the snapping fingers; she knew his profile, his limp hair. He wasn't any taller than she was. Laurie hadn't realized how much she remembered about him. She'd told the police that he'd been too far away, that she hadn't seen his face. When she'd talked to the police sketch artist she had remembered nothing but those snapping fingers.

I can take him, she thought.

After what seemed like a long time (she couldn't stop looking at his hands, what things had he done with those hands?) the Chocolate Man picked out a bottle and walked back behind the counter. When Laurie held out a twenty-dollar bill her hand was not shaking. "That enough?" Her voice was sharp. She softened her face and smiled at him.

The Chocolate Man took the money without looking at it. He seemed dazed. How could he just be standing there, making change? How could there be no mark on his forehead, no identifying sign? So that someone other than God could see his evil.

As he gave her the change his hand touched hers.

"Three forty-two," he said. Laurie's hand was frozen; his skin felt like anyone else's. "Your change," he said, and she looked into his eyes.

They were like anyone else's eyes.

"Yes," she said faintly.

Had he killed her daughter?

"What have you—" She hadn't known she was going to speak, and she stopped herself.

The Chocolate Man's eyebrows were raised, his face tilted. "Excuse me?" He suspected nothing.

The bottle was waiting on the counter. "Thank you," Laurie said, but she didn't turn to go. *Where is she? What have you done with her?*

The Chocolate Man was already waiting on the next customer. How could she walk away? The bell swung imbecilic as she opened the door (did the Chocolate Man look up behind her, did he think she had eyes like Emily's?). The door slammed, and she was outside. She had not pulled the gun and said, "Take me to her." Why? Was the veneer of civilization really so strong? That she could not threaten a stranger in a crowded place. She knew she could shoot him—it was only the presence of other people that stopped her. Her plans for the Chocolate Man were as private as a lover's.

When the time comes, she thought, *it will be as easy as moving my finger,* touching the handle of the gun in her pocket.

She looked up and down the unfamiliar street. There was a lot of sky here, and the buildings were low. A parking lot, a supermarket with big shiny windows, the red door of a Chinese restaurant two blocks down. *When she is safe it will be a pleasure to kill him.* The blue and white of a pay phone two blocks away. It held no interest for her.

Laurie put a hand in her pocket and felt the gun there. The gun metal was cool on her fingers. In her mind she talked to reason: I know I should call the police. But I don't want the police, I want *him*. I don't want warrants and probable cause, and hours of questioning before he cracks. I want him to take me to Emily.

And reason answered her: But he will not do that, he is in the store—and the inane cheery bell went off like a siren and he was there; there were shouts behind him, and some confusion—"Just where do you think you're"—and the Chocolate Man was walking out the liquor-store door directly toward where Laurie stood.

That morning, just before leaving the house, the Chocolate Man had sat in front of the television set tying his shoes, and when he looked up she was there.

"—refused to allow photographers even a glimpse of her face," a voiceover was saying. The woman looked young—twenty-eight or twenty-nine—with light brown hair and dark blue eyes. One two three four five six seven, one two three four five six seven. "But WNZW has received this photogragh from Mrs. Lookinland's ex-husband, Richard Lookinland, who currently lives in Chicago with his second wife." One two three four five six seven. The woman had high cheekbones, and a smile like her daughter's.

"The kidnapper, known to the police as the Chocolate Man, should be calling Mrs. Lookinland sometime this morning. In each of the other seven cases involving this heinous kidnapper, he has made the first call precisely—" One two three four five six seven, one two three four . . .

She was a pretty woman. Why hadn't she wanted her face on the TV? That was the only failure in his plan: the mothers got to be famous, too. It was ironic. Everybody in America knew the victims' names, but nobody knew the Chocolate Man's name.

He stood up. Emily was safe in the closet; now it was time to call Mrs. Lookinland. The Chocolate Man laughed to himself as he went to get his coat. Lauren Lookinland. Young and pretty, with a lovely smile. She probably didn't look too lovely now. He reached to flick off the recording button on the VCR.

Maybe he would show Emily her mother when he got back.

THE CHOCOLATE MAN TURNED THE CORNER. HE had walked by Laurie as though she weren't there. He was walking fast and deliberately; he didn't know he was being followed. Laurie walked deliberately, too, with long firm strides. As she walked she reached into the front pocket of her parka and brought out the gun.

One two three four five six seven, one two three four five six seven, George was walking home with numbers marching in his head. The shock of seeing the little girl's mother had apparently propelled him out the door, because he was almost to his own house and all he could remember was the numbers. Had he just seen her, right there on the corner in back of him? One two three four five six seven, one two three four five six seven, *George,* the voice said suddenly.

George stopped as though his battery had gone dead, in the middle of a step. He listened. "I don't want to," he said aloud, and the voice got angry. He looked up at his house, which was suddenly in front of him. "I wanted to keep her," he said. "Like the nursery rhyme about the woman in the shoe."

✗   ✗   ✗

Laurie carried the gun loosely in her hand: anyone could see it. She didn't speed up when the Chocolate Man disappeared. She moved with the precision and determination of a trained soldier. Ahead of her the Chocolate Man was not in a hurry; he was just walking down the street.

The Chocolate Man stopped. Laurie froze, and almost tripped. The Chocolate Man was gesticulating, he was having an argument with the air.

He was looking up at the house in front of him. It was white, bleeding gray down in great tears where the snow had wet it. He was looking toward the second floor: green shutters with tiny suns on them, closed like eyes.

Laurie could hear pieces of his voice on the air; it had a light timbre, he sounded young. His voice came to her with the cadences of a nursery rhyme: *One, two, buckle my shoe; Bluebird, bluebird; We all fall down.* Had he seen her? *I could kill him now,* Laurie thought. Her hand was firm on the gun. She wanted to kill him.

Laurie stood, bloodthirsty and still, watching the Chocolate Man make his tortuous way up the front walk of the white house.

Emily was sitting up in the closet; a moment ago she had been lying down. She had heard something, she had been sleeping and something woke her up and she had called, "George?" before she knew she was awake.

She had to go to the bathroom. It was his tread, heavy and slow on the floorboards in the hall. She had been dreaming about something nice, and then he was back. She was glad because she had to go to the bathroom and she didn't want to use the pot.

Even and slow, down the hall. He'd said he had to go to work. Emily remembered the newscasts she had seen: the little tarp-covered bundles at the side of the road. It was always night on the TV, the bundles lay in the dark until the police found them with their lights.

Was it dark out now? The boys were always dead long before dark on the second day, Emily knew; the news had said so. By the time the parents went to leave the ransom, twelve hours after the morning phone call, the boys had already been dead a long time. And where did the Chocolate Man keep them until dark? Maybe in the closet where she was now. But that was not to be thought about: the Chocolate Man said he was going to call her mother again. So it would be twelve hours after that.

Had she been sleeping for twelve hours? It was such a nice dream she was having. Her mother was holding her. It was impossible, in the closet, to tell what time it was.

There was nothing at all she could use as a weapon. The cord from the TV, the hangers above her on the rack, the scraps of carpet in the corner, would be no help. She had already tried making noise: screaming would be no help. She had prayed: *Our Father who art in heaven;* heaven had been no help. If she was going to die she was going to; if the Chocolate Man was angry when she died—

"George?" she called again, standing up to get away from her fear. But it stood with her, and closed her throat, so that all that came out of her cry was a pathetic dry whisper: "George?"

The Chocolate Man had disappeared inside the house. There was nobody on the street; most of the houses had their curtains drawn. The Chocolate Man's closed shutters gave the house a blank and eerie look, like a blind man who may not be blind.

Laurie walked down the block until she was directly in front of the house. She stared up at it, the Christmas lights on a house two doors down beating a tattoo of orange and blue at the periphery of her vision.

Emily was in that house. The Chocolate Man could not have had time yet to take her—where? It didn't matter that she hadn't been there when he called to say. It was a lie anyway. She stood looking at the house as though it might, unchallenged, give up its secrets.

Big snowflakes were falling now without rhythm from the iron sky. Laurie had no impulse to hide. There was only one way into the house. She slipped the gun back into her jacket pocket and started up the walk.

The Chocolate Man picked up an ornamental poker from in front of the parlor fireplace. It wasn't real, and the fireplace didn't work. The mantel was false-faced brick. Emily's mother was outside the house; he didn't have to look out the window to know.

The Chocolate Man lifted the poker. She would be here in a minute. The poker was heavy enough. He stood listening for a moment, he nodded his head. The voice was right. He had thought it was going to be hard, but it wasn't, not now. How lucky he hadn't done it last night! He looked around and noticed that the carpet needed vacuuming; he would have to make sure the girl didn't make any noise.

Absentmindedly the Chocolate Man swung the poker as he walked toward the bedroom. He stepped easily and unconsciously around the flowers on the hallway carpet. The voice was telling him what was going to happen. If he had killed the girl last night he would not have such a wonderful sacrifice to offer it now. He walked calmly, he didn't need to hurry. There would be time for everything.

First the child. Then let her mother come.

Laurie stood with her finger poised above the doorbell. But that was ridiculous: to come calling for her kidnapped daughter as though she were the Avon Lady.

The gun in her pocket was pointed toward the door. If Emily was alive or dead Laurie was going to kill the Chocolate Man, to save her daughter or avenge her.

Laurie's hand moved to the doorknob; she was surprised, watching her hand, that she could feel the cold metal of the knob. But she was not surprised to find the door unlocked.

He's waiting for me. There was no light behind the door. Daylight threw color onto the rug in front of her, the dim walls. There was a hallway in front of her. She could hear no sound. The carpet was patterned in blue and pink and brown. Flowers; had Emily walked on this rug, down this hall? Laurie felt suddenly as if she herself had been here before.

There was a light at the end of the hall. The rug faded out in front of her; when she shut the front door it disappeared, and she was in darkness.

There was nothing but the light ahead of her. She would go to it; there was nowhere else to go. The gun felt good, cool and somehow familiar in her hand.

Laurie walked quietly. Why had the door been left open? Had he recognized her? But that was impossible; she had not let the cameras have her picture. He was insane; perhaps he was careless, too. But Laurie knew that the man who had killed seven children without being caught was not careless. Suddenly she wished she had called the police.

There was a noise from the end of the hall. A thudding noise, something falling. Laurie stopped. "Emily?" she whispered. The light at the end of the hall did not change, flat and impassive like a wall or a door. The Chocolate Man was in that light; Emily was in that light. Fluorescent, like a kitchen. Laurie held the gun very tightly but she didn't pretend she was not afraid.

✗   ✗   ✗

Mrs. Imperle stood at the living-room window. She was nervous; she kept ground coffee in the refrigerator for when her son and his wife visited, but this morning she was drinking it herself. Hazelnut. She didn't like hazelnut. Usually she drank Lipton tea. Her husband had drunk Maxwell House instant.

There was no movement from the house across the street. That girl on the phone last night had been sweet. Mrs. Imperle was peering out from behind her curtains as though she were the criminal. She had watched the TV news this morning; at eight-twenty the Chocolate Man had called the police. So it wasn't that man across the street after all. If it had been he would have been in jail already.

But still she stood at the window, looking at his house. That little girl—because it had been a little girl, she was sure of that now—hadn't wanted to go up the front walk with that man. She could see them now. The girl had definitely been frightened. Mrs. Imperle took another sip of her coffee: too strong. What if the police hadn't gone to the man's house? Of course, that young woman on the phone had been so lovely, she'd seemed to understand.

But what if the police hadn't come?

Mrs. Imperle rubbed the back of her neck. Something was wrong—where was Mr. Linderman? Every morning at eight-thirty Mr. Linderman walked up the east side of the street and down the west. When it rained he carried a black umbrella, and when it snowed he wore his red muffler. This morning it was snowing; white flakes were beginning to stick to the sidewalk and the dark asphalt of the street.

She moved toward the phone without letting the curtain go. *They'll think I'm a lonely old crazy woman,* she thought as she dialed the Task Force number.

Well, let them. She was smiling grimly as she listened to the ringing on the other end of the line. Her son was in St. Louis; he and his wife always went to her parents for Christmas. If Sarah Louise were still alive she'd probably be busy, too.

"Chocolate Man Task Force, may I help you?" said a male voice.

Let them, thought Mrs. Imperle, *they're probably right.*

Laurie chose to be heartened by the fact that she could hear nothing. Every time she'd thought of Emily for the last unbelievable eighteen hours it was the sounds she could not bear to imagine: she had heard her daughter cry out in fear, had heard her cry with pain. But she had never heard Emily— even now, standing in the hallway of the Chocolate Man's house with cold metal retribution in her hand, she could not complete the thought.

But there was no sound at all.

Emily had told her once that American Indians always walked a certain way, on the ball of the foot and the heel, when they were tracking an animal. That was the way to walk quietly. As Laurie stepped carefully, heel and ball of foot, the memory burned. Something only a child would know.

The light was getting closer. A kitchen light always looked inviting: hot chocolate, friends around the table at parties. If she thought about what she was doing she wouldn't be able to move. Emily on Carolyn's lap, up after bedtime and flush with the excitement of a grownup party. In Laurie's memory she was drinking ginger ale from Carolyn's glass. When Laurie found the Chocolate Man it would be easy to kill him.

Ed brought a cup of coffee over to where Marcy sat, on a cot in the hallway outside the Task Force room. He stood a moment in front of her; he put the coffee cup on the floor. He touched her shoulder. "Hey. Partner." She looked up and her eyes were empty. "Fleischer—Marcy, you can't let it get to you like this."

Her eyes did not change. "No warrant," she said without inflection.

"Not yet. For Christ's sake, Marcy," pulling out his battered cigar stub, "You're spooking me. You've got to come out of it."

"She's dead," Marcy said listlessly.

"I told the lieutenant it was Riehle on the phone. He asked me to prove it. Wanted to know if the caller made any reference to last night."

Marcy only said, "How come you can never get those to light? Here," with obvious effort of will pushing herself to the edge of the cot, "give it to me."

"Marcy—I wish I could think of something to say. To do—"

"There's nothing in the world you can do."

Ed's palms were held helplessly out; and suddenly, "Goddamn it, Marcy, you get up off that fucking bench *right* now!" And he grabbed her by her shoulders and yanked her to her feet.

Marcy sagged and stumbled, and Ed was holding her in his arms, her cheek against his chest. Marcy sighed: *How nice this feels,* she thought.

"We can't give up now," Ed was saying. "Even if it is too late. We're going to get that bastard George Riehle, but I can't do it alone. I need your fire."

Marcy looked up into his face. It was pale and open; she reached a hand and touched his cheek. "I'm tired," she said.

"I know. But you can't have stopped caring. Not my Marcy."

She shook her head but couldn't clear it. "It feels like—maybe I died, too."

"No. Not you, Fleischer. You've never given up in your whole life, and I'm not going to let you give up now. You're not dead—and neither is Emily Lookinland."

Marcy's hands were on Ed's chest; gently she pushed herself out of the circle of his embrace. "How do you know?"

Ed was smiling; it didn't seem like he knew it. "Because he didn't use the formula. He didn't say what he usually says. Marcy," touching her cheek with his finger (and Marcy was sure he didn't realize he was doing it), "remember, Laurie Lookinland didn't believe him when he said he'd molested Emily? Well, I understand that now. His voice—he hesitated, just like she said. He hasn't killed her yet, I know it. I don't think he's even touched her."

Marcy felt something like heat. In her arms, her legs. "Are you sure?" Her eyes warned him; "Are you *sure*, Ed? Because," and she was walking away now, toward the room where the crime-scene map hung, "if there's a chance—Ed," turning impatiently but still walking, "when was the last time you talked to the lieutenant about the warrant? I have an idea—"

And Ed followed her, head down and smiling to himself.

When he grabbed her Laurie made no sound. She felt a hand like ice, like metal, and she instinctively ducked, and bucked her back. The Chocolate Man didn't let go. She twisted to the left as she stepped backward and the grip on her arm slackened a little, and Laurie bucked again, not thinking, and the man's weight fell against her and his grip tightened again, but she still had the gun, she could feel the gun. If she could raise her hand she could hit him but she couldn't, he had her arm and it hurt, but *Emily's here I can get my hand free I can* and he struck the back of her head, *was that his hand?* she could see nothing, there was a light at the edge of her eye. *Is Emily there,* she could see his legs, *it hurts, I can get up it hurts,* and then there was an explosion in her head and the light got bigger and there was a roaring in her head *where is Em—*

✗   ✗   ✗

Carolyn sat staring at her feet where they rested on the sofa. Emily was gone, and now Laurie was gone. Carolyn was wearing thick purple socks. Had Emily been wearing the Christmas socks Carolyn had just bought her, red with reindeer on them? What did the Chocolate Man do with the children's socks? Carolyn did not have the protective insulation of a layer of shock. Shock was what had made Laurie able to bear it—the simple belief, hiding horror, that what had happened had not happened. And, when horror ate away the shock, the belief that Laurie herself could do something about what had happened.

Carolyn couldn't do anything. She was, even now, poised for action, her feet up on the sofa, a cup of hot chocolate steaming between her palms. The police had been angry, but of course they hadn't shown it, moving with clipped efficiency between Carolyn, the telephone, and the pile of papers and notebooks stacked on the kitchen table. Already Emily's memorial had begun to be constructed, in ciphered handwriting in composition books; what were they writing now? *Friend allowed mother to leave house on hopeless chase.*

Carolyn could not imagine what Laurie was feeling now. Carolyn's distress, being less, was perhaps harder to bear. There were cracks in her disbelief; she saw the policemen's faces, heard their voices, remembered the endings to seven other stories. Her hope was not big enough to serve as a life preserver, or strong enough to block images of what surely must be over now—that was Carolyn's only solace, the chocolate mug too hot between her hands: the image of Emily lying still, at last, by the side of an anonymous road.

Was Emily really dead? Carolyn's heart told her no, but she knew she was just incapable of thinking of that child dead. The little girl who lay reading under the dining-room table every time Carolyn came to visit, who did her homework lying upside down on the rose-colored chair in the corner of the living room, who had once, years ago, asked Carolyn why an award would be called the Pullet Surprise; that little girl could not be dead. Even if she never came back it would take years for her to die: memories of Emily would be caressed until they were tattered or pushed aside, again and again, in favor of survival, until they were out of reach.

It helped Carolyn to think about Laurie, to concentrate her panic into an answerable prayer: *Let Laurie, at least, be all right*. There was no prayer that Laurie find her daughter, because Emily was lying still, now, and surely mercy would preclude the discovery of her body by her mother.

What did the Chocolate Man do with the children's socks? Carolyn's chocolate was no longer too hot; Emily loved hot chocolate. Were her small feet naked now, with a light covering of snow? Carolyn put her mug down on the coffee table; the reindeer on Emily's socks were laughing, and one of them had a big red nose. Carolyn leaned her head down on her knees and cried.

Laurie's head hurt. When she opened her eyes there was silver snow at the corner of her vision.

She was looking at a brown carpet. The pain was huge; it was an iron band around the back of her head.

Where was she? She turned her head and the pain shot into the base of her brain and the snow brightened and widened. But through the funnel in front of her eyes she saw a bed, a maplewood dresser, a low table. The bed had a lot of lace on it. Anonymous furniture. She turned her head again, ready for the pain. She was looking at a man's blue-jeaned legs.

She moved her head to look up: through the cloud of pain she saw his blue eyes. He was snapping his fingers. He was smiling as though she were a naughty dog.

"It's nice to see you," said the Chocolate Man. "I don't get a lot of adult visitors these days."

"YOU'RE HER MOTHER," THE CHOCOLATE MAN SAID. He made the word sound like an obscenity.

He had Laurie by the hair; her head was back and she was aware of her neck, stretched and naked. "Yes," she said. She thought for an instant that the force of her hatred, and of her love, would compel him to release her. "I'm her mother."

"You want to see her?" He was pulling her hair.

"Yes," she said, "that's what I'm here for." He didn't know about the gun in her pocket. Her arms were behind her back, and there was something around her wrists. A belt? Thick like that, with a biting edge. Having her hair pulled hurt more than it should, the pain a nagging humiliation: *I should be stronger than this.*

"Get up." He was yanking her; she got to her feet quickly and awkwardly, to meet his controlling hand; when she was on her feet she felt stronger. *The gun,* she thought, and *Emily,* a cacophony of images: her daughter dead, her daughter alive, this man dead, the gun.

He had led her into a kitchen with a bright light and shiny floor. "She's right over here." His voice was unctuous, like a salesperson's. He was mocking her, and that prepared her.

Emily was lying on the kitchen floor.

Laurie stopped, and almost fell; he was still pulling her by the hair. "You wanted to see," he said, no longer hiding the triumph in his voice. "Go ahead and see."

He let go of her hair. She hated herself for feeling relieved. That was her daughter's body lying there. Laurie stood above her and said nothing.

Emily lay on her stomach, her legs and arms thrown out as though she had fallen. Her head lay facing away, but Laurie could see that there was some blood at the ear. Blood in the dark curls.

"Is she," Laurie began—she knew she was being stupid, staring transfixed at the trickle of blood, "really dead?"

From behind her the Chocolate Man caught his breath. "I didn't want—" he said, and he stopped again, and his voice changed. "How does it feel, Mrs. Lookinland? How does—"

"Will you kill me, too?" She wasn't trying to find out. She was asking him to.

He was quiet for a while. Then he said, "What?" and, "Oh," and Laurie knew he wasn't talking to her. Emily's body had not moved. Laurie watched it, thinking, *Don't say anything, just do it*.

But he didn't do it; he had stopped talking but Laurie was certain he was listening to something—someone. In his head. As she waited for his decision she watched her daughter's body not moving.

"I won't kill you now," the man said to her suddenly; but he was not being kind.

"What's your name?" she asked. She didn't know why. The glare of the fluorescent light was making everything flat: for a moment Laurie lost her visual balance and everything looked wrong. What was that lying on the floor in front of her? She noticed that there was no spoon or plate in the sink, no towel hanging half out of a cabinet handle.

"You keep it neat," she said. Everything swung back into focus. That was her daughter, Emily, on the floor.

"My name is George," the man said. After he said it she heard him choke. *Whoever it is he talks to doesn't want him to tell me.* It made perfect sense to her. "So, George, what do we do next?"

"Turn around," he said roughly.

She turned around.

He was holding her gun.

"Nice," he said, the way men say, *Nice,* about a woman as she walks by. *Just do it,* thought Laurie irritably, *don't grandstand.*

"Yeah," she said.

She could run. Then he would have to shoot her. She shifted her weight to her right foot; she tensed her leg.

"Don't," said George. She did not move. "Really," he said, and the mocking tone was gone, "I want to show you something." Laurie watched as he crossed the kitchen (her gun in his hand and his head half turned so that he could see her); he stepped over Emily's body.

Laurie began to shake. The shaking would turn into a scream. Emily's body.

"Look," he was saying; he had turned back to her after a moment at the counter. He was holding another gun, big and black.

"Mr. Linderman tried to hurt me," he said. The gun looked very old. Laurie didn't care about the gun. Emily was lying there dead.

"Please," she said, and the Chocolate Man laughed.

"*Please*," he said in a mincing voice. "Do you want to know what I did to her?" He was turning the old gun absently in his hand; he didn't really seem aware he was holding it. As though it were a pen, or a flashlight.

"Yes." Laurie was going to scream soon. Maybe then he would kill her.

"Yes," she said, and the Chocolate Man laughed again.

"Yes," he repeated in the same hateful voice, like a peevish old woman's.

Laurie looked at Emily where she lay on the floor: *That's what I'll be looking at when I die,* Laurie thought calmly. The scream was very close now.

"Look," said the Chocolate Man, "at me!" He wouldn't stop laughing. Laurie couldn't help but look up.

He was standing with the old gun cocked to his ear.

"I," he said, laughing, "have molested her." He jammed the gun up against his head. "I have," he said, still laughing, and he pulled the trigger.

Nothing happened. The gun clicked, that was all. Laurie had held her breath with sudden hope. As she looked at his still-laughing face she lunged for it. She would rip it to shreds.

But she would have to step over her daughter's body.

As she stopped herself, awkwardly because of her bound hands, she realized she was crying, and she looked at the Chocolate Man and he pulled the trigger again.

The gun clicked. The Chocolate Man took the gun away from his head and looked at it. Then he pointed it at Laurie.

She froze. *I do want to live,* she thought, surprised, and he pulled the trigger.

The gun clicked again.

"Pretty funny, huh?" said the Chocolate Man, and he pointed the gun at the ceiling and pulled the trigger and the room exploded.

Laurie found herself on the floor. The Chocolate Man was crouched across the room, both hands (and both guns) protecting his head. Plaster from the ceiling was still falling, on him and on the floor and on Emily where she lay on the floor.

Emily did not move.

"Wow," said the Chocolate Man.

Laurie watched as plaster dust settled into her daughter's hair.

"Wow," the Chocolate Man said again, standing up and brushing himself off. He was awkward because of the guns in his hands.

Laurie wasn't going to scream anymore. She didn't want to die. She wanted to kill him, and she was willing to wait. So she just looked at him, and behind her back she tensed her arms against the hard leather and pulled a little.

"No," he said, and Laurie stopped; but he wasn't talking to her. He was looking, expectantly and with some trepidation, at a point just in front of her and to the left.

"I don't think so," he said.

Laurie could move her right hand a little bit. She turned her thumb toward her palm and pulled. And the belt slipped. She was looking down: if she looked at Emily she wouldn't be able to move.

"Okay," said the Chocolate Man. Laurie didn't look at him either. It was too soon to tell whether she was going to be able to work her wrist free. For an instant she forgot even Emily: there was only the pressure against her wrists, the biting leather she could not see.

"You know what she told me?" the Chocolate Man asked suddenly. "Before she died."

He was looking at her like a child with a secret to tell. Laurie thought of the last image she had of Emily. Before she died. Emily had been standing by a low bush, looking at something. A caterpillar, a beetle. If the Chocolate Man had not taken her, would she have brought it over to her mother, proud and excited? *Look what I have to show you.*

Before she died.

"She said I could never make you stop loving her," he said. "Even if I killed her."

Laurie looked at his eyes. He knew things she would never know. "That's true," she said. She wanted to know, to know everything. *Give me more,* she begged silently. *I will kill you but I will find out first. Everything that happened before she died.*

"What do you want me to do?" she asked, softly; he was like a wild dog. She could speak softly, she could wait. Because he would make a mistake, and then she would kill him. And if he trusted her he would make a mistake sooner.

She had moved her right wrist a full inch through the leather loop. The Chocolate Man was looking absently at Emily's body. "I thought," he said, "that we could all go for a drive."

"Okay." Laurie risked leaning back against the counter behind her. It was hard to move just her wrists but he hadn't noticed anything, not so far.

"Where are we going?"

"Just a second," he said, "I have to clean up." And he knelt to get paper towels and Fantastik, leaving both guns on the counter.

But Laurie made no move. *I'm not such a fool as that*, she told him silently. *I'll wait.*

Her wrist had definitely shifted. The Chocolate Man knelt next to Emily and began wiping the linoleum methodically, in circles. "You know," he said, glancing up; Laurie stopped moving her hands. "I showed Emily how to do this the right way." He chuckled. "She didn't know how." He shook his head in a proprietary way. He owned that memory.

And, as he went back to his careful circular wiping, "It won't do you any good to get your hands free." Laurie froze. "You see, I don't care if you kill me. It's all the same. But I will make sure," looking up at her with sudden cold anger, "that I kill you, too. Even if I die. So don't try anything."

Laurie looked at his blue murderous eyes and gave a hard yank against the belt behind her. She shook her wrist, hard, and the belt slipped and held and suddenly wrenched free.

Laurie leapt at the Chocolate Man where he knelt, her hand held out stiff and up against his face and he tipped easily, her other hand reached out in a blind bid for her gun on the counter. She missed (there was a sharp bark of pain in her left hand), but he was on his back, blood at his mouth.

He was profoundly surprised, no matter what he'd said: *He's never had to fight somebody who could fight back,* Laurie thought savagely, and she hit him again in the face.

The Chocolate Man made no move, at first, to resist. But as Laurie brought her hand up to hit him again with a tight fist he simply sat up, lurching her onto Emily's body.

Laurie screamed. Her clenched fist had flailed back and grazed Emily's shoulder. Laurie struggled blindly away, her fist to her mouth. She held it pressed up against her mouth, and the Chocolate Man sat there laughing.

"Oh, God," she said. "Oh, God."

He got up, still laughing. "I think it's time to go now," he said, picking Laurie's gun up from the counter.

"Why are you doing this to me?" Laurie cried. She had hit her daughter's dead body.

"Because I have to," the Chocolate Man said seriously. "You haven't suffered enough yet."

"Haven't *suffered*? Haven't—for God's sake, what do you think I've been doing since you took my child? She was my—"

"Come over here," he said calmly, "and let me tie you up again."

Why am I surprised by how crazy he is? Laurie almost laughed. "Aren't you going to say please?"

The Chocolate Man looked up and to the left and nodded. "Nope," he said.

Laurie did laugh. "You come here," she said.

"I'm not kidding here!" he screamed shrilly. Her own gun was pointed at her and his hand was steady. "I murdered your daughter, and I can kill you anytime. I know what you want," he said fiercely. "I'm not stupid. But you've got a better chance if you cooperate, don't you? I know *you're* not stupid. Emily wasn't."

And Laurie said a silent thank you as she got up off the floor and went to him. *You don't know what I want. I want your memories. Just keep giving me your memories of her.*

"Marcy, come on," Ed was saying as he came into the room; his coat was halfway on.

"The warrant?" Marcy felt as though she were coming awake. This is what she'd been waiting for, and she was paralyzed. She knew she should be moving, getting her coat on, but she couldn't; she was under water.

"Marcy, what's the matter with you?" Ed's hand on her shoulder was shaking her awake. "For God's sake—"

And suddenly Marcy was on her feet, her arm halfway down the sleeve of her coat. "Parrish came through?"

"Yeah." Ed was trying to help her; she pushed him away. "You got a car?"

"Keller gave me his. I couldn't have gotten a req until eleven." Marcy had her coat on and was helping Ed with his while she lighted his cigarette. As the comforting acrid smoke hit her lungs she was saying, "What took him so long? The Chocolate Man called you twenty minutes ago."

Ed nodded. Marcy just kept talking; "We should have stayed there," she was saying, "we should have tailed him—" as she walked quickly toward the door.

With her hands tied behind her again, Laurie watched the Chocolate Man leaning over her daughter's dead body. She did not try to loosen her bonds. He had brought a roll of carpet in from another room (keeping the door open a little to watch Laurie, but she was watching him: had Emily been in that room? With its mess of bed-clothes on the bed and the floor?). He had made her turn and kneel and close her eyes while he did something (with soft bangs and one-sided conver-sation, something at the kitchen table; it sounded like he was setting the table for dinner). She did not try to see.

Now he was bent over her daughter, about to pick her up, and there was a long white cloth cover-ing something lumpy on the table; but she didn't care, she didn't look. The Chocolate Man was about to touch her daughter again.

"Let me," she said. Even though she knew it was a mistake, she added, "Please."

The Chocolate Man looked up and smiled.

"No," he said, but he said it gently. But Laurie could not bear for him to touch Emily again.

"*Please*," she said. But he only said, "No," again, not looking at her this time.

"No!" Laurie cried, struggling up from where she knelt, hating the betrayal of her body as it lurched without balance to a stand: she could not have a body now, she had to get to her daughter.

But he was already holding Emily. He stood with her in his arms and her head hung obscenely, her mouth was open. Laurie was crying. The gun lay unwatched on the floor in front of him but she didn't see it. "Where's her coat?" she cried in anguish.

He stopped. "Her coat?" he repeated. "She doesn't need her coat."

"But it's cold outside." Laurie didn't know she was crying. "It's *cold*," she said.

The Chocolate Man shook his head. "She doesn't need it."

"But she *does*. She'll be cold." *She must not go out into the cold unprotected.*

The Chocolate Man hesitated. "Please," she said again.

He shrugged. "I guess so," he said. When he put Emily's body down it made a horrible thudding sound. Like luggage.

When he came back into the kitchen with the coat (he had left the door open again and watched her but she wasn't looking at him, she was looking at her daughter), she said, not looking at him, "Let me put it on her."

He stopped and she said, "I have to," and he

nodded, in acknowledgment to her or to his private demons she did not know. But he came up softly and she turned around and he took the binding off her wrists.

He took her hand. She did not resist. He held her hand out and put the coat in it. Emily hadn't been sure she wanted that one; she thought maybe it looked too much like a boy's coat. *Too much like a boy's.* Laurie was shaking her head.

The coat was surprisingly heavy. "But it's warm, honey," she'd said. "And you know you never look like a boy."

Laurie held the coat up against her face. It smelled like Emily. Emily lay in a heap on the floor. Laurie walked to her and knelt, and touched her neck.

Iris Imperle stood next to the phone, staring at the man's house across the street. Iris had just called the Task Force, just spoken to a calm, unconvinced voice. Yes, of course they were taking her seriously. They got hundreds of tips every day, Iris must understand, each and every one was put into the computer system and cross-indexed with more than two thousand other tips received from concerned citizens like herself.

Iris understood. *Every piece of information we receive is given the proper attention at the proper time.* That meant that if it didn't sound too ridiculous somebody would log it into the computer. *We receive hundreds of pieces of information every day from concerned citizens like yourself.* That meant please get off the phone and leave the lines clear in case anybody has some real information.

Iris lifted the curtain again, looked again across the street at the man's house. She took a sip of coffee, shook her head: too sweet. And as she let the curtain fall she saw the man's door open and a woman walk out.

And she knew who the woman was.

The body was warm.

Laurie started back in surprise—then put her hand back, fast, before the Chocolate Man could notice. Emily's neck was warm and a little sweaty. Laurie smoothed her curls; she had never touched a dead body, how could it be sweaty?

Laurie put her head against her daughter's body and sobbed.

She's alive. The blood drained from Laurie's arms, her head. She lay against Emily's warm body and cried convulsively. *You're alive, he hasn't killed you, you're alive.*

"What are you doing?" the Chocolate Man asked, and Laurie froze. *He must not see anything in my eyes,* she thought, and she turned to face him.

"I'm sorry," she said. She was certain her face must be triumphant with truth. But she betrayed nothing. Laurie sat up and began to put the coat on Emily. *Don't move, my darling, he mustn't know.* Emily's arms remained limp, her eyes closed. As Laurie turned her over she was certain Emily would move, or make a sound, but she remained soft and lifeless.

"Where are we going?" It was an agony for Laurie to let go of Emily's arm, to stand, knowing that the Chocolate Man's ignorance was her daughter's only defense.

"I'm ready," she said.

"I've got to roll her up," he said, and he knelt and reached for Emily. Laurie started forward, her mouth open—and stopped herself. He snapped the carpet from its roll and laid it flat and flipped Emily over onto it. Laurie gasped—he laughed, and made a quick motion, and Emily was gone, hidden within indoor-outdoor Forest Glade.

Laurie could not move. He was not holding the gun but he was holding her daughter.

"Laurie," he said, shocking her; she didn't know, for a moment, how he could know her name.

"Get me my gun, will you?" And she took a step and he laughed and was at the counter, Emily in his arms; "Just kidding," he said, and he laid Emily down on the counter and picked up the gun. He put her down like groceries; Laurie heard her head bang against the countertop.

The Chocolate Man picked Emily up again, with the gun hidden underneath her. "Come on," he said affably, "time to go."

"Let me carry her," Laurie said.

"Nope." She went ahead of him down the dark hallway; she couldn't see Emily; "I've got the gun pointed at you," the Chocolate Man said. Laurie opened the front-door locks herself, feeling in the dark: a chain, a bolt, a turn, it was like opening the locks at home. The Chocolate Man put Emily down again and bound Laurie's hands behind her once

more with the thick belt. He put her coat around
her shoulders carefully, almost gently; he was muttering to himself. When the door opened daylight
hit her eyes like a knife. And the bright outdoor
light, the falling snow, the strange street, held no
comfort or hope.

Iris could feel the falling snowflakes kissing the
tops of her feet. She had run out the door before
she realized it: how could that possibly be Lauren
Lookinland?

The man from across the street was carrying a
bundle of green carpet. He didn't seem to have
noticed Iris at all. His eyes were inward, cloudy; he
was talking the whole time. Shuffling down the
front walk he looked neither right nor left.

And Iris was unsure, watching these things happen in front of her as though they were no more real
than images on a television screen. Iris watched as
the man reached a hand from under the bundle to
open the passenger-side door of the car parked
there and nudged the woman in with his bundle of
carpet.

Iris didn't even know that man had a car.
There'd never been one in his driveway. She looked
in vain at the license plate on the back of the car, but
it was muddied over.

After he put the woman in the front seat the
man shoved his bundle into the back and made the
woman get out of the car again, but still he looked
only in front of him, only at the woman or the bundle or the door of the car. Even when he walked her

around to the driver's side he didn't notice Mrs. Imperle standing incongruent on the sidewalk with snow in her slippers.

The woman had a coat over her shoulders; she was walking oddly: was she hurt? Iris couldn't see her arms. The man edged the woman down the walk with the bundle of carpet. The woman stopped; she glanced at Iris; Riehle said something.

But just before she got in the car, the woman glanced up toward Iris with a ferocious hope in her eyes.

The Chocolate Man paused outside the house; he looked up and down the street. "My car's out front."

"Why isn't it in the driveway?"

The Chocolate Man smiled. "That's a silly question."

Laurie was acutely aware of the gun hidden beneath Emily's body. Emily seemed light in his arms; how could she breathe inside that roll of carpet? Laurie saw an old woman across the street. The Chocolate Man must have seen her, too, but he gave no sign.

"Mr. Linderman liked to take his walk about now." The Chocolate Man was chuckling. Who was Mr. Linderman? The old gun in the kitchen. *He tried to hurt me.* It was a nice suburban block. Laurie glanced up quickly.

The Chocolate Man saw her looking. "Go ahead," he said, "scream."

"I can't, you've got—"

"What? What have I got?" He kept smiling, she hated his smiling.

"You've got a gun." *You've got my daughter and she's alive.* Laurie could feel sweat on her palms, under her breasts; was there sweat on her face?

"It doesn't matter about her," the Chocolate Man said, stopping suddenly and looking down. Laurie looked at the old woman, who nodded, once. Laurie couldn't tell if the nod was for her. Laurie started to mouth something: "You could run," the Chocolate Man suggested. What was he trying to get her to do?

He was looking at her with innocent eyes. "I mean," he said, "I probably couldn't shoot you while I'm carrying this."

Laurie winced. *This.* Was he baiting her? Did he know Emily was alive? "I'm not going to leave her," she said.

They walked to the car, which was parked in front of the house. He walked her around to the passenger side because he didn't know he didn't have to: she wasn't going to try to get away. When she got into the car she was afraid. "Where are you going to put her?" she asked.

"In the car," the Chocolate Man said infuriatingly. And then he leaned over her to flick the back-door lock. When Emily was out of sight in the backseat he said, "Out again," and she got out. "I have to watch you all the time," he said, shaking his head; as though she were a child herself. As she slid awkwardly across to the seat after getting in again at the driver's-side door she thought, relieved, *He doesn't know that nothing could make me go now.* He got in and laid the gun across his lap.

Laurie gagged; she tried to bring a hand up to her mouth but they were tied. She was looking at the Chocolate Man's lap. *I have molested her.* Laurie bit her lip and swallowed and the car pulled away from the curb.

The siren was on, and Ed was driving as fast as he could. Marcy wanted to be at the wheel; her hands were clenched and she kept leaning forward in her seat, as though she could push the car faster herself. "Can't you go any—"

"Marcy." Ed spoke through tight teeth.

"Okay," Marcy said. Okay. Riehle's block looked different in the daylight. There were large Cape and Spanish-style houses at the sides of the road, and pale green lawns. There was a soft snow falling.

It looked like Christmas.

As the car screeched up the block nothing moved; it could have been a stage set. Ed overshot, stopping in front of the house that had had orange and blue lights blinking in the night. They were still blinking. Riehle's house was shuttered and still: no curtain moved to mark their arrival.

There was a naked rectangle of asphalt in front of the house, with a fine light powder of snow all around it, turning the dark street white.

"Think it was his?" Ed was asking as they hurried by; the windows were dark; Marcy was muttering furiously.

"What?"

"We should have gone in last night," she was saying, and her hand holding the warrant was clenched, crushing the paper. "I shouldn't have listened to you, we should have—"

"We couldn't," Ed said firmly, and he split off toward the side of the house and the back door. Under her heavy jacket Marcy was very cold.

The doorbell was cold. She could hear the sound of it echoing down the hall. For a moment Marcy was back in a dream, suddenly remembered, from last night: she could hear a terrifying, captive thud of metal against wood; it echoed in her head. Why was she ringing at all? Riehle was the Chocolate Man, he wouldn't answer.

"He answered last night," Ed called from the driveway, and Marcy smiled, looking down, then stopped herself in case Riehle did appear.

But he didn't. The bell echoed and died, and Marcy said, "I'm going in."

"Okay." She could hear Ed going up the steps to the side door. She set her shoulder and rammed the door; there was a heavy noise and a crack. She thrust again and a black line split the door, and after a third thrust the door was open.

The noise was tremendous—and then there was nothing. Marcy could see the outline of the dark hallway, that was all. There was a metallic taste in her mouth; she swallowed. She had her gun out. As always when she drew it she didn't remember doing it. But it was there, reassuring in her cold hand.

As she stepped through the door she knew there was no one there; when a house is empty it breathes differently. But she didn't turn on the light. Her eyes were everywhere: no one behind the door, no one crouched hidden ahead of her. Marcy swung into the first room off the hall, her gun held stiff-armed in front of her, and she felt a little foolish in one corner of her brain, replaying the move as she had seen it on countless television shows, where it was a simple, sweeping, balletic motion; Marcy bumped the doorjamb with her leg.

But there was no one in the room. There was a brown-patterned sofa and a glass-topped table and a bare Christmas tree; through the window Marcy could see that the snow was coming down harder.

Marcy kept her gun drawn against the emptiness. She did not run, as she wanted to, down the hall toward where the dragging noise had come from last night. She went slowly, swinging her gun out in front of her, into each room off the hallway. A sterile guest room, a dining room. There was no dust anywhere. Marcy felt sick anticipation building in her stomach. The next room was closest to the kitchen. Out of the corner of her eye Marcy could see Ed outside the screen side door; she motioned to him to wait and swung into the dark room.

There was something on the bed. Marcy went down onto one knee, her gun steady. She was aware of the kitchen behind her, the ordinary fluorescent light leaking into this room. Ed was making a noise behind her, trying to get in. Marcy saw only the shape on the bed, the coat and the pathetic bare feet. The coat was black and heavy and rumpled, so that it looked at first as though it were empty. But the white soles of the feet blared dead against the dim light.

Was it Riehle? Marcy didn't think so. Was he in the room? She moved her eyes. A pale squatting blob: a dresser. A looming white shape: an open closet. The gun remained pointed firmly at the bed. There was nowhere to hide, but Marcy moved quickly toward the closet. Behind her she heard a weak cracking and knew Ed was in the house.

There was a dirty string hanging from the closet ceiling, and a smell; Marcy pulled the string and blank light filled the small space. A little TV, a flow-ered plate with half a sandwich on it, and a black pot filled with urine. That was the smell, and something else: salami.

The closet's racks were filled with shirts, mostly white. There were a few pieces of carpet lying in one corner; there wasn't enough room for a child to lie comfortably. Emily Lookinland had been here. Ed was in the kitchen; "Look at this," he was saying. Marcy ignored him and turned toward the bed.

The man was old, at least seventy. He lay staring up at the ceiling; he looked surprised. There was something—behind her Ed turned the overhead light on and she saw: there was a Christmas card propped up between the man's legs. BEST WISHES FOR THE HOLIDAY SEASON. Silver script, with a gar-land of holly around the words.

"What the—" Ed said behind her, and she reached out and touched the man's neck, feeling for a pulse. There was none; he smiled rigidly at noth-ing; he was cold.

"His shoes," Marcy said.

"Come into the kitchen."

The fluorescent light was blinding. There was plaster dust everywhere, and pieces of plaster on the counters, the floor. There was a hole in the ceiling.

"Jesus," Marcy said; but Ed wasn't looking at the ceiling or the floors. On the white Formica table in the center of the room was a line of shoes. Seven pairs for boys' feet, each with a pair of socks placed neatly in front of it. Marcy was drawn toward the end of the line; and they were there: scuffed brown bucks, soldier-straight, and a pair of red socks; she could see reindeer smiling.

And next to them, grotesquely large and somehow obscene, there was a pair of men's black shoes with worn soles, and a pair of blue-and-yellow striped socks, neatly folded. BEST WISHES FOR THE HOLIDAY SEASON.

THE CHASE

THE LONG ISLAND EXPRESSWAY, YES. LAURIE REMEM-
bered driving on the Long Island Expressway this
morning, a long time ago before she knew Emily
was really alive. Before she'd met the Chocolate
Man. *I have molested her.* Perhaps the old woman
across the street had called the police by now; they
might already know the Chocolate Man's name.
They would soon see the kitchen, caved in now,
with plaster all over the floor. And the bedroom;
which Laurie had only glimpsed.

Where were they going? Laurie couldn't think
about Emily. She was safe in the backseat (Laurie
made a little derisive sound to herself—*safe*—and
the Chocolate Man glanced over). There was nothing Laurie could do for Emily now.

But there was the Chocolate Man next to her.
He was humming, tunelessly, and sometimes he
stopped and cocked his head: he was listening. But
he just kept driving straight.

"Where are we going?" Laurie didn't recognize
this part of the expressway. Trees at the side of the
road, sycamores and maples. The snow was falling
faster; the trees were disappearing under white lace.

"East," said the Chocolate Man.

"Why?"

"Because I told them west." And Laurie thought, *East. East of here, of my house, of his house. So we're going east. Where the police can't possibly know to come.* The trees were mocking her, Christmas green and white. She didn't want to know anything more.

The road was slicking over but the Chocolate Man drove fast. Maybe a policeman would notice and stop him for speeding. That had happened before, the criminal pulled over for a traffic violation and he has a body in the trunk.

"Christmas is coming," she said.

"I know." The Chocolate Man sounded happy. "Do you know any songs?"

Emily's voice, a clear soprano, singing "Silent Night": always before bed on Christmas Eve Emily sang "Silent Night." And Laurie read "A Visit from Saint Nicholas" aloud. Laurie had taught Emily the German words of the song, remembered from her great-grandmother in a faraway childhood. *Stille Nacht, heilige Nacht, alles schlaft, keines wacht.* All are sleeping, no one watches. Laurie stared out the window. The Chocolate Man wanted to sing Christmas songs.

Alles schlaft, keines wacht. The snow was falling fast, and the road was getting harder to see, and the Chocolate Man was singing. "On the first—" and then he stopped. Laurie looked and he was moving his lips; she hated the banality of his insanity. She had never known that she could be terrified and irritated at the same time. "—day of Christmas, my true love gave to me-ee!": loud, and the windows were open.

Laurie could feel the sting of snow on her face. It was a feeling she had always loved, and each year at the first snowfall she and Emily ran outside and turned their faces hopefully up to the sky. The air was cold; it ran down Laurie's neck like water; would Emily feel it, through her shroud of carpet, would she wake up? "Two"—a silence—"turtle-doves and a partri-idge in a—" Laurie leaned her head against the seat back and felt the air like water down her neck, and it chilled her heart.

As she came awake Emily made no sound, and that saved her. There was something wrong—it was stuffy, and there was a noise and the sensation of moving: falling or rolling.

Who? Somebody was making noise—Emily tried to roll over, and when she realized she was not in her bed she tried to sit up—and then she heard a voice, singing and halting and singing again, and knew where she must be.

The Chocolate Man was singing. "—in a pear tree-ee!" It was very dark, and she couldn't move. She could smell something completely familiar and impossible to name. She was thinking, *What's George singing for?* She was in a car, she could hear the engine. And she could feel it reverberating in her stomach.

Emily tried to move her arms. Her head hurt a lot, and she felt nauseated. She was wrapped in something.

"—three—French hens, two—turtledoves—" she heard the Chocolate Man singing from the front seat. She lifted her head and felt something scratchy against her cheek. She was wrapped in carpet. She had seen the carpet in his closet, he had taken it out when he put her in there. That's what she was smelling.

But how did she get here? She lay still; it hurt too much to move her head. She remembered the closet, this morning, half-eaten salami and *Leave It to Beaver.* She was afraid she was going to throw up. She remembered the Chocolate Man coming home, the sudden thudding fear when she heard his footsteps hesitating on the hallway rug. What happened next wasn't so clear. (She could hear him in the front seat: "—day of Christmas, my true love gave to me—" He was hesitating with every line; Emily thought of the way he paused when he spoke, the way he moved his lips.) The light from outside the closet had been too bright; she had become used to the dimness inside.

She remembered his face. It was not George who opened the door but the Chocolate Man. Any hope she had built up in the last eighteen hours evaporated before his face. Emily stopped being a child when she saw his face.

Emily knew not to make a sound. Didn't he think she was dead, wasn't that why he had wrapped her up in carpet and put her in the backseat?

But lying there she began to wonder if she had a voice. She had tried to roll away from the bright metal, ducking the pain as he hit her back, not believing anything could hurt that much, curling into a fetal ball but still able to see him, his eyes and the raised hand, what had he said? *I'll get her, I'll get her.* And thinking, *Who?* as the hand came down, *Who?* and lights burst all around her and she was here.

The Chocolate Man was still singing. "Five—" and a pause "—go-old rings!" The road thudded underneath Emily and up through her back and neck. Did she have a voice? She had never wanted anything so badly as she wanted to make a noise. *Even if he kills me, I have to make a noise.* She couldn't breathe and if she didn't at least clear her throat—

"Why don't you want to sing with me?" the Chocolate Man asked, and Emily froze. He was talking to her.

There was nothing but silence. Emily didn't want to answer. "I'm not in the mood right now," her mother said.

It's an angel, Emily thought. *It must be an angel, come because I'm going to die.* As she waited to hear the angel again she thought, *Maybe I'm already dead.* And that comforted her. She wouldn't mind being dead if it meant she could hear her mother's voice.

The road thudded gently beneath her. She forgot about clearing her throat. "I don't care what you do to me," the angel said. Blind in her bondage, Emily started to cry. It was an angel; of course an angel wouldn't care what the Chocolate Man did. Emily had spent hours and hours looking at a book her mother had about angels. They had golden wings, and they were not girls or boys. They looked more stern than Emily would have thought, and some of them had feathers. The cherubim had red feathers, the seraphim had blue. Emily's head hurt so much she was going to cry out.

"You can't do anything more than you've done already," the angel said. Emily thought she was talking a little louder than before, and was immediately still. She could not cry out; without any thought she knew that the angel wanted her to be quiet. Because she wasn't dead—the pain in her head told her that—and the angel would know she wasn't dead.

So it was the Chocolate Man who didn't know.

Emily relaxed inside her bondage. The angel knew she could hear her. Emily thought all angels were girls even if the book said they weren't. Could the Chocolate Man see the angel? "—we get there," the angel was saying. Emily couldn't hear everything, the carpet scratched her ear and filtered sound: "—not coming," said the angel.

Emily closed her eyes in the dark. Everything was going to be all right now. The angel was going to take her to God.

"—a cigarette?" the angel asked.

Emily almost sat up.

Angels don't smoke cigarettes.

It really was her mother.

"She won't mind the smell," said the Chocolate Man, and he laughed.

"No," said Emily's mother, "she won't," and Emily felt tears of happiness running down her face.

It was her mother, and now everything was going to be all right.

✳   ✳   ✳

"Well, what have we got?" Marcy stood in front of the crime-scene map. It was just before nine o'clock; she had been standing there for what seemed like a long time. Ed had been working the phones. As soon as he came into the room Marcy knew something had happened.

"Funny call came in while we were out," he was saying. "Romano tipped me to it. Seems an old lady called the Task Force. Said her name was Mrs.—I don't know, some Italian name. Says she called last night, spoke to a 'real sweet girl.' Then she says she just saw something funny—"

"Riehle and the girl?" Marcy's mouth was suddenly dry, her palms sweaty.

"No, no. Stranger than that. This old lady says she saw Riehle coming down his walk carrying a big bundle of carpet—"

Marcy gasped.

"—with a woman."

Marcy forgot to close her mouth. She looked at Ed. "Laurie Lookinland."

"Uh-huh." There was grudging admiration in Ed's voice. "She found him. Son-of-a-bitch if she didn't. Who would've—"

"Laurie Lookinland is with the Chocolate Man?"

"That's what I just said."

"But where are they now? Which way did they—"

"The old lady didn't see, she just called us as soon as she saw them."

"When was this?" Marcy felt a little ill.

"About three minutes before we got there,

Fleischer," Ed said, kindly; Marcy knew it hurt him, too.

She sighed. "Now what?"

"Now we hurry up and wait. There's an APB for all three of them."

"What, you think they're not going to get out of the city? We don't even know what kind of car he's driving."

"Marcy, there's nothing we *can* do, you know that."

Marcy turned back to the map so Ed wouldn't see she was crying. "Right there," she said, pointing to a black ribbon of street. Dogwood Terrace.

Marcy stuck a blue-tipped pushpin halfway up the block between Seventeenth Avenue and Union Turnpike: 17–84 Dogwood Terrace. Next to it was a bigger ribbon: Utopia Parkway. Two blocks over, a red pin marked Danny Angelo's abduction site; there was an orange pin two and a half miles to the northwest, marking the spot, in the dirt and grass at the edge of the Grand Central Parkway, where Danny's body had been found. The Chocolate Man had demanded that the ransom for Danny be left some five miles away, to the southeast, at a site on the Long Island Expressway. Marcy put her hand out to touch the yellow marker. "The first one," she said softly. Then she traced her finger straight across houses and stores and woods to Grand Central Parkway, where Danny's body had been found. She knew all the ransom sites, the kidnap and body-drop sites, by heart; sometimes she repeated them to herself like a rosary.

Her finger slid from the ransom drop down

toward where Danny's body had been found, and it
passed over George Riehle's house. Marcy paused a
moment, her finger on the blue marker. Then she
moved to the red pushpin marking the second
abduction: Oliver Plucienkowsky. Eighth Avenue
and Whitestone Boulevard. Oliver had been playing
in a park near the Whitestone Bridge, at three in the
afternoon on a Sunday. He had been found in a
vacant lot in Bedford-Stuyvesant, Brooklyn. His
mother attempted suicide two weeks after the body
was discovered.

Marcy's finger slid to the spot on the
Whitestone Expressway where the Chocolate Man
had asked for the money drop. "Here," she said;
she wasn't aware she was speaking aloud. She raised
her other finger and pointed to the orange pushpin
at the body-drop site. "And here," she said. She
moved her two fingers together until they met—at
George Riehle's house. "Six miles," she muttered,
"and—six miles. Ed. Oh, Jesus, Ed!" She was
shouting; when she turned and found him directly
behind her she seemed surprised.

"Ed, did you see? You think it could—"

"Here," said Ed, placing his finger on the red
pushpin marking Andrew Timmons's disappearance. The third boy. "Then we go up here," he said,
putting his other index finger on the yellow money
drop, at a particularly busy spot on the Long Island
Expressway in Sunnyside, just before the entrance
to the Midtown Tunnel.

Andrew's body had been found at the side of
Northern State Parkway, eight miles to the northwest. Marcy reached a finger as Ed slowly brought

his up from the ransom site; his hand and hers came
to rest, at the same moment, at the exact midpoint
between the two pushpins, at George Riehle's
house.

"Holy Christ," Ed said wonderingly. "The son
of a bitch does have a pattern." Marcy was checking
the ransom and body-drop sites of the next victim,
Ronald Chin. Again her fingers met at Riehle's
house.

"Okay," she said, half to herself. "Don't rush it.
We have a ransom spot here," moving to the
Delaware part of the map, which had been grafted
on as soon as the Task Force received the Chocolate
Man's ransom site, "for Emily Lookinland. Dover,
Delaware. And Riehle's house is here. That's—
what—about seventy-five miles. So he's going to
take the girl—"

"Here," said Ed.

"Here. The Long Island Expressway at about
Exit—it doesn't say. Where are we?"

"Manorville. My brother-in-law used to own
some land out there." He lowered his hand. "That's
it, then." For a moment Marcy stood, overwhelmed, and did not move.

But then she grabbed Ed's arm and said, "Let's
go."

The highway was getting icy. "I don't know if you
realize," the Chocolate Man was saying. Laurie
stared out the window without saying anything.
The Chocolate Man had been talking, talking. He
had been asking her questions, nonsense mostly.

She had stopped answering; now she couldn't tell if he was talking to her or somebody else.

"—been listening, have you?"

He was looking at her.

"Yes—no." What did he want her to say, was she supposed to be listening or not? He was definitely talking to her now.

"Well?" If he didn't look at the road ahead they would hit something. He was still looking at her; his eyes were wild. She had never known what that meant before: wild, and he was smiling.

"Well?" he said again—and there was a noise from the backseat.

"If you don't look where we're going we'll crash," Laurie said calmly. A bump, quite small; it could have been a jolt from the road. Laurie wasn't breathing.

"I like snow," she said, flat and calm. Nonsense, just to cover up the noise.

"So do I." Would the noise be repeated? The Chocolate Man reached over and slapped Laurie's face. She closed her eyes, but she didn't flinch or turn her head.

A small noise, coming from the back of the car. Laurie turned her head. "What was that?" asked the Chocolate Man.

"It sounded like your brakeshoe was squeaking." *Don't move, my darling, he will hear you.*

"Brakeshoe?" the Chocolate Man repeated. "I thought it was in the back." Laurie stared fixedly at the tops of the pine trees sliding past. There was silence in the car, no sound but the sound of the road beneath the wheels.

"If you hadn't smelled smoke you would have been dead," he said suddenly. Laurie sighed and looked out the window.

"How come you never sang to me?"

Laurie was silent.

"Your robes—they're so beautiful. I never saw so many colors. I knew you'd come." The snow was falling in big flakes, Emily liked to catch them on her tongue.

"I heard you sing once," the Chocolate Man was saying, "you were drinking that stuff with a man, Daddy was asleep at the kitchen table, and you sang. What did you sing? Sing it for me."

Emily liked to hold her arm out to catch the flakes; she would run to her mother and show her: tiny daisies, and stars, and doilies.

"Sing it for me!" the Chocolate Man screamed suddenly.

The snow felt good against Laurie's face. "Stille Nacht," she sang softly, "heilige Nacht."

"—have issued an APB in the abduction of Emily Rose Lookinland, believed to have been kidnapped by the notorious serial killer known as the Chocolate Man. The police are looking for George Riehle, of 17–84 Dogwood Terrace, in Flushing, Queens. Riehle was reportedly last seen leaving his house this morning by a neighbor. Lauren Lookinland, Emily's mother, may be with the Chocolate Man right now. The police reported—"

Ed wasn't driving fast enough. Marcy's knuckles were white in her lap, she was leaning forward, trying to make the car go faster. The siren was off, because Marcy didn't want to spook the Chocolate Man. If he knew they were coming he might go anywhere.

Ed hadn't said anything for a long time. Neither had Marcy. *We're not going to make it, we're not going to make it,* jangled in the smooth noise the wheels made. *We're not going to make it.* She rolled the window down, she needed the wind in her face.

"Ed—" she began, and he snapped, "Damn it, Fleischer, I'm flooring it already," and she lighted his cigar for him, the lighter's flame bucking wildly in the blast from the window.

The view was unchanging and somehow sad. Trees, bare tops waving, white all along the branches now, and sorry pines bare from the bottoms halfway up the trunk. There were other cars on the road, but not many; there were a lot of wheeling crows, and Marcy thought for a moment she saw a hawk, wings unmoving against the sky, but it could have been anything, another crow or a trick of the light.

It didn't seem like a holiday. Sometimes Marcy got Christmas Eve off, and she went to her sister's house and played with her sister's three boys. For years she had thought of the Chocolate Man on Christmas Eve, her nephews rambunctious and unbearably precious, rolling about on the living-room rug or wiggling on the sofa next to their aunt while she read them stories. *Winnie the Pooh* or *The Wind in the Willows,* and while she read she thought of little pairs of socks, and little shoes, and living rooms that didn't have children in them.

She was expected at her sister's house at two this afternoon. There was something at the side of the road—Marcy leaned and looked and it was nothing, two men standing next to their car, looking up at the sky.

She turned toward Ed. "I can't go any faster," he said, but he wasn't angry. He only sounded sad.

The room was dark. Her mother was singing. It was Christmas Eve and her mother was singing "Silent Night." Her voice was clear and lovely, coming from the hallway.

The covers were too warm. Why was her mother singing "Silent Night" without her? It was too dark, and her green blanket was tangled around her head. She tried to move her arms—"heilige Nacht"—Emily was frightened.

"Mama!" she called out. And then she wasn't sure: she couldn't breathe, and it was dark.

"Who?" she cried.

And then she remembered.

"Ah, Emily," the Chocolate Man said from the front seat, "it's good to see you. Won't you join us? I wasn't expecting to have the pleasure of your company again."

Laurie hardly dared look at her daughter. When she had thought her dead there had at least been no pain on Emily's face. But now—Laurie turned, and her daughter was rubbing her eyes, her nose scrunched with concentration: "My head hurts,"

she said, and Laurie said, "Oh, God, Emily, I love
you so much."

And Emily smiled.

"You found me," she said. The Chocolate Man
was humming tunelessly.

"Yes, darling, I found you."

"I think I have to throw up. He hit me on the
head," with a kind of amazement, glancing over
and away.

"Take deep breaths. Keep your face in the
wind." Laurie didn't want the Chocolate Man to
realize they were talking. He seemed very far away;
the longer Emily sat up in the backseat the more
chance there was that somebody would recognize
her.

"Okay." They would not say hello, there would
be no apologies or regrets. Her daughter's strange,
easy acceptance of the situation made it easier for
Laurie, too. Emily didn't seem to think it odd that
her mother was suddenly with her; she didn't seem
especially afraid of the Chocolate Man. Of course,
she had been hit hard on the head, in the last eighteen hours she had lived a whole lifetime away from
her mother; she was surely in shock. And yet her
face remained composed. Even Laurie's sense of
reality was beginning to shift; they were, after all,
really here in a car with the Chocolate Man. They
were really here.

There was a man about four feet away in the
next lane, at the wheel of a blue Mercedes. He was
looking ahead; if Laurie shouted, would he turn his
head? She and Emily were trapped in a moving bub-
ble; the man was worlds away.

"Thinking of making a new friend?" the Chocolate Man asked suddenly. "I'll introduce you." And he leaned over Laurie to yell: "Hey, mister! I'm kidnapping these people! Hey!" And the man's head jerked toward them, stared rigidly, and jerked back. "Don't you want to *help* these people?" the Chocolate Man shouted gaily; the man stared resolutely forward.

"Please," Laurie said quietly, "stop it."

The Chocolate Man laughed. "Don't you want to be *saved?*" he asked sarcastically. "Don't you—"

"George," Emily said from the backseat, "what's the matter with you?" and the Chocolate Man gasped and was silent. And Laurie felt a kick of horror, to hear her daughter say his name.

"You were nicer before," Emily said. *Nicer before,* Laurie thought. *What does that mean?* She didn't want to feel any hope: *I have molested her.* "You were different," Emily was saying.

"*She's* talking to me now," said the Chocolate Man.

"The same as when you were a kid?" Emily asked, and Laurie lowered her head. These two had a relationship. *She calls him George, she's talking about a conversation they had. Was this before*—there were no words to think, no images to put into words. Emily knew this man. She would always have memories of this man. George.

"Uh-huh," the Chocolate Man said. "Are you coming to my birthday party?"

Emily said nothing.

"What I really want is a dog," he said, and Laurie risked turning again to look at her daughter, who sat looking at the Chocolate Man with a confused face. And Laurie saw grief there like a loss, familiar like the look on Emily's face at Christmastime, and rage welled up in her: *She has lost someone else she thought she knew.*

George had changed. Most of what he was saying didn't make sense anymore—but it was more than that. He sounded more grownup, sure of himself. He still hesitated when he spoke; more than ever. Before, he'd moved his mouth, he said the same thing to himself over and over. He still did that (Emily didn't even have to look at him to see: she saw it again and again, in a loop in her brain that was continuous and practically unconscious). But now sometimes he seemed to be listening. Emily remembered the funny question he'd asked her: *Did your imaginary friend talk to you when you didn't want her to?* Emily knew that crazy people heard voices; once in a while, just before she fell asleep, Emily thought she heard somebody call her name. Not in any voice she knew; not her mother's voice. And that frightened her but she never told her mother.

Now George was listening to a voice, and he sounded different. He was sarcastic. Emily realized that she had never known what that word meant before. He was sarcastic; and he was calmer. As though somebody were telling him what to do. What to say. Before, she didn't ever know what was going to make him mad, but she'd been getting good at calming him down. Now he was like a different person, and she couldn't predict him. And if he got mad at her or her mother, Emily might not be able to calm him down.

"Could you close the window?" she asked George. He didn't answer. She wanted to hear him talk some more; she wanted to understand. Because she knew that what happened to her and her mother might depend entirely on that understanding.

Emily wasn't wearing shoes or socks. Laurie didn't know if her daughter had noticed that yet. It was cold in the car. "Could you close the window?" Emily asked the Chocolate Man, but he didn't answer. Laurie didn't want her daughter to be cold; she didn't want her to realize that her shoes and socks were gone. That would frighten her. Laurie knew that she was being ridiculous, but it seemed very important. Did Emily know that George was the Chocolate Man? What was George's last name? Laurie looked at her daughter; she would catch cold without her shoes and socks.

Emily was looking at her; Laurie felt suddenly ashamed. What good had she done? She was as trapped as her daughter. She smiled at Emily; she was still recognizably Emily. Laurie didn't know what she had expected. Just a little while ago Emily had been dead.

"It's going to be all right," Laurie said softly, but she was ashamed, because she was lying.

Emily didn't answer. She looked at her mother. "It's cold in here," she said. "I'm cold."

Laurie saw the roadblock before the Chocolate Man did. He was looking around, sometimes at the road and sometimes at the trees or the snow or something in his head. Often he inclined his head as though listening. And he was driving fast; any moment the car might crash.

Laurie saw them, three police cars far ahead, stopped slantwise barring the road. A fourth car was moving languidly across the highway, lights spinning. Laurie said nothing; and then the Chocolate Man saw them, too.

"They know about us," Laurie said. She felt hope like a drug, sudden and dizzying. She closed her eyes against it.

The Chocolate Man was whispering into the windshield.

Laurie whispered, too. "Just let her go. Just"—a release of breath, of hope—"pull over and let her get out."

The Chocolate Man burst out laughing. Laurie turned her head away. "You don't understand anything," he said disgustedly.

"I know," said Laurie; why was she appealing to this thing as though it had a human mind?

"George?"

Laurie started. "Don't talk to him, Emily," she said. Her voice was firm but lying: she was begging Emily, she had no power.

"Now, Laurie, that's not nice," the Chocolate

Man said, suddenly, frighteningly amiable, looking ahead at the road. Laurie saw the speedometer moving up to seventy, seventy-three.

"Emily can talk to me," the Chocolate Man said easily—seventy-seven, eighty—"whenever she wants."

He swung the car into the right lane. He was driving directly at the last, slow-moving police car; "Emily, get down," Laurie said, because the Chocolate Man was going to kill them all now.

Laurie braced herself by swinging her legs up against the dashboard; the Chocolate Man laughed.

"Emily?"

"I'm down, Mom." In a moment Laurie would be able to see the driver's eyes: he would recognize her.

And the Chocolate Man swung the car effortlessly over and around the police car as it swept to a stop.

"Thank you, Emily," he said as Emily raised her head above the seat back, "now be a good girl and sit still." Laurie could feel the police dwindling behind them; the driver had seen nothing.

"The police are always so thorough, aren't they?" the Chocolate Man said in a friendly voice. "Look behind you," to Laurie: an order.

She turned and looked back. The police car was parked now, barring the highway. "They do a good job," he continued, "but they tend to arrive"—she turned back to see him smiling at her—"too late."

✗   ✗   ✗

Ed was driving along the dead-grass meridian of the road, fast and expertly, taking the bumps hard. Marcy leaned out the passenger-side window, scanning the cars that stood waiting at the east-bound roadblock. All the faces she saw were excited and guilty. Marcy hated them. "I don't see him," she said, and she felt Ed's hand on her shoulder and didn't shake it off.

"It's not their fault," he said softly.

"I know. But they're loving it. They heard it on the radio and now they're part of it. 'Why were you late?' 'Oh, we had to wait half an hour because the police put up a roadblock to catch the Chocolate Man.' And that's all it is to them."

"No, that's not all it is. Not to everybody. Just look for Laurie and Riehle, Marcy. That's all you're supposed to do."

And so she looked for a familiar blank face; for a child's face she knew better than her own, although she'd never seen the child; for a haggard, unfamiliar female face she knew she would recognize in an instant.

"I don't want to do what I'm supposed to do. I want to do more."

"Look as carefully as you can."

"I know they set the goddamn roadblock up too late. The fucking lieutenant—" But they had reached the roadblock. Four blue-and-white squad cars blocked the road. Ed eased past them and stopped the car.

"Don't get mad," he said to Marcy, opening the door.

"I'm already mad," she said, but he didn't hear

her: he was already walking toward a policeman standing next to one of the patrol cars, saying, "Officer? How long have you been here?" He handed his ID to the policeman, speaking clearly and fast, as Marcy breathed hard to catch up.

"There'll be another roadblock," Laurie said, resigned. Rescue could not be so close, so simple; and there was no traffic backed up on this part of the highway.

"Maybe," said the Chocolate Man. They drove along; every second Laurie was racked by questions: How could she make him slow the car enough so Emily could jump out? Should she scream out the open window? Could she keep him away from the gun with her armless body? Would anybody help them if they tried to get away?

Yet she held her voice and her body still. There was nothing to gauge him by; no former, pre-dictable pattern of behavior. Maybe Emily knew. But Emily was as trapped as Laurie, even without restraints. Emily was trapped by memories.

They were whispering, whispering. Looking at him. He glanced over in the front seat. The mother. Lauren. She had a head full of bad thoughts. Emily was nice; she wouldn't hurt him.

It was like before, when he was little. The famil-iar voice in his head; he had to listen. And some-times he thought Laurie was his mother, even though he knew she wasn't. It wasn't like the other times he'd done this, when he'd been alone in the car. It was scary but he felt really powerful, too; he could do anything. *The car is full of angels, George,* the voice said. *You're going to make them all angels.* "And I am," he said to Laurie. "I know you're not who I think you are, and I'm going to do just what she says."

"A couple of cars might have got through," an older, gray-haired patrolman was saying to Ed as Marcy walked up. He seemed angry; he thought what was happening was about him. "It took—what?—eight, nine minutes to set up here." He was exasperated, too: as though Ed and Marcy couldn't know what he'd been through; as though it mattered. "There's no way we could have got any cars that went through before we set up. The Commissioner's office says go, we go. He says set up a roadblock, we set up a roadblock." He was proud of himself, executing his orders; who were these people to question him?

"We're just asking," Marcy said; Ed touched her arm. That meant shut up; she hated it when he did that, "whether any suspicious-looking vehicle passed by before you completed setting up, any vehicle being driven erratically, perhaps speeding—"

"And I'm telling you," he turned to Ed, "that we couldn't stop and check every car that went by while we were setting up the roadblock. So to answer your question—" turning back to Marcy now; "You don't know," she said evenly, and the officer went red with anger. "Listen—*officer.*

There's going to be another blockade about two miles down the road. The mayor told me to set up here, so here is where I set up. And the mayor told me to set the damn thing up fifteen minutes ago, what do you expect—" and Ed said, "Thank you," and turned back, steering Marcy toward their car with his elbow.

She was silent, but her fists were clenched. "Fleischer," Ed began, and she said, "Don't," and they got in the car and Ed started the engine. "East," Ed said. "Right?"

"There's *going* to be another blockade set up on the eastbound side?" Marcy said with disgust, "There's *going*—"

"Fleischer." His voice was stern. She turned toward him, fumbling for her cigarette pack. She sighed; she lighted her cigarette. "We're always too damn late."

She'd spit her words. "We're doing the best we can," Ed said gruffly, heading toward the road-block.

"*You're* doing. I'm not doing my best. If I'd been doing my best Emily Lookinland would be home now." She was so angry she could hardly speak. One of the police cars moved to let them pass. "But I didn't do my best."

"Marcy—"

"*I* didn't do my best, Ed. I'm not talking about you. Right now I don't give a hang about either one of us." She could hardly see the road; she blinked once and there was only snow in the way. She had nothing more to say.

"We're both doing our best now." Ed was

lighting his cigar, his voice was calm. Marcy realized that she loved him. "I love you," she said; it sounded angry.

"I love you, too, Marcy," Ed said gently. He knew what she meant.

"And I love Emily Lookinland," Marcy said, "and I want to bring her home."

Ed was silent. "He's got to do something that's familiar, something that's in the plan," she went on. "He planned to go to Manorville, so he's going to Manorville, no matter what."

She could hear Ed getting his cigar lit, could hear his sigh of satisfaction. She was looking out the window. "Do you think I'm wrong?" she asked finally.

Ed was silent for so long that Marcy glanced over. His cigar had gone out, unsmoked. His eyes were hard.

"You've been right so far," he said, "every step of the way." And Marcy felt something loosen inside her: she didn't have to cry anymore. She watched Ed push his foot down on the gas pedal and said, "Thank you," so softly that she would never know if he heard her.

Brian Devlin was standing by the side of the Long Island Expressway, freezing. It was a lot colder today than it had been yesterday. He shouldn't have lied to his mother. Brian was fifteen, and he'd said he was going to stay at his friend Ray's house last night. And he'd stayed at Melody Steinman's instead. Melody was fifteen, too. Brian loved her with his whole body. He was still punch-drunk from loving her last night, he could still smell her and he was overwhelmed by the memory of her body. Overwhelmed, and that was love. As real as anything he would ever feel. Obscurely he knew that nobody would believe him if they knew. His parents—he'd been wrong, lying to his parents, he never did that.

But he could still feel Melody's skin against his mouth.

Standing in the cold at the side of the road Brian became instantly hard and blushed into his parka, slouching his coat lower in the front. The soft snow kissed his face and that was Melody, too, the cold at his neck, the smell of the cars, it was all Melody; he knew he would remember this moment forever, just as he would remember last night.

This was a crazy place to be hitchhiking. Brian had spent all his money on wine: good wine. He worked afternoons and weekends at Hartley's Hardware; he was a good boy, a responsible boy. He'd smoked pot twice; he didn't like it. He'd never had wine, only beer; he didn't like that either. But Melody liked wine, so Brian had asked his cousin to get him some. He didn't need to impress Melody. He wanted to make her happy. And last night they'd drunk wine by candlelight, and every instant of last night was a visceral memory now, alive in his mouth and his hands and the whole length of his body.

Melody lived three miles from Brian's house, and Brian had been walking but it was cold, and getting colder. It had seemed a simple enough thing to hitch, he'd done it once or twice before. His mother would die if she knew.

But it didn't look like Brian was going to get a ride. There wasn't a lot of traffic, and people didn't really pick up hitchers anymore; this wasn't the seventies. Brian's feet were freezing, and police cars had come by, fast, with their lights spinning but no sirens. Brian had stepped back, afraid, but the police ignored him; there must have been an accident up ahead.

Traffic was beginning to slow. Brian felt stupid now, with people looking at him from their warm cars. He would just walk. He'd gone out of his way to get a ride on the expressway; now he'd just made his way longer. And he could feel the cold discomfort of standing here beginning to erode the full, physical pleasure of his memories.

So he started to turn away, and a car slid silently in place next to him, and the man at the wheel leaned over and said, "You need a lift?"

"—east on Long Island Expressway," Marcy was saying; her voice seemed to dissippate into the static of the radio. "Please notify FBI and Long Island police that suspect George Riehle may have eluded first eastern roadblock and is most likely headed in the direction of Manorville, Long Island. I advise—"

"Don't tell them what to do," Ed said from behind the wheel. He was staring straight ahead; Marcy hadn't thought he was listening. She finished quickly—"on suspect's trail at approximately sixty mph"—and signed off and heard the static abruptly die and closed her eyes and said, "Please."

"What?" Ed asked, still staring ahead; his cigar had gone out and he was twirling it absently between his thumb and forefinger as he drove.

"Not you," Marcy said, tired.

"It'll take more than prayers," Ed said flatly.

"You think I'm crazy, making you do this?" Marcy was craning her head out the window, staring into faces with fierce, frightening concentration. The occupants of almost every car shot looks of irritated unease in her direction: what did they all have to feel guilty about?

"Not crazy. Stupid. Brilliant. Brave, too. Stupid and brilliant and brave."

A little girl in the backseat of the car directly in front of them smiled at Marcy, she mouthed *Merry Christmas* and Marcy looked over to see Ed smiling. The smile stayed on his face as his eyes emptied; he didn't know he was smiling. "Marcy," he said suddenly, "why did you tell me you love me?"

Marcy almost lied: Because it's Christmas, because you looked like you needed a lift. "Because it's true," she said.

Ed didn't reply. Around them the traffic slowed as they approached the next roadblock, shifting down to fifty-five, parting and scurrying to remain unnoticed.

"And I said I love you," he said. And Marcy waited: she'd known this would happen; that wasn't why she'd told him.

"Ed—" she began.

"Pretty fucking inappropriate," Ed was saying, talking fast. "I know that what we're doing now is more important than anything either of us is feeling."

"You have a wife," Marcy said without inflection. She had known for a long time, she saw now, surprising herself; and she hadn't been waiting.

"Yes," sighed Ed. "My wife. But there hasn't really been anything between us for years—"

"Did you know I was married once?" Marcy asked quietly. It was a lie. "I was young. He made me have an abortion." She had no idea what she was going to say next. "My child would be nine years old now."

"Oh, God, Marcy, I had no idea."

Marcy breathed out slowly and breathed in. If she could be seen to be like other people he wouldn't feel obligated to love her. To make up for her years of suffering from not being beautiful. The smell of cigar smoke was Ed; she always breathed in more deeply when he was near her smoking a cigar. She lowered her head and swallowed deliberately. "I never fell in love again," she lied. "I never wanted to fall in love. I'm happy," she said, and that was true, "with my work. I do love you," eyes closed for a moment because that was true too, and true in the way he wanted it to be, "but not that way. You're my partner," and she opened her eyes and searched the faces of the people in the car next to her, because her eyes knew what was important, not her heart. "I don't want any complications, Ed. I'm sorry if I gave you the wrong idea." She was trying to kill it now, before it overwhelmed her; already the realization of how much her love for Ed was a part of her was almost too much to bear.

"Please," she said very softly, "I don't think we should mention it again." And out the window her eyes met a little boy's, and he was waving.

"Look," she said, "at that little boy."

Ed hadn't turned his head toward her the whole time. "I see him," he said at last, and he tweaked the siren and the boy laughed and bounced his hands against the window, and Marcy raised her hand to wave and Ed caught it in midair and trapped it gently back on the seat. "I understand," he said softly, "and I'll do or not do anything you ask." Marcy closed her eyes against the gentle pressure of his hand. "Anything," he said again. "Whatever you want."

There was a young man standing by the side of the road, and as soon as she saw him Laurie knew. The Chocolate Man steered the car abruptly toward the right lane and she said, "No."

The Chocolate Man ignored her. "What's the matter?" said Emily, muffled. The Chocolate Man had told her to keep out of sight, she sat hunched under the stiff green carpet, but her head was out and she seemed almost to be scenting something, like an animal.

He's just a boy, Laurie thought; he stood wearing a parka and jeans and dirty sneakers; he couldn't be more than fifteen.

"I'll scream," Laurie said, "And I'll shoot," the Chocolate Man replied in his dangerous calm voice; "Lower your head."

The boy smiled. He had seen the car. A warm seat, the air from the heater delicious on his neck; Laurie could see him thinking ahead. *He's just a baby,* she thought, and she tried to warn him with her eyes.

And Laurie's eyes met the boy's and he saw nothing. "*Now,*" said the Chocolate Man.

And Laurie bowed her head. "Emily, are you all right?" Would Emily think to run when the boy opened the door? How far could she get, would the Chocolate Man floor the gas and bolt if she got away? It was happening too fast. "Don't forget," in that quiet voice, "I have a gun." Laurie could see nothing, but she could hear that the Chocolate Man was looking at Emily as he spoke. "Emily—" she began, and her daughter said, "Don't worry, Mom," and the car bumped to a stop and the boy opened the back door and Laurie stared into her lap and bowed her back against the sudden rush of cold air.

As Brian stepped into the car he paused: the woman's face. She'd been looking at him; an odd look. Now her face was averted, looking down. And shaking back and forth, straight brown hair in a quivering curtain covered half her face. And her mouth was tight; *She's biting her lip to keep from crying,* Brian thought. *She's terri*—"You getting in?" the driver said in a friendly voice, and Brian hurried to get in, thinking, *Something's wrong,* and *I can't be rude.*

And as he slid into the backseat the woman's

shoulders slumped and for a moment her head fell forward almost to her lap. And the car jumped forward too fast and a pile of carpet next to him came alive and tumbled away from a small, frightened, familiar-looking face.

"I've got a gun," the man said with evident pleasure, "and it's pointed at you," and Brian thought, *He's enjoying himself,* and *He's the Chocolate Man,* at the same time, because the little girl looking at him from across the seat was unquestionably Emily Rose Lookinland.

The woman in the front seat lifted her head. The curtain of hair, the raised palm. "I'm so sorry," she said, and the Chocolate Man said, "Shut up," viciously, and Emily Lookinland cried, "Stop it!" Brian looked around him. Obviously none of this was actually happening. "Don't be sorry, Mrs. Lookinland," he said softly. "That's who you are, isn't it?"

"Congratulations!" said the Chocolate Man. "You're a quick learner." He was ordinary: receding hairline, watery eyes. There was nothing about him that made him look different from other people. But Brian knew that his power came from more than his gun.

Brian dismissed him. "Are you okay?" he said to the little girl. Emily.

She nodded.

"Please," Mrs. Lookinland said to the Chocolate Man, "let this boy go," and he said, "Shut up," again, and Brian said, "Leave her alone."

"Are you telling me what to do?" The

Chocolate Man's voice was eerily calm. It was all so immediate: as though Brian had been in this car forever. "You need me to get through the roadblock, right?" he asked the Chocolate Man. As though it were all scripted for him, and he already knew his lines. "Okay, I'll help you. Just—just leave Mrs. Lookinland alone, okay?"

The Chocolate Man laughed. "Call me Laurie," Mrs. Lookinland said with weary humor. The Chocolate Man snapped, "I'm talking to him," and Brian realized with surprise that the Chocolate Man was afraid of her. And of Brian, too. "Don't be sorry," Brian said to Laurie, "you couldn't help it."

"I'm glad you're here," Emily said, and the Chocolate Man laughed again. "I mean—"

"It's okay," said Brian. "I know what you mean. I'm glad you're okay. My name is Brian."

"Good God," said Laurie from the front seat, "will you listen to us."

The Chocolate Man's face was completely closed. His mouth was moving: "What's he doing?" Brian whispered to Emily. The complete impossibility of the situation made it almost easy to behave normally. Brian had never been this afraid before, so afraid that some part of him had been sheared away and floated, watching him, from somewhere up above the right side of his head. This part was curious, nothing more. It didn't plan; it didn't judge. It noticed how slowly the snow was falling. It listened to the words the Chocolate Man was saying—"Back under the covers now, Emily"—and watched as Brian's hand sought the litle girl's hand under the stale-smelling carpet. It didn't feel any of it.

And when Laurie said, "My hands are tied," explaining why she couldn't move her arms, Brian choked on a little hysterical laugh and Laurie said, "It's okay, honey," and Brian's other hand reached unbidden and touched her hair. There were other cars around them now, moving slowly toward the roadblock. Any other life seemed very, very far away. *Melody,* Brian thought, and her name meant nothing. He looked at the people in the other cars: they might as well have been ghosts. Here, with a hundred pairs of eyes around them, Brian and Laurie and Emily were completely alone with the Chocolate Man.

"I wouldn't hurt your wife for anything in the world," Marcy said. Ed had kept talking about it; like a child with a loose tooth, even if it hurt. He had broken his promise in a minute, and Marcy was glad.

"Would you hurt me?"

"Being denied something is easier than having something taken away."

"But what about you? You'll be denying yourself *and* giving something away."

"It doesn't matter about me."

"It does. What if I told you my wife was leaving me anyway?"

"I wouldn't believe you."

"Jesus Christ, Marcy, you think I'm lying to you? What kind of a woman do you think it takes to love one of us? When you know that every morning when you say good-bye it might be forever? When you've got to go days, weeks, without even seeing us? And you get pregnant and your husband's gone every night and you're stuck inside with the kid? Knowing his dad might be dead, any second you might hear the doorbell and your life ends? She couldn't stick it."

Marcy was angry: "You want company, get yourself a fucking dog."

Ed burst out laughing. Heads turned in surrounding cars to look.

"What's your problem?" Marcy asked. She wasn't angry anymore.

"Nothing," Ed laughed, "except I never heard you say, 'fucking' before. It's like having the school guidance counselor get on the loudspeaker and say, 'Fuck.' It's pretty funny. Why did you say yesterday that you were glad I'm not your lover?"

"I'm not," said Marcy, "are you happy now? Could you just shut up?"

"I will if you say *fuck* again." And he chuckled to himself as he drove.

And Marcy smiled, for the first time in weeks.

"Are you a Boy Scout, Brian?"

"No." Laurie didn't dare turn her head to look at him. He could not be here, not here in this little moving hell. "No," the boy said, and Laurie knew that he was brave. And her heart, which she'd thought broken, broke again.

"Don't get any ideas," the Chocolate Man was saying, "about being a hero." Traffic was slowing to a crawl; Laurie leaned her head against the seat back and was not surprised to feel a gentle, unfamiliar hand on her hair.

"Be careful," said the Chocolate Man, "we're getting close," and Brian said, "It's all right," to Laurie, and the Chocolate Man laughed aloud. "Yes," he said, "just like a family. It's a pity you're not a little younger."

"Don't," said Laurie, and Emily said, "George," and Brian said again, "It's all right."

They could see the second roadblock now, four police cars spread across the highway in the snow. There were three spaces in the line of cars, where officers stood checking each passenger car as it came up to the line. As Laurie watched, one car was waved to the right, past the patrol cars to where other officers stood at the side of the road, where other cars stood with their engines running and warm smoke rising from their tailpipes, ready to chase, should chase prove necessary.

Brian wished Emily's mom could know he had Emily's hand. It was small in his. Her mom's hair was soft and matted. He couldn't be a hero. He was just a kid. *And so were the seven victims:* that was from the part above his head. *And so were they, and so is she.* Her hand was warm; that surprised Brian. He had to rescue them—and himself. He was going to have to be the man here. Good doesn't always win; he knew that. But it had to here. The officers ahead would know in an instant who was driving the car. They had to. His mind could carry him no further. Even the part that wasn't him—the watcher—couldn't see past that.

But he had spoken the truth: It was going to be all right.

It had to be. There was nothing else, and the little girl was clutching his fingers with hope and courage and trust.

Emily was holding the boy's hand. It made her feel better: more real. Because a few minutes ago he had been outside the car, in a normal world, and he'd brought something of it in with him, a fresh biting smell and prickles on her skin. He was unquestionably real; therefore so was she. It was easy to forget that here, where all signs of normal life seemed as remote as some half-forgotten dream.

The boy squeezed her hand. She had her eyes closed. She knew she was close to something—to understanding. She'd been thinking and thinking, and now she knew she almost had it.

Now she knew the Chocolate Man was saying the same thing. Over and over; it was the key. The way out of here. Emily knew that if she didn't get out of this car soon she would go insane. The smell of the carpet, the back of the Chocolate Man's head, each tiny delineated melting snowflake that hit the car window—Emily hated all of it. Even the side of her mother's face, the high familiar slope of the cheekbone, the tight familiar lips: her mother was thinking every minute, Emily knew that; her eyes were huge with effort—thinking, and Emily knew that she was as helpless as Emily, and Emily hated her for it. And loved her: how kind she was being to Brian, the pain in her frightened dry eyes; Emily would already be insane if it weren't for her.

"In two or three minutes we'll be through," her mother said. Calming the children: *We'll know. Maybe we'll be free.* And the Chocolate Man moved his mouth.

He stopped. He started again. Dum dum dum dum dum dum dum-dum. Dum dum dum dum dum dum dum-dum. Emily realized she was tapping her toes to his rhythm. That she'd been doing that, every time, without noticing. Dum dum dum dum dum dum dum-dum. *He does it when we say something.* Suddenly her palms were sweaty; she loosed her hand from Brian's and rubbed her palms together, fingers held taut and out. "George?" she ventured; she tilted her head, and ducked it. "George?"

"Emily!" cried the Chocolate Man, with sickening false glee. "It's Emily! What do you want, Emily? Isn't this exciting? Aren't you having *fun*?"

Emily balled a fist to her mouth. He suddenly sounded like a child. Like he meant it. But he didn't move his mouth dum-dum.

So it wasn't his name that made him do it.

"Where are we going after this?" Her mother was looking a warning at her; she shook her head, darting a glance at the rearview mirror. He couldn't see her. But he was suddenly craning his neck, making a big deal out of looking for her in the mirror.

"Manorville," he said happily.

And it wasn't questions.

"Where's Manorville?"

"Honey, maybe we shouldn't talk."

"You'd better keep your head down," the Chocolate Man said. He sounded concerned, as if it were for her safety and not his. She hated him more than anything. "What will you do if I don't?" Her mother gasped; the Chocolate Man sighed. "I'll shoot you," he said simply: as if it were obvious.

"What if I don't care?" She started to sit up. If he was shooting at her he couldn't hurt her mother, maybe her mother could get away. "What if—"

And Brian put his hand gently on her shoulder. "No," he said. "I thought of that. That if he shot me maybe you could run. But we don't know how many bullets he has. There are three of us—that gun holds six bullets. Or eight, I don't know. But he might get all of us. Or at least two. Don't do anything, okay?"

And the Chocolate Man moved his mouth.

Emily sank slowly down, folding the carpet back over her. She could see his face in the rearview mirror: Dum dum dum dum durn dum dum-dum. Dum dum dum dum dum dum dum-dum.

"Emily?" Her mother's voice.

"It's okay, Mom," she said, peering out and up at the Chocolate Man's mouth. Dum dum dum dum dum dum dum-dum. "It's okay now, I'm okay," and she ducked all the way under, and reached out her hand and found Brian's. She had to remember, remember everything. *Six bullets, or eight. At least one of us, maybe two.* Dum dum dum dum dum dum dum-dum.

✗   ✗   ✗

There was something wrong. Of course there was, things were getting more and more complicated. But it was more than that. The girl, the mother, the boy. He could handle them. But things were changing: there were animals at the sides of the road. Not so big; nobody else had noticed them. But fast, and dark. Dark as crows. And wet-mouthed, hungry. One time one of them ran across the highway not too far ahead. One two three four five six seven. The other people didn't say anything. Not the three—one two three four five six seven—in the car. They didn't know anything. Only the one who spoke in his head. One two three four five six seven. He couldn't take it a lot longer. Like his mother, he knew it wasn't her but it sounded like her, sometimes the woman sounded like her, too. Two. One two three four five six seven. Giving him orders, yelling. *Kill them, kill them now, kill them all;* as if it were that easy. He had to get away, these people in his car were dangerous, he had to get rid of them. She didn't care if he died. She never had. The girl was talking, "—going?" and he had to answer her. They didn't know, none of them knew, they couldn't hear any of it. "—two bullets," the boy said, and the Chocolate Man counted, but he could hardly hear his precious numbers for the cacophony in his head.

Two cars now. Brian's breath was snagging on fear. "Is Emily okay back there?" Laurie asked. The Chocolate Man had quieted down; he was looking out the window, whispering. Brian was afraid he would hurt Laurie to make her be quiet. "Yes," he said. "She's fine." He was trying to say, *Don't worry.* And *Don't talk;* and *I'm okay.*

"Don't worry," Laurie said. Brian almost started to cry. She was telling him to be careful.

"We're all right back here," he said, and he saw her shoulders slacken for an instant and he was sorry.

But Emily squeezed his hand.

"Brian, do you want a cigarette?" Laurie asked; he couldn't bear her being so strong for him. "Yes," he said, surprising himself.

"May Brian have a cigarette?" Laurie asked the Chocolate Man. Civilized, as though they really were a family. No one in any of the other cars was looking at them.

"I'd have to move my gun," the Chocolate Man said, and suddenly Brian was so angry—"I'm going to kill you," he said quietly to the back of the Chocolate Man's head.

Laurie gasped. The Chocolate Man didn't even laugh. They were both looking at the roadblock ahead. The police had spent a long time with the two cars in front of them; the Chocolate Man's car slipped forward, and in a minute they were going to be next.

The Chocolate Man reached across his body with his left hand and offered Laurie's cigarette pack to Brian. "I don't think you're going to kill anybody," he said, and Brian took a cigarette. "I hope you like menthol," Laurie said calmly. In a moment—the Chocolate Man reached back with a pack of matches. Brian was whirling, physical sensation giving way to panicked thought, and thought to flayed emotion. Matches—no good as a weapon. The match packet was yellow with a vapid smile: HAVE AN AMAZING DAY! Well. He was, in a way. Brian thought for an awful moment that he was going to start laughing.

"—one for me," Laurie was saying. Brian had to let go of Emily's hand to light the cigarettes. Laurie had no arms. The Chocolate Man had one hand on the steering wheel.

As the match struck Brian froze. It was like a movie. Who had lighted two cigarettes in a movie? Emily shifted a little under the green carpet. "Here," he said to Mrs. Lookinland, and she turned to accept the cigarette with her mouth. There would be a moment; he caught her eye. There was no pleading there. But there was trust, complicity. She knew.

Brian's eye flicked to the Chocolate Man. He didn't want to look: the Chocolate Man was staring, head cocked, at the police officer examining the driver's license of a brown-haired man alone in the car ahead of them. Brian could see the side of the Chocolate Man's face, one staring eye.

And the Chocolate Man turned and looked at him. And smiled. And turned the gun on the front seat. Brian could see: the gun was pointed to the back and left. Toward Emily. The Chocolate Man unwound a scarf from his neck and tossed it over the gun. He was still smiling. "Are you fast enough, Brian?" he asked gently. "I don't think so."

Brian felt nauseated. That was anger. He started

to say something but Emily squeezed his hand. He thought she was crying; the green-carpet shroud quivered slightly and arhythmically.

"Don't even think about it," the Chocolate Man said to Brian, and "Keep your head down," to Laurie, in a savage whisper, and Laurie lowered her face until her hair covered it. The police were finished with the car in front of them; Laurie knew that they were next when she felt the wheels move. The car was creeping. Laurie had time to think a lot of things: *He'll have to take his hand off the gun when the officer looks in the car. If I scream will they be able to stop him before he shoots Emily? Or will he floor the gas pedal? And will he be able to shoot her while he's trying to outrun the cops?* Her hands were balled unconscious into fists and she could feel the Chocolate Man's terror and Emily's thin, wavering hope and Brian's brave, ignorant fear.

Laurie shifted in her seat: *I can take him*—and they were already past the roadblock, the police hadn't even stopped the car.

Laurie lifted her head. "They didn't even look," the Chocolate Man was saying with satisfaction; he turned to smile at her and he had fine beads of sweat across his upper lip. Laurie heard her daughter come out of her shroud and breathe great gulps of air. There was so much adrenaline in Laurie's blood that she couldn't see properly, everything was speckled with light.

"Thank you, Brian," said the Chocolate Man, "we couldn't have done it without you."

The boy said nothing. "Thank you, Brian," said Laurie, "for not doing anything rash," and she could hear that he was crying, and suddenly she loved him, fiercely, she would kill the Chocolate Man for making him cry. "Do you have any brothers and sisters?" she asked softly.

"Yes," the boy answered. He didn't try to hide the crying in his voice. "I've got a sister. She's eight."

"You're lucky," Laurie said, and the Chocolate Man laughed.

"I know," Brian said to Laurie, and then, "What are you laughing about?"

"Brian—" Laurie said, but the Chocolate Man was already answering: "I'm laughing at you, Brian." Laurie leaned her head against the backrest and whispered, "Don't listen," and Brian touched her hair again. "It's okay," he said, "I'm not afraid of him."

"Brian," Emily said suddenly, "what's your sister's name?"

"Mary." He took her hand again.

"That's a pretty name." It was so banal, *What's your sister's name, That's a pretty name;* Brian was looking at the back of the Chocolate Man's head, "My parents named her after Mary Astor"; he was thinking, *Maybe,* clenching and unclenching his hands, looking at the back of the Chocolate Man's head.

"I like Mary Astor," Emily said. "*The Maltese Falcon.* But I can never remember what's going on in that movie," and the Chocolate Man said, "Emily, stop talking to him," in a stiff voice. Laurie shuddered in the front seat. *She doesn't want him to say Emily's name,* Brian thought, and the Chocolate

Man went on in a monotone, "'Cause I can make you really unhappy if you do. I can—"

"Why don't you leave her alone? She's just a little kid." Brian was terrified; he really wanted to kill this man.

The Chocolate Man languidly turned his head. "Shut up," he said, "or I might really let her go. Maybe you—"

"Stop it," Laurie cried. She hated showing him their pain, but she couldn't bear it; to have hope offered with death as the price, and to wish, even for an instant—"Please," she said.

"It's okay, Mrs. Lookinland. I'm not afraid of him," again; maybe it was true.

"Would you like that, Laurie? If I let you and Emily go now?"

"Not without the boy." There was no hesitation: she meant it.

"Then tell him to be good."

"Brian," Laurie said gently, "please be careful. I don't want anyone to get hurt."

The Chocolate Man laughed so hard he started coughing. Laurie sat quite still and waited for him to stop.

"I'm not afraid of him," Brian said again.

"You should be," Laurie replied.

It was quiet for a while. Brian listened to the sound the wheels made, the engine. He'd been telling the truth. What if the Chocolate Man had Mary? He would face a hundred Chocolate Men for her.

He'd heard all about the Chocolate Man, a lot about what he did, things Brian didn't understand

and didn't want to. He'd tried to talk to his mother about it, but it upset her, she almost cried. And his father got upset, too, he started yelling about some club he called NAMBLA, something about "man-boy" love, and Brian could see that his father didn't understand either. And now he was in a car with the Chocolate Man and all his idiot brain could think was, *Mom is going to kill me for hitchhiking.*

And he lunged forward over the seat back and went for the Chocolate Man's neck.

Marcy and Ed stood at the second roadblock, talking to the police officer in charge. Yearwood, it said on his badge. To Marcy it was all becoming surreal: the unchanging highway, the police car lights, the drab, unchanging sky. And at the same time she felt an urgency that made it difficult simply to talk normally. She was snapping, at Ed, and now at the young man in front of them.

"We know he came this—"

"We have reason to believe," Ed broke in equably, "that the Chocolate Man evaded the first roadblock."

"We've been set up here for about ten minutes," Yearwood said, frowning. He was talking as though Marcy and Ed were civilians. "It's just a precautionary measure, you know. The word is the Chocolate Man is headed for Dover, Delaware. The force has got roadblocks set up all the way to the Midtown Tunnel. The first one didn't catch him, but—"

Marcy didn't have time for officious, impatient

competence. "He isn't going to Dover," she shot. "He came this way."

The officer raised an eyebrow, looking at Ed. "I'm over here," Marcy snapped. The eyebrow was amused, but Marcy went on: "Did any car get through this checkpoint without a thorough search?" and the eyebrow went flat, because Marcy was scanning the cars now; two slipped by without stopping, both driven by men with women in the passenger seat.

"We are operating," the officer said through clenched teeth, "on instructions from the Commissioner's office to stop and search any vehicle occupied by a man fitting the description of one George Riehle—as given to that office by two eyewitnesses who happen to be part of the Task Force—and a woman fitting the description of Lauren Lookinland, and a child fitting the description of Emily Rose Lookinland, or any combination of people resembling these three in any way, that is, a darkhaired woman at the wheel with a blond man in the passenger seat, a blond man at the wheel with a—"

"Listen, you officious little fool," Marcy hissed, "*we're* the members of the Task Force who gave George Riehle's description to the fucking Commissioner's office."

"Excuse me?" A black mustang had pulled up to the check-point; an exasperated-looking man sat behind the wheel, a woman leaning over him to find Marcy's eyes: "We've been waiting at this roadblock a long time, and I'd like to know if—"

"We're trying to keep things moving here," Yearwood said testily, but Marcy leaned over and put her hands on top of the open window. "Tell me," she said to the woman.

"There was a boy here," the woman said. She talked quickly, as though she were afraid someone might stop her, and low, as though she were ashamed of herself for intruding. "At the side of the road. He was hitchhiking. I was watching him because, well, kids don't do that anymore. I mean, sometimes grown men but he was just a boy, thirteen, fourteen years old. It bothered me because he was hitchhiking, farther down?" A question. "And then I didn't see him, and it seems a little crazy, I know," acknowledging with a tight smile the man in the driver's seat, "but I just wanted to make sure the police knew," and Marcy turned on Yearwood in controlled fury: "Were you aware of this?" and to the woman, with sudden calm and grief, "Thank you so much," and she turned back to the officer, and the woman and the car were gone.

"Ah, well—no," said Yearwood, "I mean, we didn't take into account the possibility that he, ah—"

"Detective Fleischer," Ed said quietly, "I think we've done all we can here. May I suggest we move on?" And Marcy, strangled silent by rage, rounded on him and he said, "A cigarette?" reaching for her front pocket, "I think you could use one," and he took her arm and wheeled her away from Yearwood, who was walking briskly away from them, shouting. "Okay, people, we've got to get cracking here! Every car, and I mean *every* car, has got to be—" and Marcy said, "I'm okay," and took the cigarette and lighted it while walking fast back to their car. She didn't say anything about

Yearwood; she could see Ed smiling a little to himself. "You think he's got the boy?" she asked, and Ed's smile disappeared.

"I think if he does he's going to get even more hell from you when we find him, that's what I think," and he slipped the key into the lock and opened the door and leaned and opened Marcy's door before she got there.

The car was wild and Brian was holding onto the Chocolate Man's neck. Mrs. Lookinland was leaning into him and the Chocolate Man; the Chocolate Man jerked his arm and Brian thought Mrs. Lookinland must have bitten it. Emily was screaming. There were horns and Brian was trying to talk: "Stop. The. Car. *Stop*." He could smell the man's hair and his skin. Brian scrabbled with his legs to get over the seat back. Mrs. Lookinland was jerking her arms back and forth, trying to free her hands. "He's got the gun!" she yelled, and Brian saw it suddenly, nothing and then silver, and he pulled the Chocolate Man's neck back as hard as he could but he couldn't reach his arm, and the silver got huge in his face and he was sitting up suddenly, arms empty in the backseat and still mouthing, "Stop." Mrs. Lookinland's head lolled back against her seat, her eyes toward the roof of the car, and silver winked at him—was she shot? He hadn't heard anything but there it was again, it grew and wavered and was still, and Brian was looking down the barrel of a gun.

Without thought he pulled at the door latch,

throwing himself toward the door: a giant sound swallowed everything, the ground out the open door was dizzy with speed, and Brian was sucked into nothing as the gun went off.

Ed and Marcy drove fast, in silence. Marcy couldn't concentrate: now there was a boy to worry about. She looked ahead and saw nothing, a stream of red taillights in front of them, and snow.

"Marcy?"

Marcy didn't want to talk anymore. Her heart was numb and her hands were cold. "Oh, Ed," she said, "not now."

"Yeah. Well." She could feel his discomfort; she turned and smiled ruefully at him.

"I just wanted to say I think we're going to get Riehle," he said quickly. "I think we'll get there in time."

Marcy snorted a little laugh. "I hope so," and then the quiet and the passing snow.

"Marcy?" Ed said again.

She massaged her forehead with the tips of her fingers.

"Marcy?"

"Yes, Ed."

Marcy sighed; "Don't get theatrical," Ed said, and she smiled and shook her head. And waited.

"Marcy—I know this is the worst possible time—"

"It is."

"—but I'm only going to ask you this one time."

Marcy started to say something, stopped herself.

"Marcy—will you marry me?"

Marcy felt something like light flow through her, it picked her up out of her seat and warmed her and eased the tension behind her eyes, and she turned toward Ed and he was looking at the side of the road, where something lay—no, something moved, and Marcy grabbed his arm and held it, watching as the car swerved toward what she now could see was a young man crouched on the white shoulder of the road, raw black dirt around him like wounds in the snow; and there was blood.

Brakes and horns screamed and they were there, and Marcy unthinking was holding Ed's hand fiercely; as he opened the door to get out he squeezed her fingers, and he and Marcy ran toward the young man, collapsed now in the bloody snow.

The door of the car was flapping wildly. "Close it, Emily," the Chocolate Man said, completely calm.

Emily didn't move. She stared with huge eyes at the banging door and didn't move. "Do it, Emily!" Laurie said, and her voice was sharp with fear.

Emily burst into tears. "Don't yell at me, Mommy."

Laurie could see the open door bucking at the edge of her eye. She could hear it; "It's all right, Emily. Be a good girl, okay?"

It was the Chocolate Man who spoke.

Laurie had never experienced pain before. This

was what it felt like: everything before this moment had been the rehearsal of a cruel joke.

Emily was sniffling but she crawled along the seat toward the open door. Laurie turned her head. The car was going very fast, at least seventy, shaky because of the wet asphalt.

"Emily," Laurie said softly, and her daughter lifted her tearstained face and said, "I'm sorry."

"No, darling." There would never be an end, a point at which she could feel no deeper pain. "I'm sorry, sweetheart. Be careful now, the car's going really fast," and sharply, to the Chocolate Man, "Slow down."

"You don't tell me what to do," he answered, dangerously quiet. But he did slow down, and Laurie kept talking to her daughter: "Be careful, honey, hold on to the seat back," screaming inside but her voice gentle and even, "Easy, baby, be careful," and Emily said, "I think I'm going to throw up," but she held on to the seat at the back of Laurie's head (Laurie turned and kissed her hand, as though her lips might secure her) and reached out into the cold air. Her hand loosened on the seat back and Laurie leaned her cheek against it, pressing, trying to hold her; she could feel her daughter's fingers crawling along the metal of the door toward the handle, it was as though it were happening to her.

"Slower," Laurie said. The Chocolate Man seemed oblivious at the wheel. Laurie's cheek was against her daughter's hand. "Please," she said, and the car slowed.

"Mom," Emily said, "I can't—" and suddenly

the cold wind was cut off and Emily was breathing hard in the seat behind her.

The Chocolate Man said something but Laurie didn't hear him because the roaring in her ears was too loud. "Darling, are you all right?"

"Uh-huh." The Chocolate Man seemed unaware of them now, speaking in a whisper to the windshield. Laurie didn't care what he did to her now: "How much longer are we going to be on this damn highway?" she snapped. Her arms were stiff behind her. The Chocolate Man didn't answer. He started to sing: "Rudolph the Red-Nosed Reindeer." His childishness only made him more dangerous; he was unpredictable like a child.

"I have to go to the bathroom," Emily said from the backseat, and Laurie thought, *So do I*. Her body was remarkable, it didn't know anything about what was happening to it. "So do I," she said aloud. An opportunity? She couldn't let her anger get in her way. Anything the Chocolate Man hadn't planned himself could be an opportunity.

The Chocolate Man wasn't paying attention. "George," Laurie said loudly, and his head jerked toward her. "Stop the car," Laurie said. "My daughter has to go to the bathroom."

The Chocolate Man looked at her too long. "George," she said, "the road," and he turned his head back like an automaton.

"Listen to me," Laurie said. "I want you to stop the car." She was dizzy with possibility. Now she had a weapon: his name.

The car was sliding smoothly to a stop on the dirt shoulder of the highway. Laurie held her breath, and then she dared look at him. He was regarding her with quiet expectation. "We're going to go into the woods, George," she said firmly, and she felt faint; and then he nodded.

The next few moments would decide everything: whether Emily would live.

"George," Laurie said with no gentleness and no anger, "reach behind me and untie this belt." He nodded; he was cowering, with his head down, and Laurie felt from somewhere outside herself a twinge of pity. But when the Chocolate Man lifted his eyes he wouldn't see that. Laurie's face felt frozen, unattached; she knew her expression remained unmoving, empty and sure without compassion. And behind her cheeks and absolute eyes she was spinning with fear and hope.

The Chocolate Man leaned toward her. "Okay, Mom," he said softly, and Emily in the backseat burst forward and screamed in his face.

"She's not your mother! I hate you, I hate you!" and collapsed, sobbing, over the seat back.

Laurie felt a chill run over her arms, her legs; "George," she said, but her voice was trapped in desperation, and he knew it. He was shaking himself out of his dream. Laurie leaned back against the seat and inclined her head until it touched her daughter's. Emily's hair was matted and wet; Laurie turned her head more and felt Emily's tears against her own face.

"Shut up," the Chocolate Man said viciously to Emily, and to Laurie, "You're not my mother," with acid disdain, and he shoved his foot against the gas pedal and Laurie knew that they were going to pay for her betrayal.

✻   ✻   ✻

His mother had been talking. He'd been dream-ing—something about a little girl—and she was there, asking him to stop the car. And somebody had put something around his mother's hands; he had to free her hands.

And suddenly the animal in the backseat started howling.

George was really scared, because the animal was loud. It wasn't very big. But George was afraid of animals. This one screamed something about his mommy—and then it was gone, and the woman was sitting next to him in the front seat of the car and Emily was crying.

"You're not my mother," he said to the woman.

Maybe Emily was crying because the animal had frightened her.

"My God," Marcy said, walking quickly toward the body, "he's just a boy," kneeling in the red snow.

Ed was at the car, radioing in. Marcy reached for the boy's neck; she was so afraid. She felt faint: she could hear a shush in her ears, and she touched him and he was alive.

The boy stirred and moaned. He said some-thing. Marcy leaned to hear him: "Stop."

She could see his face clearly now; he wasn't more than fifteen. "Stop," he said again, and sud-denly his body bucked, as though he'd been sleep-ing and dreaming of falling, and she was holding him by the shoulders as he struggled.

"He's got them," the boy said, trying to sit up, "he's got them." Marcy leaned closer: "The Chocolate—oh my God, the girl, the little girl—"

"The Chocolate Man," Marcy said. "Don't talk." She had to know but he was weak, his blood was all over the snow.

"He shot me," the boy said.

"Shh."

"But he *shot* me." The boy was incredulous. Marcy felt herself thrown outside reality: the colors were too bright, there was too much red. The boy's face was white, and his hair was white with melting snow. Marcy was holding him by the shoulders; "Don't go," she said. She had no idea how badly wounded he was. "We need you here." The snow was getting redder. "Emily needs you." The boy closed his eyes and Marcy felt sickening guilt. "I need you," she said, and Ed was behind her and kneeling in the snow, reaching past her to stroke the boy's face.

"The Chocolate Man," Marcy said; she felt Ed nod behind her. "I radioed," he said, and he put one hand on her shoulder. "It's going to be all right," he said, looking at the boy, and Marcy didn't know whether he was talking to him or to her.

"You're going to be all right," Marcy said; that was true, she saw, wiping blood: there was a clean hole through his left shoulder, but it was high above the heart. And there was a flesh wound on his right arm, from a bullet or speeding cement. There was blood from his head, but Marcy explored the wound with her fingers and it was long but not deep. When Marcy stroked the boy's cheek she smeared it with blood.

"Catch him," the boy said.

"We will. Is Emily alive?" with a patient voice and a galloping heart. And guilt, because for that instant the boy didn't matter.

"Yes. She's okay. But I—"

"Mrs. Lookinland?"

The boy swallowed with difficulty, and Marcy felt Ed's hand on her shoulder.

"They're on the way," he said, and she heard the far-off scream of sirens.

"I'm sorry," Marcy said to the boy, "but I've got to know."

"He's going to kill them," the boy said, trying to raise himself.

"No," Ed said over Marcy's shoulder, "he's not. Because we found you. We'll get him, son, and it'll be because of you."

The boy shook his head.

"Yes," said Marcy, and she surprised herself by kissing his sticky cheek. "Take care of yourself. We'll take care of the Chocolate Man."

"Mom," Emily said, very small from the backseat, "I'm sorry."

Laurie bit her lip. She nodded her head hard, so Emily would see it. She didn't trust herself to speak. She looked over at the Chocolate Man; he was looking ahead and mumbling. There was nothing Laurie could say to her daughter. Anything she said would mean something to him, too.

Laurie nodded her head for a long time. And then she felt the soft touch of fingers in her hair. Emily was close and she was whispering. "I won't say anything, if you want to try it again."

And Laurie leaned her head back into her daughter's hand and said nothing. That path was barred. "Okay?" Emily whispered, and Laurie closed her eyes and nodded again: okay.

Marcy had never been this far out on the Long Island Expressway. She had been to Jones Beach; the sign for that exit evoked incongruous cruel images: families in the sand, toddlers in the foam of crested waves. The beach would be empty now, the waves unwitnessed crashing, crashing, against the cold, stiff sand.

An ambulance had come and taken the boy away. He'd left a lot of red snow behind. He would be fine. But what about the wounds to his heart and mind? He had never stopped talking, even when Marcy pleaded; he kept saying, "He's got them, the girl, Emily, Mrs. Lookinland, he's got them and she's so brave, where's Mary? Where's Mary?" And the paramedics shushed him and put him on a stretcher and assured Marcy he would be all right. But she knew he would be different now. His bravery astonished her, his daring. He thought he'd failed. Someday he might understand that he hadn't failed; but he would never be a child again.

What did snow look like falling on the waves? It was sticking to the ground now, to the road in front of them. The sky was so dark it looked like twilight on the sides of the road; Marcy kept looking at the sides of the road. What would she finally see: a man, a car, a black snow-covered tarp? Would Emily Lookinland be lying alone or would her mother be with her? Would Laurie Lookinland's shoes wind up sitting on the cold white ground instead of a white Formica tabletop? Marcy shivered inside her warm coat. There was nothing to see at all on the sides of the road.

The car's engine shuddered and was still. Laurie looked around her. A narrow strip of faded grass, tall ragged pines, their branches white. The grass was dappled with white, and there was a crow sitting on a branch slung out over the car; it was watching Laurie.

The Chocolate Man was not talking now. "It's okay, Mom," Emily said behind her; Laurie turned, and her daughter's face was frightened and brave. There was nowhere they could run to, here at the side of the holiday highway. "Yes," she said, "it's okay," marveling at her daughter. What was it like for Emily now? To have woken to find her mother trapped in her nightmare with her. And yet she was trying to comfort her mother. They were in a looking-glass world.

Laurie turned to the Chocolate Man. He was staring straight ahead. If they opened the car door and ran, what would he do? They couldn't; it wasn't that Laurie's hands were tied; she knew she could, in spite of her bonds, reach the door handle, could open the door. But what if she did? What if Laurie were shot dead, what would happen to Emily? There were other cars going by in a spare but steady rhythm; if Laurie screamed, would anyone notice? Each passing car contained a world; she was not in any of those worlds. Emily was, in the radios tuned thoughtlessly to the news, in the memories of the people who had seen her smiling photograph on the television last night or read about her in the newspaper this morning over coffee. But even Emily was not real to the people going by in a hundred floating encapsulated worlds: she would only be a story to them, not a real girl; a celebrity of sorts on the front page, not a little frightened girl in a beige station wagon at the side of the road.

Emily was looking at the Chocolate Man too. Her skin had no color but her mouth was firm. "George," she said, "what do you want us to do now?"

For a moment the Chocolate Man only stared: a crow, the snow falling. Then he turned, and he was smiling. "I thought we might take a walk, Mom," he said to Emily. She didn't turn toward her mother, who sat, helpless. "Okay," Emily said. "Do we get out first or do you?"

Laurie was standing by the side of the car, watching the Chocolate Man help Emily out of the backseat. Laurie's hands were still tied behind her, but she knew that she could loosen the belt again, given time. Emily was saying something:

"—do you want us to do, George?"—and she sounded so normal. As though the Chocolate Man were anybody, just a man named George. Laurie wanted to help her; she watched the unprotected back of the Chocolate Man's head and almost made a move: but he was fast, she knew that, and much stronger than he looked. If there was hope now it had to be driving by, happenchance help; Laurie could see his white neck and his pale, vulnerable ear.

She had begun to work her hands loose from the belt tying them behind her. The Chocolate Man was looking at Emily, his head tilted a little; he said nothing, so Laurie knew he was listening, to Her. She wanted to go over to Emily but she had to get her hands free first.

"It's almost time," the Chocolate Man said. He spoke softly; the snow fell past his mouth and ate the words as they came out. Emily was watching him warily, tensed to run; but she kept looking over at Laurie.

The gun in the Chocolate Man's hand was pointed loosely at the ground. Laurie wanted to yell—*Emily, run!*—but she stood still, concentrating on her hands behind her: move the thumb down and pull; gently, twist the hand just so. She was looking at Emily and the Chocolate Man but she felt blind, she needed a blind woman's hands now.

She knew Emily would not run without her mother. There had been other cases, the twelve-year-old girl who allowed a kidnapper to take her out of her house without a fight, out of the room next to where her mother was sleeping, because she didn't want to put her mother in danger. That girl was later found dead.

Don't think about me, she wanted to shout; but she still had to get her hands free.

"I thought you wanted to take a walk, George," Emily was saying, and suddenly there was the miracle of a car stopping, a silver car was pulling up with a crunch onto the grass behind Emily; the driver had to have seen the Chocolate Man holding the gun.

When the car's engine stopped, the silence was enormous. Emily was still looking at the Chocolate Man, she had not turned. A crow cawed high up, twice, then there was nothing. The road was empty, a man was getting out of the car. The Chocolate Man tilted his head; he nodded.

The man was looking at the Chocolate Man's gun. "Easy, mister," he said, and the Chocolate Man brought the gun up from where it was pointed toward the ground; "Easy," the man said again, and the Chocolate Man aimed the gun at Emily.

"Okay," he said. Laurie couldn't tell whether he was talking to the man or to his private demon. She watched Emily looking at him; she had not flinched or changed expression. Laurie was shaking, but she was still working her hands behind her, faster now because the Chocolate Man wasn't looking at her.

"What's going on here?" the man asked. He didn't seem to be afraid of the gun.

There was someone else in the car. Laurie saw a woman in the passenger seat; she couldn't see the face because the window was tinted. The man was young, strong. He took a step toward the Chocolate Man.

"We're having a party," the Chocolate Man said, and abruptly the gun's muzzle shifted and there was a flare and a deep *pop* and the man fell to one knee. "You want to join us?"

The man coughed, and spit blood. Emily half turned and the Chocolate Man said, "No, Emily," in a gentle voice and Laurie froze, her left hand halfway through the belt loop, and the man said, "Run," to Emily as he tried to get up, and the Chocolate Man shot him again.

"George!" Emily screamed, and the car behind her moved, the woman was leaning over from the passenger seat to take the wheel, the car lurched forward, she was going to hit the man, who was down now on both knees, one hand to the ground, the other to his stomach; his hand was red.

The car picked up speed; the ground behind its wheels was gouged black. Emily was staring at the gun, her head held stiffly back and away, her eyes shiny like a deer's. Laurie took a step and the Chocolate Man turned the gun toward her, fast, and the car brushed by the dead man, scattering dirt; *She's going to hit Emily,* Laurie thought, but the gun did not move as the car careened, its back wheels skidding on the snow; Emily didn't seem to know it was there, even as it went by her she only flinched, staring at the Chocolate Man where he stood pointing the gun at her mother.

Hit him, Laurie thought as the car skidded, *hit him,* but the car hit the highway asphalt with a bump and a little scream, and Laurie and the Chocolate Man and Emily were alone again; there was no one else on the road and nothing near them but a silent body and black gouges in the snowy ground.

"George," Emily said suddenly, "would you like to sing with me?"

Laurie had been looking at the body in the snow. She lifted her head; Emily was looking at the Chocolate Man with something furtive in her face, something like compassion. "We can sing our favorite song," she said.

Their favorite song. Laurie's hand slid out of the belt loop; the belt slipped and she caught it in her other hand before it fell to the ground. "Don't you remember, George?" The Chocolate Man slowly lowered the gun until it was again relaxed in his hand, but Laurie didn't move. What had they sung, her child and this man?

"Do you really want to, Mom?" he asked softly; what did he think he had just seen, just done?

"Of course I do." Emily's voice was firm and warm, with the gentle cadences of a mother talking to a frightened child. *She sounds like me,* Laurie thought. There was nothing she could do to help her daughter.

"You're really going to sing with me?" the Chocolate Man asked. His voice was very young.

"Yes, George." And Emily began: "*In a wagon bound for market,*" her voice clear and unafraid.

Laurie stood, her hands held in artificial captivity behind her back, and listened. In her bedroom at night, in the sunny kitchen, she and Emily had sung this song a thousand times.

"*Why can't you be like the swallow—*"

The Chocolate Man sang with a boy's quaver;

he closed his eyes; he was smiling. And suddenly Emily stopped singing and took a big breath and yelled: "Eighteen hundred forty-seven!" very loud.

George's eyes sprang open. He froze in place with a sudden stiffness. He started to move his mouth. "Two thousand nine hundred and forty-three!" Emily screamed. "Mom, run!"

The belt dropped from Laurie's hands to the snow; she noticed the sound it made.

"Eight million three hundred thousand twenty-four!" Emily was yelling. Her fists were clenched. She spoke rapidly and without inflection, all in one breath. Laurie didn't move; she watched the Chocolate Man where he stood immobile: Emily was controlling him. "Eight zillion nine hundred three—Mommy, *run*!"

Emily's throat was getting hoarse. The Chocolate Man was just standing there. Emily's mother was standing there, too; didn't she understand? Emily was sick with victory: she was making it so the Chocolate Man couldn't move. Her brain kept tricking her, every time she opened her mouth to say a number she didn't know if she would be able to remember one.

The Chocolate Man stared in trapped horror from Emily to Laurie and back again. "Three million seven hundred thousand—" He was moving his lips, and the gun was slipping down toward the snowy ground. Laurie was struck stupid with fascination. The man could not move. His lips moved without his wanting to; she could see the struggle on his face.

"*Mommy!* Mommy, run *away!*" Emily was desperate; but the Chocolate Man was still holding the gun. *She thinks I'd really run,* Laurie thought with wonder, and the Chocolate Man began to move.

"Thirty-four! Twenty-nine and a half!" Emily shouted. Her mother wasn't moving. She didn't understand. Emily's voice was already hoarse, her mind tripping over numbers. "Thirty-four twenty-nine two!" she shouted, and the Chocolate Man raised his head and looked straight at her.

Still her mother stood. Her hands were free. "Mommy, run!" Emily cried again. Why wasn't she listening to her? The Chocolate Man stared; he moved his foot. "Forty, forty, forty," Emily prayed. Her mind could come up with no greater numbers. Everything was frozen except for the Chocolate Man's foot. It stopped: he had taken a step.

"Eighty, ninety, a hundred, Mommy, please," Emily said, quieter now. The Chocolate Man could still hear her.

And his other foot moved. "Mommy!" she screamed, in real terror now. One step; and then another. "Ten, ten, ten," Emily gasped, and suddenly her mother was across the snow and in the air, she rammed the Chocolate Man with all her weight and he fell as if he were rag and had no bones.

Laurie landed hard. The ground where her hands hit it was cold; she was surprised to notice the cold. Her arms braced, she brought up her knee and butted. The Chocolate Man bucked and lay still. He was on his back; she was lying on top of him like a lover. His eyes were closed and he wasn't fighting.

Laurie brought up a hand to hit his face, her hands bloodied, she was making a guttural noise that sounded like it came from outside herself, from the trees or the wheeling crows, a low, guttural animal sound and the Chocolate Man's eyes opened and Emily was screaming: "No! Mommy!" and Laurie turned, he was moving underneath her, raising himself, and Emily was shouting, "Get away!" Laurie didn't know who she was calling to, Laurie or the Chocolate Man; he was getting up and Laurie turned toward her daughter and saw that Emily had the gun and she was pointing it toward the Chocolate Man and her mother where they lay like lovers in the snow.

Laurie rolled away; there was cold down her back and up her sleeves. She landed on her hands and knees and stopped there, panting. Emily was moving the gun back and forth, it was shaking in her hands.

Laurie looked into Emily's eyes and did not recognize her daughter. The black hole of the muzzle stared at the Chocolate Man; but Emily was looking at her mother; she held the gun tightly in her two hands and the gun was shaking.

Laurie didn't look toward the Chocolate Man. She didn't speak. She and Emily looked at each other for what seemed like a long time, and then the shiny gun barrel exploded.

The Chocolate Man just sat there.

Emily stood, her eyes blank and crying. The gun was shaking in her hands. He was untouched; Laurie leapt up and ran toward her daughter, who was saying numbers in a soft voice and crying: "Seven seven seven six five four—" as she stood trembling violently; she would not be able to fire again.

"Forty-seven," Laurie said in a loud voice, standing up. The Chocolate Man looked at her fearfully, mouthing, mouthing. "Seventy-six, you son of a bitch," Laurie said savagely, walking toward Emily; "Two thousand sixty-fucking hundred and three."

And the Chocolate Man began to get up. Laurie didn't run. She kept her eyes locked on her daughter's. "Twenty-two," she said loudly, and, "Shh, darling, shh," to Emily. Laurie could feel him moving behind her, slowly, slowly; Laurie reached for the gun.

And Emily screamed, and Laurie turned and he was there, practically upon her, and she fired.

And the Chocolate Man fell, without a sound, to his knees.

Laurie was still looking at Emily, who stood empty-handed now, staring in animal horror at the Chocolate Man where he knelt in the snow.

"Mommy—" Emily began, and Laurie fired again, and the Chocolate Man reeled up and back, red on his shirt and his face and splattering across the snow; he let out a wild little scream and flung up a hand, reaching. Emily ran past her mother as he fell with a thud on his back. Emily skidded on her way to reach him; Laurie knelt and caught her,

Emily was flailing her arms and crying, hitting the Chocolate Man's quiet body, and he was looking up at nothing, at the sky, snowflakes like tears on his dead face.

Laurie reached to touch her daughter, and Emily screamed with wordless rage and turned on her mother, flailing and hitting, and Laurie held her. "It's all right now, Emily, it's all right," she whispered. Emily hit her face, there was blood on her hands and Laurie held on, murmuring, "It's all right," until her daughter quieted and clutched her and cried, safe at last in her mother's arms.

Laurie heard nothing; always she would remember the police car as it slid silently onto the snowy grass behind Emily, and Emily in her arms at last: there was no sound. The Chocolate Man lay with snow falling into his open eyes, and the police car stopped and suddenly there was noise all around: the slamming of doors, heavy footsteps, a woman's voice crying, "Is she all right?" The sound of a man crying, and there was a big man on his knees with his arms around Emily and Laurie; he was crying. He didn't speak; Emily half turned and flinched away, but the man didn't move away or stop crying. The woman was kneeling in the snow next to the Chocolate Man. She stared at his dead face; she reached two fingers and gently closed his eyes.

The woman looked from the body to the big man and said, "Ed?" and he nodded, his face still buried in Emily's neck, and the woman said, "Yes,

Ed. I will," and he nodded again, and his back shook and Laurie could see that he was crying even harder.

Laurie leaned back and the big man pulled free, his face contorted from crying. "It's okay, she's okay," Laurie said, and she held her daughter out at arm's length: "Emily."

"I'm okay, Mom," Emily said, but she was looking over at where the Chocolate Man lay, his hair frosted now with snow; the woman was still kneeling next to him, still looking into his face.

"The boy," Laurie said.

"He's going to be all right," said the woman, still looking at the Chocolate Man's body. "It was a clean wound."

"George doesn't hurt anymore, does he, Mom?" Emily asked; her mouth was crumpled; she looked very small.

"No, honey, he doesn't hurt anymore."

Emily breathed deeply and pressed her lips together. "Will the angels take him now?"

Laurie shook her head. "Oh, honey, I don't know."

Emily looked up, at the trees and the falling snow. "You know what I kept thinking of?"

"What, honey?" Laurie could hold her, she could listen to her voice.

"The reindeer. You know, next to our house? I kept thinking about them, the way they're running up the roof." Could listen to her voice, could stroke her hair.

"And I thought about what you told me. About Santa Claus. About the spirit of love."

"Hmm-hmm." Could feel the soft sweet skin of her cheek. Laurie kissed her daughter's cheek: "Red as a cherry," she said, "and twice as tasty." She could hardly speak for crying, could hardly see.

"Well," Emily went on, leaning back earnest and dry-eyed, "I think I understand. About love being the spirit."

"Yes, baby," wiping away tears on Emily's face that weren't there.

"And I know now. 'Cause I could feel it. Not all the time—" her face clouding, Laurie reaching to clutch her to her. "—but sometimes I felt it. Felt you." Emily leaned back again to look into her mother's eyes.

"And you know what?"

"What?" Laurie's tears were already drying, looking at Emily's brave serious face.

Emily smiled. "I guess I believe in Santa Claus now," she said.

Laurie and her daughter were quiet then, watching the police move into action. Other cars were pulling up, sirens were shrieking, the big man's face was hard and professional as though he'd never cried at all. But when he knelt next to the woman at the Chocolate Man's body he put his hand on her shoulder, and she turned and smiled at him.

"Maybe he was praying, all those times," Emily said suddenly.

"What do you mean?" The snow was falling very fast now, very hard; Emily was wearing a halo of snow on her curly head.

"George. When he was counting, every time he

heard a number." Laurie waited. She could not imagine the Chocolate Man praying.

"One two three four five six seven," Emily said.

"What?"

"One two three four five six seven," Emily said simply, "all good children go to heaven."

JESSIE HUNTER is the author of *Blood Music*. She lives in New York's Hudson Valley with her husband and two children.